"Mondragon? 'S 'at yo...

She saw a dim gleam ... in that window. Came a whispered: "Jones? Jones, dammit, get out of here!"

She hung there shaking with strain and looking up toward that dark that showed her too little, but enough to hope on.

"Mondragon, ye a'right? Can ye squeeze out some'ow?"

"No! I can't. You think they're stupid? Get *out* of here, dammit, don't—" He stopped speaking a beat or two, sounding breathless, and what eyes couldn't see, heart pictured—the desperation, the relief to hear from her.

"Don't be a damned fool! You can't help me!"

"I c'n get my gun up there—"

"Get out! Get out of here, for God's sake! Someone's coming!"

Shutters closed. She eeled down, getting splinters in her back, and soaked herself to the knees in Det water trying to get around the corner. She made it as far as her skip before the shutter banged open and lights flared above. Someone shouted, "You!" and white light stabbed down the slit and hit the water behind her.

She pulled the jury-tie, jumped in and let the Det current carry her ahead while she ran the pole out, while the light scanned the black water behind her and ran out and across the canal.

She thought, I made it worse for 'im, I only made it worse. He won't be there t'morrow night. An' I could've had a chance. . . .

C.J. CHERRYH
THE ALLIANCE-UNION UNIVERSE

The Company Wars

    DOWNBELOW STATION

The Era of Rapprochement

    SERPENT'S REACH
    FORTY THOUSAND IN GEHENNA
    MERCHANTER'S LUCH

The Chanur Novels

    THE PRIDE OF CHANUR
    CHANUR'S VENTURE
    THE KIF STRIKE BACK
    CHANUR'S HOMECOMING

The Mri Wars

    THE FADED SUN: KESRITH
    THE FADED SUN: SHON'JIR
    THE FADED SUN: KUTATH

Merovingen Nights (Mri Wars period)

    ANGEL WITH THE SWORD

Merovingen Nights—Anthologies

    FESTIVAL MOON (#1)
    FEVER SEASON (#2)
    TROUBLED WATERS (#3)
    SMUGGLER'S GOLD (#4)
    DIVINE RIGHT (#5)
    FLOOD TIDE (#6)
    ENDGAME (#7)

The Age of Exploration

    CUCKOO'S EGG
    VOYAGER IN NIGHT
    PORT ETERNITY

The Hanan Rebellion

    BROTHERS OF EARTH
    HUNTER OF WORLDS

MEROVINGEN NIGHTS

ENDGAME

C.J. CHERRYH

DAW BOOKS, INC.

DONALD A. WOLLHEIM, FOUNDER

375 Hudson Street, New York, NY 10014

ELIZABETH R. WOLLHEIM

SHEILA E. GILBERT

PUBLISHERS

Songs from this series can be heard on the tape *Fever Season* available from Firebird Arts & Music, Inc., P.O. Box 14785, Portland OR 97214-9998, phone (800) 752-0494.

DAW Book Collectors No. 857.

First Printing, August 1991
1 2 3 4 5 6 7 8 9

CONTENTS

Because the stories in this volume overlap in time they are, by the authors' consent, printed here in a "braided" format—so that they read much more like a novel than an anthology. The reader may equally well read the short stories as originally written by reading all of a given title in order of appearance.

For those who wonder how this number of writers coincide so closely—say that certain pairs of writers involved do a lot of consultation in a few frenzied weeks of phone calls as deadline approaches, then the editor, presented with the result, has to figure out what the logical order is.

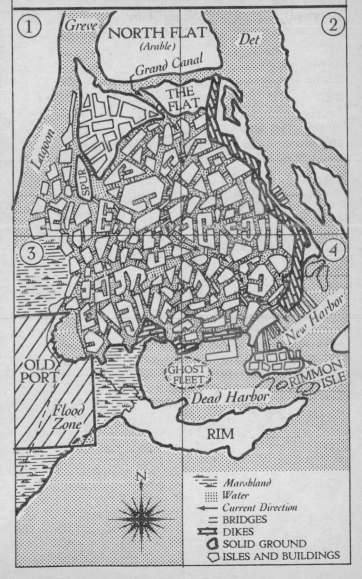

MEROVIN

① Greve
② Det

NORTH FLAT
(Arable)

Grand Canal

THE FLAT

③
④

Lagoon

SPUR

New Harbor

OLD PORT

GHOST FLEET

RIMMON ISLE

Dead Harbor

Flood Zone

RIM

N

≋ *Marshland*
⋮⋮ *Water*
← *Current Direction*
= BRIDGES
Ħ DIKES
◖ SOLID GROUND
◖ ISLES AND BUILDINGS

ENDGAME

by C. J. Cherryh

Three weeks and the bruises were mostly faded. The cuts were healing. And they trusted him with razors—give or take the large, burly servant who waited patiently for its return. Mondragon wiped the instrument on the provided linen, surrendered it to the servant, who handed him his shirt. Mondragon pulled it on and tightened the laces—silk, it was. White silk. With unstylish lace at the throat—perfectly fine in Nev Hettek, definitely out of mode in Merovingen, that made the lace. He buttoned the collar, adjusted the lace at collar and cuffs—there was nothing but time, where he was, and nothing but thinking, once the daily game with the servants and the guards was done. He straightened his hair—blond and curling and past the shoulder, the one vanity he confessed to himself. The others—the fastidiousness, the minutiae of demands he loaded on the servants—they were games. The precise order of dressing, every morning the same. The single cup of tea, exactingly hot, exactingly timed, one lump of sugar, a piece of buttered toast, one egg—

It kept the servants busy. Getting that service proved he could get it, and that small victory, in his present situation, gave him something—call it stability in his routine, call it a sense of passing time, call it a

1

sense of control in his existence, which was not in the least under his own control, on any larger scale. He was a guest in Nev Hettek's embassy, after having been a guest of Willa Exeter's inquisition, and at the moment he was a weapon on the shelf. The ambassador might decide to use him. The ambassador might decide to return him to Nev Hettek, to a prison where there were no fresh starched linens and no beds, for that matter. The ambassador might bestow him on Tatiana Kalugin, who would likely have him hanged, after other amusements paled. Or the ambassador, his old friend Chance Magruder, might decide, today, that he was simply too dangerous to use or to let surface—in which case he would die today, poison in the tea, perhaps. Or a bullet. The ambassador was Sword of God. When the Sword disposed of its own, given time and choice of method, it tended to blades or bullets.

He had his breakfast in private. He finished his tea, standing by the small slit of a window—a room with a view, Chance Magruder had joked, putting him here—and for that one favor he was ambiguously grateful. When there was no passage of time, when there was no sunrise and sunset, he slipped too easily back to that Nev Hettek prison. And such were the uncertainties in his situation that he worried even about that joke Chance had made—whether in his delirium he had betrayed that weakness, whether Chance had given him that small window precisely to keep him sane—until it suited the Sword to have him otherwise.

He had no illusions. He performed no heroics. He answered every question they asked. He answered precisely and thought how all of it connected, because he *did* hold things back: about Anastasi Kalugin, whom he served; about Richard Kamat, whom he likewise served; about the merchant militia he had helped create; about various Names, dates, and facts he had accumulated in his many times doubled career. He kept secrets about Karl Fon, the governor of Nev Hettek—many, many secrets about Fon and his rise to power. There were so many things Chance and his interrogators didn't know how to ask—didn't know they *should* ask. He thought sometimes that he should spill a few about Karl that might disturb Chance's sleep at night—it might shake Chance; it might advise Chance that he could never, having kept him prisoner this long, ever be quite safe with Karl, unless he was already privy to those things, and had agreed profoundly with Karl.

In which case, Chance should still sleep lightly, and only with the absolutely trusted companion: the lives of Karl's confidants were no more secure than his own. The lives of those Karl loved were more precarious still, because Karl hated and feared his dependencies.

God, did he know that.

He finished the tea, he rang for the servant. He stood watching the narrow dark slot of water outward from his high window; he watched the beginning sunlight on the canal, and the passage of poleboats and freighter-skips past that opening on the world. He could stand there for hours, because he knew many of the boats and their owners—he saw Suleiman's, and Rahman Singh with his wife Mary, and their daughter. He saw a hundred faces he knew not by name. And the next boat to pass might be one special skip, one that did come past now and again, *damn* the canal-rat

3

who owned her for not staying clear—if he saw it, he felt a sudden tightness in his throat, his heart beat faster, and he knew why he wanted to live; if he saw it, the sight shattered him, and he had most painstakingly to build back his nonchalance toward his fate—because, damn her, she wouldn't listen, she hadn't taken the money he'd left with Kamat for the day she might need it. Or she had it, and meant to use it for some fool attempt on a fortified embassy.

She was seventeen. She was canaler and hard-headed and if Chance swept her up, it was all over, there was nothing left, and he'd *give* Chance everything he knew—

After which Chance could kill him or send him to Karl, and beyond that he could not see. He would already be dead, whatever happened to him. Wreckage. That was all Karl would get.

He had his tea. He rang for the servants to take the breakfast tray away. Precisely on schedule, by the shadow of the embassy on the buildings across the canal.

Exactly the same, day by day. Because if he lost track of time, he was breakable. And Jones was alive, and would live so long, Anastasi had promised him, as certain things he knew never surfaced.

So he waited. He dreaded to see Jones pass through the embassy's shadow. But the days that he did see her, he knew that his silence was still buying what he'd bargained for.

4

LOST SONG

by Bradley H. Sinor

When Ethan Yeager heard the whistling, he stopped in midstep. A chill ran through him and leached his breath away with it.

The whistling continued down on the canal. A rough, uneven tune mixed in with the sound of water splashing against pilings and the regular strokes of a pole as it hit the water.

"No!" Ethan's voice was a choked whisper.

Light still lingered among the western towers of Merovingen. Down among the canals, shadows and darkness had already found their playground for the night.

Feeling gooseflesh on his arms, heart thumping, Ethan looked back at the door he'd let slam behind him. The sign nailed to the center read, "Cord and Company, Imports." At that moment he desperately wanted to see it flung open.

Please, let this all be part of some sort of elaborate joke; a bad joke, yes, but nonetheless, a joke.

Ethan knew that wouldn't happen. There was no one left in the building. He'd heard the lock bolt fall into place when the door had closed behind him. In point of fact, Ethan himself shouldn't have been there; normally he would have left two hours before.

5

Only, word had come at just past noon that m'ser Simon White's wife had gone into labor two weeks earlier than expected. So it had fallen to Ethan to handle both his own and White's duties, which included locking up.

Sitting on the walkway was a dark gray cat, missing one fang, who was carefully preening his fur. He eyed Ethan for a moment before resuming his bath.

Ethan stepped toward the railing and looked down at the canal. A dozen yards below and to the right was a single skip, riding low in the water, boxes and barrels filling every available inch of the well. At the back of the boat was a square figure of a canaler, wearing a heavy sweater, massive hands tight around his pole. He steered his skip carefully through water half-covered with tangle-lilies.

In the months since the plants had first appeared, they had become such a common sight that most people who had been cursing them, now ignored them. There were uses for the weeds, uses that the College was trying to suppress.

For him, the only thing was that song the canaler was whistling. A song the man had no right to know. A song that shouldn't exist anywhere except in his own memory. Kayleigh's song, and it had died three years ago—with her.

"You! You there on the skip!" Ethan shouted.

At first the canaler acted as if he hadn't heard anything. Then the whistling stopped and he pushed down on his pole, dragging the boat to a halt.

"If there is somebody wantin' to talk to Galen Loway," said the man, "they better have a good reason, or coin to pay for me time. I got deliveries to make."

"I've both." Ethan let fly with two copper disks that clattered onto the boat's half-deck near the canaler's feet.

" 'At's good enough fer me."

"I've got a question for you," Ethan said.

"Then might be I got the answer ye want, or might not."

"That song, the one you were whistling just now. Where did you hear it?"

The man stared at Ethan. This wasn't what he'd expected. Although hightowners were notoriously strange in their doings, any canaler could tell you that. Better to have as little to do with them as possible, especially in these troubled times: you never could tell who was working for the priests and who wasn't. Trouble with the blacklegs was the last thing he needed, especially considering what was buried inside one of his crates.

"Song? You mean that thing I was whistlin' just now? I couldn't tell you, don't rightly know. Last week or two I probably heard someone else whistlin' it and just picked up the tune without really thinkin'. Happens all the time."

"So where have you been the last week or two?"

"Here and there, mostly makin' deliveries fer Rohan. They got a couple of ships in from the Falken Isles and they definitely been keepin' me busy."

Ethan knew the Rohan Family, one of the smaller merchant companies. He'd heard something not that long since about m'sera Rohan booting her daughter out for trying to kill her.

He turned on his heel and headed off. From the canal came the sound of laughter and the muffled words, "Crazy hightowners."

7

*   *   *

Ethan sagged down in his chair. He scowled at the distorted reflection in the copper side of the mug. The bloated, dark face seemed to match the way he felt right then.

By now half the canalers in this town must be convinced I'm either a spy for the College, or demented, or both.

The last three days had jogged memories of Kayleigh and her death among the canalers. Only they knew as little as he. On one thing, all agreed: there was no way she could still be alive.

From the far side of the common room came a wave of laughter. Ethan drew a long swallow from his beer, forcing a tired chuckle. A good, stiff drink had seemed just the thing; help clear his head so he could figure out what to do.

Kay-leigh.

Ethan glanced across the sea of bobbing heads that filled Moghi's. Most were locals, canalers and the like, with a scattering of faces he didn't know.

The first time he'd laid eyes on Kayleigh had been at one of old man Greely's parties. He'd not been invited, but that hadn't stopped him from going, if for no other good reason than to irritate Simon Greely. When the two of them had met as children, they'd taken an instant dislike to each other. The passing years had done nothing to change that feeling.

Kayleigh had been part of the night's entertainment, along with two other musicians. It hadn't surprised Ethan in the least that Simon had fastened on her like a leech.

She'd protested and that had been all the invitation

Ethan had needed. "I could have handled him without your interference," she had told him later.

"Oh, little doubt you could've, m'sera," he'd laughed. "Little doubt indeed. Understand that you were a means to an end. Irritating Simon has been a minor hobby with me for years."

"An honest rogue, how refreshing! Then I suppose you'd best walk me home this evening, just in case young m'ser Greely decides to follow me."

"I'd be honored."

Six months later—the explosion of that boiler on her family's boat . . . the night Kayleigh had gone home to them because she and Ethan had had an argument.

"You're looking glum enough," said a voice from his left.

The last thing he wanted was company. "I really . . ."

He stopped right there. Standing near the table was the last person he would have expected that night, or, for that matter, any night in the last couple of months.

Nadra Ratliff.

Her short raven hair and enigmatic smile hadn't changed since the two of them were youngsters playing in the back of her father's print shop.

"Nadra?"

"Just make it Rat."

"Oh, yeah," he said. "So where's the other half of that act?"

For just a moment a shadow passed across Rat's face. "You were saving that chair for Governor Kalugin, no doubt? I'm afraid he's not going to make it. Tied up taste-testing a new shipment of wine, I suspect. So I'll take it. After all, we wouldn't want it to get about that you were a solitary drunk, now would we?"

Before he could answer, Rat had unslung the heavy bag she wore across her back. From the size and shape, Ethan was fairly certain it held her gitar. She carefully set the bag on the floor, resting it against the wall, before sitting down.

"I'm surprised the blacklegs haven't had you to the justiciar, considering the lyrics of a few of those songs that have gotten credited to you."

"It's nice to see you again, too, Ethan," laughed Rat. "As for the justiciar, he hasn't caught me yet." Waving to the waitress, Rat ordered beer for the two of them.

"A lot better for you than that watered-down canal juice Moghi tries to pass off as wine these days," she said.

Ethan sighed, shaking his head.

He could remember a very different Rat, one he'd shamed into taking her first drink of beer when they had both been nine years old. Hell, it'd been his first as well, but at the time he would sooner have died than admit it.

Had their parents had their way, Rat and he would have long ago been contract-married. The only problem with that plan was that neither Rat nor he had been consulted, and neither wanted anything to do with it.

For a long time neither one spoke. Rat finished one beer and ordered another. "So what's the matter?" she finally asked. "As if I couldn't guess."

"What's that supposed to mean?"

"Simple, the only times in the last couple of years

I've seen you looking this down is when you start brooding about Kayleigh."

"Mind your business."

"Ethan, it's been three years since that boat blew. She's gone, dead. You got to accept that and get on with the rest of your life."

"Yeah. Sure."

"Look, I know you loved her. I loved her, too. Besides Rif and you, she was probably one of the best friends I ever had. So don't think you got a monopoly on sorry. If she walked in that door right now and saw you like this, she'd probably be undecided whether to kiss you or kick your butt for acting like an idiot."

"More than like, both," he said.

"If it were at least the anniversary of the thing, that I might be able to understand. But that's another four months."

"Five and a half, but then you always were terrible with dates."

"Only when it was ones my folks arranged."

Ethan began to whistle. It was the same song Kayleigh had played for him that last night, before they'd quarreled.

"That's beautiful," said Rat. "What's the point?"

"It was Kayleigh's."

Rat arched an eyebrow.

Ethan shrugged and took a long swallow, draining his mug. "She said she'd only just finished it. Two hours later she was dead, all because of a stupid argument I can't remember the reasons of now."

Rat traced a design with the edge of her fingernail in the surface of the table. "You had no way of knowing about the boiler. Her father had been keeping the thing running with prayers and wire for years. That piece of iron was just too tired to keep on going."

"Maybe," he admitted. "But the trouble is, that song, the one Kayleigh wrote for me—"

"So?"

"Until a couple of nights ago, I thought no one but me knew that piece of music. Then I heard a canaler whistling it."

Rat sat there for a long time, not really looking at anything. "I suppose it's too much to hope for we both had a few too many tonight."

"I doubt even Moghi has enough to get me that drunk."

"All right, let's say for a minute that *is* Kayleigh's song and not just one that sounded like it. You believe in ghosts?"

For that moment every other sound in Moghi's faded away to the barest whisperings.

"Maybe," said Ethan. "Nadra, I'm scared . . . like I've never been before. Scared of what I'm going to find, or maybe what I'm not going to find. I told you we had a fight that night."

"And you think maybe if you two hadn't fought she might be alive."

"Yeah."

"Look, you'll never know about what might have happened if you hadn't fought that night. Forget that bilge. As for being scared, that's fine. Scared might keep us two alive tonight."

"Us?" he said, eyeing her.

"I heard that piece myself this week. Down harborside. Pretty piece. So was the guy singing it."

*   *   *

Set something up, Rat had said, and something else about needing to stash her gitar somewhere. Join you, she said, in an hour, near Rohan warehouse. Then she vanished into the dark of Ventani walkway.

"You're very good at that," he said to the place where she had been standing.

He took the long walk down to harborside, slowly. He lingered in a shadowed nook and waited. At this time of night, most of the honest life of Merovingen had moved far away from the warehouse district to the towers of hightown and the canal taverns. What few people were still about were lone walkers hurrying on their silent way, or couples so lost in each other they wouldn't have noticed the Nev Hettek army.

It began to drizzle slightly, bringing a feverish chill to the air. Ethan drew a breath and let it out in a long sigh.

A tall, lanky figure, wrapped in a hooded cape, moved harborward along the walkway, stopping only a dozen steps away from Ethan's hiding place. Who-ever the stranger was, he moved with swaggering bra-vado that defied the elements to do their worst. *Either very confident in this neighborhood*, Ethan thought, *or very stupid—or maybe a bit of both.*

The mist turned suddenly to a pelting rain, drown-ing the few lanterns hung along the walkway. In the east, rolls of thunder echoed among churning gray clouds. Reflexively, Ethan pulled his hood up.

A second figure stepped from the shadows, just behind the first. Two quick blows and it was over, the cloaked man sent sprawling onto his knees. Before Ethan could say or do anything, the whole of the walk was illuminated for a heartbeat by a lightning bolt.

That was long enough to reveal the face of the second figure.

"Rat!"

"Don't just stand there, help me get him into the shadow."

Ethan grabbed the unconscious figure's legs, pulling him back into the nook by the warehouse door.

"What the hell is going on?" Ethan asked. "I thought you had a bit more in mind than trying to pick up spare change."

"Yey," she said. "Besides, this young fellow and most of his cousins were broke by sundown the first day they hit port." Rat pulled the stranger's hood back. Lightning flashed. He couldn't be more than fifteen or sixteen years old. The blond hair, along with the height, were a dead giveaway. A Falkenaer seaman.

"It's a damn kid!"

"Pretty kid. Nice voice. Let's find out what other tunes he knows." She slapped the young man's face twice in quick succession. That was enough to stir a moan and set his eyes to blink.

"What th'. . . ? Gawd, what th' hell happen't t' me?"

"You got careless," said Rat. "That's the sort of thing can end you up with a knife between your ribs." One flashed in Rat's hand. The kid looked at it wide-eyed.

" 'T weren't fair, ain't fair a't all, comin' at me fra behind like that."

"You come halfway around this world," said Rat, "and you still think life is fair? Kid, this has got to be your first voyage."

Ethan asked, "So what's your name, boy?"

The young Falkenaer looked at Rat and then at Ethan. "Mathias. 'Ey calls me Matt."

"A'right, Matt," Rat said, "that's a good start. Now let's talk music."

"Music?" The kid's face was white in the lightning flashes.

"Oh, don't start with that kind of crap," snarled Rat. "The two of us are cold, wet, and tired. Ethan, give me five minutes with the likes of him and I'll have all the answers we want. The rain'll wash away the blood."

"Lad, I'd think seriously about answering the questions if I were you. Believe me, this lady can be very, very nasty."

Definite anxiousness to cooperate: "What d'ye want?"

"You sang a song yesterday," Rat said. "Want you to tell me the tunemaker."

"Yeah?"

Rat hummed a half dozen bars of Kayleigh's song. "That 'un. Who?"

To have referred to Sulaco's Tavern as a dive would have been a radical rise in status for the place.

Nobody knew exactly who Sulaco had been, or if there really was such a person. For as long as anyone could remember, a small surly man known as Morse had run the place.

Most of the tavern's trade came from sailors, and workers who frequented the docks. This included the sailors from the ships under the banner of the Falken Islands. There wasn't another tavern in all of Merovingen that'd let more than two of them in at a time.

Morse didn't care, he was just interested in their money.

"Ethan," said Rat, "I'm not at all certain you coming along was a particularly good idea."

"You may be right," Ethan allowed.

It was like walking into a steam bath. The main room was crowded, but Rat found them a table near the door.

The confusion of sounds rumbled in Ethan's ears as he studied the crowd. Here and there the shorter, darker locals stuck out like sore thumbs.

"So much for the element of surprise," he said.

Across the room, a woman with curly brown hair and a somewhat younger blond woman stepped up on a makeshift stage. They each carried gitars and struck up a slightly out of key tune. Behind them a thin, bearded man began to back their music on a small drum he held strapped around his chest.

"Looks like you and Rif have some competition."

"Not bloody likely. One of 'em's a docker, the others is a pair of bridge-way artists," snored Rat. "This place is the best booking they're likely to get."

From all around the room came various suggestions for tunes. The two women conferred for several beats before striking up a sea jig.

"Say, how's about giving us a dance, Ciara!" someone called out from near the stage.

"That's better than you deserve, you old goat," a woman shouted back from another stage.

"Oh, go on." Others added their voices. Even the musicians joined in.

"All right."

She was tall, this girl called Ciara. Men helped her up onto the stage where she stood with her back to the audience for several moments, whispering with the three performers.

The music changed, a livelier, more complicated tune this time, a ballad called "Moonfinder." After a moment's hesitation the girl started to move in sync with the music, ignoring the catcalls and yells.

Then she began to sing, a rich soprano voice that cut across the throbbing din of the crowd. Ethan's head jerked up with a start: he looked at the stage. He was listening not to the song but to the singer's voice. She turned toward his table and pulled her cap off; long red hair came tumbling out.

"Kayleigh!" His voice was a rusty whisper.

From Rat: "God, it really *is* her."

Ethan was out of his chair almost before Rat realized it. She was barely able to grab him and pull him back toward their table.

"Look, you love-sick fool, d'you want to get us killed? Not to mention maybe her as well!" Rat's voice had gone hard and cutting. "They obviously think of her as one of their own now. I know the Falkenaers, man, and if they even think you're threatenin' one of them, they'll all be on ye. Ye'll get a knife in your gut if you go runnin' up there!"

"So what am I supposed to do? Don't ask me to walk away and leave her, I won't!"

"Of course not! All I'm asking is you use your head for once. Ye'll find it a refreshing experience."

The rain had slacked off to a light mist, though gray clouds still churned and bubbled across the sky. Following Kayleigh had been Rat's idea. *Talk to her somewhere away from the Falkenaers, that's the smart thing to do.* Ethan had to admit Rat had been right.

Still, the sight of Kayleigh (what had they called her? Ciara?) up on that stage had made him forget anything but her.

"Karma, god, she's going to end up paying for all this a dozen lifetimes to come," Ethan said.

"Let's not start with any of your Revenantist crap," Rat muttered. "You'd look like hell in orange robes."

A couple of coins had bought them the location of Kayleigh's room, the far back of the hall on the canalside floor.

"I presume you've considered the possibility she might not want to see either one of us?" said Rat.

That had occurred to Ethan, more times than he wanted to admit, in the hour since they had left Sulaco's. He had pushed it into the back of his mind, something to be dealt with one if it happened.

As they walked back into the dimly lit hall, Ethan heard a scream, then a woman's voice and a string of epithets that stung even Ethan's ears. He ran down the corridor and yanked open the door of Kayleigh's room.

A large man, dressed in oilcloth breeches and a vest, held Kayleigh's arms pinned against the wall. Blood streamed from scratches across his face. "Get outta here," he growled at Ethan, "or I'll gut ye like a fish!"

Ethan landed his boot in the man's side. The impact was enough to make him let go of Kayleigh, and send him falling over a chair just behind him. Before the man could get back on his feet Ethan picked up the chair and slammed it down over his head.

"Didn't I do this once before?" said Ethan, turning to Kayleigh.

Kayleigh stared. Kayleigh screeched, "Who the hell

do you think you are, th' Angel come to save helpless little me? I'm *not* one of your pampered Merovingen pets! I could have handled this idiot, with one hand tied behind me—*and* would've if you hadn't stuck your nose in where it doesn't belong!"

Ethan started to laugh. Word for word they'd had this same conversation three and a half years before, the night of Greely's party. It seemed somehow appropriate to a reunion.

"Would some'un mind t' tell me what's goin' on?" A big man, greasy blond hair streaked with gray, filled the doorframe.

Behind him, a crowd of others, including Rat, was straining to get a look in the room. The man looked then at the guy on the floor, and shook his head. "Worden, I might a' knowt! Are ye a'right, Ciara?"

"Aye, sir, just got the wind knocked out of me. Worden was waiting here for me; took me by surprise. Nothing I couldn't have handled, but *hero* over here burst in and lent a hand."

"Yer name, lad," said the big man, turning toward Ethan.

"Yeager. Ethan Yeager."

"Well, Ethan Yeager, I'm Ian Margroff, first mate on th' Coldsmith out a' Hyei'a in the Isles. Ciara, 'ere, beside bein' one o' me best 'ands, is me adoptet daughter. Ye fought for 'er, some'at not too many people in this stinkin' city would a' done."

"You're welcome," Ethan said, shaking his hand. Then he turned to Kayleigh. "Only her name isn't Ciara."

There wasn't a sound in the entire room or the hallway outside. "You know her?" asked the Falkenaer, slowly.

"Yes."

Margroff looked at Kayleigh, running his fingers across his cheek. "Well, ye al'ays said ye wanted answers we couldn' gie ye. Looks as if ye found 'un."

"I know—and it scares me."

"Do I scare you?" asked Ethan.

"No."

That was enough for him. "Your name is Kayleigh Gallion. I thought you were dead. Then I heard someone whistling that song you wrote me—three years ago."

Margroff said, "It were three year' since th' *Coldsmith* made port in these waters. We been keepin' down among the Chat an' back."

"Where did you find her?"

"Even tide, just afore we was about t' weigh anchor, some'un said they spotted a body i' th' water. One of our'n went down t' see and found 'er, more dead'n alive. We could na'means wait the tide, sa we took 'er wi' us." He put his arm around Kayleigh, ruffled her hair. "When she come 'round she had no memory 'oo she was 'er how she fell i' th' water. Me own daughter'd died, sa I adoptet 'er."

"And that song?" asked Ethan.

"I dreamed it," she said. "Ever'body liked it and it just sort of spread around the ship. I dream it now and then."

"Then you do remember me."

She shook her head and stared down at the bed. I don't. But it feels right," she said, seeming to search for the words. "You *feel* right being here. I'm afraid that's all I know right now."

"Kayleigh, it's enough—if you want me to stay."

"I want you to stay—but my name's Ciara. Let's start from there."

"All right, —Ciara."

Ethan turned toward Rat, about to call her over, only to discover his old friend in conversation with one of the young Falkenaer sailors outside the door.

"So you all just docked last night," she was saying. "I don't suppose you got any plans how you're going to spend your shore leave."

"Not really," he said.

Ethan smiled as he watched Rat slide her arm around the sailor's waist.

Thinking, *Kid, this is one shore leave you won't soon forget.*

ENDGAME (REPRISED)

by C. J. Cherryh

Night on the Grand and Merovingen took on a glum and smoky air in this rainy, muggy night in which Moghi's Tavern was a hazed glow of light and life, poleboats and skips in plenty tied up at Moghi's porch. Inside, bare-footed skip-freighters and slippered pole-boatmen consorted with canalsiders in wooden clogs, drank, had the stew Jep served up and muttered in corners. It was a comfort, of evenings, to gather where the Trade gathered, where there were no strange faces and, on a body's life and hope of his throat remaining uncut, no spies to report chance remarks and unchance ones to the Bloody Cardinal. Willa Exeter's spies might have cowed hightown and gulled the midtown merchants with her hunt after heretics and sharrh-wor-shippers, but here in Merovingen Below, in the web of waterways and the nethermost of Merovingen's thousand bridges, canalers still spoke their minds to those they trusted.

And no few called Altair Jones a fool, like the Ancestors who had refused to leave, and been Scoured to the hills and the caves by a space-faring enemy no Merovingian today could describe or remember.

Might be she was a fool. She clung to her loyalties the way Merovingen clung to its existence, rocked by earthquakes, of which there had been the least tremor this afternoon, a wooden city poised on pilings between the flood and the shaking earth. There were people like Moghi, who said, "Jones, take my word: ain't nothing you can do. Nothing anybody can do. Forget 'im. Man's bound for Det's bottom or Fon's jails, and nothing ye can buy nor bribe can do a thing. I know."

(And Moghi knew the cost of everything in Merovingen Above and Below.)

There were those like Tommy, who said, in his gawkish way, "I'd go wi' ye, Altair, ye know I would . . . but I think we'd both be kill't."

And Tommy would—both go and be kill't—because one Thomas Mondragon was in the gut of the Nev Hettek embassy, an improvement on the Justiciary basement, so Jones hoped: the Justiciary swallowed those the light would never see again, and maintained deep in its stony gut a room where secrets got torn out of mortal bodies; after which the ax, so the penitent could go on to Revenantist rebirth, all for defying the Bloody Cardinal. The Justiciary had swallowed Mondragon down, but Nev Hettek had reclaimed him and stowed him away in its (to a canal-rat, so far) impenetrable heart. Safer there than in the Cardinal's hands—so Jones hoped.

He'd come out unscathed before, she told herself. Anastasi damn-'im Kalugin had had him in his hands a godawful while that she had been sure terrible things were going on: she'd skipped meals in her worry and gone thin and desperate, until out he walked one afternoon all hightown and clean and fine, and not a mark on him—on the outside at least.

But she knew the ones that didn't show. She knew the nights Mondragon waked sweating and shaking, in a fear he wouldn't show in the waking day, she knew the fears he wouldn't talk about, and these last weeks her own memories haunted her, the night she'd first fished Mondragon from the Det, all white and pale and scared, at first, because he'd come loose from what he knew, and drifted back to Nev Hettek prison in his mind. She didn't want to think about that, but she dreamed about it nowadays. Mondragon hated being held or shut in, and a canaler, who'd never till she met him slept with a roof over her head or on a surface that did not move to the tides and the waves— a canal-rat could understand that panic more than most. And *she'd* been in a cell once, on Mondragon's account. She knew something about nightmares, and locked doors, and not being able to do a damn thing about what other people wanted from you. Damn them.

Day and night now she thought about roofs over one's head, and doors locked and windows shuttered, and she grew grimmer and more desperate, with thoughts ranging from breaking and entering to a fire-bottle on the embassy's doorstep; but on the one hand the Nev Hettekkers weren't Megarys, to do anything slipshod; and on the other a fire could trap Mondragon somewhere she couldn't get him out of in time. And that was a terrible way to die.

She shoved the stew around looking for edible bits—she took good care of herself the same mechanical way she took good care of Mama's revolver, and for the same reason. She turned thoughts of violence over and over in her head, and she kept an ear to harbor gossip, half dreading and half fearing the arrival of a Nev Hettek ship that she was sure would take Mondragon aboard and take him away for good.

If they moved him out of the embassy and onto the canals for any reason, she had a chance, no matter how slim and desperate: that was to hope for.

But there was an equal chance then of losing him for good—to Karl Fon, who was of all Mondragon's enemies the one she least understood and the one human alive besides Anastasi that sent Mondragon sweating awake at night.

Fon had, so she'd heard Rif whisper once, depended on Mondragon for his next thought and his next ambition, in the days when they had been friends—so Rif said. Rif had said Fon was a shell these days, a crazy as sure as the crazies that poled rafts about Dead Harbor skimming for food and victims. *This* was the sherk-hearted skit that waited to take Merovingen—while old Iosef Kalugin still governed in this creaking, stinking town, and the Bloody Cardinal, Willa Exeter, used her office and the purge of heretics to pick off Mikhail Kalugin's enemies—meaning anybody in the town who favored Mikhail's sister Tatiana, who had the police, or Mikhail's younger brother Anastasi, who had the brains.

Papa Iosef didn't *want* a successor with brains: that was why Iosef had Mikhail for an heir. Neither did the old Families who liked Things As They Were want an active successor—neither Tatiana who was in bed (literally) with Nev Hettek; nor Anastasi the Chief Militiar who wasn't—who wanted war with Nev Hettek: the Old Families backed safe, simple Mikhail the Clockmaker, who wouldn't stand a candle's chance of having his own way against his advisers.

And so long as Mikhail had the votes in Council to succeed, Iosef knew his neck was safe from Tatiana *and* Anastasi.

A canal-rat had learned all too much of politics in her young life—learned it because politics and knives went thick and dangerous about Tom Mondragon. And because she'd flat ignored her Mama's advice and cared about a fool of a man and a Nev Hettekker former Sword-of-Godder revolutionary to boot.

She drank down the whiskey and got up and walked out the door, away from the light and the noise and out into the feverish night air where skips rode at tie like so many black fish, hers among them; and into the sight of the Angel who stood on Hanging Bridge, the Angel who watched over fools, the Angel Retribution who stood with his sword half-sheathed. Some swore the Angel's hand had moved of late, drawing that sword a little more—or putting it away, as happened, Adventist folk said, at every foolish or cowardly deed that set the Retribution and the return of Merovan folk to space that much further off; and at every wicked karmic debt, Revenantist folk said, that bound Merovan souls tighter to the great Wheel of lives and death on Merovin. There had been plenty of both in Merovingen—to which Hanging Bridge bore bitter witness, tonight, two corpses left there for the town's edification and the terror of anyone who might call Bloody Exeter a tyrant or a power-seeking crazy.

Two young corpses, of Rush and Basargin—not bad boys, only given to pranks, tweaks at dignity, and speaking the truth. Jones shook her head and climbed off the porch onto the Wylies' boat, and walked that on sure bare feet over onto the gunwale of her skip and so down into the slat-bottomed well, all lost in thoughts and remembrances. No cargo tonight, nor any in days previous—it was Mondragon's money she was living on, slipping ghostlike from Kamat's cut to this and that low spot in town where she recognized the regular clientele by name and habit . . . knowing that the Cardinal's slinks or Nev Hettek's could take a notion any day that she was safer for their plans at Det's black bottom; or that having her in their hands might make Mondragon easier to deal with.

Lord only knew. If they wanted her they could try. She had her knife and her loading hook constantly in her belt. She had her mama's revolver in the drop-bin of her skip. And perhaps she was too slippery and perhaps they feared the Trade, which had shut Merovingen down in time past for an offense against one of its own; or perhaps it was only that Altair Jones was too small a fish to concern them, or even that all canal-rats looked alike in the dark.

So she slipped the tie of her skip to the Wylies' and unracked the pole and moved out the old way, from before the new engines, the quiet, simple way, just a shove or two away and into the black waters of the Grand, a shove and a push of the pole to bring the blunt bow about, and a little slip downcurrent to bring the skip across the wide dark waters to the up-town lane.

The bow came toward the north, a single skip gliding along in silence under the shadows of Fishmarket Bridge, past honest family boats at night-ties, lovers tucked down in hideys, children asleep under tarps on the half-decks on this drizzly, thundery night, and the smog of cookfires making halos about the shore lights. Acquaintance with a piling or a boat-stern was damned likely if a body didn't have good nightsight.

Jones did. The night had been her Mama's time— Retribution Jones, who'd run the dark ways all her too-short life until she died of a fever and not (surprising everyone who knew her) of a smuggler's bullet. The night had been her Mama's time for her Mama's reasons; and it was hers, for her own, until she hardly dared the daylight in this town.

That she would go up to the embassy, tonight, because the fog offered a chance for slipping about— a fool could guess it. She'd gone before this to search and spy under the embassy's balconies and windows. And that there might be traps—she *could* guess it. But she meant to try again, and again till she found a way to Mondragon.

She glided up under Golden Bridge, up into the Isles of the rich and the powerful. She was sweating by then from fear as well as the work, and she took a good grip on the pole as she shoved the skip around the corner to glide into more dangerous waters, a territory where fancyboats were moored behind secure locked water-gates and watched by guards through lacy garde-ports, cat-whale faces, and sherks and the imagined countenances of sharrh.

It was the upper windows she looked to—sat and waited a moment or two as if she would tie up; and then moved on for another view, prowling around and around the hightown Isle which rented the Nev Hettekkers space near the seats of power in Merovingen.

Damn them. Damn Karl Fon.

Damn a fool, Mama always said. Mama showed up again, sitting on the bow of the ship—weighing not a thing, of course; Mama braced a bare foot against the edge and tipped back the river-runner's cap that even in her time had seen better days. Mama said, Didn't I tell ye, Altair?

"Yey, Mama," Jones said patiently. "Couldn't you be some help for a change?"

Mama said, Comes of takin' in strangers. Comes of believin' any smooth-talkin' man.

"Shut up, Mama," Jones whispered, on her next out-breath, and shoved with the pole. She didn't want Mama to go, not really, Mama being only there when things got loneliest—a figment, Mondragon would say. Which meant Mama wasn't truly there, only her memory was.

But Mama had the old pistol tonight, cleaning it and oiling it the way Mama had used to do before a run. Mama looked askance at her and said, the way she had done more than once, Ye be sure t' count your shots, Altair. Ye never fire the last.

Jones shivered. Stone walls and water and wind made a chill to the air even with the sweat running on her sides. Fever season again. Tangle-lilies in the city's veins in one long delirium of night and quaking earth.

There was one window, one, if you run round the end of the Isle and past that dark, iron-gated cut that offered tie-ups to the embassy's sleek fancyboats—and the blind shoring-up of downside's tilting pilings. If you hung just in that spot you could see into that shadow and once and twice she'd seen light there after hours. Could be a guard-post. Or it could be a man who didn't sleep without bad dreams.

She had brought a pocketful of pebbles from off Ventani Isle, the only solid rock but the Rock and Rimmon. She lapped a tie about a lesser piling, got out and soft-footed it along the walkway lowermost until she could wriggle into that water-filled slit with a trick she'd learned from a bridge-brat of a Takahashi, and with shoulders and feet braced, worked her way up and up in that narrow niche until she could see that shuttered, light-seamed window only a story above and a boat-length deeper into the slit.

She got a pared bit of greenroot from her pocket, she put that pebble on the bent-back tongue, and she let fly at that window, thinking, Yey, Mama, here's your daughter. If it ain't his window, I'm in deep water.

The pebble hit the shutter. She braced there a heart-breaking long moment and finally slithered downward in dejection.

But the light went out behind the shutter. She froze. The shutter came open, and she hung there between the sky and the water, thinking, Whoever's there—is doin' what *he'd* do.

—But so'd any of the Sword as live in there.

She didn't want to move, hoping to look like a shadow. But her legs began to tremble and her arms to shake from holding herself braced, her back was afire with pain, and she thought, He ain't *standin'* in that window, ain't no way he'd make hisself a target. He's waitin', ain't he?

She cleared her throat, said in a thin, scared, short-of-breath squeak, "Mondragon? 'S 'at you?"

She saw a dim gleam of white shirt and blond head in that window. Came a whispered: "Jones? Jones, dammit, get out of here!"

She hung there shaking with strain and looking up toward that dark that showed her too little, but enough to hope on.

"Mondragon ye a'right? Can ye squeeze out some'ow?"

"No! I can't. You think they're stupid? Get *out* of

here, dammit, don't—" He stopped speaking a beat or two, sounding breathless, and what eyes couldn't see, heart pictured—the desperation, the relief to hear from her. "Don't be a damned fool! You can't help me!"

"I c'n get my gun up there—"

"Get out! Get out of here, for God's sake! Someone's coming!"

Shutters closed. She eeled down, getting splinters in her back, and soaked herself to the knees in Det water trying to get around the corner. She made it as far as her skip before the shutter banged open and lights flared above. Someone shouted, "You!" and white light stabbed down the slit and hit the water behind her.

She pulled the jury-tie, jumped in and let the Det current carry her ahead while she ran the pole out, while the light scanned the black water behind her and ran out and across the canal.

She thought, I made it worse for 'im, I only made it worse. He won't be there t'morrow night. An' I could've had a chance. . . .

View of the wall, little else. The guard who had his wrist jammed up toward his shoulderblades didn't try to break the arm if he breathed carefully, and Mondragon took two and three breaths, now he was sure Jones was clear. New cut on the mouth. Dislocated shoulder if the guard pushed it further. He stood there with his other arm and his cheek against the wall, the guard's feet between his, and listened to what he could hear in the hallway, which was Sword officers shouting orders to check the perimeters and a team to get a boat out there.

There wasn't a thing he could do but wait, now. He could take out the guards in this room. He might get as far as halfway out of this place before he ran into a locked door or a chained gate—he knew the floor plan, he'd gotten that for Anastasi, and he knew the way out. But he knew what was between him and escape, too, and maybe he'd lost his edge, or maybe he wasn't a fool, and maybe he knew that there was nowhere to go out there—

Not to Kamat any longer. He was a liability.

Anastasi, maybe. He still held out that hope. But the Sword would go for Jones, then. He had Chance's promise and he believed it. He could get to Anastasi or he could get to Jones before they caught him—and Anastasi had the wherewithal and the motive to protect him, but Jones hadn't, and he couldn't; and he wouldn't bring the trouble to her.

If he died—then maybe she wouldn't be important enough to track down.

Or maybe they'd think he'd told her things he never had.

He heard Chance's voice saying, "Let him go."

The pressure on his arm let up, the arm fell numb at his side, and he shoved himself away from the wall with the other hand, set his back to it and leaned there looking innocent as he could.

Chance said, man who'd grown gray since he'd known him—"Jones, was it?"

He said, "Fishmonger. Saying they didn't answer downst—"

The guard lifted his arm. Chance stopped it.

"No. He knows. He does know. —Tom, what do you want? You want to see her?"

He shook his head.

Chance said: "Do you think we can't?"

He said, "I know you can. That's why I'm talking to you."

"Not as well as you know how."

"You *want* me to go on talking, you keep your hands off her."

"That's not the way it works. We know that's not the way it works."

He didn't say anything more. Not until Chance told the guards to go away. Then he said, "If you want me alive, Chance. That *is* the way it works. What do you want? Ask me."

"Tell me," Chance said, "something you haven't said."

"Honor among thieves?"

"Favors owed. Deal?"

He thought a moment. There were so many things. There were favors owed, to every side. He said, desperately, "Ask me a question."

"What broke you from Karl?"

Dangerous territory. He leaned against the wall, looked at the ceiling. "Karl wanted somebody he could control. Didn't trust me." A look straight at Chance, a half-sarcastic: "You don't trust him?"

"Does anybody trust anybody?"

"Think about it, Chance, think who's dead and who's alive."

Long silence. Mondragon's heart beat a frantic rhythm into his veins. Finally Chance said,

"Yeah. I do think about that. What else do you know?"

Time to bargain for more time. For the things that would kill him. "You want to know who really took out Stani?"

"Who?"

"Karl."

Long silence, then. Popular wing leader, Stani. Chance gave not a flicker.

"Yeah?" Chance said then. "Keep going."

There were ways fancyboats couldn't take, there were ways a skip poler had to be damn good to use, lean with the pole, step to the rim, and if the well wasn't carrying cargo, the bow'd lift and set down again around a turn a lander'd swear wasn't possible.

And by those last night she'd come to West and down by the sea-gate and Old Foundry, where there were hideouts aplenty—maybe not unknown to the Sword, but searching those would take the sherks time, time during which she'd taken her pistol out of the drop-bin, lifted the tiller-bar, started the engine and gone roaring out the Dike gate to the deep shadow of the docks, a watery dark forest of pilings— follow her there? Only if the Sword wanted a stove boat and a drink of Det water.

But that left her nothing to do but to think, and think, and, once the shakes and running sweat had gone to wind-chill and shivers, to tuck up in a blanket with the pistol in her hands and let her teeth chatter, thinking she wished some Sword agent would find her. She wanted a target. She wanted whoever'd do Mondragon hurt.

Most of all she wanted the storm to break, the earth to shake, crazy Cassie's Retribution to come before morning, because in the confusion she could go back there shooting and get him out of that damned place. She was down to hoping for the Angel to do something. And Mama had said it right, when you were waiting for the Angel, you weren't thinking any more.

So think, fool, ain't any help in Moghi. Moghi won't touch a thing like this. Ain't any help in 'Stasi Kalugin—is there?

Go to him an' gettin' out ain't real likely. Black yacht parked up on Archangel, he's prob'ly there. . . .

But goin' belowdecks, the way he'd insist, what's he got, but me, and if he could get Mondragon away from the Sword, wouldn't he? He's got most to lose if Mondragon talks. So he can't. An' I'd be a fool t' walk in there.

Call a council, get th' Trade t' move? Block the canals? But is that goin' to do anything but get Mondragon t' Tatiana's hands—that he ain't right now means the Sword is hangin' onto him real hard. He was Sword. An' he knows things they won't want Tatty t' get her hands on. He prob'ly knows things on Magruder he don't want Tatty t' hear. But Tatty— Tatty ain't the woman I'd want t' turn 'im over to.

He'd play the game, damn sure. And he'd be alive. 'Stasi'd be wild to shut 'im up. So'd a raft of others in this town. . . . Tatty's a thought.

But ain't there another? Ain't there *some* I could beg or bribe?

Yey, c'mon, we got to break into th' Nev Hettek embassy uptown?

Crazies in the swamp wouldn't buy in on that 'un.

PROVING GROUND

by Mercedes Lackey

The baby wailed, and Morgan tucked sweat-damp strands of hair behind her ears, then rocked the infant against her chest in an attempt to soothe her. She might as well have tried to stop the canal below from flowing; she got no more result than when sera had tried to feed the poor mite a bit ago. She felt her own irritation building to an irrational anger, and did her best to control it. "I know you've the upsets, child," she told the youngest member of the Kamat family wearily, "And I know your poor tummy is hurting. But crying only makes you hot as well as upset, can't you suffer in silence?"

All the nursery windows were open in an attempt to catch a hint of breeze: the stench of the canals and the humidity in the still air were punishing enough in and of themselves. The weather alone was enough to make the baby fretful, and set all the House on edge. One prayed for another storm to gather and break, and indeed, hour after hour, huge banks of clouds towered above the city and the air grew even more oppressive, heavy with the portent of storm.

A little shake just then. A tremor. One stopped. And waited. And rocked again.

Add to that the ominous sense of a storm of politi-

cal upheaval in the offing, and Marina's daily out-
bursts of hysteria, and you had a recipe for trouble as
certain as the sun shone down—even the baby felt it;
and add in her pain . . . little wonder she kept up that
pitiful keening night and day.

Morgan knew all that; it didn't make the infant's
fussing any easier to cope with. Morgan held the baby
against her own clammy shoulder, and stared down at
the dark canal below the open window. Lace-bedecked
curtains beside her moved, but only with the faint
movement of air caused by her rocking, not with any
real breeze. Thunder rumbled, but far away.

"Lord, child," she said over the wails, "your voice
is carrying right down to the kitchen. I've had to chase
that cook's helper away twice, and her thinking you
were wet or hungry and everyone too busy to see to
you. You see what you're doing to my reputation? If
you keep this up, soon even m'sera Andromeda will
think I'm not caring for you right."

"Not a chance, sera Morgan," said a rich young
tenor voice from behind her. "Everyone in the House
knows you're with her day and night. I'll take her, if
you like; I've got something for her from Dr.
Jonathon."

Morgan's heart jumped into her throat at the unexpected sound of a voice at her back, and she stiffened
automatically at Raj Takahashi's first words. A frac-
tion of a second later she recognized the voice and
forced herself to relax. She was just as jumpy as any
of the rest of the House—except, perhaps, Marina
Kamat: Marina, the baby's mother, was supremely
indifferent to everything but Mondragon's plight and
her own physical woes.

Which makes things the harder for her *mother.*

M'sera Andromeda has to think for the both of them, and somehow keep Marina from diving headfirst into trouble—which there would be aplenty if Marina brings Tom Mondragon's name to the governor. Or Lord save them, protests lodged with fool Mikhail.

Andromeda Kamat was taking a renewed interest in affairs outside the House between bouts with her deathangel addiction, and in Morgan's estimation, it was just bad luck for that interest to come now. It was a pity she couldn't have recovered months ago, when there was only Marina to worry about. Politics in Merovingen was suddenly a game where the wrong move could mean death; even Morgan knew that. Everything in the city was teetering like a drunk on the edge of a broken bridge. Andromeda was like a high-strung cat, and that nervousness was an added burden for her trusted servant-nurse-companion Morgan.

So Morgan schooled herself with a heavy hand to keep from snapping at young Raj Takahashi as she turned away from the window to face him, her thin shoes squeaking damply on the wooden floor. *The boy can't help that he moves quiet. The boy didn't mean to make your heart stop. Be nice to him, Morgan. He's always nice to you; always calls you "sera" and never a nasty word out of him—who's the little m'sera's own papa, by the book if not the fact.*

Raj held out a little round, white jar. There was a contrite expression on his thin, almond-eyed face. "Pardon, I didn't mean to startle you."

Morgan felt an instant's resentment, Raj looking far cooler than anyone had a right to on this sultry, yell-filled day, with his long black hair tied back on the nape of his neck, and hardly a trace of sweat on his brow. "Dr. Jonathan sent me over with this. We've tested it on both of us—"

"What do you mean by 'tested it'?" Morgan snapped, cradling the howling baby a little tighter against her shoulder. "What is it that it needed to be 'tested' first?"

"It's something swa—canaler folk've used for belly-ache, just not for colicky babies," Raj said apologetically, as if he held himself responsible for more than frightening Morgan. "It's not like it hasn't been used with kids before, just never as young as the little m'sera. We wanted to make sure it wouldn't be too hard for her, or put her off her milk. Dr. Jonathan's cut it plenty, put it in a sugar syrup, said to tell you he thinks there won't be any problems at all. Give her as much as sticks to your finger."

Morgan eyed the boy and the white glass jar dubiously. This young scion of Nev Hettek clan Takahashi was just *full* of herbal medicines nobody'd ever heard of before . . . but they weren't forbidden tech, Dr. Jonathan was reputed with the College and all, and she had to admit that the medicines all seemed to work. Andromeda hadn't had a bad deathangel flashback for weeks now. "All right," she said, bringing the baby down off her shoulder to cradle her in both arms. "As long as it isn't something nobody's ever used before. What is it?"

"Sugar-syrup and a decoction of something called bindroot. It'll help settle the stomach." Raj stuck his little finger in the jar, and brought it out coated with a thick, golden syrup. "I washed my hands already, sera, took off the first layer of skin. Like I said, it's used straight for belly-ache, you chew it. We thought it might ease her stomach."

There was certainly no problem with getting the baby to open her mouth: she was roaring at the top of her tiny lungs, her face, normally a soft pink, now an angry red, her open mouth taking up fully half of it. Raj stuck his finger into her mouth and let the baby have a taste before she had any idea there was something in there.

There was a moment more of ear-piercing wailing, before the child reacted to the foreign presence of Raj's finger in her mouth. Then there was a grunt of surprise—

Then a whimper, but it sounded experimental rather than unhappy. Small mouth worked busily and the little m'sera's face faded to tear-flushed perfection. Tears still stood on her cheek. She kept making dubious faces, doubtless reacting to the sweet taste of the syrup.

The boy laughed, softly, and put the jar down. "No more waking m'sera Andromeda out of a sound sleep for you, little fish," he admonished the mite playfully. "Sera Morgan, I know you've been trying to quiet her half the afternoon—I'll be glad to take her for a bit until she falls asleep. Which probably won't be long; medicine ought to take hold in just a bit. I bet she's tired herself out to nothing with all that crying."

"She's tired me out, if nothing else," Morgan admitted, letting the boy take his putative daughter from her arms. He held her against his shoulder, bouncing gently on the balls of his feet, patting the tiny back gently and just so until of a sudden the bubble got up. It was an ease and expertise in baby-handling the child's not in the least putative mother couldn't be bothered to learn. Raj was one of the few—the only male—Morgan would permit to handle the baby.

He loves that child as if she really was his own, Morgan thought, with an unexpected surge of sympathy for the boy. *And not a sign of resentment that she truly isn't his. He'd be as good a married husband and father as Nicky Kamat was, and fool Marina can't see it for that scoundrel Mondragon, and him in the Cardinal's basement, if he isn't dead.* Morgan tightened her lips a little, as the boy—no, young man, he was eighteen and maturing by the day—cooed nonsense into the baby's ear with every evidence of delight. *Well, the contract-marriage is up in a few months and she's going to lose this nice lad to that Bolado girl, a blind woman could see that—and then I expect we'll hear more wailing from her than from any colicky baby. What is it with that child that she never wants anything until she can't have it?*

"I think she's asleep, sera Morgan," Raj whispered. Since the baby's eyes were closed, and she was snoring ever so slightly, that seemed a reasonable deduction. Morgan nodded and let Raj carry her to the cradle, an elaborate froth of lace and fine linen, canopied, be-ribboned and be-ruffled. He set the pink and white mite down as gently as Morgan would have; she stirred a little, stuck her thumb in her mouth, and kept on dreaming.

"What is that stuff again, boy?" Morgan asked, determined not to show she was impressed.

"Bindroot, and Dr. Jonathan says not to use it too often, just when she starts like this and won't stop." Raj handed her the jar, as she pursed her lips. "I wish it was winter; we could get her to suck ice instead. Though Dr. Jonathan does say he'd rather use this."

"No doubt he would." She snorted. "Man isn't happy if the remedy doesn't come from a bottle. You can tell that old fraud that I've been tending babies as long as he's been killing patients, and I know what to do with them." She dismissed the doctor's opinion with a perfunctory shrug, returning her volley in the never-ending war between herself and the Kamat family physician.

The lad just smiled. "I know that, an' you know that, sera," he said, "but a doctor's got to feel like he's the one in charge—or at least that's what they keep telling me up at the College."

His eyes clouded a little when he mentioned the College, and Morgan knew very well the cause of *that*. The College itself—the whole of Merovingen Above and Below—was not safe from the inquisitions led by its Cardinal Exeter: math and the sciences were no longer the only sensitive areas of study; even medicine and art were suspect. Treat the wrong patient, paint the wrong picture, and you might well find yourself facing the Cardinal's hand-picked board of questioners, suspected of heresy.

No few of the priests at the College had found themselves in that very position. No few had vanished, never to be seen again, off (supposedly) on a sabbatical that Morgan suspected was permanent, at Det's black bottom.

And Raj Takahashi, former Nev Hettekker, must surely be under the Cardinal's eye, for all that he had passed his catechism like any good Revenantist. The times were dangerous, and if the boy had managed to grow any sense at all, he was aware and wary of the danger of new things and strange medicines. For Kamat's sake. For all of them.

Morgan shivered from a chill that had nothing whatsoever to do with the temperature of the air. M'sera

Andromeda, the whole Kamat house was Nev Hettek-ker, if one scratched deep, if anyone cared to remember that fact, and m'ser Richard had made one midnight and terrible visit to the College. A Kamat servant could as easily be under the eye of the Cardinal, as a pawn to use against the rising influence of House Kamat . . . safer to target the servant than the master, but the fate of the servant could easily become that of the master.

"Sera, I don't want to alarm you, but who was that woman in the hallway?" the boy asked, breaking into her musings. "The one in the apron, with the scar across her eye?"

Morgan caught a glimpse and sighed. *Another visit from the kitchens. Julia, this time.* "One of the kitchen staff," she replied. "Why?"

"Has she any business up here?" The boy's brows creased. "I don't want to sound like I'm prying, but— if she's kitchen help, why was she upstairs? Do you trust her? Could she be a spy, maybe trying to overhear something?"

Good thinking, boy. Not so naive, then, as he was when he came to us. "She isn't precisely 'kitchen help.' She's a legacy, do you know what that means?" When Raj shook his head, she elaborated. "When Kamat bought this Isle from the Family that owned it, the Adami, that was, they still had a few—attachments. Less than kin, but more than servants—well, that may not be entirely true, doubtless there's a lot of unacknowledged Adami blood in them. Kamat adopted them along with the Isle. The servants have all been worrying about the little one, especially with her crying the way she has been, but the legacy staff fusses more than any ten of the servants. M'sera says to let

43

them come up. They're a nuisance, but that's all. M'ser Richard's had them all checked and vouched for."

"Well," Raj said, looking relieved, "then I'd better be going. Things are kind of unsettled over at the College, still. No classes, so Justus an' me are using the time to study like anything. We figure we'd better—he needs all the help he can get with his math, and I'm still pretty lost when it comes to philosophy and history. Knowing what someone does and why he does it are two different things, I guess."

He grinned, ruefully, and Morgan smiled back against her will. It was hard not to give your liking to this boy; he tried so very hard to *be* liked.

"You need a House poleboat?" Morgan asked, as he stepped softly to the door of the nursery, catlike, to avoid waking the baby. "You might have to wait for one this time of day. M'ser Richard is down at the warehouse, and young m'sera swears she's going visiting." *Pray God it isn't to the Boregy house. We have enough troubles without Marina getting involved with that back-stabbing lot, and them related to the Old Cardinal.*

None of them would lift a hand for Thomas Mondragon. See him hanged—yes.

Raj shook his head. "Thank you, sera, but no. Sera Bolado's boat brought me over and she's waiting for me below."

Morgan's lips formed into a tight smile of wry satisfaction. *Sure enough, that fool Marina is losing this boy, if he isn't lost already.* "Then I'll bid you good afternoon, and go see to sera Andromeda."

"Give her my respect," Raj replied, "And tell her, please, that I hope her health is growing to match her beauty." It was a hightowner compliment, but in his mouth somehow the words didn't seem formula. The boy for all the lowtown cant that slipped in and out of his speech took his House obligations seriously; the m'sera truly seemed to mean more to him than his own, long-dead mother.

"I'll tell her." The corridor was stifling, and Morgan could hardly wait to be out of it. She nodded, and they parted at the next intersection of hallways, the boy heading down to the water-stair, herself to find the baby's doubtless hiding maidservant.

Raj Takahashi paused at the foot of the water-stair and looked around expectantly. "So," said a voice out of the shadowed cut beside, a voice as warm as the daylight on the broad canal and full of ironic amusement. "Did you beard the dragonelle in her lair and see the little m'sera?"

Raj jumped, then laughed, as Kat Bolado poled her family's boat out of the cut and into the canal and snugged it expertly up against the walkway. "Sera Morgan likes me, I think," he told the dark-eyed, curly-haired young woman. He stepped carefully into her boat while she steadied it with her pole against the sluggish current.

Kat shuddered theatrically and shoved away from the bank as he settled himself on the seat in front of her. "I'd rather have a skit snuggle up to me," she said emphatically. "How's the baby?"

"Colicky and crying." Raj noticed that she didn't say "your" baby. Kat bristled with resentment and jealousy every time she so much as heard Marina Kamat's name, and she would not even give lip service to the polite fiction that Raj was the baby's real and contract father.

"Which accounts for the screams I heard up above," Kat surmised, shoving hard with her pole and shooting them deftly into the flow of traffic with a minimum splash. "What'd ye do, smother her?"

Raj laughed again, since it was obvious she didn't mean what she'd said; and squinted against the dazzle of sun on moving water. It was just marginally cooler on the canal than on the lowest walkway, but considerably better than inside the House. "No, Dr. Jonathon and I came up with something to keep her quiet. That's why I was here; he figured if I delivered it, sera Morgan would likely use it without a fuss."

"What was it? Whiskey? A gag?" One of the canalers with a slightly slower craft signaled that Kat should cut in front of him; she acknowledged the gift with a wave of her hand, called out, "Yoss, Rahman," and took instant advantage of his generosity. As they pulled into the widening space between him and the next boat, Raj saw why he was so slow; his bow was fouled with a trailing bouquet of tangle-lilies.

"No, you evil-minded woman, a medicine." Raj made a face at her, a non-subtlety lost on Kat, as she happened to be looking at the traffic and not at him. "I wish those damned lilies were good for something."

"Oh, they are. They're stove-fuel. It happens you can find a place to dry the stuff, and press it down into little bricks." Kat shoved her pole against the bottom and maintained her place in the traffic with an ease Raj envied. "My family's thinking about offering a copperbit for every wet bale, and selling 'em back dry. There's some down in canalside dealing with hightowners, but nobody got a press down t' harbor.

We got contacts on both sides. No reason why *we* couldn't sell 'em to landers. We even got enough roof space . . . but . . ."

"But that's a dangerous move to make right now," Raj concluded for her, frowning a little with worry. "Could be tech. Clothes dried in the sun could be tech. Who knows?"

"Right." She shoved again, sending them out of the main traffic and into one of the side canals. That brought them out of the sunlight and into a shadow that offered a little respite from the oppressive heat. "Lord and ancestors, any hint that a Family might be trying to curry favor with the Lower Classes, and m'sera Cardinal would have every last one of them in for a 'little talk.' "

Raj shivered, only too well aware of what one of those "little talks" entailed; he thought of Mondragon, and wondered how Jones was faring. "This can't last much longer," he replied grimly. "Things are stirred up from canalside to the Rock. Something's got to give, one way or another."

Kat didn't answer at first, she just tightened her mouth and shoved her pole with a little more force than was necessary. "You're right," she said at last. "Things can't go on as they have been. Something, somewheres, is going to start an Incident. I just hope when the smoke blows away there aren't too many people hurt. Meanwhile—"

"Meanwhile we make our plans. I got two more books for the hidey." Some while ago, Raj had discovered that the chief Librarian at the College was one of those priests on "sabbatical." No one was keeping any kind of a watch on the Library, not even on the room holding rare and possibly dangerous books.

There was a room of dubious books, books only selected students were permitted access to. Tech books, half of them, holding information about devices no denizen of Merovingen would even dream of constructing.

But someone from the Chat, or Nev Hettek, or even the far Falken Islands? *They* had fewer bans on tech than Revenantist Merovingen.

Possible. More than possible. Which meant that those books had value there, value many times their weight in gold.

An advanced student like Raj or Justice Lee had every right to be in that room, for there were also books in there on medical tech which might one day be declared permissible (especially if the governor or a high-ranking priest had need of it.) There were also books whose elaborate pictures of anatomical detail made copying them difficult and the work of years for an artist-priest, for there was no way to get that kind of fine detail on a hand-engraved printing plate, and those volumes had equal interest for medical student or artist. So Raj, and now Justice, had taken to going to that room once every couple days and remaining for several hours, making their own hand-copies of those anatomical studies. But when they emerged, it was with one of the *other* books concealed in the bottom of their book-bags. There hadn't been anyone in the Library to notice them since Raj had begun the pilfering—and it didn't look as if there *would* be anybody for a while, at least.

Raj had discovered something else in that enterprise; in the confusion following the Librarian's detention and subsequent disappearance, several other books had been misfiled in the limited-access room.

There had always been rumors about another book-room, a room only the priests were allowed to enter, that contained banned and definitely heretical volumes. The fact that books existed which did not appear in the catalog of the restricted room or in the catalog of the larger, open collection, seemed to confirm that rumor.

And, as Raj reasoned, if they didn't officially exist, they couldn't officially be missed. Their value would only be that much higher. So these were, of course, the very first books he had smuggled out.

If he, Kat, or Justice had to make a run for it, there were a couple of skips waiting for them, already provisioned, in the Bolado family cut, and in their hideys, under cleverly concealed false back walls, were the books—portable wealth, better than gold, and less subject to being traced. Justice had already declared a direction: the Chat, where a decent artist could make a good living among the luxury-loving rich of the tropic. Raj's direction would depend on where trouble came from, when it came. Nev Hettek, and Granther, if there was a choice: the books contained enough information to buy his safety there from even the Sword. Or it was the Chat, like Justice, if Nev Hettek wasn't a choice. His books and his (various) skills should sustain him and Kat both for several years, and he could resume his studies—he sincerely hoped; but in Mondragon's teaching, he had other choices.

Never again was he going to face trouble unprepared. He just hoped, in a desperate sort of way, that Mondragon himself would make it. He was doing his best to get every scrap of information about the movements in the College to Jones, who was trying to get

Mondragon free before Karl Fon could send south or the Cardinal finesse him back to the Justiciary—and if anyone would know how best to use the information he had provided, it would be the former Sword agent—if he were free and safe himself.

At the moment, Raj's own best hope of safety lay in pretending he noticed none of this, that he was blind and blithe and taking the unexpected recess from classes to ready himself for the moment studies resumed, and perhaps steal a march on his fellow students. He already had a reputation as a bookworm: apparently spending all these free hours in study would only reinforce that impression.

"D' you have to go straight back?" Kat asked unexpectedly. "I mean, well, —got anything planned today?"

"M'sera Andromeda is expecting me for dinner with the Family," he replied. "I didn't tell Justus where I was going, just that I wouldn't be back till after supper. I kind of thought about taking a walk around town this afternoon, see what I could see."

"Do that as well by boat, couldn't you?" Kat asked plainly.

"I didn't want to ask you," he said, blushing.

"Well, you didn't ask, I offered." She smiled, a smile that dazzled his eyes and made his heart pound. "So, can a m'sera buy you lunch, m'ser?"

They glided into a patch of sunlight, and he smiled back at her, despite the blushes that made his ears and the back of his neck hot. "Only if that m'sera is you," he said gallantly, and she laughed and sent them back into the shadows with a shove of her pole.

* * *

They could have had lunch anywhere; from the private dining room of Bolado to the big room of Hilda's tavern. As luck would have it, they chose to picnic instead, getting fishrolls and beer enough for three from a canalside vendor and taking them off to Gallandry and the runner's office there. They surprised Ned Gallandry (who now treated Raj with a respect Raj found quite uncomfortable) with the unexpected largess of free lunch. They bribed Ned with it to let them sit on one of the uppermost walkways, and to grant permission for Kat's boat to be tied up below. So there they perched, in a bit of shade, high enough to catch what little breeze there was, close enough to the main arteries of traffic on Port and West Canals to see and hear the goings-on of the water and the walkways.

That was pure good luck; Saint Murfy smiling on Raj and bestowing his sickle blessing. Ned Gallandry, who was often among the first to hear *any* news, knew where they were—

And they themselves were in a position to see the beginning of the hue and cry, as suddenly blacklegs and Kamat blueshirts appeared from everywhere, walking swiftly, or even running along the walkways. Canalers with no particular business to conduct all seemed to be heading in one direction—the same as the provenance of the private and public police.

"Lord and Ancestors—" Kat said, staring at the canal below. "Where in the hell are they all off to?"

Raj felt a sudden apprehension as he took in the direction, the blueshirts *and* the blacklegs, and made a wild surmise. "God—" he breathed, "God, trouble at Kamat."

"Raj!" the shout from the stairway made them both

jump and turn, to see a grim-faced Ned Gallandry, hair limp with sweat and humidity, eyes angry, waving at them from halfway up the stair. "Raj!" he shouted again. "You'd better get yourself back to Kamat. They need you there. Somebody's swiped the baby."

"Boat's fastest," Kat said as he scrambled to his feet and lurched toward the stairway. He didn't turn himself to answer; just nodded and clattered down beside Ned Gallandry.

"Who?" he panted, a lump of fear in his throat. "Who took her?"

Ned shook his head. "Don't know, nobody knows. Some says it's sharrh, some Sword of God, some blame the Janes, it's every rumor you can think of goin' through town like a fire. No ransom note, no clues, no nothin'." Ned's expression told Raj that *he* thought it was a political kidnapping—which meant every known faction and cause was going to be in for some hard questioning. Again. "Need a boat?"

"Got Kat's, thankee, Ned!"

Ned squeezed over to let them pass on the narrow stair and didn't say anything more; what else was there to say? They pelted down the wooden steps from the high walkway to the canalside to reach Kat's boat tied up below, and Raj jumped into it with none of his usual hesitation. Kat was a breath behind him; she snatched up her pole from the rack as he cast off, and handed him the spare pole as he turned back to her.

He took it; she normally didn't ask him to pole with her, but they needed the extra speed, and the Ancestors knew he needed something to work off his racing nerves. He dug in with more energy than finesse; Kat's skill sufficed to keep them trim and headed, and brought them up to the Kamat water-stair much sooner than he expected.

There was a Kamat guard on the stair, who knew Raj on sight. He waved them into a vacant tie-up with a stare for Kat that took in the high quality of her otherwise plain clothing; Kat tied up where he told her, and both of them scrambled out of the boat and up the stair like a couple of scalded skits, taking back corridors and stairs to get to the big Meeting Room at the heart of the House.

The room was a chaotic muddle, Kamat blueshirts everywhere, and official blacklegs shouting angry questions at sobbing servants that got few answers. Richard Kamat stood beside the great table in the center of the maelstrom, issuing orders to those nearest them. Raj waited to be noticed, for he saw Richard's eyes rake the crowd every so often, looking for someone. That someone likely wasn't *him*, but Richard did spot him then, and beckoned him through.

He elbowed his way through police to Richard's side, and when the blueshirts vying with blacklegs for control of the questioning seemed disinclined to move even for that, the head of Kamat reached out and hauled Raj through them by the collar of his shirt.

"The baby's gone!"

"I heard, m'ser, I—"

"Sometime between your visit and half an hour ago," Richard said, through the shouting and sobbing around them. "You don't remember seeing anyone hanging around the outside when you left, do you?"

"Not at the water-stairs," Raj said promptly. "I'll ask Kat if she noticed any boats she didn't know while she was waiting."

"Find Jones. Tell her put the word out in the Trade.

You think you can contact a few of those kids to stick their noses in around town? But not to *do* anything— we don't know what we're dealing with here. . . ."

Read: The Cardinal. Raj nodded emphatically. "No problem."

"Whoever took her didn't leave a note, and hasn't tried to contact us," Richard was saying. "Unfortunately, that doesn't rule out politics. Check back in every hour; be careful; don't go anywhere without telling someone. You're her father; you're young and— well, they might contact you first. Or worse. You're not playing with rules, boy, or pity—you understand? We don't know whose move this is."

"Yes, m'ser," Raj said numbly. *They took her right after I left; they had to. While she was still sleeping, while the bindroot was keeping her quiet. Kat and I weren't out that long.* "I'll be smart, m'ser."

Richard dismissed him with a nod, and Raj wriggled his way back through the mob of Samurai and blacklegs to Kat's side. He tried not to think of the baby, alone and in unfriendly, unsympathetic hands; waking up in strange surroundings, frightened—

"Let's go up to your room," Kat hissed. "Here, I mean. Maybe there's something we can do, but we aren't going to come up with it in this nest of skits."

Raj shook his head, and waved at the milling crowd. "They've got everybody in the Samurai and the blacklegs," he said, suddenly aware that the blacklegs were among the agencies that might be *behind* a kidnapping; and gulped down one more fear in the midst of all the rest. "We don't know who has her, or why, or even how they got her. What can *we* do but get in the way, I mean?"

"I think there's something," Kat persisted. "Let's

54

go talk about it. Besides, this way if anyone's looking for you, they'll know where to find you. If somebody shows up with a ransom note, Richard can have 'em followed."

Raj gave in, and led the way into the back halls of Kamat, but Kat said, there, catching his sleeve: "I want to see where it happened. Where *was* the baby? How d' you get from there to outside?"

He blinked, got a breath, realized how she'd been pulling him out of that milling confusion and started reasoning past the shock, himself, about Morgan and the room, about doors and hallways and stairs. He took her arm, himself, and said, "Come on. I'll show you."

The corridors felt like dark ovens. Once again, they took back stairs. When they got to the heart of Kamat, and the corridors that housed the rooms and suites of the Family, Raj paused to let a bevy of maids pass. One door opened and shut ahead of them, and when they reached Marina's suite, they could hear Marina weeping hysterically as they passed her door, the crying penetrating even the thick wood of the doorway, a babble of feminine voices trying to soothe her. Raj hesitated there, keenly aware of Kat's presence, of obligations to Marina—and of Marina's all-too-active imagination, and all the possible gruesome fancies Marina might have made herself by now—but there was no helping here. He walked Kat past that door toward the nursery.

"Where's that go?" Kat pointed at a shut door, behind which echoes sounded. "And that one."

"This one—this one's down to the water-stairs. *I* was there. The way we've come—that's the water-stairs again. Longer."

"And the other?"

"Servants' quarters. Couldn't anybody get through there without someone seeing."

Kat met his eyes. "Anybody?"

Foolish question.

Kat asked. "Where does it let out directly?"

"Upstairs to the walkways. But that's through the front hall."

"Downstairs?"

"Kitchens."

"There wasn't a soul out there on the water then that I didn't know on sight," she said, "But that's about right, isn't it? A stranger wouldn't have come in by water, and if it isn't a stranger—"

Raj watched the comings and goings of anguished servants, thinking how, in the quiet, frantic preparations of Kamat to desert Merovingen, someone might have betrayed Kamat intentions. Or changed loyalties. But he could not tell that possibility to Kat. Not even to Kat. He owed Richard that much loyalty. "She's gonna wake up in a strange place with her stomach hurting, and she's gonna start right in screaming. We could set Denny's friends to listening—there's the pipes. We can get word out."

"There's ways to quiet a baby," Kat said glumly, and that made him think of some a Cardinal's man might use.

But he kept looking at that door, and thinking on a woman in the hall, and Morgan saying: . . . *M'sera says to let them come up. They're a nuisance, but that's all*. . . .

"If I was some kind of agent, the *last* thing I'd pick to kidnap would be a colicky baby," Kat persisted. "You can't reason with it, and you can't shut it up without hurting it, and people get real worked up about babies. *Bad* karma. So what if this isn't a kidnapping like Richard thinks it is?"

"Not Megarys, damnsure." He thought it over some more. "You know, Kat, you keep saying 'when in doubt, try the simplest solution first.' It doesn't always work—but everybody else is trying the hard stuff already. Nobody else has tried the simple answer—"

"Which is?" she prompted.

She isn't precisely 'kitchen help.' She's a legacy, do you know what that means?

"Who would want a baby—except a mother?"

"Like somebody who'd *lost* a baby?" She pursed her lips and sat up a little straighter. "And you've got a little china-doll right here, 'bout as pretty as anybody'd ever want. All right, that makes sense. But who?"

"Somebody from outside would have gotten noticed," Raj said firmly, and grabbed Kat by the hand, hauling her for the door and the stairs. "Which means it's got to be someone from Kamat Isle. Sera Morgan said that 'bout everybody's been hanging around the baby's room."

"Everybody is a lot of people."

"Somebody in Kamat. That would account for why nobody saw the baby taken. Sera Morgan told me there've been people she called 'legacies' up there, too, poking their noses in—"

"Adami legacies?" Kat demanded, as they headed downstairs. "Lord!"

"You know anything?" Raj asked.

"What a midtowner knows." They were going down in a clatter of steps, down and down the turns. Family servants were gathered at the landing. One said,

"M'ser Raj," and the others whispered as they passed, speculation run rife, God, him with Kat, *in* the house, and m'sera Marina upstairs crying her eyes out—

Raj got the downstairs door open, out on the water-stairs. The cut was crowded now with boats. A black-leg moved to detain them, but the Kamat blueshirt on duty there intercepted him while they got into the boat and untied.

"What's a midtowner know?" Raj asked as they eased out onto the water. "What about *legacies*?"

"Listen, when you get a Family as old as the Adamis were, you got sort of other Families attached—of servants, spare cousins, you understand, them the Family has to care for, that can't care for themselves—people who've served for generations; hangers-on, old staff—most of 'em unspoken *relatives*, you understand, even in the lowest of the low in the kitchens; them that'll say and do things no hired servant would dare, because they consider themselves *responsible* for the Family—*part* of the Family. The Kamats haven't been around Merovingen long enough to have legacies of their own, but they took on the Adami legacies; and the Adamis—" Kat touched her brow, and took the pole out of the rack.

"You mean crazies?"

"Listen, the Adamis birthed no few. And deathangel made the rest. If there are Adami legacies around, they'll know things about this island no Kamat would ever find out."

"Like where to hide a baby?" Raj asked, grimly.

"And how to get her out of the nursery without anyone seeing," Kat said by way of reply. "Remember, Raj, we're most likely looking for someone who isn't entirely bow t' th' wind, but it's also probably someone too careful to give 'erself away by skipping work. Lord only knows *why* they took the baby—"

Raj felt a finger of ice trace the line of his spine. "You don't—you don't think they'd hurt her, do you?"

To his relief, Kat shook her head. "No, I don't think so. We Bolados have legacies of our own. A few of them are crazy as any swampie, but they wouldn't harm anyone on purpose."

"Which leaves by accident." His heart sank again. "Ancestors. If the baby starts fussing again, wakes up and starts crying—Lord, they can't feed her. . . ."

"We don't know that. And that crying's the only place we're lucky. If it *is* some legacy that has her, they've been sheltered in Kamat all their lives—they won't *know* the canaler tricks that could hurt a baby, like a dose of whiskey and sugar, or bindroot straight on. They'll just do what Morgan did; *exactly* the kind of things Morgan did. . . ."

"Which means she'll cry herself into a fit again," Raj said. "Let's put the word out, get folk all over Kamat Isle and 'round about, listening for a crying baby!"

It took every last bit of his set-aside, and he wished to the Ancestors he had Altair Jones and her karma with Moghi and the Trade, if it came to the convolute underside of Merovingen-below, but Raj had Kamat and the several Isles around covered and surrounded by forces more slithery and less forceful than the blacklegs that poked and pried into corners: every roof-climbing rascal friend of Denny's he thought marginally trustworthy, and every Kamat runner he could recruit, and a couple of the workers' and servants' kids he knew well enough to trust—all bribed and sent to standing in odd corners or perching on the walkways till the blacklegs moved them on, and then circle about to perch elsewhere close: while Kamat called in political favors and dreaded what this all might portend, Raj and Kat and their motley army patrolled the length and breadth of Kamat Isle by water and by bridge, by rooftop and by the tangled undersides of wooden walkways.

Raj and Kat tied up below Kamat East's Bluewater Bridge and slipped along the half-flooded waterside, following yet another youngster who'd heard the wail of an infant. Though sunset couldn't be far off, neither of them had eaten or rested since putting this plan in motion. The turmoil had communicated itself to the tenants on the Isle, and there was no shortage of crying babies. This was where Kat proved her worth: blacklegs and blueshirts might have barged in and demanded to see the infant in question; Kat just politely rapped on doors, presented herself to the woman of the house, and gossiped what little news there was in the search, while Raj stayed in the background but kept a sharp ear for his newborn daughter's particular wail.

Kat's easy speech and calmness quieted fears the blackleg searchers roused; her plain clothing, bare feet and canaler's breeches conveyed no particular class, and no threat; Raj's looks and hightown dress were distinctive enough to lend him immediate credence as Kamat's contract husband—his strained and anxious face enough to win him sympathy from every female and most of the males. Here was the baby's young father, shunted aside from the police and the in-laws, but nevertheless *trying* to do something.

This time was no different from the rest. The young mother in Kamat's East underside showed no sign of alarm at their presence, and no nervousness, and the thin wail that emerged from a half-barrel in the corner that served as a cradle was nothing like the youngest Kamat's outraged bellow: the thin child taken from its bed couldn't have been more unlike his daughter's pink-and-white perfection. Raj leaned wearily against the woman's doorpost, while Kat fished verbally for information, using gossip gathered in a dozen other similar encounters as bait.

The rumor-fishing wasn't particularly good; Kat waved him on, and he bade the young woman a civil good evening and made his exit, hoping it didn't look as hasty as it was. *Living like a hightowner has got me spoiled*, he reflected, as he breathed in careful, shallow breaths, trying to avoid inhaling as much of the stench of rotting tangle-lilies as he could. *Time was I wouldn't have noticed the stink. Time was, that little apartment wouldn't have made me feel like I was about to smother. The old place Denny and I had wasn't any bigger—might have been smaller, I disremember. Could I go back to that now, if I had to?*

He looked back over his shoulder at the apartment door, both shadowed by scaffolding and lit by pole-lamps on the walkways above; mere inches above the waterline, likely to flood, and always damp and crowded. He thought about all he'd been through until now—and decided that maybe it wasn't that bad after all.

I could do it. Beats not being alive, that's for sure. I could even go back to the swamp if it came down to it.

61

"Hey!" called a high voice from above them. "Raj!"

Raj looked up. Crouched on a rickety walkway stair that should have been condemned was a girl clad in cast-off clothing four sizes too big for her, short hair standing up in spiky points from the damp; she twisted her head sideways so that her cat-green eyes and high cheekbones caught the feeble light, and he recognized her immediately. This unmanageable, willful adolescent, pretty as a feral kitten and as wild, was one of Denny's smarter young friends from the bridges. She went where she pleased and did what she willed—and today it had pleased her to accept Raj's coin and go baby-hunting for him.

But once she made her bargains, she was as trustworthy as Jones and nearly as wily.

"Lady-o," he called. "You got something?"

"Maybe," she said cautiously, her voice just above a whisper. She shifted again, bringing her face back into the shadows. The sky above was blood-red with the dying sun, but down here on canalside it was full night, except the lamps above. "Yey, maybe," Lady-o repeated. "A light where there shouldn't be none, an' a baby cryin' where ain't never been one afore."

"Where?" Raj and Kat exclaimed simultaneously.

The child-woman jerked her pointed chin sharply upwards. "Above. Just by old Foundry-Kamat bridge. The Kamat bridge-house."

"The bridge-house?" Raj bit off what he had almost blurted out—that it was impossible, that no one could get to the old bridge-house that had once guarded the Kamat side of the hightown Kamat Foundry bridge. Lady-o would take offense at doubt—Lady-o took offense very easily, and let no man, woman, or child call her a liar. But right now Raj needed her, needed her climbing expertise very badly. Lady-o could climb like the cat she resembled—she frequently had no other choice, being too small to defend herself from bullies and blacklegs. If anyone could find a way up there, Lady-o could; Lady-o would *have* to, for the old Kamat-Foundry bridge had collapsed from the Foundry side in the last major quake, and had never been rebuilt. The stair leading up to it had disintegrated in the aftershocks and was never replaced, in favor of two new, open-air bridges. The old bridge-house, a small, round, two-room shelter meant to house bridge-guards, had been abandoned to the elements when the stair collapsed. The Kamats held the Isle by then, had other concerns than salvaging wood from a perch that precarious, and after the scavengers were through with it there was nothing of value left in the shelter. *Not even the bridge-brats use it for shelter*, Raj recalled, *because everyone knows the floor is rotten. Everyone knows. —And who was the first to spread the story, I wonder?*

Lady-o got up off her stairs and led the way along the flooded margin, and around the corner. She pointed. Raj looked up, and could just see a sliver of the place, black against the darkening sky. The bridge-house remained outwardly intact, a little round turret tacked to Kamat's wall, with a lonely tongue of bridge-timbers sticking out from beneath it. The bridge itself had long since been pulled down from below as a possible hazard to traffic on the canal.

"You're sure?" Raj asked the child.

"Sure as flood an' th' Retribution," she answered firmly. "There's a light up there, I seen it. A little light, slimmer'n a canaler's candle, but I seen it. An' by the wailin' there's a baby up there too."

"Someplace no one can get to," Raj murmured. "A place nobody looks at even when they're looking right at it. It's walled off from inside. And if anyone should *hear* something—"

"They'll figure it was a trick of the echoes along here," Kat finished, as Lady-o nodded.

"Ever'body knows ye go up there, ye fall through th' floor," Lady-o said, in an unconscious echo of Raj's earlier thought. She looked up, following Raj's gaze. "Ye wanta get up there?"

"Yey," he answered, grimly. "If you can find me finger and toe-holds, Lady-o, I'll be right behind you."

"Raj," Kat protested, and Lady-o started to snicker, then turned around and got a look at his face. Whatever she saw there must have convinced her; she closed her mouth and nodded. And Kat shut up.

"Les' think 'bout this a minute," Lady-o said, and studied the face of the building. She pointed, and Raj squinted against the dying light. "Lookee—we got up here, this drainpipe. Then catch that ledge, an' up where they put them scallops on the corner . . . then cross t' that balcony an' up th' support an' we're at th' right floor. An' see that winder, right up 'bove the balcony roof? What you reckon that winder gives on a room or summat what goes t' th' bridge-house? Bet it ain't *all* walled off."

Raj traced the way Lady-o had described, ending at the window. It was dark—which meant it might well belong to an unused access, perhaps now relegated to storage.

Kat stepped back as far as the walkway would

allow, and eyed the area of the bridge-house. "I'll see if I can find anybody to listen to me in there, and maybe we can find the entrance to the thing," she said. "Damn sure nobody went climbing up the side of the building in broad daylight with a baby. There *has* to be a way to the bridge-house from the house itself; maybe one of the Adamis will remember it."

"And maybe won't," Raj said, thinking how the Adamis might feel more allegiance to their own, how the Adamis might have overheard too much, or have purposes of their own. "If there's a way in, I think it's nothing they've told Kamat. We might not find it—go tell Richard. *Not* the blacklegs. Richard."

Kat gave the bridge-house a second, misgiving look. "Raj, be careful."

"May not be any time for careful." Raj bent to strip his shoes from his feet and leave them for Kat to take with her. "Ye comin'?" Lady-o hissed, and he hurried: Lady-o flitted for the rickety stair, and he was not minded to lose her in the darkness.

He caught up with her just below the bridge-house. It was a full three stories up from here, and mostly blank wall, except for the windows and decorative balcony Lady-o had pointed out. The Adamis that had built the House had not been minded to have the noxious smokes and grime of Foundry blowing in their windows. And by now it was full dark.

"Watch," hissed the child. Raj looked sharply up, and saw a furtive flicker, more a glow than a light, in the middle of the dark blot of the bridge-house.

Someone's put a rag or something across the window—a dark rag, or it'd be noticed by day. But when they go by it with a light, some still leaks through.

At precisely that moment, a baby cried. A fierce

howl of pain, and frustrated anger. It might have come
from across the water, from ramshackle apartments on
Foundry's failing high story—but Raj knew very well
that it had come directly overhead: he *knew* that cry,
knew that baby-voice. It was *his* baby, *his* little girl—

Anger he'd been carrying inside since the abduction
exploded into a white rage. He was scrambling up the
side of the building, fury carrying him, before Lady-o
even realized what he was doing. His hands and feet
found crevices and protrusions he couldn't see, and
his anger gave him strength he never knew he had—
not since he'd clambered pilings at swamp-edge. A
moment ago he'd looked up at the climb and wondered how he was going to manage it. Not now—

He paused for a breath, halfway to the bridge-
house, and Lady-o scrambled up beside him. "What're
ye gonna do when ye get up there?" she hissed at
him. "Ye better think 'f that *now*, afore ye get yerself
in trouble!"

He wedged himself in the false balcony, and peered
upward. Canal-water lapped and gurgled below. The
tide was coming in, and wooden Kamat shifted a little
and groaned on its pilings. "I'll get in through that
window, and see if it really does give out on the
bridge-house," he said slowly. "If it does, I get in and
get the baby and wait for Kat. If it doesn't, from there
I can get on what's left of the walkway. There's a door
there—I guess what I'd better do is just bust it down.
Then get the baby, and wait for Kat again."

"What 'f those skits has a gun?" the child asked
shrewdly. "Ye go bustin' any door down, ye c'n well
get kill't."

Raj shook his head, though he knew she couldn't
see him. He could barely make *her* out, and she wasn't

in the shadows of the false balcony. "Don't think there's going to be a gun. Anybody with enough money for a gun or a reason to even own one would have taken the baby someplace else. Keeping her here is too risky for a sane kidnapper."

The child shook her head. "Then ye don' think it's Janes or summat? Or mebbe old Cardinal Willy? I thought that was the word."

"Sometimes the word can be wrong," Raj replied, studying the next leg of the climb as well as he could in the uncertain light from the pole-lamps below. "I'm thinking it's a woman—an Adami woman that wants a baby so bad she'll do anything to get one."

Lady-o's dark head bobbed then in slow agreement. "Yey, Tree's Mama got like that afore she died. Carried 'round a rag-dolly she said was 'er baby. Kept walkin' off wi' peoples' babbies till they wouldn't leave 'er alone wi' kids. They says it was deathangel got 'er."

"And there's been enough of it in this town," Raj said sourly. *Deathangel. Deathangel never did me a favor but once—*

He found he could no longer clearly remember the assassin that had nearly killed him, out in the swamp, the one who had died himself. It seemed a lifetime ago now. But fear didn't.

"Let's make for the window," he muttered, and grabbed for the next set of handholds.

This time he let Lady-o go ahead of him, and paid close attention to where her hands and feet went. She looked like a strange kind of wall-climbing lizard, dark against the gray-weathered wood. He eased along in her wake, getting some minor scrapes on his hands and feet, and ignoring them.

A couple of timber-ends that might at one time have supported some portion of the bridge gave them a place to perch beside the darkened window. Peering into the shadows of the recess, Raj saw that it was roughly boarded over from the inside. His heart sank, as Lady-o reached out and ran her hand gently along the bottom of the frame.

"Took out th' glass," she said softly. "Lessee if they was as lazy as I think they was." With that, she flicked her hand to her side and when she brought it up again, a thin blade glittered against the darkness. "Grab m'belt," she said shortly, and hardly waited for Raj to do so before leaning out toward the window.

She did *something* with her knife hand, as Raj clung to her belt with one hand and a cracked place on the wall with the other. She was a *lot* heavier than she looked, and his arms were screaming with pain before she hissed satisfaction and pushed at the window.

The boards swung back. She waved at Raj, tossed her knife inside, and grabbed the ledge with both hands as he let go of her. She swung herself over the sill, dropping into the shadows as silently as a falling feather. He looked longingly at the sill. It was just out of reach; he'd have to go completely off balance and grab for it—and hope.

The baby cried again, and he lurched for the strip of wood, found himself clinging to the sill with both feet dangling out over nothing. Sweating, he managed to drag himself up and over, and fell heavily to the floor inside.

The window hadn't been boarded up, after all. The interior had been fitted with wooden shutters held in place with a catch. That was what Lady-o had meant by "lazy"—closing up the old shutters, not even sparing a board and a nail. Or somebody had pilfered the metal. The child had simply flipped the wooden bar up with the blade of her knife, and allowed the shutters to swing open.

"Ye didn' see that," she hissed out of the darkness. " 'F some knew I got them cat-tricks, they'd be after me t' help 'em B 'n E, an' I ain't lookin' t' end up on Hangin' Bridge."

"I don't blame you," Raj whispered back, and stood up, slowly, letting his eyes adjust to the deeper darkness inside this room. He wished now he'd brought a lantern or something. The tiny room seemed to be empty of all but dust—which was odd, definitely odd.

Lady-o hissed again. "C'mere—" He fumbled his way as quietly as he could to where she was crouched against the wall, the worn boards were age- and use-smoothed, and still warm under his bare feet.

Wall? No—it was a door, and she lay with her eye level with the sill. He imitated her, and saw a very faint, furtive gleam of light somewhere beyond it.

"This's like a hall or somethin'," she breathed into his ear. "Like there was this private entrance t' the bridge, through th' bridge-house. Ev'body else had t' take the walkway an' stairs, but the old Family didn't have t' go outside till they got t' the bridge proper. Figger they closed it up when there weren't no more bridge."

"Can you get the door open?" he whispered back. She rose to her knees, and felt along the doorframe. He suppressed a sneeze as she stirred up dust.

"They took th' hardware," she said, "an' they nailt a couple 'a boards across. But that frame's rotten. Bust 'er open!"

So it's down with the door after all, he thought, and rose and balanced for his best one-legged kick.

Wood splintered: the door held—but as Lady-o had observed, the frame didn't. The whole door tore away and fell on the floor with a boom like thunder, startling a scream both from the baby in her crude, make-shift cradle and the woman in Kamat livery who rocked her.

Though there was only a single lantern in the room, its flame turned down to almost nothing, to Raj's eyes the place was as brightly lit as any of the Family rooms below—and no doubt of it, she was one of the Family servants; he remembered her vaguely, an odd little mouse with a plain face and hungry eyes—and now he knew what she had hungered for.

She snatched the infant up from the cradle, retreated holding it so tightly against her that the baby howled in protest.

Raj froze where he was. She edged away from him, step by step, until her back was against the rotting door that had once led to the bridge. Before Raj could stop her, she shoved the latch up and dashed out onto what was left of the walk.

Torches and lanterns lit her eerily from below. Revenantist, Adami, and believing implicity in karma and the wheel of rebirth. "Get away," she cried, looking back to the light, her eyes wild. "Get away from me!"

Raj edged across the rotten floor of the bridge-house, then out onto the creaking stub of the bridge, one slow step at a time. "I won't hurt you, sera," he said as quietly and calmly as he could and still be heard over the baby's screams that echoed now off the walls of Foundry. "I've just come for my little girl. I'm her papa, you know—"

His heart pounded painfully in his chest, and his throat was too tight to swallow as she backed up another step. A cool, reasoning corner of his mind was calculating footing, the length of his own lunge, the amount of planking still behind her. The rest of him wanted to shriek and grab for his baby, now.

"You can't have her!" the woman said, shaking her head violently. "She's mine, not yours! You'll leave the Isle—you'll run away and leave; but you'll not take the heir! She was meant for me, I saw it—I saw it in my dreams—"

"What dreams, sera?" Raj asked, edging another foot closer. The wood creaked dangerously underfoot, Kamat Isle groaned on its pilings, and the whole building swayed again—

"The dreams, the holy dreams," the woman babbled, clutching her hand in her hair while the baby subsided to a frightened whimper, as if she somehow sensed the danger she was in. "She's mine, she was meant for *us* It'll be Adami Isle again . . . and my little one, my little m'sera will never go away."

He was almost within reach.

Boards cracked. Her eyes fixed wildly past him as bright lamplight streamed from the door behind him.

"Raj!" Kat called. There was a murmur of shocked and frightened voices, and someone stifled a cry of despair.

"Stay back," he warned sharply, not taking his eyes from the woman, who took another two steps backward onto wood that moaned under her weight. "Sera," he said urgently, recapturing her attention. "Sera, the dreams. *What* did they tell you?"

She transferred her attention from whoever was

71

behind him to his face. "You don't care about the dreams," she cried. "You just want my—"

The wood gave.

Raj made a desperate lunge as the woman shrieked and teetered on the brink of the black gulf over the canal, one arm flailing wildly, the other still clutching the baby. He reached her—she fell, just as his hands brushed cloth—

He grabbed for it and held, as he was falling himself. His gut meeting the bridge planks knocked breath and sense from him, but he had a handful of linen fabric, and he held onto it past all pain and sense. The universe spun, then came to rest again.

He was dangling face-down over the canal, so far below that he could only sense it was there by the errant flickers of light on the black water, and the murmur of the tide around the foundations. With one hand and both legs he held to the bridge-timber that had saved him. The other hand was clutched in the linen and lace gown of his tiny daughter, who was likewise dangling head-down over the empty darkness, wailing at the top of her lungs.

He edged back until his chest was supported by timber, then drew her up. Only when she was safely cradled against his chest did he breathe again.

And held her, carefully, like the tiny precious thing she was, murmuring her name over and over, hardly daring to believe he had her back safe. He might have wept tears of his own at that point, but suddenly the others were on him, hauling him to safety, praising him to the skies. Kamats, Kamats everywhere, pounding his back, touching his sleeve, exclaiming over the baby—Richard foremost among them, his mother

Andromeda beside him, her face as white as fine por-
celain—Marina was conspicuously absent.

He ignored them all. All but one, the only non-
Kamat in the lot; Kat, standing at the edge of the
crowd, her eyes shining with tears and pride.

They traded a look that said more than words could
have, and a smile bright with relief and promise.

Then Raj gave Morgan the wailing infant, and let
the Kamats carry him away.

Raj put his arm about Kat's shoulders, as much for
support as for affection. It was past midnight, and he
was too tired to think clearly. All he wanted to do
now was get home to his rooms behind Hilda's tavern.

He shook off the last of the Kamat cousins, and got
the door closed before anyone else took it into his or
her head to follow him out and tell him how brave he
was—again. If this was being a hero, he'd far rather
be anonymous.

"Well," drawled a voice, slurred a little with drink,
out of the shadows beside the tie-ups. "Ye're sure th'
man of th' hour."

A dark shape uncoiled itself from a larger darkness
of piled-up tangle-lilies. It staggered a little, then
walked unsteadily into the light of the single lantern
over Kat's poleboat.

Rattail, Rif's partner, looking oddly naked without
her gitar, a bottle in one hand. Raj could smell the
whiskey on her even before she came close.

He let go of Kat and backed up a step.

"Hey, it's all right, boy, I didn't mean it sarcastic."
The raven-haired singer ran her free hand through her
short cap of tangles. It looked as if she'd been getting

into fights again. "I watched that last bit from Foundry-side. That was quite a save."

"Thanks," Raj replied, not sure of what else to say, doubly unsure of what she wanted.

"I—I came over here looking for ye, boy," the musician said, looking vaguely past him. "When's that brother of yours coming back?"

"Any day now," Raj told her, a chill deep in his throat. *What's she want? Is she going to get him in trouble? He—*

"Lord." She looked at the bottle in her hand, as if she hadn't expected it to be there, and took a swig. "Listen, you keep him away from Rif, you hear? She's gone clean crazy, an' Black Cal with her, and she's nothin' but trouble. She was bad before, but now—" She shrugged, and her eyes showed the pain that must have driven her to the bottle tonight.

That was the *last* thing he expected to hear from Rif's erstwhile partner. "What happened?" he asked, unable to help himself. "What do you mean?"

"She's just—I dunno. Religion, I guess—I mean, every time somebody gets religion, seems like his brain turns to muck." She shrugged again. "Me, I don't believe in nothin'—Revenantist God's a cosmic accountant, Adventists' is a maniac, Janes' is just a pack of cheap tricks and a sweet line. But Rif, I guess she bought into it even if she *knows* the tricks. Took to dosin' herself with the stuff that Raven crazy brought out of the swamp—next thin' you know, she's got Black Cal on it too, and they're both babbling about talkin' to cat-whales. Shit, when a cop falls, he falls *hard*."

"Talking to cat-whales?" Raj could hardly believe his ears. Rat laughed, but it sounded like a sob.

"Yey, they got themselves some old hulk, got themselves talked into thinkin' it's a real ocean-goin' boat—they're tied up out on the Rim right now, convinced they're out on the Sundance, talkin' to cat-whales. I—"

She turned her head away for a moment, and rubbed the back of her hand angrily across her eyes. "Shit. And I get left holdin' tangle-lilies. *She* can't make the bookin's, 'cause she's stoned out of reality, and nobody wants me alone—I'm part of a set, and not even Hoh wants a solo act. I've been livin' on savin's—anyway, kid, you just tell that brother of yours that Rif's gone clean bad, and t' stay away. I'm gettin' out of this town, gettin' somewhere they don't know I'm supposed to be half of a duet. The Chat—"

"But—" Raj *knew* the cost of passage to the Chattalen, and his mouth dropped open. "But—"

"I know what you're thinkin'. An' I *don't* have it—yet." She held up her hand to forestall him. "I didn't come here to put the touch on you. I'm gonna do one last job. A special job. There's a captain down in the Harbor that'll do about anythin' for what I'm gonna bring him. I just came to tell ye, 'cause in the mornin' I'll be gone. And to warn ye to warn your brother. Aye, and that Jones, too. Keep 'em away from Rif; she's steerin' for the reef, she's gonna run aground, an' I don't plan on bein' here to see it."

With which, she finished off the bottle in one long swig, threw it into the canal, and vanished into the dark.

ENDGAME (REPRISED)

by C. J. Cherryh

The rim was a spooky place these days—and at night damned dangerous, not mentioning the crazies that lived out in the marsh near this spit of rock and sand and straggling weed. There were skips and poleboats hereabouts in every nook of the Rim, campers on that Rim that weren't fishing, no, not, at least, on take-five from hauling freight. There were fires where people didn't want to be approached, where another skip pulling up was like as not to get a bullet into the bow.

And finding somebody that didn't want to be found wasn't damned easy, on an island with one face to the Ghost Fleet and one face to the crashing sea, and it large as all Merovingen. She'd collected one bullet today, she'd outrun a pack of crazies not so many hours back, a reed raft bristling with boathooks.

And she'd only the faintest notion what she was looking for, poling along in silence on the rim, no notion what manner of structure, or where found, except the word was, a place where marsh and Rim meet, and she'd *tried* the seaward side, on which she would have bet, on a chance word of Rif's. So it was the harborward side—where the crazies were thick. *Nobody* went this deep into the crook of the rim and the marsh—and maybe, she told herself, maybe that made it the reasonable answer.

Mama said, keeping her company, Altair, what'd I ever tell ye about this place? Ye never let the crazies get atween you an' open water. 'Ware how the shore curves there.

She said between her teeth, on harsh breaths, "Yey, Mama, I'm watchin' 'at, best I can, Mama."

Glad of Mama's company, she was, in this place of ghosts and crazies, and she could only think, I can't get lost out here, I can't get kill't, and leave Mondragon with no help. . . .

Something stuck up out of the dark, some dark hump, and she let the boat glide a moment, in doubt. It looked like the kind of hidey crazies put together out of reeds. Could be a raft with a hidey in the middle of it. But it didn't move.

Shallow around here. Skip was floating only a couple of hands above the silty bottom. Place stank of rotten weed.

Couple of those humps. *Big* one yonder. You didn't like to make noise out here. Racket of an engine or a gunshot'd draw crazies quicker than a lamp drew bugs, but she was powerfully tempted to let fly with a shot and see what stirred.

Wasn't the only choice, though. She thumped the hull with the pole and stood ready to chuck it in the well, start the engine, and let fire with Mama's pistol, that she had stuck in her waistband.

Nothing happened. Which made a body think about some crazy who might have heard her coming and who might just about now be lurking just off the side of the boat, ready to grab the pole, next time she put it in—

She drifted, she hardly breathed. And she drifted close enough to reach out with the pole and give the reed hummock a thump.

It didn't rock. It was solid.

Second thump.

"Weird 'un, Mama."

Third thump. A try at lifting it with the pole. The skip rocked, but the reed shelter resisted. Solid as stone.

She fetched it a solid whack with the pole.

Nothing. The pole bounced. She shoved the skip closer, and stern about, so she could lean off the half-deck and poke a knife into it.

The point hit stone. Or something like. Just under the reed covering.

The boat rocked of a sudden. She caught her balance and jumped up as there was an arm over the rim of the well and there was a dripping-wet man crawling over the side.

And a batch more about to try.

She pulled the gun in a fright and let fire. Did for that one. But the boat rocked to the other side. She let that one go and punched the starter on the engine. It whined and wanted priming.

Man was aboard, a gangling shadow headed for her down the slats of the well. She flipped the choke and punched the button again.

He was still coming and she grabbed the throttle lever as the engine caught. Shoved it hard.

The crazy went flat in the well, waving arms and legs and yelling.

And white light showed across the water. Blinded her. Sent the crazies howling.

She looked at the edges of it, most she dared. One

shot came back. *Boom*! across the water. And the crazy in her well scrambled lizard-fashion for the side and crawled over it, splash! into the swamp.

The light was dead on her, whitening the deck and the well, fast as the skip was traveling, and she was blind. She thought, They got me pinned, whoever. And she swung about again and throttled down, heart thumping.

Mama wasn't anywhere about to give advice. Mama didn't take to bright lights and shots flying. Mama's memory just said,

Here's a fool. . . .

Man's voice said, Who's there?

And she called out, over the beat of the idling engine: "Jones, Altair Jones! Is Rif about?"

The skip was tied upside of the big hummock. Inside—

Inside it was a seeping stone well, the sides all black and oozing with water, and wooden steps black and treacherous—she could see that in the electric hand-light the man behind her had—had her gun, too, and gave her no promises except the man topside was going to be sure the crazies kept away from her boat.

Could be a nest of sharrists for all she knew. Damn, she didn't like this pit—it was *worse* than roofs. There was a thumping sound that had to be a pump deep in its guts, and her knees shaking made her have to hold tight to the slimy rail, because her feet weren't at all reliable on the dripping steps. Break a body's neck, yey, Mama. *Don't* like this, no way.

Down in the dark something creaked like the gates of hell, and another light showed through black, dripping stairs and blinded her.

"I can't see the steps!" she yelled at whoever it was. But she kept going, because the man behind her was coming down and she was scared of a fracas on the slick steps, in which she was apt to break her neck. She was feeling her way when she got down into the blinding light, and the man behind her caught up with her and caught her arm.

"Blindfold," the second one said. And she didn't like that at all, but it meant them wanting her not to see things, which meant it mattered. Which meant she might get out of here. So she stood still while the one set his electric light on a step and pulled out a scarf and tied it.

"You leave that," he said, and she said, "Yey, you just watch it I don't break my neck."

"I got you," he said, and took her arm while she tried not to be shaking like a fool. Her teeth wanted to chatter so she clamped her jaw and thought how Mondragon was in a worse place than this. Not as scary, maybe. But damn-all worse.

The door groaned open again—right close this time. The man pushed her head down, said, "Duck," and she ducked, and went where he guided her, onto footing that echoed worse—*metal*, God, metal that boomed and shook and echoed deep down in this place. Cold, damp air and rusty metal smell. "Step," the man said. "Rail an' your right."

"Got 'er," she whispered. Her teeth *were* chattering, she couldn't help it; and the man's grip was bruising her arm. But she held with the other hand, she felt her way down, and he didn't hurry her, didn't get rough. That was encouraging.

Encouraging when she got to the bottom and Rif's voice said: "Well, well. Here's a fool."

BOOKWORMS

by Nancy Asire

"You really should tell the boy," Stella said. "You really should. What if he were to find out from someone else? How do you think he'd feel?"

Alfonso Rhajmurti sighed quietly and looked up at the dimly lit ceiling as if he might find the answer to her question there. "I know . . . I know. It's been hard not to tell him, sometimes. In fact—"

"You're making excuses again, Alfonso." Stella's green eyes, so like her son's, caught the last gleam of afternoon light that penetrated the second-level shops on Lindsey. "Way things are going here in town, who knows what might happen? Lord! The whole thing could turn topsy-turvy on you and you might never have the chance. And *he* might never have the chance to know who his father really was."

"You're not telling me anything I don't know," Rhajmurti said. "It's . . . let's put it this way, Stella— much as you're aware things are a bit unsettled in Merovingen, you don't know the half of it."

"And by that, you mean. . . ?"

"By that I mean things are worse than you thought." Rhajmurti looked across the shop, out the opened door which let in the barest hint of a summer breeze. Few people were on the walkways now, most headed home from work or whatever endeavors kept body and soul together. He gestured and Stella joined him at the counter. One eye on the doorway to guard against a possible intruder, Rhajmurti lowered his voice to a half-whisper. "There are eyes and ears everywhere, mostly where you'd least expect them. Exeter isn't letting anything get by her these days."

Stella's lips thinned. "Are you in danger?"

"Me?" Rhajmurti snorted. "I'm not nearly powerful enough to worry the College."

"But you and Trevor—"

"*That* business is under wraps. It'll stay that way." He glanced toward the door. "But not even the Householdheads are safe these days. Exeter's people are everywhere. The least little infraction and . . ." He let the sentence die, gestured futilely.

In his mind's eye, he saw the gaps that had recently appeared among the priests and, yes, even the cardinals, at the College. Some of his colleagues were reported as 'off visiting family,' while others had taken supposed sabbaticals. Such was the official word, the image Exeter and her cronies wanted to convey to the world at large, to the cloistered world of the university itself. Rhajmurti knew better. So did everybody else, devout as they might be.

How to explain the absence of those priests who'd had a reputation for open-mindedness? How to rationalize the disappearance of many of his friends who taught in the arts and go on believing in the holiness of the church, if not its servants? He mourned the lost, not knowing if it was loss of a permanent nature, or whether these men he had known for years would reappear, chastened, fallen in rank, and echoing Exeter's policies and politics.

His own caution and careful footwork had saved him until now. But tomorrow?

Why can't I just come out and say it? What's holding me back? I can't lose trust in everyone *or I'll go mad!*

"Stella." He reached out and took her hands in his. "I want you to think of leaving this place. Not *maybe*. Really. I want you to start cutting loose. Now."

Her eyes widened. "This shop, or—"

"The city itself. Adventists aren't high on Exeter's list of favorite people right at the moment, though she's concentrated on dissent in her own flock. No . . . I don't mean leave today, nor tomorrow—gods forfend. Just make sure that *if* the time comes, you're not caught without an escape plan. I want you able to walk out that door at any moment, no hesitation and no question where you're going and what you're going to do."

"Are you serious?" she asked, her voice gone very, very quiet. Her face hardened in the fading light. "You *are*, aren't you?"

"Stella." He dug in his wide sash and shoved a small leather purse toward her. "Take this, and hold on to it."

She lifted the purse, heard the clink of metal and frowned. "Alfonso . . . I don't need—"

"Yes, you do, and you know it. You make enough to keep this shop going and to maintain a modest lifestyle. Tell me truthfully, how much have you saved? Enough to get you and Justice far enough from this city in case all hell breaks loose?"

"How far is far?" she asked, opening the packet. The glint of gold made her gasp softly. "Lord and my Ancestors! How *much* is in here?"

"Sufficient to buy you and Justice passage on a ship

headed for the Chattalen—don't look so puzzled. That's the best place. Down there, they don't seem to care what religion one adheres to, and we have no involvement in their politics. They value the arts. The government's stable—at least steadier than this one. With your knowledge of shop-keeping and Justice's talents, the two of you could look forward to more than just a living."

Stella drew the purse shut. "Why not Nev Hettek? At least we'd be with civilized people."

"Ah, Stella, Stella, you're smarter than that. If Merovingen goes—with Fon in power in Nev Hettek, *civilization* isn't what we'll have. Gods only know what's going on with the Sword of God—but they're here. They're already *in* the city. People are going to die, Stella."

She weighed the packet in her hands. "There's more in here than necessary to buy us passage, Alfonso, if it's all gold. It *is* all gold, isn't it?"

"Yes, it's all gold." He reached out and touched her cheek. "Do you think I'd send you off without a chance at a decent future? You'll have to live on something, get established somehow. And you're not going to do it without something to line your pockets. Money gets respect and respectability. I intend for you to have that. You *and* Justice."

"But you must have saved for years to—"

"Stella . . . we've been over this time and again. I could never marry you, though I wanted to. The College frowns on such things. But I'll never stop loving you or Justice. He's turning out to be more than I'd ever hoped. The two of you are my family . . . do you understand? And, by Rama, Vishnu and all the gods, I'm going to do my damnedest to help you. Don't worry about me, I'm more than taken care of at the College. What do *I* need money for? All my meals, my clothing, my room . . ."

"Aren't you coming with us?"

His heart gave an odd little twinge. "If I can," he said. "But I don't see how that will be possible. I'm hardly a big fish when it comes to College politics, but I *do* have a position of some power. I'm stuck in the middle . . . not important enough to be 'noticed' by Exeter and her friends, but not insignificant enough to be ignored. I'll be watched. I may not be able to get out. But I'll manage. And *you* have to get our son out of here."

"Alfonso." Her chin lifted. "I won't leave you behind . . . *if* things turn bad. I'm not going to a new life somewhere and leave you here, not knowing whether you're alive or dead. Don't put me in the position of having to choose between you and Justice. Don't do that to me."

"You won't have to choose, love." He smiled slightly. "When the time comes, you'll know it. And then, my darling Stella, you'll do only what is right."

Back on the walkway of second-level Kass, Justice heaved a very real, though quiet, sigh of relief. He shifted his backpack on his shoulders, ran a hand through his damp hair and tried to look to all the world like nothing more than a College student going home after a long day at the books.

Books.

He cringed inwardly. In all his life, he had never, *never*, contemplated dishonesty. Being honest and truthful were as much a part of him as breathing. Between his aunt and Father Rhajmurti, he had learned the lesson well: don't lie, don't cheat, don't steal. Don't do to other people what you wouldn't want them doing to you. If you find yourself placed in a position where another person would lie, keep your mouth shut. Diplomacy is a pardonable escape from utter honesty. But now. . . ?

The backpack seemed to weigh heavier on his shoulders. Oh, he understood *why* he was thieving . . . understood all the reasons for his dishonesty, understood that if they were right in what they feared they were *saving* something that was in deadly danger, but the whole pattern of subterfuge and fear still rankled. He and Raj had sat up late night after night discussing the alternatives. Theft was the least dangerous and the least damaging solution to their problems—because the time was coming when anyone who wanted to pursue a career in art or science would have to do it outside Merovingen. Cardinal Exeter was making sure of her grip on the city by an intellectual reign of terror. Even the high and mighty were not immune, to say nothing of the students, like himself, who had no Family connections above the middle tier.

So he and Raj had taken to thieving books from the Library, books they could later sell for a handsome price—books that might be in deadly danger from Exeter—or be a deadly weapon themselves in other hands: there were plastics in those books. There were electrics. There was space travel and physics and chemistry. They were getting these things out to sell to those that would pay. And they had no foreknowledge to tell them whether what they were doing was good or bad, or utterly, wrongly foolish. It was their way to survive. They'd argued their way into it as a moral act. They had snatched a goodly few already, being above suspicion as top students and daily frequenters of the Library. With the Librarian himself off for an alleged 'vacation,' many of the books from the off-limits, secret room of the Library had refiled themselves in places no student would have expected them.

Tech books, some of them.

Worth their weight in gold in certain places.

Worth death, if a student happened to get caught reading them.

Never in his life had the atmosphere of Merovingen seemed more stifling, and the dismal weather was hardly the culprit. The students at the College had grown uncharacteristically silent as of late. He had seen the furtive glances among the students when a new priest had turned up at a class to teach—sometimes a class got an explanation for the former teacher's absence . . . sometimes not. But everyone, from the lowliest beginning student to those like himself, on the verge of graduation, knew whose were the hands that moved people like game pieces on the College board.

Justice shivered. He and Raj had passed their catechism classes with flying colors, and thereby removed themselves from the list of the 'most watched.' All the study, the God-given gift of intelligence, and the 'luck' of having Father Rhajmurti instead of the dreaded Father Jonsson as their examiner, had gotten them past that. They were devout Revenantists on the College records—thanks to Sonja's intervention (and her wealth) without which Lord only knew what might have happened.

He crossed the last bridge, walked down the steps and along the board walkway to Hilda's, territory in which he felt a bit more secure—on an even keel, so to speak. If Exeter had spies in Hilda's, they would hear nothing damning from the patrons: when storms, real or figurative, blew into Merovingen, most folk knew how to keep their heads down and their mouths shut—and Hilda tolerated no fools.

"Justus."

Sonja was sitting at Justice's usual table, a limp and sleeping Sunny sprawled on her lap. Justice waved at Hilda, lifted a finger to Guy the bartender in an order for beer, and turned aside from his direct course to his room. But as he took a chair beside Sonja, his smile froze. Her eyes were shadowed and unhappy.

"What's wrong?" he asked in a hushed voice, placing his money on the table top as Jason deftly deposited the beer and swept up the fee with one practiced hand. "Gods, Sonja . . ."

She shook her head, mutely instructing him to keep silent. He sipped at his beer, glanced around the room, but found few patrons occupying the tables who weren't known to him as regulars. No chance for Exeter's secret police here, unless one of his acquaintances had been suborned.

What could be bothering Sonja? She was out of Family—the Keisels *and* the Borgs, good Revenantists all. She had passed the Testing, as he had known she would, with far less coaching from Rhajmurti than the other students had needed.

Sonja, meanwhile, sat nursing her own drink, listlessly stroking Sunny with one hand. The large gold cat's purr was so loud Justice could hear it from where he sat.

"Justus," Sonja said in a voice very little above a whisper. "We've fallen under the Eye."

Justice nearly choked on his beer. The Eye? Code language among the students for Exeter and her slinks. He licked his lips and kept his own voice low. "K or B?" he asked, meaning Keisel or Borg.

"Both."

He tried to make the connection that would make that reasonable, handicapped by his less than perfect knowledge of the web of hightowner Family interconnections. Borg he would have thought above reproach; fine Revenantists, they had been pillars of Merovingen society for generations. As for the Keisels, *Sonja* was the Borg/Keisel link. He knew only that . . .

The connection snapped into place.

Beef.

Dealings with Nev Hettek.

O Lord and Ancestors! No . . . now even thinking in Adventist terminology was dangerous. Gods, gods, gods!

"Mother made a Trip," Sonja said. Translated: Nadia Keisel had been summoned to talk with Exeter.

Justice asked, "Did it come off well for her?"

"So-so." Sonja took a long sip of her beer. Her dark eyes met his. "Some of her business partners are having a bad year. You know how that goes. Father says she shouldn't worry."

Translation: Nadia Keisel was under suspicion because she dealt with cattle ranchers to the north who had ties to Nev Hettek. Sonja's father, Vladimir Borg, in Borg, had caught Exeter's eye because of his ties to Family Keisel. Nonetheless, he had offered his support to the woman he loved, and implicitly, to their mutual daughter.

"I hope he's right," Justice said. "Would you like some dinner?"

Sonja made a face. "I suppose so."

"Let me treat," Justice said before she could offer. "I sold another painting today. I feel flush."

He lifted a hand and Jason came to their table, took their orders and disappeared into the kitchen.

For a while, the two of them sat in silence, Sunny's purr all the louder for that. Justice shifted position in his chair and his foot bumped the backpack he had placed beside his chair. Gods! He had totally forgotten about the books. If someone were to catch him here with—

"Have you seen Raj?" Sonja asked.

"Not today. He's probably in Kamat."

"You might want to tell him about Mother."

He nodded. Raj had become somewhat of a specialist on the hightown Family alliances since he had entered House Kamat. Maybe *Raj* could see something he'd missed.

"Storm's coming," Sonja said. "A bad one."

"It might hit sooner than we think."

Jason brought their dinners, set plates, knives and forks on the table and, taking Justice's coin, returned to his place behind the bar.

"But you're well protected, all the same," Justice said, cutting into his fish. "Better than those on canalside."

"This storm may have little regard for addresses," she murmured. Sunny had lifted his head at the scent of fish and Sonja pushed him from her lap. He gave her a totally disgusted look, hopped up into a chair next to Justice, and commenced his silent begging.

Justice lowered his eyes, took a drink, then looked up again. "I know this will sound stupid *and* presumptuous . . . but if there's anything I can do to help. . . .''

For a moment he thought he had insulted her—he, a nobody from second-level Lindsey, offering help to one of the Names of the city. But, no . . . she smiled slightly.

"I'll keep that in mind, Justus," she said, "and you might be surprised one day to find me collecting on that."

They finished their dinner in silence, Justice finally relenting and giving Sunny the last few bites of his fish. The books at his feet called out for attention, or at least removal to a safer place. He glanced at Sonja, weighed in his mind the ramifications of telling her what he was doing and why, and made his decision.

"Come to my room with me," he said, pushing his chair back from the table. "I've got a new painting to show you."

Sonja lifted one eyebrow, but followed readily enough. Once in his rooms and after nearly shutting the door on an appreciative Sunny, Justice set his backpack on the couch.

"Raj isn't here," he observed, nodding toward the dark doorway to his right. "We're as safe from observation as we can be."

"What's all this about?"

He shook his head, opened his bag, and pulled out several textbooks, which he set to one side. From the very bottom, he pulled out an old volume, battered by time and worn by the many hands that had held it. Sonja's eyes widened.

"Where—?" She reached for the book, ran her fingertips over the old cover. "Justus . . . where did you get this?"

He told her, told her what he and Raj were doing, and why. Told her his fears for the future, his concern that if he had to make a run for it, he wouldn't have the money to get himself or his aunt out of Merovingen—or live once they did. He told her where he and Raj had been stashing their hoard—skips tied up at the repair docks of the Bolado family. And then he waited for her judgment.

Waited.

And waited.

"Justus," she said, and sat down in one of the two chairs that graced the small sitting room. "Do you realize the price one of these books could command— elsewhere? Do you realize the danger you're in merely *having* this book?"

He swallowed. "Yes. But they'll never be missed, Sonja. No one even knows their location anymore, the Library is all upside-down." He spread his hands. "My aunt's no more than moderately comfortable, and gods know *I* don't have much. If the whole city goes to hell and back, it's going to take more than we could ever put together ourselves to get out of here with a whole skin. I know this sounds idiotic, but I won't resort to doing anything flagrantly dishonest . . . *this* is bad enough. I won't rob, I won't deal drugs. I won't cheat people by asking ridiculous prices for my artwork. And Raj won't take it from the canalers, either, for his medicines."

"The Kamats should take care of Raj," Sonja said, her face expressionless. "By now, he should have saved quite a bit on the allowance they've given him."

Justice nodded. "And he has. But if the break

comes suddenly he can't get at it: it's tied up in the Kamat accounts, not easily accessible. And you, yourself, said that this 'storm' we both see coming won't respect addresses."

"If you needed money," Sonja said, "why didn't you come to me?"

Justice felt his ears go hot. "That's . . . that's taking advantage of our friendship! I could never—"

"What the hell are friends for?" she demanded, setting the book down. "Without sounding conceited, I've got enough money to fund both you and your aunt's passage out of Merovingen—without noticing."

Justice stared at her for a moment, then sat down on the floor at her feet. "Sonja," he said, "try to understand. Our friendship means more to me than— well, than just about anything. And when one friend takes money from another friend . . ."

She smiled, reached out and touched his shoulder. "You silly man. Do you think I'd offer if I didn't care for you?"

Justice remained silent, his heart beating so loud it was a thunder in his ears.

"What you're doing—" She gestured at the book. "—borders on the foolhardy. If you happened to be caught carrying it, or the others you say you've got hidden safely away, you could be hanged! And I don't want to see that . . . gods know, I don't want that."

"What I owe you already I can't—"

"A debt is only a debt if the lender expects it back."

Justice scrambled to his feet and turned away from her. He closed his eyes, calmed his breathing, and rubbed his sweaty palms on his trousers. "I've been called a lot of nasty things in my life," he said, hearing the choked sound of his voice and hating it, "and I've long since achieved the ability to ignore them. But lately, I've had people say that I'm nothing more than a social climber, that I've become friends with you merely for your connections with a world I could never enter on my own. And that hurts, Sonja. It hurts bad!" He folded his arms and turned to meet her eyes. "I have *some* pride, and that pride won't let me take advantage."

"Who's been saying such things?" she demanded, and stood up, her dark eyes snapping anger. "Who would dare? You're one of the few people who've ever accepted me for *me*: not a Keisel, not a Borg, not a hightowner, not an heiress! You've always treated me like a friend and never once, Justus Lee, have you *ever* presumed beyond that friendship!"

"That's because I don't want to lose it."

"Then sell the books to me. I'll pay you for them."

He blinked, feeling stupid and slow. "I couldn't do that, Sonja. What if *you* were caught with them? Gods . . . some of them are *tech* books. I don't care how powerful your Family is, if Exeter even caught wind of you having such books . . . Sonja, forget I even told you about it. You and your Family are already under Exeter's scrutiny. . . ."

"And you think *you're* not?" She laughed bitterly. "Anyone I associate with is marked. That's why I came here today to let you know—about my mother. If you weren't being watched before, you are now. Don't you see? It's not only dangerous for you, it's dangerous for me, and for my Family, for both my Families, if you're caught carrying one of those books!"

"Then why in all the worlds did you offer to *buy* the books from me?"

She bit her lip. "Justus . . . there are some secrets the Families hide from anyone *not* Family. Say there are places Families have that no one outside Family knows about. I can hide them."

"Let's slow down here," Justice said, lifting a hand. "If I promise this is the last book I'll ever take from the Library, will you forget I ever mentioned it?"

"Only if you'll take the money. Only if you'll sell me those books. I've been in your aunt's shop and I've seen what she sells. Don't look at me that way . . . I wanted to know something about your family. What she sells are old, worn-out and thoroughly read and re-read books. Gods know there's trade in it, or she would have starved by now. But none of these books is worth much, and if the time comes everything's going to hell and you have to get out of town, you're right, you haven't got it. Let me buy books from your aunt. I can do it—say I'm giving them to needy shut-ins. It's something we Keisels have done time and again, and it won't be anything out of the ordinary."

He stared at his feet. "People would wonder why it was only one shop you traded with. People are already talking."

"Let them. Unless you're afraid of association with *us*. I'm not all that important to be watched every single second of the day, and it's not out of character for Families to do charity."

"All right," he conceded. "Buy books from my aunt. But, Sonja . . . please, be circumspect about it. For both our sakes."

She lifted an eyebrow. "You're telling one of *us* to be circumspect? Gods, Justus . . . we learned such things in our cradles. No one will know. And so they

95

don't—" She pointed at the book on the floor. "—I want you to unload this book as quickly as possible. When were you going to take it to Bolado's?"

"Tonight."

"Rama protect! Are you *serious?* You could end up at the bottom of the canal!"

"It's safe. I've done it before," Justice said, "and I've never—"

"Have you ever gone alone?" she demanded, "or have you and Raj gone together?"

"We've gone together," Justice admitted. "But it's just south of Bent which is just south of here—"

"You don't need to give me directions." She chewed on her lower lip a moment in concentration. "We'll go together."

Justice felt as if someone had hit him in the stomach. "You're out of your mind, Sonja," he sputtered. "I could *never* let you go into such dangerous—"

"You just said it was safe," she pointed out. "So, why don't you and I go for a walk? It's just going on twilight, and it's definitely the time that young lovers take to the walkways."

"Young lovers?" Justice all but choked.

Sonja laughed, retrieved the book and slipped it into her own book-bag. "And who would think twice to see us on the walkways? We've been together everywhere else. Besides, I know the Bolados and it won't seem all that strange for anyone to see me there."

"But—"

"Oh, come on, Justus, or it *will* be too late for us to walk safely. I want to get this book out of your hands."

He sighed, remembering what Sonja had said once about being a Keisel and Keisels usually getting what they wanted. It had never done him any good to argue with her before, and he was damned sure it wouldn't help him now.

The city grew quieter as the sun set; fewer people were on the walkways and the canal traffic slacked off—in these grim times, hightowners stuck to hightown and more and more shops shut at sundown. Rhajmurti stood leaning on the railway of second-level Spellbridge, torn between going back to the College or visiting Justice on Kass. Stella's words kept going 'round and 'round in his mind; Tell him the truth, she'd said.

She was right, he knew it, but the very notion of confronting Justice with the truth about his parentage made Rhajmurti question whether now was the right time.

Was *any* time the right time?

It had been an easy lie to spin when Justice was young. Telling him his parents had been lost in a boating accident was a story neither strange nor all that unusual. It was not major news when someone drowned in the canals: it happened all too often. But as Justice grew older, maintaining the lie only got more difficult: he'd perpetuated the untruth, shown only scholarly interest in the talented boy he'd sponsored at the College. Only natural a closeness should develop between teacher and student, but on one side it was a deeper bonding. And maybe Justice felt it; or maybe Justice wrote it down to seeing in his teacher the father-image he'd lacked since he could remember.

Stella's right. I'm going to have to tell him, sooner or later. And the way things are going, there might not be a later.

He straightened, then subsided against the railing again.

If he were to tell Justice tonight, then if order in the city deteriorated to the point that escape was the only option, how might Justice react? Would he stubbornly refuse to leave without the father he'd only just found?

Or would he go more willingly if he thought Stella was his entire family? Tell the boy he had to get Stella out? Lay it on him that way?

No. That was being unfair. Justice was a man now, able to deal with life and life's ups and downs. But if Stella told him then *who* he was—

Rhajmurti sighed softly. Stella knew him far too well; she could pull strings and make him jump better than anyone he had ever known. He *wanted* Justice to know who his father was and she knew it. He'd dreamed of having closer ties to the son he was so proud of. And, as Stella had accused him, he was making excuses again.

He'd tell Justice.

Tonight.

He started off down Spellbridge walk, putting his mind to a calming mantra.

Not the easiest thing he had ever done—finding a path back through all the lies—with the boy he'd lectured about truthfulness.

And could Justice still act the part, keep on treating his father as his teacher and his friend?

Or even respect him, once he knew he'd lied.

Rhajmurti's feet dragged to a stop. He stood for a moment at the edge of Spellbridge-Kass Bridge, unwilling to take the first step.

Then he *saw* Justice . . . Justice and Sonja.

Relief and regret poured through him. He could certainly *not* tell Justice anything in Sonja's presence.

But that association suddenly worried him. Nagged him with the awareness of Exeter—and Exeter's sudden interest in House Keisel. Sonja looked worried, walking along arm in arm with Justice. And knowing the reason for that—one could ask oneself where they were going, in that unusual direction, and what Sonja might have told Justice about her family troubles—

What attention Sonja might focus on Justice—and from what quarter.

He hesitated, undecided, then leisurely crossed the bridge and followed them. They seemed to be out for an after-dinner stroll like a few other folk. But with a school book-bag? Going away from Hilda's? He could not hear what they were saying at this distance, not the slightest whisper of conversation, but from the angle of the heads, the gestures, he knew them deep in conversation.

Justice's relationship with Sonja had delighted him—yesterday. He wished only the best for his son, and a friendship struck with one of the Families of Merovingen certainly would not have hindered Justice's career, no matter the alarm of Sonja's parents.

Sonja had come to him once, not long after the Governor's Ball, to speak with him in his office of priest, not as teacher. What should she do? Her parents were not overly happy with her association with an un-Housed man—however she protested they were only friends. She'd agreed to contract marriage, she had to go to it with no whisper the promised child would be other than Jorge Kuminski's; once she'd fulfilled that contract and given Kuminski a child, she could have any man in Merovingen for a lover—

A relationship with Sonja Keisel could make all the difference in the world to Justice in the future. If it didn't create scandal in the upcoming marriage.

If—

And what future? All he could see were dark clouds on the horizon. It was plainer every day that the reactionaries who surrounded Exeter would have their way, that Mikhail the Clockmaker *would* succeed Iosef Kalugin, the machinations of Anastasi and Tatiana notwithstanding. They'd waited too long, they'd lost the votes in council—Exeter had killed the staunchest and terrified the rest: Boregy had left Anastasi's camp and gone to Tatiana's, but Cardinal Boregy was dead, most horribly, House Boregy was powerless to control mad Cassie, and wavering between pandering to Mikhail's fond folly and fearing for their collective necks: Exeter was both baffled and frustrated with Mikhail's one act of self-will. But look to Exeter to find an answer—before Anastasi and Tatiana's sudden appearance at a state function arm in arm, with deathly smiles painted on their faces, could rally any support against her. He knew the rumors. He knew the *facts* inside the College: the gossip that passed among priests was quick, and accurate, and lately terrifying. He had had no doubt when he'd told Stella to prepare for a sudden departure. The signs were everywhere—that some faction was going to move.

Sonja's mother had been called in—Vladimir Borg was somehow connected—

He did *not* like playing the spy. He didn't like following his son like a thief. But, damn, he had to know.

Ahead, Sonja and Justice were crossing over to

Bent, not all *that* unusual a path to take if out for an evening walk, give or take the book-bag: they seemed to be in no unusual hurry. They were keeping to second tier—not especially dangerous in early evening, until lately.

He breathed a prayer to Vishnu, the protector, to grant him strength: the young fools took the steps down to Bent canalside.

"Who's your contact at the Bolados?" Sonja asked, leaning closer to Justice as she walked. Justus' face was shadowed in the twilight of bottom tier.

Justus said: "A fellow named Stet."

Stet. Where had she heard that name? She thought back to her Family's dealings with the Bolados, going through the names of everyone she knew who was connected to that House. Stet, Stet. Ah! She had the man now. Stet was the boatman who worked for the Bolado business. From what she could remember of the man, he was a quiet fellow—not the sort she'd have marked for intrigue with college students.

Though she would rather have died than admit it to Justus, she was terrified. She was quite sure he had no idea of the value of the books he and Raj were stealing. Justus and Raj had come up with an idea that was, on the surface, utterly sound. And utterly, fatally dangerous. They had to get that cache of books out of there. If he or Raj had ever been caught . . . or mugged . . .

Priceless, secret articles every so often changed hands among the powerful and the wealthy—and, feeding that market, thieves abounded in the underworld of the city, none of them hesitant to steal a rare painting, book, jewel or the like from one Family and then sell it to another. Many of the Families knew very well they possessed stolen goods; the irony of it was that if they lost something and then later discovered it in another's house, they could hardly cry foul without admitting they themselves had passed off as theirs something stolen from gods only knew what Family had owned it originally. People of good breeding simply kept their mouths shut about the silverware.

And in that market—books like this—

She cast a sidelong glance at Justus. Damned if she knew why she was so attracted to the man; he had no Family, no wealth, no future other than the one his talent would make—and *never* the resources a future Househead like Jorge would have. But there was something about Justus Lee that pulled at her. Honesty—first and foremost. Integrity (if one discounted his forays in the Library). And his ability to treat her like a human being, not a bank account.

Their friendship had deepened beyond that now: she sensed he felt the same toward her, but he was still too shy and too unsure of himself to voice his feelings.

Damn Jorge Kuminski! Damn all contract marriages! It had looked like a smart move—before she'd cared about someone else. She didn't have to live with Jorge. Just pay a damned year of her life being circumspect. Which she wasn't being tonight. In any sense. If someone raised a question about their whereabouts tonight the marriage could be extended another year and she might *have* to live with Jorge to dispel the gossip.

Twelve excruciating months, never alone with the man she *really* loved.

*　　*　　*

Justice surreptitiously touched the hilt of the knife he wore sheathed at his belt and felt the reassuring constant weight of the other knife at his boottop—these days he went armed to the teeth, had a third knife sheathed at the top of his spine, hidden by both his hair and his collar. He had learned, not without a few blows and bruises, that the walkways he and Raj used after hours could be deadly dangerous.

Sonja was nervous. He saw that by the quickness of her gestures, heard it in her voice. He doubted she had ever done anything so foolhardy in her life, or ventured this far at night in the nether walkways without some bodyguard of House Keisel accompanying her. And he wondered how he was going to talk her out of any deal about the books: He and Raj were sure that the books were valuable, but after Sonja's reaction he began to think they might have underestimated the worth of what they had taken. And the danger of the game they'd thought was a small one.

No one ahead on the canalside but a couple of tradesmen. He didn't want to overtake them, he didn't want to attract attention by hurrying, but, dammit, he wished they could make better time. He hadn't lied when he had told her he and Raj had come to the Bolados before to hide their ill-gotten gains, but she'd rightly guessed he'd never come alone—tell the truth, most times neither he *nor* Raj had made the trip. Kat Bolado herself had taken the books home with her—on her boat.

The workmen went around the corner. Thank the gods. Bent-Bolado Low Bridge was only a few steps ahead now. And, at the moment, deserted. They were in bridge shadow from two tiers above: fog hazed the few lights showing. Their steps echoed on the bridge.

"Will Stet be there?" Sonja asked, shifting the bag with the book to the other hand.

"He always has been, this time of evening. He lives there."

"Watergate?"

"Yes."

They were on the floating walkway now. Steps sounded behind them, down from the upper tiers. Someone on the stairs. Justice took Sonja's arm and hurried her, never mind looking casual.

Steps on the walkway behind them.

"M'sera Keisel?"

Justice's heart threatened to jump out of his chest. Sonja stopped dead, turned and stared wide-eyed at two large men.

"And who might *you* be?" she asked, in her best hightown accent, her posture taking on all the attributes of the rich and powerful.

The man stepped closer, his face moving in and out of the light past by the lamp that hung on middle-tier above. His companion stayed behind, a faceless shadow in the stair-supports.

"I'm the one asking the questions, m'sera, not you."

"Now see here," Justice said, placing himself between the man and Sonja. "We're out for a walk, and hardly in the mood for company. I suggest you go bother someone else."

The man laughed coldly. "Young bully . . . get back to your den where you belong. My business is with m'sera here, not you."

Justice drew a deep breath and settled into a fighter's balanced pose, up on the balls of this feet, his arms hanging loose at his sides.

"Stop it, both of you!" Sonja's imperious voice rang off the walls around them. "Once more . . . what is it that you want?"

"Just a few questions, m'sera," the man said, all false politeness, "and then you'll be free to go."

"Ask," she said.

"I'm afraid you'll have to come with me, m'sera." He shot a look in Justice's direction. "Your—body-guard—can wait for us here."

"Don't give me that tone, ser," Sonja spat, *all* high-town. "And you'd best treat him with the respect he's due. Who are you? Who do you work for?"

Laughter came from the shadow waiting in the stair-way. "All *he* deserves is a swim in th' canal, don't ye think?"

Justice's mind was racing. Not blacklegs, these men. Nothing he'd ever run into. Middle-tier accent. Or higher. And Exeter with an interest in Borg and Keisel. . . .

Nobody coming from any side of these men. The whole waterside was deserted; and in the silence, he could hear no one behind him on the walkway. Nothing moving on the walk over their heads. If he could stall these men, *someone* would come along. Surely. The hour was hardly late enough to drive everyone indoors.

"Why don't we just discuss things here?" he said, trying to keep his voice steady. "If you're about hon-est business, I don't see why you would object."

"Our business is *our* business, boy." The man moved closer. Sonja backed up to Justice, her harsh breathing loud enough he could hear it. "If you want to push it, we can make you our business, too."

"Just who do you think you are?" Sonja demanded.

The man grinned mirthlessly, held out his arm. He and his companion were dressed in dark colors, but in the lamplight, the saffron College sash around the man's upper arm shone all too clear.

Exeter's men. There was no way out of this but a fight. Justice realized that now and, knowing who these two men worked for, he knew why the walkways were deserted.

"Sonja," he whispered, trying his best to look terrified—no chore, that. "Get out of here. Run."

"Come, m'sera . . . be cooperative," the man said, gesturing toward the stairs. "Just a short talk. Then you'll be free to go."

Sonja said, "We'll talk here, or not at all."

"M'sera—I'm through asking. You either come peaceably, or I'll drag you." He came closer—Justice threw Sonja behind with his left arm and faced the man with his knife glittering in the lamplight.

"Oh ho!" The man stepped back. "The young tom's got teeth!"

A sword whipped out from beneath the cloak, cloak wrapped around the other arm, fast and smooth. Justice's heart sank. Sword against knife: he and his opponent were of a height, equal reach—*bad* disadvantage. Keeping his eyes locked with the other man's, he pulled his second knife from his boot top.

"I was right," the man commented over his shoulder to his companion still waiting in the stairway. "Canal scum. Fah! No . . . get Keisel. This one's easy."

He and the man began to circle each other on the walkway. The man stabbed out with his sword, a careless gesture and one Justice blocked easily—blocked the other man's advance on Sonja from the bridge too, and hoped Sonja kept behind him. *He's toying with me . . . trying to see just how good I am. Damn! Of all the nights to leave my sword at home!* "Sonja? Get out of here. Go!"

Another stab, another angle. Justice kept his breathing easy, measured the man's reach, water close on one side, blank wooden wall on the right, the whole floating walkway heaving underfoot and slick from the passage of some boat. Steel rasped against steel as he countered a downward slash with crossed knives, tried to twist the sword out of the man's hands, but the sword flexed free—snapped helplessly aside and Justice lunged through the guard, but the man jumped back and clear.

"Hand it to you, kid . . . you're not bad. Maybe next life you'll come back as a duelist!" A talker. Justice had seen the type before. Talking to shatter an enemy's concentration. Ruin his timing.

Another attack. Low and high. He blocked both, heard a yelp from behind him and realized Sonja hadn't run. "Sonja—*get help!*"

Point, edge . . . the blows came quicker now. Pushed him hard. Parry to the weak part of the blade. Slide in. Never far enough fast enough. If only he had his sword. The man brought his sword around in a slash at his head. Justice ducked and parried, but the limber blade swept under and Justice jumped back, a little ground lost. "Sonja, get *out* of here, dammit, you're in my way!"

He had to win, had to kill this man . . . him and his companion. They knew his face now. They'd go back for reinforcements. His gut quivered . . . he didn't want to kill anyone. But he had to. For Sonja's sake. For his and Aunt Stella's now—

Kill a swordsman with a knife—

Another succession of attacks. Justice refused to back up, kept parrying, carrying himself low as he could, maximum trouble to a tall man, called upon all his training, the hours he'd practiced, the time he'd spent with Raj trying to pick up what Raj had learned with his hightown fencing master—

Breath came short. Sweat poured into his eyes; he shook it away with a sharp jerk of his head, blocked another slashing blow, and jabbed for the man's groin—forced him into an awkward parry and a jump back.

Keep your thoughts centered. Strike the balance within yourself. Let your enemy defeat himself. Stay in the fight. Be the last to quit.

Words from Raj's weapons instructor. Words a fighter—a truly talented fighter—lived by.

Or died believing.

Sonja huddled against the wall of some shop, her arms around the book-bag, saw Justus again and again turn away the sword of the man who had attacked him. Exeter's men—gods, Bolado daren't help—the blacklegs wouldn't intervene. . . .

Or *were* they Exeter's?

Might they be mere bridgeway ruffians, thieves who wore the cardinal's badge to disguise themselves and to ward off intervention?

Whoever they were, thieves or slinks, if they discovered the book she carried, both she *and* Justus would be dead. One way, or the other.

"Sonja!" Justus' voice pleaded with her.

He couldn't run. He couldn't hold them forever.

The second man kept trying to get at her and Justus kept maneuvering the fight to prevent it.

She gasped as Justus went to his knee. In a backward cut too quick to see, the swordsman opened a long gash across Justus' arm. She yelled something, not quite sure what, saw Justus slip and catch himself on his hand—the swordsman stabbing out—

Justus' knife came up. The stab into the swordsman's brain was either a move of exquisite placement or sheer desperation. The effort that tumbled that man back and put Justus on his feet was raw strength—

But it was the last. Justus staggered, waiting for the swordsman's companion to rush him. Rama help him . . . wounded, winded—as the second man drew a sword. She flipped back the cover to her book-bag, frantically rummaged the bottom; her fingers touched the cool metal of what she carried at her mother's insistence—

Nothing to arming it: pull back the spring, aim, and hope—the gun held only one dart. And if she should miss—or hit Justus. . . .

The two men danced with death on the walkway, Justus refusing retreat, then pushed back, bumped her. The other man lunged.

She fired as steel rang on steel—and steel stung past her arm.

Gods . . . weigh my karma against the deed!

The sword whipped back, aside, spun into the canal. The man was clawing at the dart in his chest, screaming . . . a high, inhuman wail that ended in a choked cry and tortured gasping. It seemed to take an eternity for the poison to do its work, for the man to go to his knees at their feet. Violent spasms shook him . . .

he fell forward, twitched uncontrollably, and then lay still.

Hands trembling so she could barely put the dart gun back in her bag, Sonja felt her knees threatening to fold, but she locked them and found a handhold on the rope support of the walkway, staring wide-eyed at the motionless body of the second man to die on the walkway this night. There was silence, silence so profound all she could hear was the lap of the water at Bolado.

"Lord!" Justus panted. "What did you do to him?"

Sonja swallowed heavily. "Deathangel."

Justus sheathed one of his knives. "Sonja . . ."

She closed her eyes as he took her in his arms, and buried her head in the small of his shoulder. *I've killed a man. I've taken a life. Gods, O gods, the karma . . .*

Her deed was far darker than Justus': he had killed in self-defense; she had chosen to kill when she herself could have run.

And a wicked man's karma was all hers.

Rhajmurti stood rooted to the middle tier walkway, unable to move, unable to call out. Oddly detached, he watched as if it were some morality pageant to educate the innocent; and while everyone else had vacated the walkway, turning a blind eye to what happened, he had stayed, frozen in time, forced by some power, or lack of it, to watch.

The cardinal's men. If he had intervened—Stella would have had no help, no warning—if he had intervened—

The karmic consequences of those two separate actions were enormous. Justice and Sonja had bound themselves to each other and to those men. For all lives to come.

So his Revenantist beliefs told him.

They told him he should have stayed on that walkway. They told him he should walk away now—pretend he'd seen nothing, *not* go down those steps.

He walked them—caught Justice's wary, on-guard stance; and Sonja's white face. Now that the fight was over, shock surely set in. Or his presence added it.

"Justice. Sonja."

Justice still held his knife, had a protective arm in front of Sonja. Perhaps they only saw the priestly robes in the shadow. Or trusted no one now. He came off the stairs.

"Father Rhajmurti!" Justice lowered his knife. "Thank the gods."

"Yes . . . thank the gods it's me." He reached for Justice's bloody sleeve. "You'd better let me look at that."

Justice held out his arm, grimaced, and nodded. "I don't think it's deep . . . not bleeding much."

"Huhn." Rhajmurti gently parted the split cloth of Justice's shirt. The wound was indeed shallow, and the blood had already started coagulating. "You're lucky, you know that . . . damned lucky."

"How much did you see?"

"All of it."

Sonja's glance screamed silent accusation.

"I . . . I could have helped, but—" Karma seemed a weak excuse. Stella was the worst one.

"They're wearing the cardinals' colors," Justice said, shoving the closest body with his foot.

Rhajmurti said: "We've got to get out of here. Now."

"Get rid of the bodies first," Sonja said. "No evidence."

Spoken like a true scion of a House. Justice kicked one man's body off into the canal. Rhajmurti nerved himself and shoved at the second corpse, rolled it over the edge into inky water and wiped his hands.

"Move," he ordered, then. "Over to French and then to Borg."

He hastened them toward Bent-French Bridge, glancing over his shoulder and above. No one had braved the walkways yet. Fights used to draw crowds in the Merovingen of old; he thought back on one notable altercation between Justice and Krishna Malenkov in front of Hilda's when people had gathered and actually placed bets.

Not any more. Muggings, murders and other crimes drew only silence now—especially when people saw priestly colors. But sooner or later someone would venture forth on the walkway to see what had happened.

Exeter was growing bold to accost a member of one of the Houses in Merovingen on an open walkway. Rhajmurti prayed as he hurried along behind Justice and Sonja . . . prayed there had been no witnesses. If anyone had seen, he prayed they had not seen the attackers as more than overly bold bridge thugs. And that, if Exeter herself was waiting for them—Exeter might go on waiting, thinking Sonja just a bit harder than expected to lay hands on.

Justice and Sonja hugged the shadows of Bent-French Bridge on the way across. A few people lingered in the gathering twilight, going about their business in total ignorance of the death that had stalked canalside. Rhajmurti prayed as he walked, prayed to every god, saint, and power he believed in that nothing would come of tonight's calamity.

At last, the relative safety of Borg. Sonja stopped, leaned up against the railing, and set her book-bag at her feet. Strands of her dark hair lay plastered to her forehead; her face was pale in the lamplight; her dark eyes were pools of shadow. Justice felt at his wounded arm, lifted his fingertips, and smiled slightly that they came away clean.

"All right," Rhajmurti said. "I want some answers."

Justice looked up. "To what?"

"Why were you attacked?"

"Gods only know," Justice said. "They came out of the dark at the stairway. I've never seen them before, and I'm sure Sonja hasn't either."

"*Were* they Exeter's?"

"You saw the armbands," Justice said. "They weren't hesitant to show them."

"That tells me everything and nothing."

"Lord and Ancestors, Father!" Justice exploded. "D'you think *we* were responsible?"

Rhajmurti lifted his hands. "Settle down, lad. Settle down. And if you're going to curse, *please* use Revenantist deities—I need to know these things. If those men *were* Exeter's, I need to know everything I can about what happened. If I have to lie, I'll want to have my story straight. And if they call you in, Sonja,—go. Peaceably. Lie to them. You don't know a thing. You got no message. You never saw these men."

Justice and Sonja exchanged a glance.

"My mother was called in," Sonja said quietly.

"I know."

Sonja said: "I—k–killed someone."

"Your karma—"

"Karma be damned!" Justice growled. "I won't go down without a fight, and you should know that by now."

"And *I* won't see my friend murdered before my eyes and not do anything," Sonja said. "If I've heaped karma on my soul for what I did, then so be it."

Rhajmurti shook his head. "Go home," he said. "Now. Separately. And Justice . . . make sure you clean that wound. Do you have anything to put on it?"

"You forget who my roommate is," Justice said. "Raj will have three or four things to put on it, believe me. Sonja—"

"I'll walk her home," Rhajmurti said. "Myself."

Justice hesitated on one foot, opened his mouth to object. And shut up.

"Sonja," Rhajmurti said, holding out his hand. He thought: *I nearly lost my son. Tomorrow! Tomorrow I'll tell him . . .* this *time, no excuses!*

Maybe Sonja was still shaken. She swung her bookbag to the other hand. And lost it. It splashed into the canal.

Rhajmurti looked after it in dismay. Justice had stopped and turned.

Sonja said, "It's nothing. Nothing worth going after."

So he walked her home.

ENDGAME (REPRISED)

by C. J. Cherryh

"Karl's got all the documents," Mondragon said. The voice was going. Chance's interest might, soon—the two of them, alone, into the small hours, dawn, by now, maybe. Two days Chance Magruder had chased the trails of question and question, picking over the bones of old quarrels, old murders, old business of all kinds that Chance heard for himself, and took occasional notes. He'd had sleep yesterday afternoon. The sessions were on Chance's schedule, since Chance didn't trust his own staff to hear what he was saying—and Chance told him nothing, not where Jones was, not whether she was in their hands, not what the situation was. Chance just asked his questions, one after the other, and Mondragon answered without argument, elaborated when asked—no coercion. He'd no reason to suffer, no reason to court discomfort that might fog his wits and make logic difficult: he thought Chance might at some point apply force, precisely to do that, just as a matter of curiosity. He hoped not. He hoped that, as Chance no more than hinted, he was buying Jones' freedom and her life.

He said, finally because he'd reasoned his way to that point, "Do you mind telling me where things stand—with our two principals? What's Anastasi up to?"

"Why?"

"Curiosity. He should have gotten me out of here."

Chance's mouth quirked at the corner. "You never believed that."

"I believe he would if he could—for his own sake."

"You want to talk about Anastasi?"

"Where's Jones?"

He hadn't asked that till now. He hadn't wanted to make it a direct issue, for Jones' sake. He watched every reaction Chance showed now—little as Chance let the mask of no-reaction slip—and there was a little calculation, a little interest, maybe Chance wondering whether he was cracking or if he'd been leading him down some course all along. From Anastasi to "Where's Jones?" in one leap, and Chance had to sum that up for a beat or two and figure how to navigate that unmapped connection.

"We don't have her," Chance said with a shrug, and watched him.

He said, "Do you know where she is?"

"What's Anastasi Kalugin have to do with it?"

Mondragon shrugged. Said, "How do you feel about Anastasi?"

Shrug from the other side: "He's a problem."

"Karl's problem, someday. On the other hand, if he and Tatiana put their support together in council—"

"They still don't outvote the governor's."

"You're sure of that."

"We know who's bought. And with what. Like what hold Anastasi's got on you. You're worried he's got her."

Chance knew, then, what he'd thought Chance might know. Or guess. Chance said, "What if I told you we're reasonably sure he's got her?"

"I'd say he should've found a way to tell me. Or he can't. In which case it was a waste of effort."

"Maybe he thinks he's told you."

He hadn't expected that. He hoped he kept it off his face. Chance said,

"The guy he thinks did—is ours."

It sounded plausible. Worrisomely plausible. He made up his mind he didn't believe it. And shrugged. "So you want me to keep his secrets to myself? Is that why you're telling me?"

"You asked."

Chance had a quirky sense of humor. Hard to tell when he was enjoying himself. Unwise if he was enjoying himself—instead of keeping strictly to the useful. Or the session had gotten to the point he really wasn't valuable to Chance any longer—because Chance knew enough now: and Chance had never batted an eye—which meant it was no news and he was in with Karl to the hilt; or Chance had added it up fast and knew he'd better hear what Karl would believe he had.

He was a fool to keep you alive, Chance had said last night. Which might have been an indication of Chance's own thoughts at that point—or now. Which, till Chance had played this little maneuver, had been a risk he'd decided to run—scare Chance into an alliance or make it clear Chance didn't *need* Jones to get the truth out of him. And Chance came up with this tossed grenade.

Damn him, he was lying. Anastasi *didn't* have Jones. But Jones hadn't come back. He'd stood by the window as long as he had the strength, as long as he dared keep awake—and there hadn't been any sign of her. Too smart to come back, he kept telling himself. Or there were obvious guards outside the narrow slit of water he could see.

But Jones could've run for help. Could've gone to Anastasi, never mind he'd told her never, ever do that—

Chance just sat and sipped his tea. Excused himself for a moment then, and left him to sit and to think, and to think—he couldn't help it, and that was a bad sign—that if he went to the window it might just be the right moment and he might catch sight of her.

He was cracking. He couldn't do that. He had to shrug it off. Had to make Chance believe he couldn't get any action that way. But Chance had seen the reaction. Chance had left him to think about it, and jerked the timing and the choices and the questions all out of his control—

A bullet was better. Chance didn't need to go to this trouble, except to win a point. Or to win him. And if he could sell his much-trafficked soul one more time if Chance was buying, yes, he'd do it, he'd do it and mean it, at least as long as it got him one try at shaking Jones til her teeth rattled.

Or seeing her. Even from the window. Just once, to know she was free and outside anyone's concern.

The door opened. Chance walked in, sat down, poured himself another cup of tea. "You?"

"Thanks," he said, and pushed his cup over. Chance filled it.

"So what about Karl?" Chance asked. "You were talking about the Tanner affair."

It wasn't what he was ready for. He dragged the

118

cup back over. He couldn't pick it up. Wasn't sure he could hold it steady. He drew a couple of breaths, said, "Just that Tanner leaked the date."

"You worried, Tom?"

"About what?"

"You just look worried."

He looked Chance in the face a long, long moment. Waiting. And with a pain in his gut. Chance wanted him to ask. It could go on another day like this. Or maybe there wasn't time, on Jones' side.

Chance got up then, walked for the door. Lingered there a moment, but Mondragon found distraction in the other wall. Chance said, "A man in love's a damned fool, Tommy-lad."

"So?" Rif said.

Jones said, "Ye do me this 'un, Rif, an' there ain't nothin' I'd deny ye."

Rif grinned, the two of them squatting over a map in a place the like of which no Merovingian alive but the Janes had seen, Jones reckoned: in a place that had survived the fire of the Scouring and the seeping corruption of Dead Marsh. All metal and something like plastic, its metal parts the ransom of any House-head, Lord, of the whole damn *city* out there, and reaching up through the ooze in a caisson the Janes had built around a ventilation shaft. Rif said it was some old remnant of the starport—she was *in* a place that the Ancestors had built, no, *not* the Ancestors, who'd been fools and stayed, but the real space-farers. Astronauts—Jones liked that word—had come and gone here, technicians who *knew* what all those dead, water-stained panels used to do—they'd handled the evacuation from here, and there might even be, out there in the ooze, some ship that hadn't made it off—

Mondragon should see this, Jones thought, hugging her arms about her knees. Her feet were cold. Water leaked in here and the lower level was, Rif said, all full of water, but there was something about sealed electrics, so the lights up here worked just fine, except one or two. Rif said there was something in the deep-down gut of this place that got its electrics from the center of Merovin itself. Which sounded unlikely, but after she'd seen this place she'd seen everything.

Only fault with it, there weren't any guns or such from the astronauts. But there was her mama's revolver. And Black Cal, who squatted down to take another look at the map—that gun of his wasn't any blackleg issue, for all Black Cal was, himself.

Black Cal pointed a lean finger at the backside of the Nev Hettek embassy, and said there was all the standpipes and the chimney and such on the roof about there. But there was a guardpost, too. He knew that because he'd been Tatty's once. He said he was still Iosef's. But mostly he was Rif's, and the way when they were thinking and planning he took hold of Rif's hand and their fingers locked, the two of them not even thinking about it, made Jones ache with lonesomeness, even with five and six Janes lurking about and offering advice on *doing* something, for the Lord's sake, finally there was this thread of a hope, even though Rif said they hadn't the hands right now, and last se'nday they would have—they were doing something upriver, you didn't ask.

But Rif gave that funny laugh of hers and said, hunkering there over the map, that the time was coming, that was an odd thing to say: the time was coming

and Jane'd provided, and the seeds she'd sowed were
going to bloom.

Wasn't what Adventists talked about, seeds and
blooming. Adventists talked about the Retribution,
about the ships coming down and fighting off the
sharrh that might be circling around and around the
world to be sure humans didn't build new ships.
Adventists talked about a day of reckoning, and
thought and thought about it, until some of them got
the Melancholy and went and *did* something, even if
it got them hanged.

Maybe she'd got religion. Because that was the way
she was thinking. They'd got her man and they
wouldn't let him out, and she'd use the Janes' help or
anybody's, they weren't going to carry Mondragon to
Nev Hettek and put him in that prison again.

"Chance t' rattle th' Nev Hettekkers?" Rif chuckled, rubbing her hands. "Yeh, Cal and me is in. How
'bout a fire-bottle?"

"I ain't riskin' fire with him! I ain't havin' him
trapped in there! Ye say yourself we can't anyways
get a floor plan—"

"Na, calm down. We got t' get t' uptown." Rif had
got this odd look, then, grim as grim. "Fast. 'Cause
there ain't all that lot o' time, Jones. Cal an' me goes
with ye t'night. Rest of us got to stay here."

"Why? What d' ye mean?"

"All I'll say. Can't take hands nor eyes from th'
things we got movin'. But ye got favors due an' this
little favor fits right in, Jones. Trouble for th' Sword
ain't a bother t' us a'tall."

FAMILY TIES

by Nancy Asire

"You're my *what?*" Justice asked, his voice shaking.

"Your father," Rhajmurti repeated.

Justice tried to say something, tried again. He slowly rose from his chair and turned away, staring at the wall.

"Justice." Rhajmurti's voice radiated calm. "Look at me. Is the fact so distasteful you can't face it . . . or me?"

"But why?" Justice faced Rhajmurti, blindly sought his chair. He banged his shin on it, cursed, caught its arm and sat down. "Why haven't you . . . God, why tell me now? You've had my entire *life* to tell me!"

"Many reasons, some of which you wouldn't understand. First and foremost, I'm a coward—I proved that this afternoon. On the bridge. Didn't I? And don't look at me that way . . . this isn't easy for me either."

"A swordfight's not your best talent. Words are. Quit dodging. Why wouldn't you tell me?"

"Maybe fear of the way you see me now. I put it off, I kept thinking it was going to be easier to explain when you were older. It wasn't; the lie only got more complicated. I didn't want to unbalance you when you were beginning College. I didn't want to put the lie off on your shoulders, pretending one of your teachers *wasn't* your father. Or have you think it was nepotism that got you in."

Justice shook his head as if that would sort his thoughts. "And it wasn't? *Tell* me it wasn't."

"No. You could have been anyone . . . any child I happened to come across—who happened to win the board's approval. Who happened to pass the tests. Your talents are your own, Justice. They're more than enough to qualify you."

"But . . ." God, the unanswered questions. The maze of wrong assumptions. "If you're my father, then who—"

"Who's your mother? Your aunt, Justice."

"Oh, Lord." Justice buried his head in his hands and listened to his own ragged breathing. He heard Rhajmurti get up, saying,

"I think you need something to settle you down. I'll be right back."

Rhajmurti left the room. Tears Justice would never have believed he could shed spilled down his cheeks. He lowered his hands, absently noting that they shook violently, then wiped those tears away.

Father Alfonso Rhajmurti, Priest of the College, Instructor in Fine Arts . . . his father? And Aunt Stella his *mother*? Neighbors had always remarked how they looked alike—and how much had they known? His coloring, especially his eyes, he had surely inherited from her. She'd given him his outlook on life—and the Adventist leanings he'd so carefully concealed from Father Rhajmurti . . . *Father* Rhajmurti. What a damnable joke!

He stood, paced up and down the room; he leaned his head against the wall, closed his eyes, and rubbed his hands together to stop their shaking. So nepotism hadn't propelled him through the College doors? What else was it? The tall, kindly man in priestly saffron, watching his childish attempts at a rat on a sunlit walkway edge, offering encouragement—telling him he was going to the College school when he got older.

He drew a deep breath. Was what Rhajmurti . . . what his *father*, said true? Could he have gotten into the exclusive world of the College without familial help? Was he good enough? Rhajmurti was a damned good liar. He'd just found that out. So was Aunt Stella. Their relationship had always seemed warm, verging on tender. He'd never questioned it. It had always been there. Friendship, he'd always thought— a shared interest in old books. Now he understood the glances they'd traded over his head, at the edge of his adolescent awareness. Or the lingering of hand on shoulder in farewell. Religious consolation, hell!

He'd thought his parents dead from before he could remember. Aunt Stella had even given him names for them—neighbors *talked* about his mother dying—

So Aunt Stella must have had a sister. And people died in boating accidents—people did die that way. . . .

He stared up at the ceiling, lost in flickering shadow and light. His entire life rested on a lie. Everything he thought he'd known was untrue. The entire foundation of his being was shattered. And without that to stand on, what could he trust for true?

Truth: he *was* still Justice Lee. It was Stella's surname, too. He *was* still an artist. And a damned good one—if he could believe what other professors at the College had told him. Maybe they knew Rhajmurti was his father, and complimented him accordingly.

No. He couldn't believe they knew. That was the

whole point of the silence, wasn't it—protecting his father's reputation, his priestly karma—wasn't it the catechism his father had taught him: priests were celibate because the more personal ties one had in the world, the harder it became to break free?

Rhajmurti could say that and look him in the eye? And Stella—

Stella, who'd held him, comforted him, protected him from the bumps and bruises—

Stella the martyr, who'd lived a quiet, uncomplaining life, telling the world that she could do no more for her poor, dead sister than raise her son? Damn!

But she'd taught him to read, surrounded him with her books, guided him through the pages—she'd put up all his pictures over the kitchen counter. She still had them. Wouldn't give them up, no matter he painted her better ones.

She loved him. *She* had stuck by him. In spite of everything.

He heard footsteps in the hall, hastily wiped his cheeks of lingering tears.

"Here, Justice." Rhajmurti closed the door and extended a glass of wine. "Drink this. It should help."

Justice reached for the glass; his fingertips brushed against Rhajmurti's, and he flinched.

"Better?" Rhajmurti asked.

He lowered the glass and licked his lips. "Why now?" He stuck to his original question. One had to do that, with Rhajmurti. He'd learned that years ago. "Will you answer me?"

Rhajmurti gazed down into his own glass. "Because, Justice, it's now or never, and I'm tired of living a lie; I screwed up my courage to the extent I thought I could tell you without falling apart. Events outside this room made it necessary."

"*What* events? Something in the College?" He recalled the incident on the walkway, wondered if someone *else* had seen. . . .

"Nothing we trusted before is reliable. The situation's going to go from bad to worse, very soon now."

A chill ran down Justice's spine. "Are you in danger? Is it something I've done?"

"I'm not in danger—no more than anyone else of my rank and calling. But you are. Your mother is. Listen to me, Justice. Just listen. I've given your mother money to get the two of you out of Merovingen. There's a Falkenaer ship in port and its destination is the Chattalen. It sails in two days. You're going to be on it. I want you out of here as soon as possible."

"But . . ."

"That attack on Sonja—her family's troubles—they're contagious. Interest in her may have been on a subordinate level, do you understand me? And it might fall quietly if circumstances change. Or it might go higher, fast. And spread. We *say* there weren't any witnesses out there last night. But there were. There were people who got out of there. And some gossip moves on slower feet these days, but it does move, and it all gets to Exeter. Do you hear me?"

"Then Sonja—"

"Sonja's got her own resources. Trust the Families to make their own protective moves—above my ability. Or yours. You're my concern. Your mother is. She's balking. I want you to get her out of here."

Sonja was *still* an issue. But he didn't like the other thing he was hearing. He asked: "What about you?

126

Are you coming?" and for the first time since Rhajmurti had come into his room, saw Rhajmurti avoid
eye contact.

"I'll be there if I can. Or later."

"If you can? What's that supposed to mean?" Tangles upon tangles. "You haven't given me the straight
truth yet. First you suddenly have to tell me you're
my father because you want me out of here, and now
it's an 'I'll be there if I can?' Excuse me, but *hell*—
Father . . ."

"Calm down. There're many ways events can go,
Justice, many paths into the future. I'm not saying I
won't go."

"So my—mother—is balking," Justice said slowly,
"and *that's* why you've told me. You know everything
Exeter's doing and you *don't* want them calling my
mother in—is that what you're saying?"

"You have a vivid imagination. No. I'm not involved
in anything. That boat is a sure way out of here. I
want you and your mother on it. I'll be there if I can."

"You're not through holding things back. I want to
know the truth, dammit, you're not going to escape
me like that. Do you want me to come to the College
after you? I will."

"No. Let's not be irrational."

"Irrational, is it?"

"If I can, I'll meet you at the docks." An expression
of intense sorrow passed over the dark, lean face.
Which was his heredity, dammit. His own expression.
"I don't see any way of saving things, Justice. I don't.
But I can't turn my back on my fellow priests. They're
my brothers . . . my friends."

"What about your family?" Justice demanded. "What

127

about us? You stood up there on that walkway and *watched*, last night—"

"It wasn't my kind of fight. This is. The same as I'd have been doing if you'd been arrested. I've have gotten your mother out. And you, if I could. Question of fencing styles, Justice."

He had the niggling instinct he was hearing truth now. Not all he wanted. But enough to make this Rhajmurti agree with the one he thought he'd known.

"So know when to quit. Get out *with* us. Or is there more I'm not hearing?"

"Settle down, Justice. I'll do my best to go with you. I promise you. If it doesn't work out, if I can't join you, I'll follow you. I'll find you."

"In all the Chattalen."

"You and your mother are to disembark at the first port you reach. It shouldn't be hard to find you."

"You've thought this whole thing through, haven't you? From beginning to end."

"I've *had* to." Rhajmurti downed the last of his wine. "I'm going to visit your mother now. Gather everything you can that's portable and not obvious. I want you to be ready to leave on a moment's notice. I don't know how you're going to get to the harbor. Or when. I'll arrange something safe. Where's Raj?"

"I don't know. Kamat, I suppose. God,—*he's* linked to me. . . . Is it *my* trouble? Or whose?"

"I shouldn't worry about that lad," Rhajmurti said, a smile softening his face. "He probably knows more about what's happening than I do. But if you *do* see him tonight, warn him. Tell him I'm afraid not even his ties to Kamat will protect him much longer."

For a moment, Justice held Rhajmurti's eyes in

silence. Then, as if at some mutual impulse, he and Rhajmurti moved and met in a fierce embrace.

"Be careful," Justice whispered, and felt Rhajmurti's lips on his forehead.

"Always. And you, too, son. Take care of your mother. I'll send word when. But if anything goes wrong—if you *feel* anything wrong—get to Hilda's and stay put. No matter what. Hear?"

What to take? What books, clothes, paintings, supplies, mementos to pack?

Justice stood in the center of his room at Hilda's, taking survey of his possessions. Abundance was hardly the problem, but it would still be difficult to choose—no way to take anything out but the bookbag, maybe a parcel. Nothing to attract attention.

Someone came down the hall. Knocked at his door. Such sounds were to dread now. "Who?" he asked.

"Package just come for you, Justus."

Hilda's voice. Justice opened the door. Hilda said, extending a medium-size parcel wrapped in brown paper: "Letter with it."

Justice took the package, blinked in surprise as he felt the unexpected weight of it, and took the letter.

"You be wantin' dinner, lad? Ye've been in here past supper hour. Got to wash up soon."

"I'll be out in a little while," Justice replied, and noting Hilda looking over his shoulder at the sketches laid out on the floor: "Picking out a portfolio. I've got a potential buyer."

"So. Now ye come out soon, hear? I'll save ye some fresh greens."

"Thanks." He broke the seal. Shut the door and gave his attention to the letter.

Raji's hand.

Time's now. Go. I send you the smallest and most valuable. I'll be all right. Maybe I'll look you up someday. We've had a good friendship. You've been more than fair with me and my brother. My House doesn't forget such things. Take care of yourself. Think of me often.

Justice lowered the letter. A sudden, hollow feeling coiled in his heart. Lord. He might never see Raj again. Raj was the first close friend he'd ever had, the closest he might ever come to a brother. Even the revelation that Raj was Nev Hettekker and a Takahashi hadn't shaken the friendship. Nor had the strange friends Raj kept company with. Or his marriage in Kamat, to cover a friend's indiscretion. The future seemed a lonely place without Raj in it.

Time's now. Go. Rhajmurti was right. Lord knew Raj had enough ties with the underside of Merovingen, and a warning from Raj after what Rhajmurti had said—was damned serious.

He took a deep breath, tried to figure what to do with the letter, then decided to tuck it in a book: if the slinks got it there, they already had him. He would take with him only the most precious of his possessions. Take the best of his paintings off their stretchers. And get to his mother's shop—

Quick, light steps in the hall, a frantic knock. Trouble, Justice thought, and *not* the heavy tread he had to fear. But the noise was to fear. He snatched the door open.

For an instant, he hardly recognized Sonja as she whisked inside—she wore dark, simple clothing, and the hood to her black cloak was drawn close. "Close the door!" she whispered hoarsely. "For gods' sakes, close it!"

"Sonja . . . what's happened? Why—"

"Exeter's moved against my family," she said, pushing the hood back from her face. The tears on her cheeks glittered in the lamplight. She swallowed heavily, tried to speak, and finally croaked out, "They've taken my mother, Justus! Taken her!"

"Lord!" He tossed the package and the letter into a chair and gently took her into his arms. "When?"

"I came home this afternoon, later than I'd expected. I found the house in disarray, the servants terrified. They said Exeter's men came to the house and took my mother and four of my cousins to the College. They said the Cardinal wanted 'further inquiries' into House Keisel's dealings with Nev Hettek. I . . . oh, Justus! What can I do?"

He tried to concentrate on her problem, pushing his own aside. "What about your father?"

She buried her head in his shoulder. "I don't know," she said. "I went there. No one's seen him all day. I'm afraid they've taken him, too!" She lifted her head; tears stood in her dark eyes. "Some of the servants have run. It's terrible out there, Justus . . . terrible! Have you been out this evening?"

"No."

"Gods. It's quiet. Terribly quiet. Blacklegs. A few people. Fog's come up. *No*body on canalside—you don't *see* a boat. I thought I'd lose myself in the

131

crowd—but there wasn't one. I just—just came ahead. And nobody stopped me."

"You came over here by yourself?"

"I had to. I slipped out of the house—I was afraid the slinks would come back—I'm afraid to go home—gods, Justus . . . what do we do?"

Justice drew a deep breath. *How much can I tell her? How much right have I to trust her—if she turns me down and gets caught and spills it all—it's not just me, it's Stella—it's Rhajmurti—and Raj—everything leads back to everybody. . . .*

He said, "Sonja, there's nothing you *can* do. Come *with* me. I've a way out of town."

"Where?"

"For the Chattalen."

"Gods." She straightened back in his arms, seemed to pull herself together, to look at him as if she didn't know him. "What are you saying?"

"That the threads lead everywhere, Sonja. You're helpless as I am. You have to leave."

"But Mother . . . Father . . . I can't just go off and leave them—"

"You're one less for them to worry about. And if worse comes to worst, you carry two Names. You can get *out* of Merovingen." He pointed at the books. "That's money. That's the books. That'll keep us alive after we get there."

She stared at him. Thinking desperately, he was sure. Then she said, her voice shaking, "More than alive. More than alive, Justus." She backed away from him, pulled back her cloak to show a heavy bag slung from her shoulder. She opened it, and inside—

Jewelry. Jewels of every kind, color and size. More jewels together than he'd ever seen in his entire lifetime. *My God*, he thought. *Did she know she was running? Is that why she came?*

She said, shakily, "I took these when I left the house," she said, and folded the bag shut again, hugged it close. "Mother's jewelry. Mine. I was scared to death coming here. But I was scared the servants would steal it—or Exeter's slinks take it. I can buy help in the Chat. I can set up Keisel there. . . ."

The ambitions of Family. Intrigue was in the blood. This was the girl an artist had fallen in love with.

"There's a ship in port," he said. "I'm going. My aunt is. God, I've got things to tell you—Rhajmurti's arranging us to get out of here. We're to stay put here till he sends for us. . . ."

ESCAPE FROM MEROVINGEN

Finale in two acts by
Janet & Chris Morris

Act One: THE FOOL MUST DIE

Kenner and Jacobs wanted to wait until sunset before they murdered the governor's son. That way, the tricky light of the twilight hours would help obscure their identity. Kenner liked to use every natural advantage, and the poor visibility available in the city built on stilts was even poorer when night began to fall and the canal water met the chilling air.

You could call the result "lake effect," if Merovingen had been built on a lake. Kenner called it canal effect, the first time he'd seen the billows of white mist rising from the canals and covering the dockside like a horde of ghosts.

Today, the canal effect had started early, and the mist was as thick as smoke from a raging fire. It sparkled when the late day's sun hit it. It swirled. It skimmed the surface. It eddied upward, toward the blue sky above. That sky, where he could glimpse it through the crazily-canted tiers of the stilt city, was already beginning to lower toward dusk.

Sunset was the ticket, Kenner had insisted, and his

henchman Jacobs, pale and fair and still smooth with baby fat, had gone along with the plan.

But now Jacobs was clearly musing, mulling things over. Kenner knew it was dangerous when subordinates had time to think. Kenner had led death squads back home in Nev Hettek when Jacobs was still a privileged child shielded from the Revolution by his parents' position, before the Revolution had become Karl Fon's Revolutionary government and all of Nev Hettek had gone Fon's way.

These days, Karl Fon was Nev Hettek's ruler and Fon wanted Merovingen brought into the fold—or had wanted it. Kenner wasn't included in the elite councils of the revolution. He was a weapon in its hands. He'd been sent down here to help Chance Magruder, Nev Hettek's Ambassador to Merovingen, teach the Merovingians that they didn't have to suffer under a corrupt religious state.

They could do some damned thing about it, these Merovingian fools, if only they had the nerve. The plan had been subtle, at first. But subtlety didn't seem to work where karma was involved, and the Merovingian majority believed in karma—when they believed in anything at all besides greed and making sure the other guy didn't do any better than you did. Karma was the excuse for all prejudice, greed, envy and more: for all corruption, the rationale behind all bad fortune, the justification for all the oppression in Merovingen. Karma was the driver that powered Merovingen's ruling class, an unholy merger between the mercantile elite and the religious bureaucracy.

This being the case, or so the reasoning had gone in Nev Hettek, karma could be made to work for the revolution.

That was where Kenner had come in. Shipped down here with Dani Lambert, a high official of the revolutionary council, Kenner had been put to work by Magruder immediately, dispensing karma in the form of favors, low-interest loans, technical quick-fixes, and death.

So Kenner hadn't minded his job description as a machinist, or his real job, that of a covert Sword of God agent in Merovingen. After all, Magruder had put Kenner to work doing what Kenner did best: assassination and incrimination.

As soon as Kenner had gotten into town, almost, Magruder had sent him off to murder a cardinal in the College. Kenner had taken Mike Chamoun, Magruder's pet Nev Hetteker agent, along with him, to share the blame and the risk.

Having thrown Kenner into the thick of Merovingen intrigue, Magruder had then waited to see how Kenner performed. Once Cardinal Ito was dead, Kenner had been put away, seemingly forgotten, minding his cover in the Nev Hettek machine shop that provided Merovingians with marginal technical competency.

Until now. Now Something had changed. Maybe everything had changed. Even Jacobs could feel it. Kenner's big, soft assistant wandered away from the pier, to a fish stall.

Jacobs soon came back with fish and chips he didn't have the stomach to eat. The chubby kid sat on a moldy barrel and looked rebelliously up into Kenner's watchful eyes as he chucked chips off the pier, into the white swirl of mist. There the bandit-birds dived to catch them before the morsels fell into the water, where hungry blue-gills were congregating in hopes of a feast.

ESCAPE FROM MEROVINGEN

"Quit lookin' at me like that," Jacobs snarled, when Kenner watched but didn't say anything.

"Like what?" Kenner asked quietly, taking a quick look around. Behind his back, over his shoulder, up the pier and down, all looked quiet. Too quiet: There weren't even the usual number of folks around, today.

Maybe the reason for that was simple caution in Merovingen-below: Everybody stayed indoors if they could, since Cardinal Exeter's Inquisition marshals had begun arresting folk for congregating without a license or for saying the wrong thing or for looking indigent or for any damned thing at all.

So maybe it wasn't smart to be out here, on Ventani Pier. But the boat would come, the way Magruder promised. Then he and Jacobs would get in it and motor to the kill zone, and on, up to the embassy, the way they were supposed to. There they'd leave the boat, for somebody else to take, the way they'd been told to do.

"Yer lookin' at me funny. Lookin' at me like I was dead already, is how," Jacobs growled.

"Eat your dinner. It may be the last time we get to eat for a long while," Kenner advised. His own mouth was too sticky to even consider putting food into.

Kenner could never eat right before an operation. Magruder had told Kenner to leave the boat for "somebody." Somebody who couldn't be seen to be leaving on his own recognizance, or seen leaving openly at all. Leave the boat for whom? Magruder himself? Dani Lambert, Magruder's old girlfriend? Tatiana Kalugin, his new girlfriend, who was the governor's daughter and a power in her own right in Merovingen? Or for Vega Boregy, Mike Chamoun's father-in-law and Magruder's unwilling ally? Or for some-body even more sinister?

You could never anticipate Magruder. It was futile to try guessing what the ambassador had up his velvet sleeve. Kenner, who admired nobody and respected nothing but his own ability, had come to possess a grudging admiration for Chance Magruder.

Magruder was the closest thing to a role-model that Kenner had ever stumbled on, and not just because Magruder had made it clear to Kenner on their first meeting that if Kenner screwed up—any way at all—Magruder would kill him.

Magruder was determined to have an error-free environment in a covert venue. Kenner had to admire the guy's guts. And Magruder was getting what he wanted, it seemed. Until now.

Now, something was so wrong that even Jacobs could feel it.

Jacobs looked up at Kenner, a greasy chip halfway to his pale lips, and said, "So are you sayin' this is my last meal? You gotta give me a chance to get through this, Kenner. If I messed up, you owe me a chance to make it right. I been a good long time takin' your orders, doin' whatever I was told. You can't just . . . waste me. . . ."

The pudgy Sword of God agent was nearly in tears. Jacobs' chin became two chins. Both chins quivered as if they were made of gelatin. A trick of the late-day light made the sun sparkle on Jacobs' sparse whiskers.

"Retribution protect me from fools and cowards," Kenner swore softly, aloud. But there was nobody in Merovingen to protect Kenner but Kenner's own self. "Look, Jacobs. I know you've been hearing lots of rumors. So have I. So what? We do our job, and we do what we're told. Both of us. Then we get the hell out of harm's way. Just like Magruder wants. Both of us. Get me?''

Kenner couldn't say 'I don't have orders to kill you, Fatty—not yet, anyway.' Because you couldn't tell who might be listening—under the pier, behind a barrel or in one, or hidden in some doorway. But he came as close as he could, then and there, even joining Jacobs and picking out a piece of greasy fish to pop into his own mouth.

"Get me?" he said again.

The fat agent made a noise that was part sob, part grunt, part moan. Jacobs was actually shivering.

Well, it was chilly out here, and the wind had oncoming winter's bite in it. Some place else, not so cursed crazy, the damn sky would have given up some snow. But it wasn't going to snow here. It was just going to spew cold white mist off the canals as if there were steam engines with billowing smokestacks down there under the murky water.

This place didn't deserve any better than it got. When Kenner had first come down from Nev Hettek, Magruder had told him that Merovingen had exactly the government it deserved. The crack had seemed strange and inappropriate at the time, but now Kenner had been among these superstition-ridden crazies long enough to agree.

If these folk had their freedom, they wouldn't know what to do with it, Kenner sometimes thought. If they had control of their fates, they'd start killing each other in droves. Most of the factions here misunderstood freedom as the ability to force your will and beliefs on anyone and everyone else with impunity.

Freedom wasn't worth crap without judgment, fortitude, forebearance, and strength of character.

As Kenner understood from the last revolution he'd helped manage, real freedom wasn't the freedom to force your will on everyone else; real freedom was the freedom from having everyone else's will forced upon you; real freedom was having some say in and making sure the rules were obeyed equally by all. And that took restraint on the part of citizens. Tolerance. Control over prejudice and greed—self-control, not state control.

If you destroyed the current regime here, you'd have civil unrest, ethnic violence between minorities, and religious wars among the currently ruling Revenantists and the Adventists and the Janes and all the other sects waiting for their turn in the catbird's seat.

Magruder knew that revolutionary fervor without guidance would just lead to bloody anarchy here. He just didn't seem to care any longer—if he'd ever cared. Kenner had realized long ago that the power brokers didn't always believe in the causes they promoted; they just believed that they should have the power to call the shots.

Maybe Magruder was no exception. Kenner had seen the singleness of purpose in Magruder's pale hazel eyes when Chance had given Kenner the order to take out Mikhail Kalugin.

Mikhail Kalugin was a dimwit, a fool, an idealist, and the governor's annointed successor, whose primacy was endorsed by the strongest cardinals. If Mikhail was dangerous, he was so only to the factions in his family and allies of those factions—those who didn't want Mikhail to succeed Iosef Kalugin; those who needed to make sure that the status quo would stand.

But Nev Hettek had aligned itself against the status quo here. Giving Kenner the order to assassinate Mikhail Kalugin, Magruder's head had been high and defiant: *Don't ask me any questions that aren't operational, kid. Don't question my judgment. You and I know that killing is going to rip a new asshole in Merovingen. So we do it. Because those are my orders.*

Magruder's eyes had seemed to say, *We don't generate policy; we execute it, remember?*

But Magruder had a personal stake in this: he was sleeping with Mikhail's sister, who'd have a chance at the helm if Mikhail was out of the way.

So Kenner began wondering if those orders Magruder had given him had really originated in Nev Hettek, or in Magruder's ambassadorial bed here in Merovingen.

With Mikhail out of the way, Tatiana Kalugin and her brother Anastasi could fight it out for their father's power base; with Nev Hettek on her side, Tatiana was bound to win eventually, either *before* her brother Anastasi got Merovingen into an all-out war with Nev Hettek, or after. Either of those results would suit Karl Fon. But maybe Magruder was playing favorites.

Magruder had never said outright to Kenner that the assassination order had originated in Nev Hettek. Could be it hadn't. Could be it had originated with Magruder. All the briefing had covered was the likely result of Mikhail's death, once discovered. And how to make sure the death was discovered. And their secondary action plan, which included putting the blame on Cardinal Exeter; using the rumor mill to explain that Mikhail was out of the cardinal's control and under the spell of the drugged-out prophetess, Cassie Boregy; that, and setting a couple fires.

Leave it to Magruder to come up with a coup de grace so complex you needed a scorecard to tell the players.

Set a couple fires. The right fires, at the right time, in the right places. That was why Kenner had wanted to do this at sunset. Cassie Boregy, Mike Chamoun's wife, had been prophesying a fiery revolt in Merovingen for so long that some well-timed arson would result in the whole power structure of Merovingen going up like a tinder-box.

Those fires were going to look so pretty in the sunset.

Kenner couldn't wait.

He chucked his fish over the side of the pier and said, without looking back at Jacobs, "Let's go, Jacobs. We'll feel a lot better once we get moving. We got a timetable to meet."

The fires were going to be so pretty, all those orange and gold and green flames against a purple sky afire with sunset. A little blood, a little death, a little destruction, and Kenner was going to ride out of this hellhole without a single regret.

After all, somebody had to light the fuse to blow this powderkeg to the karmic hell it had imagined for itself. Let Magruder worry about the repercussions: Kenner was going to give Magruder his error-free environment, a perfect operation, and get the hell out before the flames got too hot to survive.

Mikhail Kalugin wanted to go see Cassie Boregy, but that was easier said than done, these days.

Son of the governor or not, Mikhail would need the

permission of a College cardinal, or of someone high in Boregy House, to see Cassie alone. He'd been caught smuggling deathangel to Cassie in a clock, and now no one trusted him.

Standing in his fancyboat's stern on the waterway in sunset, Mikhail glared defiantly around at the mist and the city beyond, gilded in sunset. Coming to see Cassie like this, he might not be allowed any time alone with his magical, mystical prophetess.

But he was going to try. He was still the governor's son. He wasn't going to knuckle under to the College, inquisition or no. Not to Cardinal Exeter, who had even Mikhail's arrogant sister and murderous brother frightened. Certainly not to Cassie's father, Vega, who ought to know that Mikhail's wishes were more important than the orders of the Nev Hetteker physician brought in to tend Cassie in the wake of childbirth.

Just because his beloved prophetess was married to some Nev Hettek bean-counter, that was no reason to keep Mikhail from the counsel of his beloved.

Cassie was the only person in Merovingen whom Mikhail trusted implicity. She would look up at him from her sickbed, her beautiful eyes huge and her hair spread upon her pillow, and say the truth to him from between her pale lips.

Mikhail Kalugin had heard more truth in the last few weeks from the young girl in her bedroom festooned with ormolu cherubs than from all the counselors his father had appointed to tutor him.

When Mikhail became his father's successor, as Cassie had assured him he would, then Mikhail would declare Cassie Boregy's marriage to the Nev Hetteker, Michael Chamoun, null and void.

After all, Vega Boregy would understand that a

merger not to the interest of Merovingen—a merger with a foreign power—was one the state could nullify, on the request of the woman in question.

If not for the baby—Michael Chamoun's baby—Mikhail would have convinced Cassie to see things his way by now.

He couldn't stand the thought of that lout of a foreigner in Cassie's bed. She was so ethereal, so delicate. He almost wished he could believe that her baby had been immaculately conceived.

Mikhail wanted Cassie only for her mind, to see those eyes look into his soul and tell him the truth. Together, they would remake Merovingen. He had promised her. And the time was nigh.

Papa was not well. Sister Tatty and 'Stasi were becoming daily more bold. The cardinal in her lair was acting as if she *was* the government of Merovingen, terrorizing the populace. And Cassie had looked up at Mikhail and told him, "You are the only one who can stop the terror, Mikhail. By sacrificing yourself, you can bring Merovingen into balance with its karma, to make things the way the universe wants them. It will be fiery, and bloody, and we will not—"

Then she'd broken off and bitten her pale lip.

"We will not what, dear prophetess? Tell me. Tell me. I can take it."

But Cassie would never tell him what horrors she saw when her eyes grew wide and she shut her mouth. She'd only turn her head away.

Tonight, Mikhail was determined, he would hear the rest of the prophecy. He'd sent word two days ago to Vega to announce his coming, formally. He was determined to enter Boregy House without subterfuge. He was demanding an audience with his seeress.

And he'd let all and sundry know he was determined to have one.

But the night seemed to be telling him that he'd been too bold. The tiers of the city hunched over the canalways seemed to be trying to close over his head. Merovingen's very buildings were crowding him, as if they could conspire to shut him away from the sky, the sunset, and Cassie.

Of course, it couldn't be that inanimates were inimical. The canals were just spewing mist, a thick mist that made visibility difficult, traveling treacherous, and spun out the sunset into a fey fantasy that seemed drenched in blood.

The fancy boat throttled down, approaching an intersection. Someone lost in the mist shouted, " 'Ware!"

Beware, was right. Beware the night. Beware the might of right in the night. Beware the arms of fate holding you tight, tonight, beloved. . . .

If karma had been kinder, Mikhail would have been a poet. But true talent had been denied him. So he made clocks, in homage to the wheel of fate and to propitiate time itself, which always to him had seemed to be chasing him like hunters on his track, soon, embracing him, enlacing him, facing him to eternity's grim smile. . . .

Mikhail pulled his cloak tighter around him and stamped his feet on the deck to warm them. He was not going to Boregy House like a furtive lover, or a thief in the night. He was standing tall in the night. He was standing tall in the stern of his boat and he would be standing so when they pulled into the watergate of Boregy House.

He was, after all, a Kalugin, not just in blood, but

in nature. He was conscious that what he did was the stuff of history. He liked the poetic, historic figure he made, cloak wrapped about him, standing, feet wide-spread, in the stern of his boat wrapped in mist. A painting of this moment would adorn the governor's office some day. And as with all State portraits, in it his shoulders would be broader, his jaw firmer, his hairline lower and fuller, and his gaze more command-ing, than it was tonight.

But his head would be no higher. Mikhail was going into Boregy House with his head high, and if anyone tried to stop him from partaking of Cassie's counsel, he was prepared to demand that the prophetess come live in his father's house, as counselor to the State. He had it all planned.

He—

A crack sounded, a sharp bang that bounced off the surface of the water and boxed his ears with a painful loudness. No sound could be that loud but the sound of a collision—

The sound came again, and this time the pain that accompanied it was hot, red, direct, and blew his skull apart so fast that only the beginning of the pain tele-graphed from his skull to his brain before his brain, itself, ruptured and splattered out through the back of his skull like the pulp of a melon.

Mikhail Kalugin fell. Heavy as stone, he collapsed from his standing position in the back of his fancy boat, backward, to hang limp over the stern with what was left of his head trailing in the water.

The shot had blown out the back of his skull, but the small entry hole above his eyes looked, at first glance, like no more than a penance mark at festival. The bullet hole was like a black smudge, centered over lifeless eyes staring through the swirling mist at the setting sun and the leaning towers of Merovingen-above.

But those who scrambled from the bow of the fancyboat to catch the corpse before it slid into the water knew what they'd witnessed.

The boat that sped away in the mist, carrying cowled assassins, safely out of reach, had the unmistakable insignia of Cardinal Exeter on its stern.

If an argument hadn't broken out on the fancyboat, among the retainers, as to whether Mikhail's body might still have a breath of life in it, the governor's boat might have given chase and followed the assassins.

But it did not, and those who'd seen Exeter's blazon on the stern of the boat duly reported what had happened as soon as they returned with the corpse.

Thomas Mondragon kept looking out the window of his room in the Nev Hettek Embassy, waiting for his boat to show.

All the while he dressed, in new, warm, velvet and leather that Magruder's people had provided, Tom Mondragon watched the waterway for a sign of the boat. Even while he cleaned his sword and belted it on, while he counted the gold that Magruder's smug staffer had left him, he watched for that boat.

If it didn't come, then Magruder had betrayed him—would betray him. Again.

It wouldn't be a surprise, given their history. But it would be a disappointment that Mondragon truly feared more than death. He didn't know why he'd let Magruder suck him into this scheme of final destruction and bloodshed. He regretted everything, as he waited. Mostly, he regretted being a part of some plan he didn't understand.

Nothing new about that. Every fool repeats the errors that marked him inarguably a fool in the first place.

Mondragon had come down to Merovingen to get away from Revolution, away from Karl Fon and Chance Magruder and jail cells and inquisitions and hostile factions and sharp blades in the night.

Run to Merovingen just in time to watch it happen all over again. From the beginning. He'd run scared, and he'd run right into the most extended déjà vu of his career. Sometimes he thought this nightmare was truly a dream—that he was mad, in some cell somewhere, creating a punishment for himself to fit his endless crimes. But then he'd admit to himself that although he was a good duelist and a passable operator, he wasn't creative enough to have conjured Chance Magruder, et al, from whole cloth.

When Mondragon had seen Dani Lambert come down to Merovingen, and set up shop by Magruder's machinations in Boregy House, attending to Cassie Boregy's new baby, he'd known that the end was near.

Dani Lambert was the most capable woman he'd ever met. She was Revolution's mistress. Some said she'd slept with every major player in Nev Hettek's revolution, until she'd ended up at the top, with Karl Fon himself. Mondragon didn't know if she had; she'd never slept with him, when he was high in the Nev Hettek revolution's hierarchy.

But Mondragon did know that Karl Fon would never have sent Dani down here to do a situation report firsthand if he wasn't tired of waiting for Magruder to show results.

Mondragon had fallen out of favor with Fon, and out of love with Fon's tactics, and all the misery he'd lived subsequently had been a direct result of that.

When Fon frowned on you, people died. When Karl got impatient, blood flowed in the streets. And now Magruder was going to help Mondragon: "Escape Merovingen, save that canal-girl of yours while there's still time."

Still time? Magruder said this to him? Chance, who'd nearly killed him when first they'd met in Merovingen, used him and abused him, manipulated him and sent him out this final, pay-all time?

The top was about to pop on this revolutionary brew, and Mondragon knew it. He just wished he knew what benefit Magruder saw to letting him run ahead of the tide of death.

Maybe, just maybe, Chance was getting old and sentimental. More likely, Thomas Mondragon was a distraction to misdirect the energies of any of a number of players and factions.

For all Mondragon knew, Magruder would pass the word in certain quarters that he'd escaped, forsaken the sanctuary of the embassy. Magruder would probably announce it, as soon as Mondragon had enough of a start to make a chase interesting.

So Mondragon wanted to change the game plan just a little. As soon as he saw that boat come in, he was going to slip down to the water gate. Nobody would stop him: everybody in the embassy knew what was about to come down. With luck, nobody would even see him.

When he got there, he was going to take the little boat ahead of schedule. Maybe he'd need to kill to do that. But to stay alive, he needed a head start on whatever Magruder had in mind for him.

He was ready to kill if he must. He had two daggers as well as his borrowed sword in its scabbard, and extra blades in his kit bag. And doubt as he tried to believe Chance's story—he had to take it for the only hope he had in the kind of violence that had to be at the heart of whatever Magruder was planning.

Mondragon knew Chance's style. If he hadn't known it so well, he'd have been dead long ago. Staying alive had become Tom Mondragon's profession.

If he lived through this, he was going to add to his professional skills the skill of staying out of jail, out of penury, and out of trouble. But first things first. Since he was incapable of staying out of love, he was going to do what he could to bring that dirty, arrogant, semiliterate brat of a Jones out alive—out of Merovingen altogether and into an unknown future that was, by any reckoning, better than what lay in store for Merovingen now that Karl Fon had grown tired of waiting for Revolution to catch fire here on its own.

Beyond the window, Mondragon thought he saw the white curl of wake on the waterway. It was hard to be sure at first, because of the thick mist. Visibility was a problem now. It could be his salvation later.

He looked harder. He opened the window to the foggy cold and peered out, staring until his eyes ached from the effort.

Still, he couldn't be sure.

But his pulse was pounding in his ears and the urge to act was on him like a physical ache that he couldn't endure.

Every muscle in his body would cramp from inactivity if he didn't do something soon.

So he did. He circled the room once, like a doubtful cat, snatched up his kit bag and shouldered it, and swung open the unlocked door. Simple, everyday movements.

Not the sort of thing to dry your mouth and constrict your throat and make your fingers tremble— unless you knew what those actions signified. When you were a prisoner taking refuge in the embassy of Chance Magruder, you understood what was dangerous and what was foolhardy.

It was foolhardy to be at the watergate too early. Foolhardy to be caught with your kitbag on the stairs. But it was dangerous in the extreme to do exactly what Magruder suggested, on the Sword's own timetable.

Chance would spend Mondragon in a second, without blinking an eye, for the smallest possible advantage. Mondragon had learned that when he'd been accused of treason back in Nev Hettek and Chance had led the team that came to apprehend him.

Clouds of memory, which had mercifully obscured those details for so many years, parted and Mondragon was once again at home—the only home he'd ever known—on the day, long ago, when Chance and his thugs came bursting in, weapons ready.

A million years. A cat's eight lives out of nine. In that sudden, painfully clear moment of memory, the present dissolved. And:

"Move," Chance suggested in that death-rattle voice. "Just give me an excuse to save the revolution the time and trouble of trying you publicly. Traitor."

Mondragon saw Chance's eyes again and realized again that Chance hadn't believed a word of what he said or what Mondragon heard. Chance's eyes that day had been full of ice and calculation—and a sort of abstract pity.

One revolutionary mover was offering another a chance at suicide. Only a formal gesture. A suggestion. A courtesy extended to a man once his peer.

Mondragon had never shared Chance's cavalier attitude toward life.

Tom Mondragon struggled back to his present, and his present danger. He'd never shared Chance's expedientist nature. He didn't share it now. But Mondragon still didn't know if Chance had been right to offer him a quick, clean death that day, and whether he'd been wrong to choose life at whatever cost, only to face death so many times and cheat it so many times, thereafter.

After all, death would win in the end. The game was fixed. The dice were weighted. The deck was stacked.

Death would come, finally. It always came. Mondragon reminded himself he mustn't fear death, only men anxious to mete it out.

Death would come when it willed. He must be ready.

Some Merovingen cultures believed that the quality and success of a man's life could only be judged at the moment of his death, and by that death. So when Chance had come, a few scant hours ago, as he had once so long ago, offering Mondragon escape—salvation, an opportunity to cut and run—Mondragon had looked over his shoulder and said, "What's this, Chance? History repeating itself?"

"Could be. That's up to you. Make a move, Mondragon. Do what benefits us both. It beats sitting around waiting for misfortune to befall you."

They both knew that malevolence, rather than simple misfortune, was at issue. Misfortune didn't come into it—unless you cared what happened to Merovingen or its folk.

Chance didn't. He'd come here and moved only among the powerful, mentally twisted, amoral players of hightown, who used the beliefs of the ignorant and religious as crowd control mechanisms. No wonder Chance despised those he'd met here.

Mondragon had found good folk down on the canals, in Merovingen-below. But he couldn't argue that their ignorance made them slaves and that they were unwilling to give up that comforting ignorance: freedom wasn't granted from without, Mondragon had learned. And it came at great price. To free these folk, rather than just herd them toward new masters or toward death itself, you'd have to wrench from them all the comfort of their primitive belief systems— without offering any replacement but the revolutionary ethic.

And Mondragon, a product of that ethic, knew it wasn't enough. But he didn't know what was enough. Unless it was love.

So, for love, he was letting Chance manipulate him one more time.

Time to go. Time to roll the dice. Time to test your luck.

Luck, like time, runs out.

Out in the halls of the Nev Hettek embassy, he felt naked, exposed. Every footfall was painfully loud. His breathing was far too fast.

At somewhere shy of thirty, he was getting old. Too old for revolution. Too old for brazen feats of derring do and hair-rasing escapes from the jaws of death. All were young men's games.

He moved down the hall with every muscle in his body aching as he asked it for stealth and it reacted too slowly, too clumsily.

A door opened as he reached the landing and he stopped breathing altogether.

If it was Chance, who saw him like this, it was all for nothing. Chance could look at him, read the signs, and kill him on the spot in that tight, decisive rage of the thwarted operator.

But it wasn't Chance, only one of the Nev Hetteker chambermaids. She smiled a countryman's smile and he smiled back, then hurried on.

Hurry. Don't creak a floorboard with a misplaced step. Come on, body, behave and earn the right to breathe another day.

Take me safely out of here. Carry me, one more time, through the danger ahead and I promise, I'll treat you better. Feed you. Keep you warm. Let you rest.

He was floating above his body as if it belonged to somebody else. As if he could survive, somehow, even if it perished.

But he knew all too well that he couldn't.

Steps. Steps winding down. Steps to hell or steps to salvation.

Down a flight of steps, onto another landing. Here were voices, those of the staffers who lived on this floor. Here he could not hope to avoid questions if discovered.

He started down another flight, and his ears produced a high, internal tone which was loud at first, then fading: the tone was his body's reaction to the stress of not bolting down the stairs three at a time.

He kept trying to envision Jone's pinched, dirty face, eyes wide at seeing him.

What would it be like to hold her again?

He gave himself the promise of her flesh against his, of her touch, of the smell of her hair, as if he could bribe his body into giving him the strength and quickness he needed for this one more, desperate deed.

And then he was down those steps, on the lowest working floor of the embassy. He heard a woman's voice, a throaty laugh. Dani? Tatiana? Chance played dangerous games in his bedroom these days. If Karl Fon had left Chance here much longer unsupervised, Chance might have ended up in the Merovingian seat of power, with Tatiana on his lap.

Karl had realized it, no doubt, and thus sent Dani to keep watch and tabs on Chance. If Mondragon had been Karl Fon, he'd have worried more about Chance installing himself as Merovingen's ruler than about any religious state with fanatical tendencies on his border.

So push had come to shove, and Chance was the man with all the cards in his hand, on site. He had helped in that.

Chance was a pragmatist.

Chance had known that Mondragon would read this opportunity for what it was: the beginning of overt revolution, and perhaps the end of Mondragon.

But Chance Magruder was a man who believed in fighting chances, and Tom Mondragon was a man who believed in fighting.

So maybe it would be all right.

When Mondragon made the floor landing, he saw a Boregy cousin, in lace and velvet, waiting in the hall, and nearly stumbled over his own feet, so quickly did he turn his head away and continue downward.

Downward. Down into the darker underbelly of the embassy. He was still on Nev Hetteker territory. He was still subject to Nev Hettek law. Chance could still change his mind, and send the house guard after him. If Mondragon was killed by Chance's people, and his corpse hidden, Chance could always say he'd escaped.

Thanking Chance for something was like thanking the wind for blowing a storm your way—a storm that might kill you or save you and cared not one whit about which it did to you.

Mondragon was shivering in the dark now, trying to force his eyes to adjust to the dimness, forcing his weak knees onward.

He *was* getting old. Or maybe he'd finally used up all his nerve. You could run on nerve only so long.

When he got to the watergate, he was dripping with sweat and shaking all over.

But he was alive. And alone, facing the iron bars, with freedom only a hand's breadth away.

Kenner and Jacobs came in the watergate of the embassy jacked up and sweating, snarling at one another and looking over their shoulders.

"Should have got him with the first shot," Kenner kept muttering. The bullet that had gone wide might be anywhere. In Nev Hettek, a bullet lodged in a piece of wood could hang you. Ballistics weren't unknown there.

He kept trying to tell himself—and Jacobs—that a bullet, even if found, wasn't going to hang you the way it would back home. Tech here was lower than a whale's belly. The Nev Hettekers weren't the only ones with primitive firearms. That was why the fire-arms *they'd* been issued were so primitive.

But, for safety's sake, they'd chucked both of their guns over the side in the middle of the remotest damned canal they could find.

They'd detoured to do just that. And so Kenner was wet to the skin and shivering with cold. Probably catch the flu and die, because of Jacobs' incompetence.

How the hell could Jacobs have missed, at point-blank range? Kenner hadn't been willing to trust Jacobs to do any damned thing if he couldn't shoot a fool standing in the stern of a boat. So Kenner had had to do everything else himself—had gone over the side, to pull off the fake stern insignia and send the plank to the bottom of the Grand.

Nothing but his first steak in the embassy kitchen had looked as good as Kenner's first sight, tonight, of that watergate—not since he'd come to Merovingen. Nothing would look as good to him again until he left here, for good.

The gate came down with a satisfactory clank of rusty metal and he scrambled to help Jacobs make the boat fast.

Jacobs was up on the quayside already, looking like a skit about to bolt for a hole, when a malevolent shadow stepped out the dark.

Kenner wasn't sure for a moment what was happening: the shadow moved. Jacobs dropped the rope he had in one hand and swung around, holding a grapple like a weapon.

The shadow drew a sword, just as Kenner yelled a "No!"

But the sword in those hands had hissed out with a duelist's competence and it was too damned late to do anything about Jacobs, who was swinging with the pronged grapple as if he had a chance against the level of professional he was facing.

Kenner didn't see more than a glitter of errant torchlight off the duelist's sword before he dived overboard, into the water, holding his breath and swimming for his life.

He didn't know what had happened up in the embassy, or why Thomas Mondragon was on the loose, lethal and lurking here. He didn't bother to stay around and argue.

Maybe you could have talked your way out of a quick death or a nasty wound if Jacobs hadn't started swinging, but you couldn't stop that kind of fight between men any easier than you could between stray cats.

And Kenner wasn't willing to risk himself to save either of those sons of bitches: not Mondragon; not Jacobs. Not after tonight's cock-up.

All he wanted to do was hold his breath long enough to live through this.

The water was brackish, deep and cold.

He had to get to the surface.

His ears and heart were pounding.

He wanted to surface as far away from the boat as possible.

He kicked his feet as little as he could, and kept his hands close to his body, and headed for what ought to be the watergate wall.

Then, with red dots spinning before his open eyes, fighting the pain in his chest and the desire to gulp water, he let himself slowly come to the surface.

Slowly.

Just your nose. Just get your nose up there.

And then his nose broke water and it was all he could do to breathe through it without letting instinct overwhelm him and sticking his head up.

If he stuck his head up, Mondragon was going to cut it off. You didn't kill one man of a pair and not make at least an easy attempt on the other—not when the living one was witness to what happened to the dead one.

Kenner knew that Jacobs was dead, the way a mother rabbit knows it when her babies are killed. And even if he hadn't felt it with an operator's keen instinct, he'd seen the start of Mondragon's deadly stroke. He knew Jacobs' abilities. The result was only logical.

Breathing through his nose, he listened as hard as he could. Sound traveled through water better than air, and his ears told him everything he was afraid to let his eyes see.

He heard the watergate begin to winch up. He heard the boat cast off. He heard the putt of its motor starting up.

And he dived.

If he got chopped by the motor, it would be his own fault.

When he surfaced again, he couldn't hear anything of the boat.

So he stuck his head up, very carefully.

No boat. No Mondragon.

He swam for it. Something brushed him, under the surface, bumped his thigh.

When he clambered up onto the floating dock, he didn't see Jacobs' body anywhere. So, maybe his instincts weren't as keen as a mother rabbit's. Maybe Jacobs escaped somehow.

He wanted to believe it. He kept trying to believe it, as he dripped his way along. Then he saw a little blood, diluted, in a puddle of water as if someone had made a hurried attempt to sluice down the bonds.

And then he knew what had bumped him in the water: Jacobs' corpse.

Corpses float unless you gut them and weight them right, and sometimes they float even then.

He vomited, retched on his knees until all the water he'd swallowed and all the bile he had was mingled with the blood in the puddle.

When he staggered to his feet and away, Kenner didn't look back. He headed up the watergate stairs, and then out through the kitchen.

It was deserted. And the stocks were a lot leaner than they should have been. Shelves nearly empty. Funny.

He needed to change clothes. He was going to freeze to death. He couldn't find anybody down here to help him. That was strange, too.

Magruder would skin him alive if he showed up on the business floor in sopping black night-action clothing.

He almost snuck out the back, but he was so hungry he grabbed a hard roll and started gnawing on it, trying to catch his breath and stop sneezing. He ought to go get on with his job, wet or not.

But Magruder needed to know what happened here—about Mondragon, about Jacobs.

Or did he?

The mission wasn't over. Kenner still had some things to do.

Just as he was deciding to get about his business, wet clothes or not, one of the cooks came in and

Kenner jumped, startled, and spun around, hand going to the knife at his waist.

"Ya! You scared a' me, boy? What the—lookit ye, yer sopped!"

"Yeah. Get me some clothes from upstairs, okay? And have one of the boss's people come down for a second. I gotta leave a verbal message."

The woman wasn't listening. She was telling him he needed a cup of tea and he should get out of those clothes so that she could dry them for him.

He wanted to wring her neck. Instead he said, "Listen to me," very quietly, in a voice that brought her up short. "I need clean, dry clothes—now. Matches. Money. Boots. Get one of Magruder's people down here now or I'm going up there."

She went with wide eyes, calling back in a wheezy whisper, "Everybody's getting ready to leave, you know. You should, too," as if she was giving up a state secret.

"Leave?"

Because of what he'd done? Had they botched it that bad? Was the assassination being blamed on them?

Kenner panicked.

He was supposed to be out on the canals, right now, with Jacobs, blaming Mikhail Kalugin's murder on Exeter and starting as many rumors as he could, while he did some selective arson that had to be completed before dawn.

In the end, Kenner didn't wait for the cook to come back, or for Magruder's people to come down so that he could give an interim report. He couldn't. He didn't have time.

He took some cooking oil, a flour sack, some

matches, added bread, and cheese for good measure, in case he was searched, and grabbed a handful of the petty cash fund that he knew the cooks kept in a rice barrel.

Then he went running out the delivery entrance, hunched over and still sick to his stomach.

He got to the rear gate before he started to retch again. Jacobs was dead. He kept seeing Mondragon's sword stroking down. He kept feeling the corpse nudge him under the water.

Damned canal water was pestilential. He'd tried not to swallow any. But he'd swallowed plenty, from the way his stomach was behaving. Jacobs was dead. They'd been a team for so long. . . .

FAMILY TIES (REPRISED)

by Nancy Asire

Lights haloed in the fog. The air had a bite this evening, and the walkways suddenly seethed with people, most of them with no apparent goal. Rhajmurti gathered his dark cloak closer and dodged through, head bowed, trying to escape notice of the blacklegs who forged through the steady stream of foot traffic. Something was going on. He sensed it with every nerve he possessed. He picked up bits and pieces of scattered conversations as he walked, most of them exchanged in low voices.

"—Exeter's crazy. *Why?*"

"—was the College. The College—"

"—can't know who's on what side—"

"—shot Mikhail."

He stopped, nearly tumbling forward as someone behind him ran up on his heels. He apologized, sought the inner wall, and followed the press of traffic, his heart pounding against his ribs. Mikhail, dead? Gods! Shot? When?

By what side?

"—some slink blew his head right off. Yey, they *saw* the boat—with the Bloody Cardinal's own seal. . . . Yey, I *know*, I know it ain't reasonable—but 'at's what they seen!"

He stopped and hovered next to the wall of Spellbridge. He'd been headed for the College. But a major player dead—assassinated by his own side—and the ripple of panic and speculation would run like fire through the town . . . he daren't go back to the College now. If Exeter *was* making a grab for power—if partisan violence had gone that far and Mikhail was dead, a priest could find himself answering more questions than he wanted, questions he had no more idea of than anybody else on the walkways. He clutched his cloak closer, thanking every god he knew he had worn dark colors this evening. Not a hint of saffron showed; at the first opportunity, he'd get rid of the sash that marked him as a priest.

Exeter—against Mikhail? With witnesses? Instinct said not, instinct and his own knowledge said not. It could be pure rumor—the sort that could fly in an instant through the tiers of a nervous town. It could be the wrong name—might be Tatiana, or Anastasi dead. Or some Signeury clerk who'd fallen on a stairs.

But what it started was real. And deadly dangerous if it kept going. He heard the name of Cassie Boregy. Heard Mikhail had died right outside Boregy.

He had to get to Stella's shop, get her, and get back to Kass and Hilda's. If the gods loved him, Justice would have followed orders and stayed there.

He only hoped that in the spreading panic and the movement of police of every faction, they weren't going to seal off the walkways.

Or order them completely cleared.

Justice stood for a moment at the edge of the common room of Hilda's Tavern, his eyes moving slowly. This time of night, the tables were usually full, the place awash in conversation. That was nothing new.

But this crowd wasn't the usual mix of students, and it was sudden and mostly standing: unnatural quiet had given way to a gathering of shopkeepers and students and a scattering of poleboatmen, Guy the bartender was dispensing drinks, tables were partly full, while Hilda—Hilda looked grim: she kept darting glances over her sudden wealth of customers as if she suspected devils in the shadows.

She smiled as Justice approached the bar, but the smile looked forced.

"What's going on?" he asked.

She hesitated, then leaned closer. "Mikhail's dead."

He put out one hand to the bar for support. "How?"

"Word is, he was shot, though some say he fell an' knocked hisself into his next life. Some are sayin' th' cardinal—" She lowered her voice further. "Some is saying She done it. Word is th' blacklegs is movin' on the College."

"God. How long ago?"

"Inside th' hour." She nodded toward one of the men seated at a far table: "Jonas come flyin' in on th' edge of—"

The lights swayed. The building jolted and there was a panicked silence, then a nervous ripple of oaths.

" 'S *all* we need," Hilda breathed, hand to her heart.

"Just a shake," Justice said, his own pulse fluttering. Someone was talking about Mad Cassie, how she'd *said* there'd be fire and earthquake, how there'd be blood—

Hilda said, "Ye take my advice, lad . . . don't go out. An' the lady who come t' visit ye . . . tell her the same. If that's the one I'm thinkin' of, the hightown

165

lady, she for *sure* don't want t' be out right now."
She crossed her arms on her ample bosom, her hands
nervously rubbing her shoulders. "Truth t' tell, I ain't
felt nothin' like this in all my days. Bad feelin'. *Bad*
feelin' in this crowd."

"My aunt—"

"Lissen. *You* stay in here. She's got enough sense
t' stay off th' walks. She's a grown woman an' she
ain't a fool, is she? So don't you be!"

Rhajmurti forced himself to stand still and substituted rocking from heel to toe for overt motion. The
noise of people standing and talking on the walkway
outside the shop had grown to a steady thunder of
wooden clogs and hightown boots. A sudden, loud
boom rattled his nerves, but it was likely something
bumping into the wall outside.

Stella looked up, clutching her canvas bag. "*That*
wasn't a shake. I think it was a gun."

"Rama protect us. Come *on*, Stella."

"I—" She looked about her, at the shelves, at the
shop, looking lost. "I guess we don't need to lock up.
God save us."

"Come *on*," he said, and took the bag from her,
took her arm. A fast change of clothes, he'd thought
on the way here—something of Justice's might fit him;
but he'd decided against it: they had the ship's captain
to deal with and priestly saffron might be out of favor
in some quarters, but it still meant rights and immuni-
ties. He wrapped his cloak close, snugged the bag
against him. "We've got the gold?"

Stella pressed a hand to her bosom. "Here. I'll be
dead before anyone takes that from me."

He opened the door on a walkway resounding with

hurrying people, no few of them carrying bags. Shop-keepers. Scared students. A man went running past, took the stairs, knocking others aside as he disappeared into the dark and the obscuring glow of fog-hazed lanterns.

"Stay with me," Rhajmurti said sharply, and with a firm grip on her hand headed down to the bridge as fast as they could. Somebody was yelling, "They're closin' the high tier! Lindsey's closin' the night-gates!"

"If they close the bridges . . ." Stella gasped, on the stairs.

"Don't talk. Stay with me! Don't get separated. . . ."

ENDGAME (REPRISED)

by C. J. Cherryh

Wasn't what they'd looked to meet—her and Rif and Black Cal. Hard as they'd tried, them with their black powder and their few guns, slipping halfway up to Hanging Bridge before the word hit canalside, before the crowds hit the walks all hurrying away from uptown.

"What's goin' on?" Jones asked, hailing a passing skip, and when she got the answer, shoved the engine open wide and moved, no matter she had a fearful load of powder and a damn dangerous package: wasn't any need slipping up on the embassy, now, all hell was breaking out, and Rif and Black Cal with their fancyboat lurking off by White were going to see it, too.

She cut past and yelled a follow-me as the first shots rang out from the roof of the Signeury, and whatever had happened uptown, the moment she rounded the corner she could see the black smoke rolling out of the embassy's second tier door and mixing with the fog.

She had her gun in her waistband, and fog and smoke and load of explosives and all, she steered straight for the embassy's frontage and its watergate—

Fire, mama, God, if they shoot me we're all goin' t' hell t'gether—

Blow Mondragon a hole t' get out of, if nothin' else, he ain't goin' t' sit around if he's got a way out—

An' if he ain't got one, there's Rif an' Cal ahind me. They won't lay back, they won't leave 'im t' burn, they ain't that kind. If I make 'em a hole, they'll use it—

She throttled up into a sharp turn into the open watergate and into the dock, she hauled mama's pistol out and thumbed the hammer back, despite her eyes running and that she couldn't see clear targets in the smoke. She had the throttle wide before she saw the dockside clear and empty of boats, the building door standing wide—she yanked back and reversed the prop hard, thinking, God, I'm going to be blown t' hell an' the skits've already left this place—

Goin' t' hit 'er . . . God!

Bang went the bow on the buffers and she found herself with a cut lip, lying belly down on the powder-barrels in the well, didn't even register that she wasn't dead, just her body was trying to move, her hand still had a sweaty grip on the gun and she was scrambling off the barrels, got a grip on a low-hanging help-you rope to bring the drifting skip to the buffers again, planted a precarious bare foot on the cracked bow plank and kept her balance through it breaking under her. Second stride was on solid floating dockside and third was going for that doorway as hard as she could.

Nobody shot her. She was halfway up the stairs before her breath ran out and she had to slow down and pull her way up by the banister, coughing in the smoke, tears running on her face. God, you couldn't breathe in here, you couldn't see. There wasn't anybody left. The Nev Hettekkers had taken out some-wheres, maybe slipped up the northward direction, never gone to harbor at all, just—took him and got out, and everything was for nothing—

She felt her way to a hallway of doors about the level of his window, she yelled out, "Mondragon!" at the top of her lungs, wiping her eyes and coughing. Wasn't an answer but the roar of fire. Smoke was pouring through the trim-boards, coming out every seam of the place. They took 'im, she told herself, and then had a more terrible thought, and went down that hall and started rattling doors, scared to death she was going to find him lying shot dead in some room. "Mondragon!"

Female voice. Downstairs. "Jones, ye fool!"

She went on looking. Her lungs ached from the smoke. She yelled and she opened doors, but she didn't panic or shoot when two murky figures came running up onto that floor and grabbed her and carried her out of there. By that time she'd figured she needed rescuing, she needed somebody to yank her around the waist and make her go, because she'd stopped thinking, she'd go searching till she died, because he was gone and it didn't matter any more.

But they got her downstairs and got her air again, between coughing. They were trying to haul her into their fancyboat when Cal lifted his gun of a sudden and Rif cried, "Don't shoot! It's Raj! —Ye *fool*, what're ye doin' here?"

"Trying to help Tom," a shaky answer came back. "Kat and I—Jones, Jones, did y' find him?"

She shook her head. Struggled to see him and the Bolado kid in the electrics and the smoke of the dockside, but her eyes were running and it hurt too much to look long. "Gone," she managed to say.

"We got eyes," Raj said, "hundreds of eyes. Somebody's got t' have seen where they went."

It was a hope, damn, it was.

"Get you out of here," Rif was saying, pulling her for the outside of the boat dock and clean air, and Raj was saying how he had something in Bolado's skip might help her lungs, but she shook her head and waved for silence.

"Get in *my* skip," she said. "Got th' powder. Raj, ye help me—"

"Kat," he said, "get the word out. I'm goin' with Jones."

"Yc'rc fools! Rif said.

"You *help* me," Jones yelled at her, struggling free. It came out a cracked, strange sound. "You get up on the North Flat, ye see if there's been any ship—"—Up there, she was trying to say, but coughing prevented it. "Got t' get clear," she managed to say, headed for her skip. " 'Splosives."

ESCAPE FROM MEROVINGEN (ACT ONE REPRISED)

by Janet & Chris Morris

Kenner wanted to go lie down, if he couldn't report. But he'd done what he'd been told, out on canalside, he'd spread the rumors he'd been told, just as Magruder wanted them.

Jacobs was dead, so he had to spread twice as many rumors, go to twice as many taverns.

He drank a bit in each and he got drunk, on an empty stomach. So he enunciated very carefully, spreading his rumors:

"Mikhail's been shot. Killed out on the Grand. One of Exeter's slinks. Just like that. No warning. Just shot in his boat."

And elsewhere: "Yeah. I heard. They're arresting Nev Hettekkers, arresting anybody—sayin' some of *us* did it. *I* don't want t' end up in some Justiciary cell accused of what Exeter's thugs did. I give fair prices at my shop, I give fair service, I pay my taxes, what d' I get? Dragged in on this? The same folks'll be lookin' fer the killers as did the killin'. Is that justice?"

He did that till he ran out of likely places, and he was too drunk to keep his tongue from tangling. He was getting the first rumors, riot uptown, people starting to move fast on the walkways. Then he set the first of his fires, down near the fish and chips stall on Ventani, where Jacobs and he had met the boat tonight.

He saw a dirty chip squashed by somebody's heel near a barrel, and closed his eyes. Jacobs was dead. Here, where he'd been so alive only hours before. It was hard to believe that he'd never see the fat kid again.

Jacobs would come walking out of the shadows and the fog any minute, with another dirty paper full of fish and chips.

But Jacobs didn't, and setting the fire felt good, because Jacobs was dead. It was like setting a funeral pyre, for Jacobs and this fogbound excuse for a city.

It felt good to raise a little hell here. This place, as much as Mondragon, had killed Jacobs. All Kenner could do for Jacobs now was make sure his friend hadn't died in vain. Do a perfect job. On schedule. Make Magruder proud of them both.

He was on his way now to the second of the arson sites on his list, his own machine shop. *Second* time it had burned. Mondragon again.

Damn him.

The shop was an easy place to torch—and he had to burn it. Jacobs' ghost was most alive here. Confused, it was sitting around on an oil drum wondering where its body had gone.

Scat, ghost, you're dead. Go find Jacobs a resting place. Not here. Here's for the devil. Here's for the Retribution.

The fire burned hot as hell. The ghost looked at him reproachfully from the midst of it and finally turned its back and walked away, into the flames.

When it disappeared, Kenner found himself sober enough to find the doorway. To scatter the cans and the rags outside. Magruder wanted it to seem like the Bloody Cardinal's people had come down here and hit the shop—come after the innocent Nev Hettekkers, who helped the canalers and gave good fair service to the poor. Magruder wanted clear arson.

Arson was a good pretext for any response Magruder wanted to make. Kenner made damned sure that this fire looked real suspicious.

But for some crazy reason he got all choked up when he was leaving, wishing he had Jacobs' body so he could chuck it into the flames and give it a decent burial. Adventist burial. Sword burial. Not have it for fish food, like Merovingen did with its dead. Fire. The way the spacefarers had done with theirs—tossed them into the burning hearts of suns.

But he didn't have it, he couldn't. He'd sent Jacobs' ghost packing, hadn't he? He had to get on with his tasks. He must be running about an hour late. He had to hope that an hour late was going to be all right with Magruder.

Otherwise he'd end up right beside Jacobs, floating around in the embassy watergate.

What in hell?

Big glow on the water. Fog lit up. Shots rattling. Kenner knew that sound. It was coming from uptown.

Steps running for him, down the boards. Kenner blinked, reaching for a gun he'd lost somewhere. He caught himself against the corner of the building. Heard shouting from the walkway overhead, people yelling about Cassie Boregy, about Exeter's assassinating Mikhail, about Cassie Boregy's prophecy coming true, the fire was coming—

He ran for the steps, he staggered up to middle tier, saw the sky glowing uptown.

Damn, it was really working. Chance's scheme was off and running. Now if Kenner could just connect with his own people—

Except he'd lost Jacobs.

He started walking, kept looking for somebody to take his report. The harder that was, the more he learned as he moved through the crowds that bumped him, the more determined he became.

Now there was, according to the crowd, a full-fledged move by an Exeter conspiracy against the Kalugin power structure. Willa Exeter had betrayed Iosef Kalugin. Killed Mikhail and set the fires.

Common folk, who'd never cursed the Church, cursed the priests, cursed the governor too, for a fool, cursed the Ancestors, who'd forsaken the stars and stranded them in hell—

If Kenner wasn't scared to death of crowds and mob psychology, he'd have been giggling at the swiftness and completeness of the plan's success. His, and Jacobs'. Hey, Jacobs, check this out!

Hey, Jacobs, we did great! Magruder's going to be friggin' thrilled.

Hey, Jacobs, rest in peace.

At least Jacobs didn't have a body to risk being trampled by the mob.

Kenner knew a lot about mobs. More than he wanted to, learned the hard way, back in the north. He knew enough to stay the hell away from them, to never get caught up in one, and to respect them like a force of nature.

Hand grabbed his arm. "Kenner!" He nearly killed the guy before he heard his name. He leaned against the railing of some mid-air bridge and blinked at the guy, one of the embassy staffers. Accident, the meet-

ing, a piece of luck. Or the manipulation of Jacobs'
ghost, trying to run interference for Kenner from
beyond the grave. "Kenner, where the hell you
been?" the man yelled, as a mob surged past them.
As he leaned there over the dark and the water.

"Doin' my job," he shouted back. "Where's
Chance?"

"Down at the docks, where we should be. I've been
hiking all up and down here looking for you! You're
late!" The man wasn't happy. His face was soot-
smudged and his eyes were wild, and not just from
the lamplight reflected in them.

A warm feeling of belonging flooded Kenner from
head to foot, almost enough to banish the shivers
racking him. At the same time he was shivering he was
sweating. He wiped his stinging eyes with a forearm.
"Docks, is it?"

"We're to report there! The embassy's burning. We
can leave as soon as we find Jacobs!" The man gave
him a shake. "Hear?"

"Take your hand off me!"

Even Kenner was surprised at the deadliness in his
tone. Mob violence. It was as contagious as the worst
plague. Or maybe he was reacting to the man who
wanted to wait for Jacobs. Wait until hell and Merovingen froze over. "Take your friggin' hands off me!"

The man did, hands up, clear of his body.

"Good." Kenner stood clear from the rail. "We
can't wait for Jacobs, unless you want to wait till
Retribution comes." He couldn't say it. Then he had
to. "Jacobs is dead. Killed by Mondragon in the line
o' duty. Let's go. I'll explain to Magruder when we
get there."

He had no intention of reporting in depth to the

staffer, but he got the man moving. They'd left this guy behind to make sure the whole team got out clean. Down at the docks. The embassy afire. Maybe things weren't going right.

But they were. Maximum disorder. Ships must be coming in. There was a new day, after this one.

But salvation was canals away. He and Chance's staffer had to get through the fires and the mobs and the looters they began to see as they trotted along the middle tier.

Kenner had the queasy, satisfied feeling he always had when he'd run death squads against the tide in the old regime—you'd find yourself moving through crowded streets, sometimes the opposite way to what folk were going, and if you were alert and careful and good at your job, you never got caught up in the fights at the barricades or the looting at the doorways or the police actions failing to restore order. You were moving against the tide, but it was your tide.

You kept your head down and you stayed in the shadows and you moved along. And since what you wanted wasn't at odds with what the crowd wanted, you usually did okay.

They kept within arm's length of each other, and they moved across the spindly bridges and through the crowds as if they were moving through a herd of animals—carefully, respectfully, but with a different purpose: Kenner had seen his boys die because they stopped to help a fallen child or grab a bit of loot—or because they saw one more opportunity to do some extraneous bit of violence, because violence is such a contagious high that you can find it hard to resist.

Kenner had no trouble at all resisting the urge to pitch in and destroy anything Merovingian. He just wanted to save his own life. He'd lost a friend tonight, he didn't realize how good a friend until Jacobs was dead. He didn't dare ask himself for what—

He knew for what. So had Jacobs. They'd had a job to do. They'd had to kill a fool tonight, so they'd killed one. Usually, to kick off a revolution, there was some fool who had to die.

He wasn't angry at Merovingen. He wasn't even angry at Mondragon. He was angry at himself, for not having found some way to keep Jacobs alive. Jacobs had known he was going to die tonight—had felt it. Had tried to tell Kenner so, back there on Ventani Pier. But Kenner hadn't been listening hard enough.

And now the mission was all there was left. Doing the job they'd come here to do, was all he could do for Jacobs. He didn't have to do it with hate.

In his way, he was doing it with love.

Whatever was left of Merovingen when this night was done wasn't his concern. Now that he knew the whole embassy was being pulled out, he figured not even Chance was going to try to make some stable transition out of this free-for-all. Nev Hettek was pulling out, pulling back, leaving behind a legend of fellowship with the poor, an example of industry and progress. And Jacobs' ghost.

When the smoke cleared, maybe Karl Fon would send down a second contingent, offer aid, offer help rebuilding Merovingen, deal with whoever was in charge.

But right now, you couldn't tell who that might be. All you could do was your best to get out alive.

FAMILY TIES (REPRISED)

by Nancy Asire

They'd gotten a table in the common room, near the door. Their single bag was under it. Justice and Sonja sat scanning the crowd that milled in and out the doors. "They'll be here," he swore, and clenched her cold fist in his. "They'll make it." Sonja looked like hell, white as a Dead Marsh ghost, smudges under her eyes that spoke of worry for her parents. *He* had no problems. *He* would be leaving Merovingen with his father and mother. He had packed all he could carry, but now the talk was gunfire uptown, and at the College a student had come in all bloody and said he'd climbed down off the Justiciary walkway, that Anastasi's regulars and Tatiana's blacklegs were shooting at each other; and Justice had quickly revised his packing—he was down to the books, the paintings, rolled in sketches, thank *God* his best were small ones. He had his sketchbook for ideas, he'd a precious few jars of reds and blues he wasn't sure he could replace in the south—necessity finally came down to that one bag, and Sonja's jewels, and the hope Rhajmurti and Stella were going to come through that dark doorway any moment.

"God," he said suddenly, "I haven't paid Hilda."

Sonja squeezed his hand, said, "Go do that. I'll watch."

He got up, felt for his wallet and walked to the bar, attempting to look as if nothing more was on his mind than another beer. "Hilda. I need a word."

"Eh?" She looked at him, her eyes momentarily unfocused, looked at the coin he pressed into her hand. Tried to shove it back at him. Hilda didn't handle gold.

He closed her hand on it. "I'm paying out, Hilda. Going to be leaving town."

"Not comin' back?"

"I don't know. Hilda, you take care of yourself. Keep your head down. Maybe lock up the next couple days."

She stared at him. "Me? Lock up? Ain't never locked. What'd you students do, go to John's place?" Her expression changed from confusion to concern. "What've ye heard that I ain't?"

"Nothing. I swear to you. Nothing more than you know?"

"Where ye goin'?"

He hesitated to tell her the truth. Someone might care to ask. Someone of Keisel's enemies. God knew. "Where I'll be safe. Where I'll paint."

Hilda's eyes shifted beyond him, toward Sonja. "Yer young m'sera?"

"My young m'sera."

"She's a fine 'un," Hilda said, God, her chin was trembling. She darted a fierce, moist look his direction. "Figger then ye can afford th' coin."

"I can afford it."

"Ye been th' best of my boarders . . . an' that Raj boy— Aint' seen him t'night. . . ."

"He's all right. So am I. I wanted to let you know, so you won't think I'm at the bottom of a canal somewhere. And thanks for all you've done for me. I might come back, you know. Might get homesick for your sillybit and greens."

Hilda laughed, short and sharp, wiped a glass and set it down. Justice returned to his table, sat down beside Sonja, and watched the doorway, along with everyone else in the room—Krishna Malenkov had just come in. Krishna bullied his way through the crowd to the bar and swore they were fools out there, shooting at random—"They knocked down the gates at the College," he said, and the room got quieter. Krishna found himself with an audience, picked up the beer he'd ordered, and turned to the room at large. "Blacklegs atop the Signeury, shooting at anything that moves, Kamat's shut its gates—"

A murmur of panic that had to do with people's routes home. Kamat was a key isle for anybody going Eastside. Shut up, somebody said, so we can hear! and Krishna waved his mug and said, "Mikhail was definitely shot—blew half his head off."

"Aw, then he ain't even wounded," somebody quipped. There was a grim mutter of laughter.

"What about the governor?" somebody asked Krishna. Krishna was hightown, the Rimmon Isle elite. Krishna had contacts to have the real facts of what was going on and Justice was all attention.

Krishna said, "Governor's shut his doors and waiting for his heirs to sort it out. Tatiana's holed up in the Justiciary, Anastasi's on his yacht on Archangel, not doing damn much, but he's got one hell of a gun on that boat. Figuring is, he's moving his militia in toward the Justiciary, just waiting to back that big boat up along Kass-side and blow that door down—"

Sonja's hand jerked. Sonja's parents were in that building. God. And the battle was shaping up on the Archangel side of the very Isle they were on. "I'm getting out of here," someone said, and no few left.

The walkways were clogged with people. The boards thundered and Rhajmurti forged ahead, one arm linked through Stella's, elbowing his way through the men and women who blocked his path—no care now for the saffron showing: it was dark, it was shoulder to shoulder through the spots of lantern-light along shop and warehouse frontages and everybody was in a hurry. There was the faint pop of weapons-fire from somewhere, echoing crazily off the walls so there was no telling where it was coming from. They were on Deems and headed breathlessly for Mansur and North, hoping Mansur and North were open canalside to Spellbridge and then Kass, where Hilda's sat on canalside—there wasn't a boat to be had, you couldn't *see* one from Deems, and they were lucky to be this far: Vance had shut all its gates, was closing off its bridges, and people were panicking, taking convolute routes as rumor proliferated of night-gates shut, shots fired—

Blacklegs forced their way through the crowd, and for a frightened, exposed moment Rhajmurti had felt like a target, but they shouldered past. A single boat did pass, a fancyboat, loaded with people, roared under Deems-Mansur Low, and throttled back sharp for the turn. Another pop of gunfire, a series of them. And the crowd on Bois was moving east, so Bois East must be open. Rhajmurti offered up a prayer of thanks to Rama, Shiva, Vishnu and all the gods above and below.

Came a sudden cracking of wood, a splintering sound over the noise of the crowd. Screams. Bodies hurtled past, hit the canal with a splash that drew screams from the crowd. More followed—a rail had given way above—the press of bodies up there shoving people over the edge. Screams proliferated, echoed off the shuttered faces of Bois and Deems—people who'd survived the fall were flailing out toward the canalside, trying to climb up on the bank past a tangle of floating wood.

"Those people—" Stella cried, trying to look back. But Rhajmurti saw Spellbridge ahead. And open bridges. The crowd spreading out, going around North—some poured off to Yesudian, but Rhajmurti took the chance and went around the corner for Spellbridge. Something boomed, rattled shutters up and down.

More of Krishna's friends came in, white-faced and sweating—said they'd outrun a mob, lagoonside— fighting at the College and Kamat's shut gates eastside had sent panicked people trying to get around and home by lagoonside when Lindsey shut its gates. Justice listened to the gunfire and explosions that rattled out from the Archangel side of Kass and sipped his drink—on the house, Hilda said, for him and Sonja. Desire for a clear head fought an urge to down it and go numb. The worst of the fighting was on Archangel. Where Rhajmurti and Stella had to come to get here. Sonja sat in silence beside him watching every movement in and out the door.

Make a break for Rimmon, some of Krishna's

friends were saying. "No," Krishna was saying, "no, fool, you want to get—"

Militia came through the door. Two of them, with guns, headed straight for the bar, demanding, "Is there a stairs here?"

"In the back," Hilda said, still washing glasses. "Wipe yer feet, ye crazies."

The one militiaman said, with a wave of his hand, "Students over against the wall. The rest of you clear out of here."

There was dead silence. Nobody moved, except two people came through the door—Rhajmurti and Stella, who suddenly had the whole attention of the militia. "Priest," one said, and a gun clicked.

Glassful of dishwater sailed out and the gun blasted at the far corner of the ceiling, raining splinters. A flash of silver and the second soldier arched his back and yelled, already in a tumble to Krishna Malenkov's feet. The first soldier was in a battle for his rifle. It went off and Samad Cohen went down, holding his stomach and yelling.

Justice whipped a knife out, the one from the collar-sheath—launched himself with a shove at the table. The soldier spun around with the gun leveled at his face.

Krishna lunged and the point came out the black-leg's chest. The gun went off and the wind of the bullet passed Justice's cheek before the gun fell, and a dozen hands scrabbled for it.

Justice caught his balance, stood there frozen, looking at Krishna. Krishna Malenkov, rich brat, drugrunner, duelist, and bully of the high walkways. And heir to Malenkov. "Not bad for a beginner," he said, a superior smile on his face. He flicked blood off the

sword with a whip of the blade. Spattered the bystand-
ers. "Not bad at all."

He thought Krishna might make it a third. The
night was that crazy. They *weren't* friends.

"Karma's paid," the hightowner said then. He
bowed slightly to the group at the door. "Father
Rhajmurti. Apologies. Going on a trip, I see. Justice,
too? Don't let me keep you."

Justice hesitated, in the silence in the tavern. Felt
Sunny rub about his legs. With two dead men on the
floor and weapons rattling up and down the canal.

Sammy Martushev ducked through the door, white-
faced. "The launch's *here*, Krishna. C'mon, f' God's
sake! It can't stay!"

"My ride," Krishna said, and sheathed his sword
with a single motion. He bowed to all and sundry,
gathered his couple of friends, and strolled for the
door.

Stopped, facing Rhajmurti, with that same smug
attitude. "Drop you anywhere, Father? Dangerous
out there tonight."

Rhajmurti made a nervous, small motion, inclusive
of him, Stella, Sonja—Justice. "We're four."

"We seat eight," Krishna said, and nodded toward
the door.

Damn, Justice thought, and felt someone bump his
elbow, saw Hilda holding Sunny. Hilda pushed Sunny
at him. "Ye go," she said. "Ye go. Ye take him, too."

He sheathed the knife, he took Sunny. He didn't
know what else to do. There was a glistening track on
Hilda's seamed cheek.

"Karma 'twixt us," she said. "I got t' see ye again.
This life or th' next."

A lump in his throat stopped him talking. Sonja

185

had grabbed the baggage. He mumbled a good-bye, ducked out after Sonja and Stella, holding Sunny tight in his arms, stuffed Sunny mostly into his coat as he scrambled after his family to step down into the big Malenkov fancyboat rocking there in the fog.

Hand grabbed his coat. He dropped helplessly into a too-cramped bench seat between Sonja and Rhajmurti, Stella next to the stern; and held Sunny tight as the boatman throttled up and took off with a roar. Krishna eeled his way back to lean on the boatman's station as the walls and walkways shot past faster than sane.

"Paid is paid," Krishna said. "Need a roof, Father?"

"If you could just let us off at the harborside—"

"Ah."

Justice said, it almost choked him to say it: "We've got passage out. The Falkenaer ship. If you need to get out of town—"

Krishna rocked with amusement. Said, over the motor's roar, "Over that? They're our own damn faction!"

"Still—" Rhajmurti said.

"Mikhail's dead, Tatty's under siege—It appears we're in for interesting times here in Merovingen. Whatever wins—whatever works." They broke out into the Grand, wide expanse of black water. "Call it opportunity, Father."

Justice tucked Sunny closer under his coat, scratched Sunny's chin to calm him, and reached for Sonja's hand. Saw her looking back, profiled against a glow of fire, along the wide pattern of their outbound wake.

ESCAPE FROM MEROVINGEN (ACT ONE REPRISED)

by Janet & Chris Morris

When they reached the docks, Kenner saw boats— boats everywhere across the harbor, fancyboats with people in evening dress and nightgowns, skips towing strings of poleboats with scared passengers aboard.

And Mike Chamoun's *Detqueen* and *Detrunner* both at the end of the pier, just shy of a couple of Falkenaer deep-water craft.

Even Magruder couldn't anticipate everything. But he must've damned well planned this one ahead. *Two* riverboats waiting. Panting, the staffer put a hand on Kenner's shoulder and gestured. Kenner saw a little catwalk with a rope across it: Authorized Personnel Only.

They sure as hell were that.

And when Magruder, seeing him come aboard, left a knot of men, including Michael Chamoun, and came toward him, Kenner knew he'd done the right thing. He straightened his shoulders. He palmed his eyes. He tried to scrape the stains of vomit off his mouth and chin and shirt.

"How'd it go?" Magruder said. His face was sooty. The whites of his eyes were fluorescent in the firelit, foggy night.

"Good enough. Jacobs is dead—Mondragon killed him and took the boat when we brought it back through the watergate."

Magruder's bright eyes closed for a moment. "Get with Mike Chamoun, see if he can use your help. Stay with him. We can't have him wandering off."

"Yes, m'ser," said Kenner, using the Merovingen honorific for what he hoped would be the last time. *Watch Chamoun. Make sure he doesn't break for his wife's place. You bet.*

New orders. Kenner understood perfectly well what he was to do.

Magruder shook his hand and slapped him on the shoulder. "Good job, so far. I'm going into town to get something. When I get back, we leave. If I don't get back by midnight, leave without me. Understood?"

Kenner squared his shoulders. Magruder trusted him. Kenner was damned sure he'd be worthy of that trust.

Field promotions were one of the things that could come your way if you moved just right in times like these.

"Yes, sir," he said, and grinned at the ambassador as Magruder slid by him into the night.

Kenner stomped across the planks to take up his watch on Michael Chamoun, totally committed to his new purpose. Chamoun was his to watch over and protect. This time, he'd be more careful. One ghost was plenty for tonight. He'd keep Chamoun safer than he'd kept Jacobs. And the others.

As far as Kenner was concerned, the whole contingent of Nev Hettekers was his to watch and protect, if Magruder didn't make it back.

The staffer had heard Kenner's new orders, and fell in behind.

"M'ser," said the staffer, "anything I can do to help?"

"Yeah," said Kenner. "Get me a steak. And some clean clothes. And set sentries down here. Chamoun's wife and baby are back there in town. We can't have him sneaking off to find them."

Command felt good. Kenner knew that taking the initiative was risky, but it was also the only way to win, sometimes—and, in times like this, it might be the only way to survive.

And Kenner was determined to survive. Death had bumped against him tonight under the murky waters of the embassy water gate; death had come as close as he was willing to let it. He did a quick head-count and saw that Dani Lambert was also missing from the Nev Hettekers gathered for evacuation.

Then he thought he knew where Magruder had gone. And he knew damned well that Chance might not make it back alive. Otherwise, Magruder wouldn't have put the evacuees' lives in Kenner's hands.

But they were safe with him. Even Chamoun was safe with him. Kenner was determined. No more ghosts tonight. Everybody was going to stay alive. Kenner had never been more alert to danger in all his life.

And Mike Chamoun seemed to know it. Magruder's pet agent blinked at Kenner and said dully, "I suppose you're calling the shots?"

"Takin' orders, friend. Just takin' orders."

Chamoun, who was the agent around which all of Merovingen's destruction had been spun, went to the rail and looked into the deep water lapping there.

Kenner followed. "Don't get any ideas of jumping, Mike. I'm here to see you make it home alive."

"My wife and baby—"

"Magruder's gone back to town. He'll do the best he can. We don't want any more dead. Anyway, your wife predicted all this, didn't she?"

Chamoun looked up at him with sudden fury so intense that Kenner took a step backward.

"She did, yes. She predicted all of this, Cassie did." Chamoun's fury faded and he seemed near tears.

Kenner remembered that Chamoun liked drink more than a man should, and hoped the fool wasn't going to drown himself in some fit of inebriated remorse. Drunks were such a waste of time. But Magruder wanted this one alive.

"So, if your wife predicted it, Mike," Kenner said with savage cruelty meant to slap the other man back to reality, "then don't worry: it's all karma, right? Everything's working according to some higher plan, right? You must relax. Our higher plan says we get you back home in one piece. Everybody's going for themselves, out there. Even that scum, Mondragon, got away before the embassy fire started. So karma's on our side."

Chamoun stared at him, blinking.

Kenner stared back, until the other man looked away.

So far as Kenner was concerned, there was nothing more to say. Behind Chamoun's back, the flames of Merovingen reached toward the night with hungry fingers, crackling and muttering a song of revolution as they consumed all that stood in their way.

ENDGAME (REPRISED)

by C. J. Cherryh

The fires lit up the fog and rolled it away with smoke. The fires shimmered on the water and danced in the shimmer that age made in Mintaka's eyes. Oh, she was old, old as had seen a lot come and go on the water, but, Lord and her Ancestors, she'd never seen the like of this. She sat in her skip and knitted, because that was what she did, could do it in the dark, all the pretty bright yarns scraps that she got from weavers and a couple nice shopkeepers, nice 'uns, yey. And Jones. She did work for Jones now and again, special work, being as how her eyes might not be so good, but she put things together real clever sometimes—being as how she'd learned from her years, as some never did. Old Man Muggin now, he'd gone, just his boat turned up empty. And nobody noticed till the rope rotted and the boat come adrift, and nobody aboard. Old Man Muggin wouldn't have nothing to do with no one, and when he went nobody knew, and nobody found out till that rope just rotted off its tie-up.

Hell. Old Man Muggin was always like that. But people liked Min Fahd. Knit 'em gloves for wintertime. Lots of gloves. Poling wore 'em out. And socks. People needed socks.

Jones brought her this nice yarn. And that was real fine. People'd pay nice for them sweaters, yey. But in secret—Min never said it to Jones, because it didn't sound grateful—in secret Min liked the yarn scraps, because you never knew what you were going to pick up in the dark, always making splices, and when the dawn came you'd see what you'd done. All that pretty colors in those gloves. Kids liked 'em. Kids'd say, I want *that* pair, no doubt. Min knew why. Maybe when you got old you understood things again, like how beautiful the fires was. Other people were running away, but Min, she went uptown to look, in the color and the red shining on the water.

Because grown-ups, they'd be afraid, they'd see the city going down, they'd know they were losing all they had, but kids who didn't know better, even when they was looking out from some boat, all scared and cold, they'd see the water shine and they'd stare and stare, because kids could understand: kids'd remember the dying and the fire, but they'd remember how the water shined that night, and how the air was glowing, and feel confused, till they were old, why they'd thought that way, when people were dying.

The pretty, pretty sparks, that drifted over rooftops, wicked sparks, that laughed like snowflakes and whipped around corners and drowned themselves in the Det, that made them safe. Out they winked, one by one. Shimmered in Min's eyes. Stung, too. So she had another drink, the needles crooked in one arthritic finger, oh, the body went, yey, aches and twisting. And she didn't have to be pretty. She let the fires be that. She could be comfortable and mostly safe here in the deadend next to the towering Dike, at Romneyside. Folk wanted away from the fires, they went the other way. So she drank, and she knitted, and her heart ached so the tears spattered onto her fingers, but she just watched, and drank some more.

Boat came up out of The Hole, fancyboat out of Romney North, she figured, seeing that sleek bow. Just lazing along. Most folk hurried tonight. Them that was on the water did. The lookers, they just gathered up on Eastdike, but they didn't stay. Smoke drove them off. There'd be voices, faint and distressed, then they'd go away.

Boat would turn, yey, just come out to have a look—hightowner trying to figure how to route hisself to southside, maybe, maybe trying to figure if Grand End was open or if the fire had it blocked—she called out, "Ye can't make it in the boat!" being helpful. And maybe drunk. Wasn't always a good idea to talk to hightown folk. Didn't want to deal with them and their notions.

And it wasn't a good 'un now. Because the hightowner boat throttled down and then that bow come around toward her tie-up, real slow, real powerful engine on that thing, yey. Hightowner pulled up alongside, standing there in the fireglow, and he said, "Min? Is that Min?" in a voice real hoarse, like he had a cold.

Or maybe—he was all black and tall against the fire—maybe it was the Angel hisself calling her by name like that. She'd been expecting Him.

But she wasn't ready yet. She said, "I ain't. Ye got th' wrong one." Angel had a lot of work tonight—lot of work. He might forget. "Go 'way."

"Min, dammit!" He leaned out and grabbed hold of her skip's side tie that she wasn't using, to starboard side, and dragged the fancyboat closer real sudden, jolting the skip so she snatched up her bottle. Lord, that wasn't the Angel, that talked like that, that was bang against her side, that was a mad hightowner asking, "Min, it's Mondragon. Where's Jones?"

Lord and the Ancestor fools! Mondragon? Jones' man was deep in trouble, locked up in the Nev Hettek embassy that was burning.

Maybe he'd died and the Angel had him out helping, tonight, looking for her and Jones. . . .

Looked like the Angel, he did, pretty man, prettiest curly hair—

"Jones—" She had a hiccup coming, made it hard to talk. A lot of excitement for an old fat canal-rat. She thumped her chest. "Sorry. Ye give me a fright, Tom."

He gave a heavy sigh, still holding to the rope, was down on his knee inside the fancyboat, and she could see now he was closer how he'd got his pretty hair covered, the way he'd do if he was being discreet. "Min, Min, *please*, have you seen Jones?"

"Not since two days."

He kind of slumped down, said, after a moment. "D' you know where she *is*?"

"She was lookin' fer you, Tom, last I saw. She was goin' uptown. Said—said something—"

"What?" Mondragon asked, upset with her, and she tried to think, damn, she'd talked with Jones so many times, Jones was always in some kind of trouble, like her mama, Retribution.

Like her mama, same old cap, same—

Retribution'd died of fever. Altair was Jones. Altair who'd banged her nose with the pole and broke it, poor kid, trying to handle that skip alone after her mama died. Wouldn't take no help—wouldn't sell that boat, wouldn't take any man—and there was a damn lot who'd tried.

"What did she say?" Mondragon asked. "Min. Min, a whole damn *barrel* of whiskey on it, she came by the embassy. Two nights ago. Did she get back?"

Min shook her head, trying to think. "Went out of Moghi's, I seen 'er, seen her go uptown. . . ."

"Did she come *back*, Min? Have you seen her?"

She understood the question then. Didn't like to understand it, no. She choked down another hiccup and pressed a hand to her chest. "No. Nobody's seen 'er. Just dropped out o' sight."

He didn't say anything. He just sat there so long she kept thinking over what she'd said and wondering what he was thinking. Except all Jones' friends was worried, because they kept saying she was going to go up there once too often and she was going to end up in that place with Tom. . . .

Which was burning down there. Which was all the fires. And the banging and the gunshots you could hear far off. It was the embassy was burnin', with all those pretty fires. . . .

She tried to think why Mondragon wasn't in there. Sometimes she forgot things. She tried to think if she'd had one of those blank spots or was having one now.

She said, "She ain't *in* there, is she, Tom?"

He said—she'd never think she'd hear a shake in Mondragon's voice—"I don't know, Min. I don't know."

Lord, pain hurt. She knew. She felt tears in her own eyes and an empty spot in her own heart if Jones was gone like that. She tried to get up on her knees, made a clumsy try at reaching the side where she could reach Mondragon. But all she could reach was his hand on the rope. She said, "She's a good 'un, Mondragon, her mama was."

"I've got another place to try." A steadier voice this time. "If they lied to me, I'll kill them. Min—"

"Yey?" She wanted to help. She'd helped before. She was another year older, but she wasn't worse.

Mondragon said, steadier and steadier now: "There's a chance, too, she's just lying low. At Moghi's, maybe. In the Room."

"Tom. I been around there. Moghi asked *me*, You seen Jones, he ask't, an' I said, no, I ain't. Not fer two day, now. That's what I said."

Mondragon didn't say anything for a couple breaths more. Then he took her hand in his young strong one, Lord, he felt good. . . .

He said, quietly, "Min, you ever want a fancyboat? You can have this one. Sell it. Do anything you like. I want your skip."

Didn't make sense. But Jones' doings and his always started out sounding crazy. Just sit here and watch, Min. Min, you wait here a few minutes, then you just pull crosswise of that canal. . . .

She said, "Ain't real fair, Tom. Ye're jokin', right?"

"That's one thing I want. The other's your getting down to Moghi's and giving Moghi a handful of sols, tell him I want the pickup out on Jones. Hear me? If she's laying low, tell him get her in. Anastasi could be looking for her."

"Oh, damn!"

"—if he hasn't got her, Min. You do that. The boat's yours. Free and clear. Right of salvage."

"She's got to be empty."

Mondragon got up and dragged the boats up close. Stepped down into her well and held the big boat steady with one hand. Held out the other to her, and helped her like she was some hightown m'sera, getting into her boat. He said, "You get down there, Min."

"Yey," she said, trying the wheel. She'd not stood on a fancyboat in years. And only once in her life. Hightown man, she'd had, when she was young. He'd take her in his boat. They'd ride in the harbor, to the Rim—

"You all right, Min? Can you turn her around?"

"Oh, yey, ain't no problem."

He'd let her go. She backed the prop, she backed a little hard. Took her a while.

By the time she was full about in Romney West, she was out of breath, so she sat down. Just let the engine idle a bit. And steered with the little way the idle gave her. Just till she caught her breath. She was sweating. And cold.

But she drifted backward out of Romney West, on the strong Greve current, and back onto Grand End, seeing a skip all lonely against the fire, black against the shimmery red. Seemed to her a curious sight. Seemed to her she knew that skip. And that poler. Long time ago. Sammy Elgin was his name. Pretty, pretty hair he had.

Bang! against a Dorjan piling. Dreadful way to treat a boat. A pretty boat. Couldn't figure what she was doing here. So she took it slow. Didn't want to bang the sides. And it moved faster than she was used to.

Wasn't safe to take this big boat through the fire. There were skips and Farren's fireboat shooting water down there, and floating booms and all, and this a wide, high fancyboat. So she decided she should back

197

again, the current and the piling having turned her mostly about, and go up Romney, the way up by the Rock. That was where.

Only getting across the Grand above Zorya was a mortal nightmare, there was fire and drifting timbers, and shooting everywhere, and cannon booming. She knew that sound. She throttled up and got the Justiciary corner and there was shot falling into the water. So she stopped. Something whistled overhead and fell into the water by her bow, and there were blacklegs shooting ahead and behind now.

So she backed and she turned and she backed and she got the bow around while the shots were still flying and whistling and falling, and she shoved the throttle in and took a scary turn down somewhere, she wasn't even sure, the way the walls flew by. But there was shooting that way, too. So she found herself a cut and swung way out and suddenly she knew where she was. Knew the archway and the watergate.

It was Elgin. It was Sammy's watergate. And she was at the wheel. She powered right in, where people were getting out of another boat in the dark. She called out, "Sammy?"

Bad trouble tonight. She could still hear the shots. Retribution and her had ducked a few. But she stood up and waved her hand to the hightowners in the dark. She said, "I come here for Sammy Elgin."

Clank of chain. Watergate was shutting. Electrics came on, blinding bright. Min winced, and off in the outside, cannon boomed.

"Who *is* that?" someone asked.

"Min Fahd! I come fer Sam Elgin. Ye tell 'im, hear?"

They came alongside, they caught the bow-rope and

drew her snug. They all looked scared. There was this wounded boy they were taking inside, up the stairs.

But they helped her ashore. They said she should come inside, and, Lord, she remembered this. She said, "I got t' wash. . . ."

They said she could use the kitchen. So she did. But then a cook showed up with a pretty robe and said she could put that on, she was going to have to come upstairs.

Long, long walk that was. Long climb. She was breathing hard when she got to the top. Dizzy. But there was a servant girl to steer her for the sitting room.

Old man sitting there, old and wrapped in a lap-robe. He said, squinting at her, "Min Fahd?"

"Yey."

He said get tea. He asked her to sit down. He said she still had pretty eyes. He said it was a shame what was happening out there.

She said so, too. It was kind of strange, sitting here. She said she had to go, soon, she had to get down to the Grand—

"They're shooting out there, Min. They're crazies."

"Yey," she said. "Don't never change, do it?"

Sammy looked at her a long, long time. "Lot of things change, Min."

"Not on th' water. Always th' same."

Sammy said, "You still running that skip alone?"

"Yey." Then she remembered. "Traded 'er. Sammy, I got t' get t' Ventani."

"You can have another cup, can't you?"

It was like a dream. Sammy's folks had had a fit, him bringing her inside. But this time they could sit here. Sammy told a servant bring the tea. Sammy said,

"It's not a night for going out, Min." Cannon shot boomed close. Something hit the roof.

She looked at Sammy, remembered him poling down the canal. Liked to help her with the skip, he did. Such a pretty 'un, he'd been. She wished she'd fixed her hair.

He said, "God, Min."

Hard to know what to say. She sat there with this fancy cup, opposite Sammy Elgin, and he was talking about how the time they'd watched the sun come up from out on the Rim.

God, yes, she remembered. . . .

"You aren't afraid," he said. She laughed, rolled a glance toward the wall and the thunder. "Hell, I out-run 'em. You remember Retribution? No, you was off th' water, then, had yourself a wife—ye wouldn't a knowed 'er, ye hightowners. . . ."

"Tell me," he said. "Talk, Min, I want to hear."

ESCAPE FROM MEROVINGEN

Finale in Two Acts
by Janet & Chris Morris

Act Two: ESCAPE FROM MEROVINGEN

Magruder moved through the night and the smoke with a feeling of predestination. The sky was alight with fires, blurred with mist, and low with ashes. The waterways and bridges were transformed, this night, into a dream or a nightmare Merovingen, lit with fury and rage and fear and metamorphosis.

Through this altered cityscape, Magruder slipped as if he were an astral traveler, devoid of even a body to risk. The real world had become one of Cassiopeia Boregy's prophecies, lock, stock, and crashing timbers. Chance felt removed, detached, disconnected.

His work here for Nev Hettek was done. What he did now, he did for himself and for his people, those whose futures were in his hands. Always, at times like these, ennui overswept him. Once plans became reality, they took on a life of their own. You could no longer steer them. The best you could do was steer *by* them. Keep the wind at your back. Keep your people safe. Get them out of the path of metamorphosis alive.

These times of actual revolution never much resembled the plan of revolution envisioned by men like

Magruder during preparation phases. Once the wave
of revolution crested, no one could control the result.
So for the architects of change, the reality of change
was always unfamiliar, sometimes deadly, inevitably
suffused with an air of unreality. Survival was suddenly the only real thing in a phantasmagorical world
full of death and destruction.

In a moment, any person or place or thing here
could cease to exist, finally, completely, inarguably.
Death and destruction brooked no argument; real
change could not be appealed, only obeyed, outrun,
or eluded. The safety of personnel was all that mattered to Magruder at times like these.

On this particular occasion, he had too personal a
stake in the fates of his people to think as clearly as
he wished. Yet instinct and training prevailed. So he
moved, as he must, to stay ahead of the tidal wave of
revolution.

He moved quickly, seemingly without thought or
plan, trusting to instinct and training to bring him
where he must go without incident.

He moved. Along empty walkways Eastside, avoiding
crowds, avoiding barricades. Along hightown bridges
where neither looting nor fire had so far changed a
thing. It seemed as though he was moving between
Merovingen of the Past and Merovingen of the
Future, in some timeless space where change was
holding itself in abeyance until he'd passed by.

Twice, when he was safely across a bridge, trouble
started there. Once a fiery torch hit the planks where
he'd just walked and he smelled creosote and oil. But
he was safe by then.

He was as safe as a man in a dream, armored by

fate and purpose and knowledge of what was happening here, and how, and why.

Some of his own were safe, already. Chamoun was safe on the *Detqueen*, if Kenner could keep him there.

Safe was a nice word. For some, it meant removal from danger. Magruder had always aspired to that state. But "safe" wasn't a word or a state that came naturally to him. He understood its desirability, but it was always somehow incompatible with his needs, desires, responsibilities, gameplan, and interim projections.

For Magruder, safety was a state of relative excitation that came only in the midst of deadly risk, a surety of survival that was a concomitant of not caring whether he himself survived. You put yourself in the hand of fate and moved on, content to let caprice decide if you were fit to live another day.

Safety, when it was his, came because it was beside the point, a corollary of moving faster than events in order to take control of them. Or moving in harmony with the time so that you were its instrument. He who broke the laws of nature was destined to be broken upon them; he who let himself become one with the force of nature, acting in harmony with the time, survived.

Or so it had always been for Magruder. If he was out of harmony, out of sync with the universe as he perceived it—as he might be, this time, because he was too concerned with particular people under his care—he would be crushed by the forces he'd unleashed here.

He hadn't been distressed when Kenner had told him that Jacobs had been killed after the assassination of Mikhail Kalugin. To light a fire, you had to burn a match.

He'd felt almost relieved. The time had demanded a sacrifice, and perhaps Jacobs had been enough. Magruder was a pragmatic man, but his mother had named him Chance, and a man with such a name couldn't help but be touched by it.

If he had a religion, it wasn't one he could proselytize; it was a sense of the violence of natural evolution and the order of chaos. If this religious sense of natural selection was a religion, then, without ever meaning to, he'd become its high priest. There was safe harbor for his flock, so long as he stayed alive to steer them to it.

Change was the thing that steered all things through all things, and change was Chance. Chance knew what to do in moments like these with a preturnatural clarity and a sense of purpose that separated him from everyone else and everything that was happening as if he were some omniscient observer.

Take tonight. He absolutely did want to be safe on one of the Chamoun shipping vessels, headed out of the harbor toward Nev Hettek. That was the whole point of this exercise. After that, he wanted to be safe in Nev Hettek, having given an acceptable account of himself and this enterprise to Karl Fon.

But Change was master here, and it wanted certain things from Magruder, as from everyone else. He could have what he wanted, he knew, only if he was willing to give up his life to secure the lives of those he loved here. So safety, as an abstract, was beside the point.

Before he could go back to the ships, he had to find Dani Lambert, and they, together, had to finish up the job here. He wasn't looking forward to facing Dani and telling her what he now must tell her. But he couldn't leave her behind, and he couldn't leave the part of himself behind that still was here, smoldering slowly on the fire-licked canal, as if it might burst into flame at any moment.

He changed course; it was always easy for Magruder to find another way to go. He wished he could have found another way for Merovingen. He'd tried to bring hope, dreams, new ways of thinking and of acting. But places and populations had their own ideas about what they were and who they were, and often you could not shake them from the course their nature determined.

Ahead of him, a small riot was in progress: looters and locals with something to protect, plus a few harried blacklegs with clubs and shields, trying out riot-control techniques they'd never really expected to bet their own lives upon.

He changed course again, climbing higher, up where he'd have a better view of what he'd wrought here.

Merovingen was growing up tonight. When the flames had cleansed the town of infection and rot, maybe it would have a shot at becoming a living society, instead of a tracing from some forgotten temple's wall.

People went through the motions of life here, promised an afterlife for which they were paying in advance, and expecting to be punished by an inimical universe for all the wrongs they'd done in previous lives.

At first it had been hard for Magruder to respect these people, who let themselves be duped out of their current lives by fictions constructed to control them and keep them in misery.

But now, maybe because he'd finally been ordered to kindle this blaze—figuratively and actually, he felt a deep pity, a fatherly regret, and a wish that somehow it could have gone differently, here—peacefully.

But he shook out of it, as best he could. He was getting soft, in his dotage. He was thinking like a parent, and looking at these dangerous, untutored oafs as errant children. Any of these maddened children would kill him tonight without a second thought if he made the mistake of resembling or embodying an authority figure, or reminding them of someone who could be blamed for their furious misery, or merely getting between a looter and his next acquisition.

Dani was going to give him one serious hard time. He couldn't think ahead, or penetrate his own feeling of detachment. His mind was shying away from everything unnecessary to keeping Chance Magruder alive.

He'd done this so many times that he slipped around the worst of the fires and the worst of the rioting as if he had foreknowledge. But he had only honed instinct, sure knowledge of the twisted, multi-tiered maze city with its bridges and its classes.

He was up in hightown before he knew it, and stopped only when he found himself facing a choice between heading for Boregy House, where Dani was, and the Residency, where, he hoped to hell, Tatiana was.

Tatiana Kalugin, the governor's daughter.

If Tatiana and he could have staved this off just a little longer, they might have given everybody—Karl Fon, the vicious Cardinal Exeter, Iosef and Anastasi

Kalugin—a run for their money. All Merovingen wanted was a chance to realize its hopes.

It had gotten a chance: Chance Magruder.

You couldn't have everything. And Magruder wasn't a free agent. He might have been, with Tatiana—or more of one. But in the end, he'd chosen the Nev Hettek way, because it would free these people, those who survived, more surely than Tatiana's way. Although he'd have had a nice life with her. Power. Wealth. Sex. But she was a creature of the old guard.

He could never have changed her. And he couldn't change himself. Seeing Dani Lambert again had reminded him of that.

He struck out for Boregy House with an odd foreboding, as if he'd made a final decision only at the moment when he turned his back on the path to the Residency. Magruder had been in this business too long. He'd begun to believe, somehow, that all these people were souls in his care. He'd begun to think that the loss of some lives in order to provide better lives for the majority and the unborn might be worth it.

The obverse was the continuation of a grindingly cruel system because the people living under that system had become ignorant, invidious, and grasping—and because, if there was no disruption, all those souls would stay alive.

Violent revolution is never more clearly immoral than when you've fomented that revolution and you step over a corpse of your making in your path.

The corpse was before him: a real corpse, with its head at an odd angle, and some debris from a scuffle around it. In its hand was a sack which once might have held loot. There was no sign of perpetrators, or current violence, on the walkway or anywhere around.

In his separate space of responsibility and knowingness, Magruder stepped over the corpse and passed on, without stopping.

The corpse was a sign, a symbol, a cull; it was of nature's choosing, as much as of his doing.

The corpse was, most of all, dead. Magruder wasn't trying to shirk responsibility. He was a surgeon, cutting out a disease and hoping the body would not only survive once it left his care, but not reproduce exactly the same killing conditions and symptoms he was removing.

Tatiana Kalugin believed that there was no right and wrong where the lives of others were concerned; that there was only a process of life and death, a hierarchic, natural process that justly put some at the top of society, and some on the bottom.

Magruder remembered the night she'd told him that. Her words had made him realize that he'd been closing his eyes to too much about her, trying to pretend that she was not only useful, but more like him than she was.

He wasn't willing to argue the point, but he wasn't willing to live a lie, either.

Being unwilling to live with injustice, lies, and compromise was Chance's worst personality flaw. It had kept him solitary and lonely and full of regrets for far too long.

In the midst of this fiery destruction and rebirth, he was finally going to do something for himself. He was, after all, a person, too. He was not some caretaker appointed by Nature itself to see to the needs of everyone but himself. And he was tired of so much death. To decree the sacrifice of others, you needed to be sure that such sacrifice was worthwhile.

Magruder wanted to make peace with himself, over Merovingen, before he left it. Maybe that was why he was luckier than Mondragon: he understood what he needed. Tom never had allowed himself the room to be human—

When Magruder came to Boregy House, he saw to his relief that Vega had done everything humanly possible to protect his holdings: the House had been soaked down: pumps lifted water to the roof, sent it sheeting down the walls. Guards were posted everywhere.

He walked up to one and said, "Ambassador Magruder. I'm here to see the family."

Magic words, and he was ushered down a double row of wet sandbags as if he were being presented at one of Tatiana's dress balls.

He and Tatiana had parted amicably enough. She hadn't known what tomorrow would bring. He had. She'd invited him to a dress ball in three days' time, as her escort.

And he'd changed the subject, asking, as he stroked her long thigh, "Why is it that Merovingian mice have such small balls?"

"I'm sure I don't know," she'd chuckled, going along with the joke.

"Because so few of them know how to dance."

She'd laughed, and he'd laughed, but he'd seen the concern in her eyes. Knowing he was failing at pretending there was nothing on his mind, he'd left early.

"You're worried," she'd said. "You're almost . . . desperate with me. Can you tell me what's wrong?"

He shook his head. "I'll handle it. If I could tell

you, or you could help, or if it would help if you knew, you know I'd say something."

She was a professional, was Tatiana, so he didn't lie, just chose his words very carefully. And when he was done, knowing he wasn't lying, she'd seemed relieved, and kissed him once more before she'd let him slip out the door and back to his work.

He'd left her, out through the slate and tan and velvet and flocked grandeur of her office sitting room, and gone back to his work.

His work of causing all this. On the Boregy doorstep, he looked behind him, for the first time.

From this vantage, the city seemed as if it were celebrating a mad holiday. The tiers were backlit. Red glows touched the sky in places. Smoke hung like veils over hightown Houses. It was corrupt, clearly.

It was being cleansed, by its own folk, as he watched.

Chance wished there was some easier way, some more civilized way. There might be, when folk were more civilized. Somewhere. Somewhere the poor were not so full of hate and the rich so full of disdain.

The door opened, and a stooped old man let him in and muttered, "This way, Ambassador. The master is this way."

He hadn't come to see Vega, but there was no way around a courtesy call.

Boregy was sitting at his gilt-encrusted desk in the green room as if this were a normal evening. But on no normal evening would Vega Boregy's eyes have been red and deeply circled with shadows, or his skin so deathly pale, or the blue veins standing so high on his temples.

Boregy said, "Chance, what news have you? Sit. Have a drink. Tell me why you've come."

Okay. Have it your way,. Boregy was either cooler than the glass of wine the servant handed Chance, or in some sort of shock.

"I need to see Dani. We've been burned out—the Embassy—I'm sure you've heard."

"Yes. Let me apologize for my . . . for Merovingians. This is . . . a difficult hour for us."

One your daughter created from her drug-induced ramblings, you fool. And you know it. "Don't apologize. We're none of us in control of everyone or everything. But I'm collecting my people. We're going back to Nev Hettek, in anticipation of a recall order that must surely come."

"I see, Ambassador." Noncommittal.

So now you know why I'm here. Or part of why. And if you argue with me, Vega, I'm going to slit your throat, personally. And I'm not going to mind it a bit, no matter how messy it is. If not for this family, into whom Mike Chamoun had married, none of those roasting in the flames or coughing in pools of their own blood out there—none of them would have had to die.

Cassie Boregy had been the wild card that had skewed all plans. And she was probably still up there in her blue and gold bedroom, doped out of her mind, high as a kite, muttering about fiery revolution, in her bed, with a baby that wasn't even hers clutched to her breast.

"I see. Well, I'll be sorry to see m'sera Lambert go, of course. But I understand that you must care for your citizens here, as I must care for mine."

Did Magruder sense relief? Was Vega worried that

the presence of a Nev Hetteker in his household would bring the mob down on him? So far, this place had escaped harm. "That's right, Vega. My citizens are at too much risk here. If I can get them home without casualties, when this is over, perhaps we'll be able to send another contingent back."

The unspoken matter of Michael Chamoun, Nev Hetteker citizen and husband of Cassie Boregy, hung between them as Vega sipped his drink and Magruder merely turned his in his hands.

Finally Vega said, "I'm not going to ask you to do anything differently than you may have conceived it, but I'm concerned for my House, of course. And everyone's safety."

"Of course. Well, I'll just run upstairs and collect Dani and be on my way." *I won't mention Michael if you won't.*

But Vega had to broach the subject: "Shall I tell Cassie, later, when she's gotten over the shock of Mikhail Kalugin's death, that her husband went along to see his countrymen safely home? Or shall we arrange a more serious severing of relations?"

"Vega, I want to do whatever suits your needs. We'll want to be informed, of course, if you wish to declare the marriage nullified and the merger as well. My assumption is that it's too early for you to tell what you may wish to do."

And you know as well as I, there's no telling that any or all of us endangered Nev Hettekers will make it back upriver alive. You wouldn't want to risk Cassie's inheritance—either through nationalization of Nev Hettek assets here or through that "daughter's" claim, however the wind blows.

Vega got up, came around the desk, and Magruder rose to shake his hand.

The man was impressively calm, in a deadly situation. Magruder said honestly, "It's been a pleasure knowing you, m'ser. I hope we'll meet again. You won't mind if I don't stop back in on my way out. Dani's going to find it hard to leave her patient, whom I'm sure she'll say still needs her. I may need to force the issue."

"I understand. Good sailing, m'ser Magruder."

"And good fortune to you, m'ser Boregy." All nice and neat and not a feather ruffled.

Chance was sweating under his collar by the time he got out of there. He half expected to be stopped on the endless staircase by young, strong guards who'd grab him and keep him from the third floor because Vega had seen through Magruder's subterfuge to the truth and decided to stop him.

But nobody came running after him. When Chance reached Dani Lambert's door, he took three deep breaths, closed his eyes, and then knocked resolutely.

"Come," she said.

And when he opened the door, Magruder saw that Dani had her baby in with her. The natural mother of the child substituted for the stillborn Boregy heir was cooing at the baby, playing with little Hope. Dani's face was swollen from crying and tears had made her cheeks flushed.

But she wasn't crying now. "You."

"Me." Magruder closed the door and leaned on it, crossing his arms. "You must have known I'd come. Let's go. We don't have much time."

Dani Lambert got up from the bed, brushing her

Janet & Chris Morris

short hair back from her eyes, and snatched up her baby—the baby they'd been passing off as Cassie's.

"I won't leave Hope. You can't make me."

"I don't want to make you. Bring her. Just hide her. Pray she doesn't cry and get us both killed while we're sneaking her out of here."

Dani took a step back as if he'd threatened her. Her face turned white. She said, "You know, then?"

"That Hope is my baby? I've always known. What was I going to do about it? You didn't want my help. I'm assuming you'll accept just a little help, now— enough to get the two of you out of harm's way."

She had the baby's head against her breast. She was still walking backward. "That's all you can say to me? After—what you've done. After all this time. This . . . revolution out there, it's all your doing. I suppose you just *assumed* I'd be able to take care of Hope and keep her safe enough, without any help from you—or any warning. I know your style, Chance Magruder. You precipitated this horror out there as surely as if you lit the first fire yourself."

"Ssh! Please. Or do you want to end up as one of the first retributional killings? Those will be starting soon enough. I couldn't tell you. I couldn't move you out of here prematurely. Either would have endangered you. I played the odds. It's what I do."

"I can't stand to look at you sometimes," she whispered, still not making any move to find some way to smuggle the baby out.

What am I going to do about that now? Surely not leave my own child in Boregy House and you with it. You didn't have to bear that child unless you wanted it. You're a physician, damn you. Don't do this to me. Let me help us all.

He could barely make his tongue work, part his lips. They seemed glued together. "What can we use to smuggle Hope out?"

"Oh, I'll give her something to make her sleep. We'll put her in my carpet bag. Don't worry about that. I won't let anything happen to her. And I can take care of myself."

"Just like old times."

"Not quite," she said venomously, and began preparing the baby to leave.

He stayed there, leaning against the door, fearful that anything he said or did might set her off, make her do or say something neither of them could survive. If only she were as bloodless as she pretended, none of this would ever have happened to either of them.

But it had happened. And in the end, he couldn't live with it. He couldn't have his own child reared by a dope-addicted Merovingian spoiled brat, no matter how he cared for the revolution, and no matter how much he'd done to put Mike Chamoun in place, and no matter how much great sex he had with Tatiana Kalugin.

If Karl wasn't so good at keeping them all on track, one of these days a man like Magruder was going to slit his throat. Maybe Magruder would do it himself, just so that Karl could get an understanding of what karma really meant. And Mondragon had named the names and given him the keys.

Magruder thought about that, as he watched Dani put the baby to sleep with an injection and pack her between blouses and underwear in a bag.

He'd never been able to bring himself to touch the child. He'd thought that if he did touch it, something in him would shatter beyond repair.

But now he knew that wasn't so. He was doing the best he could, for some life he accidentally brought into this world. But he was doing this more for Hope's mother. And what had shattered in him where Dani Lambert was concerned had shattered long, long ago.

So he could handle it, whatever happened: if he couldn't get them safely to the boat, by himself. Or even out of the house. Or if they all died between here and Nev Hettek.

Whatever happened, he'd deal with it the best he could. He could feel the coming together of his body and mind that meant he was on the right track.

Dani wouldn't let him come near her, or touch her. That was fine. Her cheeks were flushed. She looked like the model physician, hustling down the stairs, being almost forcibly removed from her putative patient—Cassie.

At the last instant, when they were on the landing and Magruder could feel the sooty wind of escape in his nostrils, Cassie called out upstairs.

Servants called Dani. Dani stopped and handed Chance the bag with little Hope in it.

Chance Magruder held his child for the first time. He could hardly breathe. If he jostled the bag and she woke and screamed, they were dead. All of them. There and then.

Dani started to go back upstairs and Vega stuck his head around his office door: "It's all right, m'sera Lambert. We understand your peril. We'll tend to Cassie now."

"What? Oh. All right. If you're sure?"

"A Merovingian physician is safer for all of us, under the circumstances." A wisp of black hair fell over Vega's eye. He brushed it back, cold as ice.

"Your ambassador is right. We thank you, but your services are no longer required."

Vega wanted them out of his house before their presence brought down a mob, or blacklegs, or any other part of this holocaust upon the Boregys.

Dani came down the stairs at a measured pace. Chance had never admired her more. Her jaw was set. Her head was high. There was fire in her eyes and the strength of her made him want to grin.

But he didn't.

He stepped out the door first, carrying the carpet-bag with the sleeping baby into the night.

He had to make sure there wasn't anyone lurking out there, waiting for them.

When Dani followed and the door closed with a thump of finality, she coughed in the air full of smoke and char. "Well?" she asked. "What now?"

"Now we catch a boat for Nev Hettek, m'sera," he said, and she took the baby in the satchel from him as he walked with her through the wet sandbags and into the revolution.

Michael Chamoun saw Chance and Dani running down the gangplank, seemingly at the last instant. The lines were cast off and the engines thrumming.

He saw the baby, too. And then he knew it was over. He didn't even go up on deck to ask why Cassie wasn't saved, somehow.

Cassie couldn't be saved. Cassie couldn't come with them. Cassie was of Merovingen, as Mike Chamoun had never been. He'd come down here, so long ago, to live a lie and then found himself believing it.

Michael Chamoun, who'd been nothing until the

revolutionary council had groomed him to marry the Boregy heiress, was about to become nothing again.

Chamoun felt the deck shudder under him as they made way. Escape was nigh.

He put down his glass of wine and it fell over, to drip on the polished floorboards. Maybe he'd had enough to drink. Now that he didn't need to live the lie, maybe he didn't need to stay half drunk.

He wanted to talk to Chance, though. About everything.

To do that, he'd need to go up on deck. So he would. He'd face Dani Lambert and the baby that really wasn't his, and Kenner and the carnage they'd wrought here.

He would.

When he finally climbed up to the foredeck, where Chance was, the baby and Dani were nowhere in sight. Merovingen blazed with lights and fires and sparkled with water in arcing plumes from the fire-fighters' boat.

They were nearly out of the harbor. No one had yet come chasing them. Magruder was staring behind him, looking for pursuit, his face grim.

His eyes flicked over Michael, and away. Mike Chamoun was just a tool to Magruder. He'd always known that.

Michael turned his head away. And then he was looking at the Angel of Retribution, its sword half drawn from its scabbard, that guarded the harbor.

Cassie had said the angel looked just like him. The angel's name was Michael.

It hadn't meant anything. It hadn't needed to mean anything. He'd loved his wife and almost failed the revolution. But Chance had saved him even from that.

His eyes were smarting from the fire. He rubbed them. "Chance, it'll be better, won't it? We did the right thing?"

"It'll be different," he thought he heard Chance say. "Maybe that's better." Then, louder: "You did fine, kid. You did the best job you could. Let it go."

"But . . . Cassie's my . . . wife." She'd killed their baby, with her drugs. She'd killed his heart, and all his hopes to make something lasting out of this venture.

Magruder said, "Trust me, kid. Let it go. You're going to be a hero."

Mike Chamoun couldn't believe that heroes felt the way he was feeling. He had a mouth full of tragedy, a gut full of guilt, and a heart as heavy as a stone.

But then, maybe that was what being a hero was all about.

He stayed up there, with Chance, without talking, until they'd passed out the harbor and their way was clear ahead.

Chance's eyes never wavered from the stern. When Chamoun realized that Magruder was going to spend the night there, keeping watch for pursuit or danger, he gave up and went belowdecks.

Dani Lambert's cabin door was open. The baby was asleep there. As he passed by, she motioned to him and said softly, "Come on in, Chamoun. Have a drink. All's forgiven."

"No, thanks," he told her. "I've had enough drinks to last the rest of my life. I've got to get some sleep."

He tried to sleep. He really did. But every time he drifted off, he saw Cassie, his beautiful, crazy Merovingian wife, standing on the highest balcony of Boregy House as it burned, her arms raised to the sky, crying revolution to the heavens.

Then he'd wake up, sweating and shivering, and remember where he was.

On his way home. At last. And he'd remind himself that he wasn't Cassie; he didn't have to believe that every dream he had would come true.

Cassie had the knack, not him. If only she'd listened when he tried to tell her to be careful what she wished for.

But she hadn't. And it was over. He'd done a service to his country. And to the folk of Merovingen as well, probably, in the long run.

But he'd never thought it would cost him his heart. His life, maybe, but not his heart.

Sometime in that long night, once when he woke up yelling hoarsely, Chance was standing over him when he knuckled his eyes.

The former ambassador to Merovingen sat on the foot of Chamoun's bunk for awhile, before he went back up to the foredeck to keep watch.

Chance didn't say a word, the whole time he was in Chamoun's cabin. Not until he started to leave.

Then Magruder said, "Freedom costs, kid. Just try to remember who you are and what you aren't."

Chance left, and Michael Chamoun started trying, with all his might. Mike Chamoun was an agent of the Sword of God, who'd given all he had to bring revolution to Merovingen—given his heart and soul.

So even if it hurt, because he'd done so damned well, then that was okay. He'd learned a lot. Learned about freedom. Learned about discipline. Learned about sacrifice. Subterfuge. Loss. Despair. Tragedy. Triumph.

Tragedy and triumph were seemingly synonyms, right now. But he was still learning.

He'd started out as Magruder's green protégé, and ended up a revolutionary hero who drowned his guilt in drink and bumbled his way to success. Chance was right: he had to find himself, reclaim himself, and not let Cassie's ghost stalk him for the rest of his life.

He'd learn how to manage, once he got home. Home to Nev Hettek.

Chance was one hell of a teacher.

ENDGAME (REPRISED)

by C. J. Cherryh

"Swallow this," Raj said. "It's cut with whiskey. Do you good."

Jones took the bottle, not because she wanted the medicine, but because whiskey sounded like a good idea right now. Unconscious sounded like a good idea, but the whiskey burned her throat so she had to double over the tiller and wipe her eyes. "Lord." A cough, and another sip, that went down easier. Raj offered her a grimy handful of something fried, and she shook her head. Couldn't eat. Throat wouldn't work. But the whiskey was all right.

Chased a rumor all the way to harborside, near killed themselves, and they hadn't a damned thing but the lights of those boats going out. And a sick fear.

If he wasn't on one of those riverboats he could've been in some part of the embassy that she hadn't searched. She'd only been on that one floor, and Lord forgive a fool, the floor he'd been on wasn't likeliest, not after she'd gone and gotten things stirred up that night—they might have moved him. Where did they move people they were mad at but down where there weren't any windows. Or any way out. And that Isle had all burned, every stick of it, down to its sodden pilings, that was the report she'd had, not a thing left but a smoking ruin. And if he'd been in that, and died like that—

God.

She took another swallow. Sat there staring at the bottom of the boat, then staring at the powder barrels and thinking how, if Mondragon was gone, and dead like that, she didn't want to live in a city where she'd have to pass that place, and go one working and living and growing old like Mintaka Fahd, drinking her liver away and talking on and on about the handsome young men she'd loved and lost. Wasn't the life she wanted for herself. And she stared at those barrels and stared and thought how if Mondragon had died like that she'd have slim chance of tracking down Chance Magruder and making him pay. Or going to Nev Hettek and collecting from Karl Fon. She'd like to. But it wasn't real likely she could do that. Skip didn't handle worth much on the open Det. Didn't carry near enough fuel. Could sell the boat, maybe, get passage. Just her and a gun.

Black, black thoughts before the dawn. Sipping whiskey and whatever Raj put in it. And, poor lad, he'd Kat Bolado running about collecting rumors and risking her boat and her neck and all, and he was probably scared about her, but here he was with his medical bag, doing such as they could in this stirred pot of a harbor—he gave out bandages, he gave away his medicines, while Kat was off somewhere like Rif and Cal, doing what they could.

Meanwhile she had a boatful of gunpowder, the crying of kids in the dark, the stink of burning about this town she'd grown up in, and a sure knowledge of certain people responsible.

Mondragon could've gotten free. Could've. He'd an

C. J. Cherryh

eel's ways, she'd always said that. Like Merovingen's cats, he was fast and he knew when to lay low. He'd go to Moghi's, if he was looking for her. He'd use the back way. Nobody would see him there. And there'd been fire on Ventani, but they'd got that out, all right. He'd know. He'd go there. Which he hadn't, last she'd heard. And she'd sit there, except Cal and Rif had argued her into staying here and gone off searching about the harbor—she was to coordinate information, that was what Cal had called it. Meaning if they found him they'd bring him directly here, and here was about as easy to find her as there. So she waited, while her bruises went stiff and her bones ached.

Finally she said, in her whisper of a voice, "If he's alive and if he ain't at Moghi's it's because he can't. And if he can't it's because he's hurt or he's up to somethin'. And if he's hurt, there's people he knows he could hail."

"No question," Raj said earnestly.

"An' if he's up t' somethin', it's politics. It's *business*. An' I know where t' look." She moved. First time she had moved in a while and it hurt. "We got to get us some fuel, boy. Got t' find someone who'll give us a tank or two." A glance at the barrels, innocent as the barrels she'd run all her life. "I got me a delivery to make."

224

ONCE WAS ENOUGH

by Lynn Abbey

When a ruddy glow appeared in the eastern sky over Merovingen, Richard Kamat was not the only citizen whose eyes clouded with dread. After a long night manning hastily erected barricades, watching every passing boat with undisguised suspicion, and enduring the twin terrors of fire and earthquake, many exhausted residents mistook the ruddy aura of dawn for conflagration on Eastdyke. Self-conscious laughter erupted here and there as the sky brightened to a pale gold.

"Hail, Murfy! We made it!" a workman exclaimed, clapping Richard on the shoulder with the familiarity and equality only shared nightmares could bring. "The worst is behind us."

Richard grinned and returned the comradely salute, wondering as he did if the night of rioting would ever be behind them.

Many hours ago, at the top of the second watch, Richard had commanded all the able-bodied folk under Kamat's protection to pile up barricades on all their bridges. There had been ample material on hand. Until yesterday evening Richard's foremost concern was ridding the family's island home of the wreckage from his sister Marina's wedding. That the island was a firetrap had nagged at the Househead's thoughts

225

these last six weeks, but a seemingly endless parade of circumstances kept him from commissioning the workcrews. Now Kamat had what were undoubtedly the most daunting set of barricades in the entire South Bank quarter of the city.

The folk of nearby Tyler came calling at midnight. They said Kamat owed karma and begged for lumber to shore up their own defenses. Richard offered them the remnants of a painter's scaffold and said nothing about the quirks of fortune that had left his family so well-prepared for the unforeseen. An old Revenantist proverb proclaimed that there were a thousand kinds of karma, then added only ten forms of karma could be perceived by mortal minds. If Kamat had karma, that karma was one of the 990 unnameable varieties.

Kamat's barricades hadn't been seriously tested. Across the water on four of their five exposures, they were reinforced by mercantile houses as devoted to the preservation of life, order, and property as they were themselves. Kamat's primary concern—indeed one of the primary concerns of the whole South Bank quarter of Merovingen—was the abandoned Wayfarer's Hostel which Kamat faced alone on their fifth exposure, and that was where Richard spent the long hours between midnight and dawn.

Somewhere in the middle of the third watch a rowdy gang tumbled out of the hostel carrying petrol-soaked torches and promising death to all oppressors. But the gang was fired by brandy, not revolution, and balked before any of them set foot on the fortified bridge.

A torch had been thrown at the carved mid-level door, but that entrance—even more than the many, many others—had been thoroughly drenched with canal water. The torch had guttered before the bucket brigade could assemble itself. Richard did not know if their Eastdyke warehouse was similarly intact, but Kamat had survived the loss of its warehouse before.

If the aftermath of Mikhail Kalugin's assassination could be compared to the aftermath of one of the fast-rising, powerful sea-storms of late summer, then the worst was indeed behind Kamat and all Merovingen. They could pick up the pieces, get on with their lives, and have the city almost back to normal by sundown. If last night's aftermath was comparable to a hurricane. If it was an aftermath at all and not, like the mild tremblors which rattled the city's foundations during the night, a pointed reminder that things could get much, much worse.

For the moment, though, with the sky growing steadily brighter, Kamat's defenders listed toward cautious optimism. Cheers went up across the canal on Malvino Isle. The chorus was picked up by Tyler, St. John, and Kamat, but not by Kamat's weary househead.

The usual morning mist was sticky and foul with soot. Richard coughed and covered his mouth, leaving another dark smear on his chin and cheek. His clothes were stained with canal water and sweat. He stared at the wispy pillars of smoke rising into the bright morning sky as if they were omens he alone could read.

Merovingen had been a Revenantist city since its refounding. Its leading citizens however, with a few notable exceptions, wore their religion casually. Trade, they were wont to say, was more important than dogma. But Merovingen trade, with its ledgers and balance sheets, its credits and all-important debts, was inherently Revenantist. Richard Kamat could not watch the sun climb above the rooflines without calculating who had won during the night, who had lost, and who was to blame. He couldn't measure the winners or losers yet, but he certainly knew where to place the blame.

Iosef Kalugin, the governor and protector of Merovingen, had been too busy protecting himself from the predatory children he'd sired and raised to do his duty to the city entrusted to him. Of all the night's rumors none had been more prevalent than that of Iosef, the Lion of Kalugin, abandoning the Signeury the moment he learned of Mischa's death, abandoning Merovingen to the partisans of his surviving children and worse.

Yes, Iosef was to blame, but the Angel of Merovingen and the ghost of Murfy himself knew that there was blame to spare after the Lion took his portion. Tatiana Kalugin had completely corrupted the already tainted blacklegs. Along the way Tatiana laid the city open to Nev Hettek influences, including the thrice-damned Sword of God. Anastasi Kalugin was no better than his sister, but because he did not control the local blacklegs and had not, so far as anyone knew, gone to bed with Nev Hettek, he was somewhat more palatable to the mainline Merovingen Houses than Tatiana. Still, Anastasi looked out for his own welfare above all else and would sell Merovingen to the sharrh if the price were right. There was even a bit of blame left for feckless, assassinated, and unlamented Mikhail Kalugin who, no doubt, would still be alive and playing with his automata if he hadn't mistaken Willa Cardinal Exeter's attentions for admiration. Once Mischa started preaching his own garbled brand of Revenantist mysticism, his days were strictly numbered.

All in all, Merovingen's anarchy had festered just out of sight for more than a year now. Everyone in trade agreed that the rivalry among the Kalugins was out of control. Everyone feared the growing Nev Hettek influence in their city. But the trade Houses hadn't done anything directly or in concert. The Samurai—the private security force Richard, himself, had founded—was an expedient compromise to protect mercantile property, not Merovingen itself.

Richard shrugged his shoulders to accommodate his own portion of Merovingen's melancholy karma. He was one of the many who succumbed to omnipresent intrigue. He'd given Tom Mondragon—vanished Tom Mondragon, late of the Sword of God and the dungeons of Karl Fon—shelter within the Kamat house. He'd looked the other way throughout his sister's unrequited infatuation with the handsome, charismatic, and utterly amoral Nev Hetteker. And when the time came, he'd had no qualms in using his sister's innocent child, Tom's almost-acknowledged child, to further Kamat's fortunes in the great game being played throughout the Det River valley. In point of fact, Kamat's young, inexperienced Houschead had been as smitten by Tom as his sister had been—or at least by the roguish aura of excitement surrounding the pale, deadly aristocrat.

For a time, Richard had fancied himself a power in the dangerous game the Kalugin siblings played. In the smoky morning mist, he recognized that he'd been a pawn, not a power, and that, above all, when chess was played for Merovingen's future, the city lost no matter which individual or faction won.

"All the barricades are secure, Dick," twenty-year-old Paul Kamat informed his twenty-eight-year-old cousin with breathless urgency.

Throughout his life Richard had been Dickon to his

intimates, Richard to his peers, and m'ser to everyone else. While some of his contemporaries had a new nickname every season, Richard resolutely refused to acknowledge them—until this summer when his cousin Paul graduated from school. In the usual course of events, Paul appeared on the audience side of the Househead's desk the following Monday morning to receive his first formal position in the family business. In the three years since his father's death, Richard had consolidated his position at the top of the family hierarchy and grown accustomed to both its power and its responsibilities, but in Paul he faced the first member of his family whose career was entirely in his hands.

Paul was easily the cleverest, most aggressive of the Kamat cousins, the antithesis of his mousy, bookish father, Patrik. Richard had readily assigned Paul to the Underhead position which he, himself, held until Nikolay's sudden death. Paul was grateful. He devoted himself to his work, as Richard had when he was Underhead, but where Richard could always address his Househead with a correct and respectful *Father*, Paul seemed at a loss for the proper title. For a month Paul had initiated conversations with a mumble, then *Dick* appeared, and spread like fire through that small, but growing, group of contemporaries who owed their present and future positions to Richard Kamat, Househead.

"I've been down to the kitchen, Dick. There's tea and breakfast ready for as many as want it. I checked the pumps; there's fresh water settling in all the filter-cisterns. One of the clients, Fowler, Canalside, asked me about moving supplies and barrels from his back-room to somewhere more secure. I didn't know what to tell him. No sense wasting time carting stuff all over the island, right? But we shipped a load of dyed wool around the Horn for weaving when the womenfolk left for the *stancia* the other day and the wool lofts are empty right now. They're about as secure as anywhere in the city. The clients could use them, if you thought they should. The tenants, too. If you thought it was necessary. What do you think, Dick? What should we—I do next?"

A few moments passed before Richard's night-numbed brain made sense of Paul's rapid-fire words. "We should get some sleep," Richard replied after grinding his knuckles against his eyes. "Wake up your brother and everyone else who went off guard at midnight. Tell them to eat a hearty meal, then come outside to relieve us so we can eat and sleep ourselves."

Paul nodded. "I'll see to that, Dick. What should I tell Fowler?"

The Kamat family's relationship to its eponymous island was typical for Merovingen. The family who gave the island its common name owned it outright from the below-water bilges and cisterns to the highest iron-crowned spires, but generally occupied only a small portion. Family clients operated their diverse businesses on every level except the highest. Independent tenants, who were often clients of other Merovingen Houses, rented the rest and had little contact with the island's ultimate owners. House Ventani had a generation-lease on Kamat's easterly exposure which predated Kamat's arrival in the city's aristocracy and from which they ran a wholesale produce market for the northeast quadrant of the city. Richard didn't need to know the names and numbers of the Ventani clients living above the market so long as Benjid Ventani paid the rent on time. But these were not normal times and Ventani over on the Grand Canal might just as well be across the ocean or amid the stars for all the good they'd do their clients right then. Romney and Amparo also held generation-leases; Richard racked his brain without success to remember where or why.

"Remind me to tell Greg when he gets out here to conduct a census of the island. I want to know everyone who's here, what rights they've got, and what they might need from Kamat. Don't let me forget. In the meantime, if Fowler or anyone else asks, tell him he can haul whatever he wants to the lofts, so long as men don't leave the barricades to help him."

"You don't think it's over, do you, Dick?"

Richard tried to keep the full extent of his doubts on that matter from showing on his face. "The sun's well above the roofline and there's been no morning peal from the Signeury bells—has there?"

The younger man spun on his heels to study the smoke rising in the northwest. The wedding-cake islands of Sofia, Eber, and White concealed every part of the Signeury, even the tall campanile tower, but Kamat always heard the bells.

"Empty? Overrun? Anastasi, Tatiana, some other faction? The Nev Hettekers. . . ? Do you think they *burned* it?"

Richard shook his head. "The Signeury's built of rock and on rock. It will still be standing when the rest of Merovingen's swallowed by the sea, Paul—but whoever's in charge there this morning isn't thinking about the rest of us, we can be sure of that."

There was a peal of sorts to prove Richard's point: the unmistakable crack of gunfire rather than the ring-ing of the great bell. The gunfire was followed by the sound of a high-power engine roaring flat-out down the Grand. Paul levered his torso over the railing, although there was no way to see the Grand from Kamat Island.

The Househead felt obliged to fasten a hand on the younger man's belt. "Don't worry about it. Whatever's happening up there doesn't matter," he said firmly. "Make certain Greg's awake, and tell him not to dawdle over his tea."

A chastened Paul disappeared into Kamat-proper through one of the lower house doors.

Of course it did matter who controlled the Signeury and the rest of the city; it mattered very much. If Tatiana had secured the upper hand, she would seek reparations from her brother's erstwhile allies. And when all illusion and subterfuge was stripped away, as it surely had been during the night, Kamat would stand revealed as one of Anastasi Kalugin's many uneasy allies. Kamat could breathe easier if Anastasi were in control, but not much: 'Stasi would expect his allies to support him in every imaginable way.

If neither of the Kalugin siblings had achieved a victory the situation was bound to get a good deal worse before it got clearer, or better.

Richard had, however, learned one important lesson during the night: In no event would he, or his kin, or any of the folk of Kamat Isle influence the outcome of the struggle. Family, clients, and tenants alike, they were just another island riding out the storm on their own resources.

Richard made a complete circuit of the levels of his ad hoc fortress ending up on the slick canalside planks of the dye-room freighting gut. A dozen skips and poleboats that normally relied on Kamat for their trade had take refuge in the cavelike gut. The lives and livelihoods of the canalers depended on free traffic through the city waterways; they were the first to feel anarchy's pinch. None of the boats carried more than a day's food or water, and their sanitary facilities, in a close tie-up, were worse than nonexistent. Richard moved steadily from one deck to the next, arranging fresh food and water for them from the Kamat kitchen in exchange for their promise to use the house privies.

Doing his arithmetic in an absentminded mutter, Richard calculated how many casks of bacteria cultivate to add to the island bilges. He'd just about convinced himself that the burden of the canalers was adequately offset by the coincidental absence of his female relations and their respective entourages, when he spotted Paul and Greg loitering on the dock. His cousins looked uncomfortable and very out-of-place upwater of the family's polished tealwood boat slip. Richard wished the canalers well before climbing the cantilevered ladder to the dock.

"Are you letting them stay?" Greg asked once Richard's head was above the planks. His tone implied what his own answer would be if he were the Kamat patriarch.

"We've always let canalers tie-up in the gut during heavy weather. I know these boats and these people." He bounded off the ladder which, at low tide, was quite steep.

"This isn't exactly 'heavy weather,' Dickon." Greg thought that using Richard's childhood name emphasized his own nearness to the peak of Kamat's hierarchy, but, as Paul had correctly observed, it only made him seem like a petulant child. "Any one of them could put a torch to the pilings and burn us to the waterline. You can't know who, or what, they're hiding in their holds—even if you think you know them. They'll all stick up for each other."

Richard unrolled the cuffs of his trousers, establishing the relative importance of his cousin's opinions. "You're right. They *will* stick up for each other. I'm counting on that—even if I don't know all of them or what's in each and every hold. They look to us for shelter and safety, so long as we provide that, so long as we keep faith with them, they'll make certain no harm comes to us through our gut. They may be poor and ignorant, Greg, but they're not fools." Richard straightened and managed to look down on his cousin, though, in fact, Greg was a good six centimeters taller.

"Are you saying I'm a fool?" Greg demanded. "Are you?"

At midnight, when Richard realized that the crisis would likely last longer than anyone could stay awake or competent, he'd divided his forces into two watch-crews. He'd seriously considered making Paul, not Greg, crew-leader of the second watch. Gregor Kamat *was* a fool of the highest order, and just enough aware of his deficiencies to bridle at the least slight, real or imagined—as his younger brother, Paul, was swiftly learning. And it was necessary that Paul learn his brother's failings without Richard's obvious interference. So Greg, by right of seniority in the family, was in charge of the second watch, and carefully surrounded by house retainers and clients who knew him too well to be cowed by his tantrums.

"Dammit, Greg," Paul hissed, just before Richard was out of earshot. "Dick wasn't talking about *you*.

He just said that the canalers won't let anyone burn them out of a safe tie-up. You're the one who's foolish for being so thin-skinned."

Richard swallowed a smile: Paul was learning fast. He paused by the mid-level door to confer with Ashe, one of those trusted retainers who was immune to Greg's shortcomings. After telling Ashe about the need for an island census, Richard left orders to be awakened at the first sign of renewed disorder although he expected his sleep, when he finally got it, to be undisturbed. The most opportunistic rioters would be at least as tired as he was—if they weren't passed out drunk already. The truly dangerous people—the Swordmen from Nev Hettek, the Kalugins, and that ilk—would reconnoiter the city thoroughly before the sun set and they became active again.

Before climbing the stairs to his private apartment, Richard visited the kitchen to make certain there was ample food in the pots and on the table. In the long run, Merovingen was painfully vulnerable to food-siege, but because Kamat was no more vulnerable than the rest, and because so far as he knew there was no blockade threat in the harbor or on the Det, Richard didn't want to dull his household's wits by starving them. He satisfied himself that there was enough in the larder to feed the whole island—household, clients, and tenants—for several days, if worse came to worst, but as he was filling a plate for himself one of the housemaids tugged on his sleeve.

"There's St. John folk in the vestibule and Ralf says they won't speak to anyone but you, m'ser."

With a sigh Richard left the kitchen for the sloping corridor to the mid-level entrance. He expected to greet the St. John Househeads, Christen and his sister,

Amitra, and he expected them to offer Kamat aid and assistance—which he would gladly accept. St. John's island was roughly the same size and overall population as Kamat's island, although the House of St. John—parents, grandparents, children, aunts, uncles, cousins to the third degree, and body-servants—was considerably larger than Kamat. Moreover, St. John's island had half the number of bridges to watch, being more regularly shaped and disconnected from Sofia on account of a previous generation's piece of sour business. But the "St. John's folk" turned out to be Pradesh St. John, the Underhead of his house and Richard's closest confidant.

Prad looked worse than Richard felt. "We're bailing out," he announced as soon as Richard shut the door. "I thought you'd want to know. The high tide changes tonight at the bottom of the first watch. We mean to leave with it. And not just us alone. We'll be forming a convoy down the backwaters to Eastdyke with Eber, Chavez, and Dorjan. Kamat's welcome to join. There's safety in numbers."

Richard was incredulous. "Bailing out? You're leaving Merovingen?" The idea had not occurred to him. "All of you? All of St. John—the whole island? How in the stars will you get everybody out? Did a Chat freighter heave across the horizon during the night?"

Pradesh raised a hand to forestall the stream of embarrassing questions. "Dorjan settled badly during the 'quake; one whole wing broke loose. It was a family wing. There were casualties. They came to us as soon as they could, saying they wanted out of the city. M'sera Jane Dorjan—you know she's one of Cassie Boregy's circle. I guess the last things Cassie said were that there'd be death, there'd be fire, and the ground would tremble before the end. We got three of the four by the end of the first watch and, I guess, the Dorjan folk aren't alone in thinking the *end*—whatever it will be—can't be far off."

The Underhead of St. John grinned sheepishly and shook his head before continuing. "I've never had much time for Boregy prophesying, Christen hasn't neither, but Amitra. . . .Cassie Boregy may be mad as a drunk skit, but she's on the mark right now. After a while, Dickon, you've got to start wondering if maybe she isn't onto something—"

"I'll tell you what Cassie Boregy's been on—" Richard retorted.

"No need to tell me." Prad lowered his eyes and his voice. "She's a symptom, a catalyst, not a cause— I know that. But there *has* been death, there has been fire, and there has been a quake. There's also been looting on Dorjan, and Boregy, too, by the number of broken windows we can count. And more gunshots and cannonfire than I've heard in my life, nor my uncle's life, for that matter. I don't believe in Cassie's apocalypse any more than you do, but, Dickon, Merovingen's not safe, and we've got a whole lot at risk here. We've got to get the family out at least, and, putting it bluntly, our strongboxes, too."

"Let's talk about this, Prad," Richard said soothingly, reaching to guide his friend to the greater privacy of the doorman's empty closet. "It was a bad night, but it was just one night—"

"That's easy for you to say. We're not you, Dickon, we don't have Kamat's karma. Your family's never kept its wealth in the city. You're still sheep-farmers at heart, just like old Bosnou. Don't tell me you didn't load up his boat once you got it hosed out from the sheep he brought for the wedding-feast. I've known you too long. That ship was riding right on its water-line. And, as if that weren't karma enough—'Talya gets kidnapped. Angel knew, it put the fear of God into all of us—but you got 'Talya back *and* sent your whole damned family out to Bosnou's *stancia* on the next tide. And *that* ship was wallowing like a leaky bucket." Pradesh shed Richard's arm. "I'm not saying Kamat knew. We've been friends too long. If anybody had told you something, you'd have told us—" Prad was referring to Kamat's sometime client, Tom Mondragon, who had been known to untangle a rumor or three in lieu of rent. "—But, Dickon, your karma—Kamat's karma—must be clear as crystal."

Richard shrugged awkwardly. Crystal karma was the purest of the ten named karmas. It was rarely bestowed on mortal souls, especially Merovingen souls. "Hell's bells, Prad, you know how long I'd been trying to get my sister out of Merovingen. I wanted her to go before she got pregnant. I wanted her to go with Great Uncle Bosnou. It was luck—blind coincidence—that we'd find ourselves with a deranged woman in the nursery. The rest was trade."

"What's luck but unpaid karma?" Pradesh retorted.

Richard thought of a reply and rejected it. He raked his hair, seeking another tack: "Luck, karma, whatever. You're right, if they were here, I'd be trying to get them out. But *I* wouldn't be leaving, Prad, and I wouldn't let anyone who could help me maintain order on the island leave. This is my family's island, my family's city. This is where I live. It's going to take more than one night of crazed Kalugins fulfilling Cassie Boregy's drug-dreams before I'm ready bail out. Come on, Prad, give it another thought. This is Merovingen: *home*."

Pradesh St. John retreated until his shoulders struck the doorframe. "I have, Richard. I thought you understood." His voice had gone soft and distant with disbelief. "I thought you were with us all the way. We're crowded together here. We're like sheep in a pen— you said so yourself: A city of hostages no different than our ancestors were. I thought you agreed with us: *Once was enough*. We waited until Juarez finished the transceivers. After that all we needed was opportunity. The transceivers are all shipped. When will we have a better opportunity?"

Once was enough.

Richard heard nothing clearly after those words. The phrase had become an oath of sorts: a trio of words fraught with meaning for a clandestine group of educated Merovingian citizens, of which both Richard Kamat and Pradesh St. John were members.

They saw Merovin's history repeating itself in Karl Fon's strongman ambitions and their own cardinals' rabid rejection of any innovation that might strengthen Merovingen against her undeclared enemies. Praddy's fierce, dark eyes held the three words in the air between them. Richard blinked and looked away.

"Not like this, Prad. This isn't a Scouring; this is anarchy and it can become an opportunity if we all stick together to fight it. . . ."

"You swore, Richard, when you accepted the first transceiver," Pradesh reprimanded his friend. "Once was enough. No second times. No half times. No weaseling distinctions or retreats. Once was enough."

Once the Sharrh had come to Scour Merovin. They'd swept through the skies on fire-spewing ships, sterilizing their possession after humanity's taint, then the star-faring bugs abandoned it. Those men and women who survived the Scouring—those few individuals, self-selected for inborn stubbornness, tenacity, and fatalism—staggered out of their boltholes and set about rebuilding their shattered world. They dreamed wistfully of their ancestors soaring between the stars, and their increasingly distant cousins who, one hoped, still maintained humanity's tradition of exploration and colonization *out there*. But in their daily lives the survivors looked up at the stars with foreboding.

Once was enough.

The renascent society of Merovin was a society of denial: they denied themselves the technological wonders diagrammed in those archives so carefully preserved in the locked storerooms of Merovingen's College and similar fortresses of abnegation. Technology cast a shadow which might bring back the sharrh and the days of fire. They would never forget the philosophy of progress which carried humanity from Earth to the stars and from the stars to Merovin; but Merovin would never be allowed to progress.

Once was enough.

If the societies of Merovin *had* forgotten their origins—if they'd allowed themselves to forget—they might have known peace. Neither progress nor technology was an imperative coded into humanity's genes like eating, sleeping, or reproduction; wondrously complex societies could, and had, maintained themselves quite nicely without it. But the abandoned inhabitants of Merovin would not forget and invention lurked beneath the surface of their society like a stubborn infection. Each outbreak was fought and purged; each left scars of innovation. Progress occurred. Technology reappeared, subject to formal prohibition: it must not leave a trail.

Once was enough.

Richard recalled the afternoon he and Pradesh became friends. Karma, nothing more or less, had kept Richard from harassing Pradesh the way the other boys did. Murfy knew, Richard had greater opportunity to shout "Cat-nose" or "Rabbit-lips": The houses' nurseries faced each other and a voice did not have to be raised much at all to be heard across the canal separating them. But karma had held Dickon Kamat and Praddy St. John apart until they met on the flatland north of the city where their Houses administered adjacent farms. Dickon was searching for additions to his mineral collection; Pradesh was chasing a native butterfly with a net. Pradesh tripped over Richard and Richard hadn't said the first thing that popped into his mind.

By sundown they were friends, and hours overdue at the flatland pier. Men from St. John and Kamat formed a joint search party. The boys were found together and thrashed on the spot for the grief they'd caused their respective families. Shared punishment cemented their friendship for life.

So Richard knew the depth of Pradesh's rage against Merovingen's Revenantist hierarchy as no one else did. Praddy was not a St. John cousin, but the much-younger, half brother of Christen and Amitra who was denied his birthright. The cardinals had decreed his split lip was the karmic manifestation of the sins of a previous incarnation. The College would not, therefore, sanction the surgery necessary to repair it, and St. John would not acknowledge a congenitally deformed infant.

All that had changed when Amitra's legitimately contracted children drowned in a boating accident. The House of St. John had needed an heir. The cardinals had reconsidered their earlier decree; they retracted it before the mourning banners were removed from the high door. A flawed and unwanted younger brother was supposedly shipped off to a client's estate; a high-priced Nev Hettek surgeon was secretly summoned to the same estate; and some months later St. John legitimatized a supposedly distant cousin with the same name and a fresh scar between his nose and upper lip.

No one was fooled—least of all Praddy's schoolmates. Richard had many friends; Pradesh, to this very morning, had just one. In spite of his exhaustion—or perhaps because of it—Richard was uncomfortably aware he was far more important to Pradesh than Prad was to him. A part of him, an admirable part under most circumstances, wanted to find a compromise: he even reconsidered his own decision to remain in Merovingen.

As Richard's eyes darted from side to side, pursuing vagrant thoughts, and the silence in the vestibule lengthened, Pradesh became desperate and irritable. "It *is* karma, Dickon. Don't you see? Juarez's wireless transceivers are all in place now, we don't need the city any more. Every estate is in the network. We're closer to each other than all the bridges put together. It's time to go. Time to leave Merovingen to the Kalugins, the cardinals, and all their enemies. Let them destroy each other—but not us: Wex, Raza, Yakunin, Balaci, Martushev, all the others, *and* Kamat. We don't need Merovingen to trade with each other. A free confederacy of trade—remember,

Dickon?—a *free* confederacy of free Houses, trading freely with each other, with no one to tell us what we can or can't do, and spread so far over Merovin that not even the sharrh could Scour all of us. "It's what we've worked for, what we've been *waiting* for. Don't break ranks now we're so close to the dream."

Richard came back to his original decision. "Merovingen's my home," he said flatly. "I won't be driven out by anyone. If Kamat leaves, we leave in our own time, of our own choosing."

Pradesh released Richard's arm as the intangible chasm between them widened. "You still want to win their game with their rules."

Richard shook his head. He was beyond games and rules. His reasons for staying in the city were as simple as he claimed they were. He reached for his friend's hand. "I'm not breaking with you, Prad; I'm just not ready to abandon everything my House has stood for. The situation's not hopeless. It could even turn to our advantage. . . ."

But there was no persuading Pradesh St. John, nor any of the others whose disillusionment with all Merovingen stood for had been complete long before Mikhail Kalugin blundered into an assassin's trap. Richard let his arm drop.

"Tell any of your clients and tenants who stay behind that Kamat's staying too, and that they're welcome to join us. We'll preserve your island—in case you decide to come back."

"Burn it for all we care, Dickon. Burn it to the waterline."

Richard flinched to hear anyone seriously invoke Merovingen's ultimate curse. Pradesh had his rage to sustain him in exile, but what of the rest of his house, and the other houses joining the exodus? Some island families had never set foot on the estates to which they now retreated. Richard spent part of each year visiting Kamat's far-flung estates and *stancias*. He'd even lived a shepherd's life for a whole year under his uncle Bosnou's watchful eye. Merovingen could become much, much worse before it would be worse than the truly insular life of rural Merovin after the sharrh.

Although rural life had just changed tremendously with the introduction of wireless transceivers built by Juarez Wex from schematics smuggled out of the College library. Some nights the sky above Merovingen was quite congested with invisible messages. Juarez's transceivers had ended a six-hundred-year isolation.

"It won't come to that," Richard said with forced cheerfulness. "I'll keep you informed with the wireless. We won't burn bridges, or anything else, unless we have to. . . ."

Pradesh shuddered. For a moment Richard thought he'd found the means to stiffen the St. John spine and keep them on their island. Then Pradesh let his breath out slowly and the moment passed.

"Keep in touch, by all means, Dickon, but don't worry about the Isle."

Richard told himself that Praddy's condescending tone was fueled by a trace of shame or regret that the St. Johns were abandoning Merovingen quickly, completely, and without even a token of resistance. But, at best, it was only a trace.

Richard had understood the usefulness of the wireless transceivers from the moment he'd seen them demonstrated in the St. John cellars several months earlier, at the height of Willa Cardinal Exeter's orthodoxy campaign. He'd paid for the construction of six of them, the last of which had departed Merovingen with Bosnou after the wedding. The wireless was a good idea, an overdue resurrection from before the Scouring. It promised to bind Merovin's isolated pockets of humanity together as they had not been in six hundred years. Richard Kamat saw the promise of a better future in the devices, but Pradesh and others, it seemed, saw them as a way to escape from the present.

"I'll do what I can, Prad," Richard said finally. "May the tradewinds fill your sails and carry you south to port before Murfy knows you're on the sea—"

Pradesh responded with a different timeworn platitude and cranked the big latch handle to open the door. "There's still time, Dickon—if you change your mind. Kamat's always welcome. You're always welcome."

"Thanks." Richard's voice was hollow. Emotional weariness had joined forces with physical exhaustion. All he wanted to do was lock the door and drag himself up to the top of the stairs where his bed was waiting for him. He wasn't going back to the kitchen for breakfast and he wasn't going to leave Merovingen on the next tide: the two decisions balanced in his mind with equal importance.

Richard shoved the wide iron bolt through its brackets, sealing Kamat's formal entrance to all but the most determined intruder. He stood at the bottom of the stairs, reminding himself that more than ninety steps were between him and his bed, and wondered if, perhaps, the leather sofa in the library wouldn't be just as comfortable.

"M'ser! M'ser—come quick!"

Richard turned slowly. "I left m'ser Greg in charge," he muttered. "Can't he handle whatever it is?" His thoughts were running behind his mouth. The houseboy, whom Richard hardly recognized, hadn't come up to the mid-level of his own volition. Someone had sent him; probably Ashe or one of the other senior retainers, and Greg, undoubtedly, had already demonstrated that he *couldn't* handle it.

"Please, m'ser . . ." The boy writhed anxiously. "I waited 'til you were done talking with m'ser St. John. You've got to come quick now, *please.*"

Belatedly Richard realized the houseboy had gotten himself hung-up between his orders and his reluctance to interrupt his Househead's private conversation. "All right, I'm coming—"

The boy darted away like a shot arrow.

"Hold on, there. Wherever we're going, I'm not running until I know more about it!"

The boy's rope-soled shoes skidded to a halt on the polished wood floors of the upper house. "It's bad, m'ser. We got to hurry—"

Richard took the boy's sleeve. "Walk beside me and tell me everything you know." The conversation with Pradesh was locked behind a door in Richard's memory before the boy said his next word.

"There's been fighting up on the North Flat. The farm steward says he wants to leave his children here and take household folks up to the Flat in their stead."

Richard could imagine the rest: Greg had no instructions regarding the farmland and its residents; in the crush of events Richard himself had forgotten them. But, sure as the Det flowed south to the sea, Greg would have assumed a lack of specific instructions meant those people, and the valuable land around them, were unimportant. The narrow-minded young man had probably refused to let the steward's children into the house, and he almost certainly had refused to send house folk up to the Flat.

Wrapping his hand around the newel posts, Richard propelled himself down the stairway to the kitchen where the situation was every bit as sour as he feared. Greg's face was knotted with fury, his cheeks were an angry red, and his voice cracked as he tried to enforce his will by screaming at the frightened farm steward and disapproving house retainers.

"There's no room on the island for a lot of dirt farmers! We've got our own problems to worry about. Let them worry about themselves for a change!"

The steward, a bald man with a weathered face who looked to be somewhere on the far side of fifty, was clearly cowed by Greg's explosion. He crumpled his cap from one hand to the other and moved his lips without opening his mouth. But there was a second man with the steward, a younger man who'd carried his pitchfork all the way from the fields to Kamat's kitchen and looked like he might consider using it.

Richard interceded from the stairway. "Stand down, Greg!" There was no time to spare for his cousin's easily-bruised ego. "Any man who lives under a Kamat roof is as much a part of Kamat as you are! Their problems are our problems, and we'll do everything in our power to resolve them." He gave Greg a look that stung like the buckle of a father's belt.

The flush spread over Greg's face from his neck to his hairline. His emotions were easily read as they flowed from shock to humiliation and outrage. For a heartbeat the kitchen was quiet enough to hear the Det lapping at the pilings beneath the floorboards.

"Help them!?" Greg's hands folded into fists and rose slowly in front of him. "Help them!? Angel's blood, cousin, we can't help ourselves! There's fire, death, and destruction across our bridges and you want us to worry about *farmers*? They're on *land*! They can hitch up to a goddamned cart and get away from here, while we're stuck on this shaky little island waiting for our deaths to find us!"

"Gregor Kamat—that's enough!" Richard sensed the situation beginning to slip away from him. "If you can't stand as an example, go upstairs to your quarters—"

"I'm not going upstairs. I'm not going to be thrown out of my bed again. I want to get out of here, Richard! I want to get out of this house, out of Merovingen altogether!"

Throughout its history the city had been prone to earthquakes: one more thing the living could blame on the long-dead starfarers who'd brought humanity to Merovin—and botched the survey. There were the major ones that set the whole Det River sloshing and carving new channels—usually to Merovingen's detriment. There were the middling ones that happened maybe once in a lifetime and rearranged the city's architecture. And there were the minor ones which hit like a bad storm, one without wind, rain, or clouds.

In point of fact, Merovingen was nowhere near as fragile as its jumble of spires and bridges implied. Revenantist aversions notwithstanding, natives had learned a thing or two about keeping their city standing through flood, mud, hurricane, and the occasional earthquake. They'd had, after all, seven centuries for tinkering and experimentation. If Dorjan Isle had lost its family wing last night, then House Dorjan had only itself to blame: the previous night's quake had been neither major nor middling and far less destructive than a Turning gale.

A gale, however, heralded its coming. Seething clouds could be seen coming over the horizon and when it was gone it was over. Quakes came without warning. They might come alone, or in a series: ascending or descending. They were a betrayal of both logic and instinct: the ground was not solid, not strong, not safe. They were the clergy's favorite metaphor for the impermanence of mortal endeavor and the power of karma. And most people took both the sermons and the quakes—at least the minor ones—in thoughtless stride.

Richard had had the same reaction as Greg and everyone else last night when the ominous, yet familiar, heaving began beneath his feet. Was this the truly major one? Was this the karmic dividend to tear the Det valley apart—to dwarf assassination, fire, and all humanity with its power? He'd grabbed onto the railings and feared for his life. He'd held his breath without realizing it, until his world was spinning and heaving both. And then he'd filled his lungs with air, braced his feet, and called for a report of damages.

If the Lord had seen fit to spare him, his city, and his world, Richard Kamat wasn't going to waste precious time wondering why.

Of course, he'd been awake when the ground quaked—outside the house with a railing beside him and torches all around him—not dreaming in a dark bedroom, walls away from the next living soul. When the circumstances were right, when a man was already pushed to the limit, a storm or quake could unleash all the doubt and nightmare he'd hidden away since the moment of his birth.

Looking across the kitchen, Richard realized that his cousin Greg was just such an unfortunate man and there was nothing he could do for him except make matters worse.

"Go up to the library, then, or go outside and sit on a bench for a while. But *go!*"

"You're wrong, Richard. You're wrong to keep everyone here while there's still time to get away. Merovingen's *doomed*—don't you understand that? You're dooming everyone with your damned Revenantist karma. St. John's going! Dorjan! Eber! Zorya burned down last night! What's wrong with you, Richard? Does everybody else have to die first?"

Greg bulled his way past the farmers. His bootheels echoed against the floorboards until he reached the dock door which slammed behind him. Then Richard had the undivided attention of everyone in the kitchen. He'd have preferred to explain their neighbors' impending departure in his own way and at his own time—if he was going to explain or acknowledge it at all—but Greg had just forced his hand and judging by the expressions scattered around the room, a sizable number of Kamat folk were ready to abandon the house and the city.

The farmers had precipitated a crisis among the house folk that threatened to sweep Kamat and its worries aside. Richard stared at them with their rigid, stubborn-child expressions and distinctive homespun clothes. He wished to Murfy, the Angel, and the Lord himself that they'd simply go away and let him tend to more important affairs.

But they didn't budge.

"They're coming out of Merovingen-proper like rats from the flood," the steward said flatly. "We stood on the walls and held them off 'til the sun was up. —Course, me and Willy left right after that, so there's no telling what's happened since. But if it's half as bad as these folk say it is in town, there's no way we'll hold the barns or the crops for harvest. Swampies and canal-rats—," he meant the two-footed kind, "—be like to trample anything they can't kill or eat right off."

Richard thought of the boats in the Kamat gut, and the Ventani market on the island's northeast exposure. Riots led to looting, looting to hoarding. While he was still a child, Richard had seen that spiral threaten when floods rose at the wrong time and the view from the Rock was broken dikes and fields drowning in brack water. In those times the Lion of Kalugin had earned his keep: confiscating House warehouses, farms, and markets until the next harvest, if necessary, to keep the peace.

That wouldn't happen this time. The Houses were isolated from their warehouses and markets. The farms on the Flat were sitting pretty and full of food behind their easily climbed dikes. Merovingen could run out of food *long* before Karl Fon or anyone else managed to set up a blockade.

Should Kamat leave its wooden fortress to defend its food supply? The farms on the Flat could feed the Isles. They couldn't shelter people on scarce cropland. Should they confiscate the Ventani market? Should they pull the steward and the other farm families to Kamat Isle and leave the farm to looters? Or send reinforcements to the farm from the Isle? The problems and their solutions were equally obscure. The only thing that was clear was that Richard Kamat *was* Kamat; and all the decisions—and all their consequences—belonged to him.

The Househead's heart was pounding faster than it had during the quake, and he wanted nothing more than to escape to the free air outside the kitchen as Greg had done. He wasn't old enough, or wise enough, to hold the lives of some four hundred people in his hands. They should know better than to stare at him the way they were staring, expecting him to have the answers. Or to take the blame for his ignorance.

That sniveling thought was no sooner growing in Richard's mind than he saw the downcast eyes and twitching lips on the faces of Ashe and Ralf, who might well have come to the same conclusion. Even Eleanora Slade, who shared his bed and privacy and who'd slipped down the back stairs without anyone already in the kitchen noticing, averted her eyes when her househead looked at her. Then a contradicting thought erupted: Richard *liked* being the head of his house and suddenly found his doubts an insufficient reason to surrender that position.

And as humanity was always disposed towards doing what it *liked* doing, doubt ceased to grow in Richard's mind.

Richard had karma—crystal clear karma, Pradesh said—and maybe he was *thinking* like a Merovingian, clinging to it in a faith that his web of accumulated debts would take him safely and swiftly to a decision no reason could find, transcend the adrenalin panic in his body and the stagnant doubts in his mind. Like the generations-native in front of him, he opened himself to receive whatever bolt of inspiration karma would fling his way.

Gunshots: the hiccups of small arms' fire and the deeper cough of a cannon. There were cannon emplacements above the New Harbor and more up on the Rock, but the repeated cannon coughs had a closer source: the Spur, where Anastasi's blackleg militia had its armory, and the Justiciary where Tatiana's blackleg civil force had taken shelter and fired back.

Guided by karma, Richard's thought turned from whatever skirmish might be boiling on the Spur to the panic those sounds must be causing wherever Families were piling their valuables onto boats. And the panic among those who were being left behind. God knew, most people *were* being left behind. Adventist God and Revenantist karma—

"It can be done," Richard said as the plan unfolded in the light of karma owed. Debts everywhere. It was the *essence* of Merovingen. Interdependency. "There are more than enough upright men and women left to keep Merovingen upright. All it wants is bringing them together and giving them common purpose—" He was unaware that he spoke aloud, and unaware for an instant he'd captured the imagination of the upright men and women around him. 'Til he saw their faces.

"But *how?*" one of them asked.

Richard's exhaustion vanished along with his doubts. He had answers, and he gave them freely.

ONCE WAS ENOUGH (REPRISED)

by Lynn Abbey

Throughout the remainder of the morning messengers trooped in and out of the Kamat kitchen. Some wore Kamat livery and tried to deliver Richard's hastily-written vellum letters to those Househeads who remained accessible to receive them. Some wore the livery of other nearby Houses and carried documents of transfer and pewter seals in their letter pouches. Many were lesser clients and tenants cut adrift from their house contracts. Barricades on the bridges between the central islands of the South Bank quarter were taken down and replaced by cross-canal blockades along their perimeter. A deputation of fifty men and women armed, by and large, with the tools of their erstwhile trades made their way to the North Flat farms to reestablish a useful sort of order. There were signs that the Ventani had come to the same conclusion as Kamat—at least a purposeful militia in Ventani colors had been spotted going up the Greve toward *their* farmland. This last could not be confirmed: Ventani was not answering any of its doors and Richard's messengers reported the whole West End was buttoned up more tightly than Kamat's South Bank quarter.

Paul Kamat, awakened from a six-hour sleep, went up to the farm to act as Richard's hands, eyes, and ears. More importantly, he took the St. John wireless transceiver with him to establish communications between the North Flat and the house.

"It's the least you can do, m'ser, to protect your karma as well as your House," Richard had said to Christen St. John while pointedly stirring another glass of tea that had steeped so long it was black as the Det herself. "You'll hardly need it where you're going if you don't intend to look back."

The transceiver itself could be hidden inside a nondescript wooden chest, but its generator and antenna—disguised these last few months as a copper-clad lightning rod—could be identified by the knowledgeable and were all the more eye-catching on the deck of a canaler chugging upstream as fast as its motor could move it. The battered, besieged College was not completely moribund and, as individual spies scurried to their individual masters, was not pleased by this public display of often-rumored, strictly-prohibited technology, though envy vied with orthodox outrage as the source of their displeasure. The College was, however, in disarray—as evidenced by the four separate messengers admitted through the blockade to Kamat's kitchen, each of whom claimed to speak for Willa Cardinal Exeter herself and each of whose warrants confiscated the technology in the name of a different, non-Exeter, house.

Richard Kamat politely ignored them all.

There were defeats as well as victories as the sun arced overhead. One of Kamat's messengers, her throat slit from ear to ear, was thrown from a speeding fancyboat. Two others had not come back at all. Despite Richard's personal arm-twisting, none of the other South Bank families decided to stand with

Kamat; their heavily guarded convoy passed through
the blockade several hours behind schedule, too late
to catch the first watch tide. Gregor Kamat was with
them in a Kamat-owned skip, along with his father,
Richard's uncle, Patrik. This despite Richard's promise to send them to Bosnou when the Kamat packet
boat returned in four days' time.

"There won't be anything left in four days' time,"
Greg insisted, wedging another parcel of god-knew-
what into the bulging cubby. "What the Sword doesn't
destroy will be swallowed by the quakes and the sea."

Richard didn't argue. The fewer nay-sayers he had
in his own house, the better. He was hurt, though, to
see Ashe among departees. Ashe was neither a client
nor a tenant, merely the major-domo who opened the
mid-level door and delivered the morning mail. He
wouldn't even live on Kamat Island, though he'd
worked long enough and loyally enough to earn sine-
cure housing. But he took Richard's offer to pay the
passage for anyone under Kamat's shield. Richard had
taken it for granted that the dour retainer would stay
in Merovingen and the sight of him crowded shoulder-
to-shoulder with the St. John entourage, clutching his
life's possessions in a black canvas sack like some
storm-racked refugee sapped the young househead's
confidence.

Richard's hands began to tremble as the convoy
passed under the Kamat-Sofia bridge on its way to the
Grand Canal. He rested them on the walkway railing
as waves of nausea brought a cold sweat to his face
and back. The planks shifted beneath his feet, as they
had during the quake—but no one else noticed. He
clutched the railing to keep from falling over and

tried, unsuccessfully, to gulp back the bile rising from his stomach.

It was the tea, he told himself. He'd had nothing to eat or drink all day except rot-gut tea with honey. He could taste it at the back of his throat. It was tea, not karma, that was making him weak in the knees. Tea and Bosnou's wedding brew which had scarred his stomach.

"You look poorly, m'ser." A stout, motherly woman with her hair bound in a kerchief and with a stained white apron around her waist tried to guide him gently from the rail.

Richard knew her—she was the family cook in whose kitchen he'd sat most of the day—but, for his life, he could not remember her name. The failure of memory was more disturbing than the thing forgotten. Meek and mute, the househead allowed himself to be led to a bench where he sat wondering if he had suddenly gone mad.

The cook put a hard-crust knob of bread in his hand. "You didn't eat, m'ser, and you haven't slept. You've been strict enough with the others—keeping 'em fed and rested—but you're cheating on yourself."

"Tonight will be crucial," Richard said, confiding in her because she was there and he was not fully aware of himself. "If we can keep the gangs out of South Bank—if we hold the farm— All *ifs*. There's no guessing what anyone else will do . . . or who anyone else *is*. I can't let go, can't leave things to chance."

"Might be better, m'ser." She caught the bread as it fell from his fingers. "Chance is even and, m'ser, you're not."

Richard recalled her name. "Alice. Alice Maihall. You live above the kitchen . . . with your man and five children. . . ." His skin was clammy and it seemed for a moment that his body's whole strength and purpose was dedicated to his heart which he could feel thumping rapidly against his breastbone. He wasn't going mad—he was having a coronary seizure. He was twenty-eight years old, and having a heart attack. Karma.

"Dickon— Boy, what's the matter with you?" Richard stared into the face of the family's longtime physician, Dr. Jonathan.

Alice said, "He's burned himself up." She brandished her fresh-baked roll for the doctor before putting it once again in Richard's hand. "Some fool scullion left the leaves to steep the whole live-long day and the tea's fit to stand a spoon in—and he's been drinking it like water."

Dr. Jonathan's lips puckered at the thought. "That's the source of it, all right. Go upstairs, Dickon—m'ser, and have a bit of a rest until the acid passes."

He was not going mad and he was *not* having a heart attack; it *was* the tea, after all, just as he had thought when the nausea struck him. He smiled wanly and tried to rise—thinking that knowing the cause of his illness was the same as being rid of it. Dr. Jonathan tapped his shoulder lightly and he sat back down with a thud.

"Doctor's orders, m'ser Househead. I'll see you to your room as soon as you eat that nice fresh bread you've got in your hand."

That, the eating part anyway, was suddenly irresistible. Richard tore off the shiny brown crust with his teeth and chewed it slowly. As the bread sweetened in his mouth, the nausea and the cold sweats retreated. "I'm all right," he insisted. He felt strong enough to push the doctor aside. "There's work to be done. I'll have something more to eat in the kitchen."

"You'll have it upstairs," the physician disagreed, refusing to be shoved aside. "You're no good to anyone right now, m'ser."

"There's no one else. Paul's up on the farm. Ashe is gone. I'm needed."

"You're needed *healthy*, m'ser, not vibrating like an overheated skit. You are as important as you think you are, and this is no time for heroics."

Richard could have ordered Dr. Jonathan to stand aside, and wanted to—except he knew the man was right. He'd done exactly what he'd forbidden Paul and the others to do: squander himself without food or sleep. And the over-steeped tea, coming on top of everything else, was the final insult.

"The sooner you rest, the sooner you'll be yourself again," Dr. Jonathan said, putting his thumb on the proverbial scales.

"All right—I'm going." He tore off another mouthful of bread.

This time the doctor allowed Richard to rise, but kept his hand lightly on the younger man's arm to steady him.

"Murfy's ghost," Richard complained, shrugging free. "I'm a grown man. I can get to my room by myself."

The physician and the cook exchanged furtive glances, each confirming the other's diagnosis: too much tea, too much stress, and too far gone to know it. But neither of them wanted to cause a scene—not outside the house where there'd be a hundred witnesses and who knew what in the way of disastrous consequences.

Dr. Jonathan held the door open. "You could use my room, if you prefer, m'ser. It's below the mid-level—not so far to climb."

Richard shook his head and, chewing on the last of the bread, began the long climb up the back stairs to his private quarters in the tallest spire of the island. He regretted his stubbornness before he was above the mid-level, especially when he heard the ropes and pulleys of the dumb-waiter ferrying his dinner to the heights above him. He'd burned through the bread; the nausea was back, though not as bad as before. His hair stuck to his forehead and he was panting by the time he reached the landing where the back stairway joined the main stairway for the final twelve-step ascent to his bedroom suite.

Eleanora Slade was waiting for him. "I heard the food trays . . . Dickon—you look terrible!"

Wiping his sweaty face on his sleeve, Richard decided Eleanora didn't look much better: her face was pale and tight with anxiety. But he wasn't so far gone that he'd say *that* to her. "Tea's gone acid on me," he said instead. "Nothing worse than that. A few hours, a bit of spongy food in my stomach—"

"Can you come upstairs to your office, then? Your uncle's been hammering up a storm on the wireless."

Richard's weight settled on his heels. He gripped the handrail and pulled himself forward, upward: twenty-four steps instead of twelve.

The wireless, using bits and pieces of approved tech from in-house tappers, completely covered a large table in Richard's office. The generator, with its banks of acid storage batteries, was outside on the walkway under its own shelter, and the antenna, like St. John's, had been incorporated into the lightning rod. The hammering to which Eleanora had referred came from a brass device inside a glass dome. The device recorded incoming messages by translating the electronic code into marks on a narrow strip of paper, which fed through the dome from a neatly wound roll to a tangled heap on the floor.

Eleanora gave the tangle an unfriendly look. She came from a different stratum of Merovingen society, a layer where Revenantist teachings about the evils of progressive technology went unchallenged. The wireless was certainly progressive technology. In the part of her that still lived in an airless two-room flat, Eleanora knew a telegraph was one thing—the Houses did use them (even between Isles, what time that thieves hadn't made off with the wire). But a transceiver—*that*, she knew was a monster and evil, and apt to draw the sharrh back from wherever they were waiting. Still, the part of her that had been raised up to share Dickon's life—a *househead's* life—bravely resisted that knowledge: Richard trusted her as much as he loved her and so, when circumstances had dictated that he conduct Kamat's urgent business from the kitchen, he'd sent her up to his office to transcribe the messages coming in from the North Flat and everywhere else.

"May I wait for you downstairs?" she asked, her Revenantist fear of the machine showing clearly now that Richard was here to lift the responsibility from her shoulders.

The weighted, balanced, and razor-sharp brass arm within the glass dome began to chatter. Paper spewed out of the dome's base and the snaky mass on the carpet began to rustle with its own false life.

"I'll take care of it," Richard assured his unacknowledged wife. "You go ahead downstairs and relax. You've earned it."

She was gone before he drew another breath. The brass arm rose too high, striking a restraining bar which even casual observation could tell was a jury-rigged afterthought. The paper strip jammed. Richard sighed with resignation, not panic, and disconnected the toggle switch that directed the electric signal from the transceiver to the recording device. Perching over a clerk's high stool, he reached for a set of leather and wire earmuffs and fastened them over his head. Then he winced and fiddled with one of the many odd-shaped knobs.

The Voice of Doom, Bosnou Kamat had named it when Richard brought him to the spire for a demonstration after Marina's wedding—when the crews and construction necessary to install it were indistinguishable from those repairing the damage the wedding feast had caused.

The Voice of Doom—but that hadn't stopped the old man from learning the archaic moss code it used to reduce words to electric impulses. Moss code, so called, one presumed, because moss plants were as primitive and spreading as the signals the wireless transmitted. Bosnou swore he'd never permit the wireless into his house—and he'd kept his word. The *stancia* transceiver was in its own building on a hilltop almost a kilometer from the main house.

Richard wondered why—unless his great uncle wanted to escape from his ever-expanding family. Bosnou sent all the messages himself—there was no mistaking his heavy hand on the spark-key, which, coupled with the position of the antenna made the *stancia* signal one of the strongest and clearest ones in

the newborn network. It blasted everything else in the
sky, including Paul's signal from the much, much
closer North Flat farm.

Richard opened the log book and began transcribing
the message.

—*Wrong. Kamat home, this is uncle. Where are you.
What is wrong. Kamat—*

He held the spark-key down for a five-count—the
conventional request for quiet. He'd gotten no more
than a few words into a terse, cautious response when
his ears were assaulted again.

F-O-R-G-E-T K-A-L-U-G-I-N!

The wireless was ideal for the lightning-swift trans-
mission of short messages: when the packet boat left,
what it carried, when it would arrive with his niece
and sister. It was less well-suited to conversation about
subtle or sensitive matters. And, not to be forgotten,
it was not private: the signal sent by one transceiver
could be received by all the others. Could be, and
probably was, and although Richard knew which families had taken custody of one or more of the devices
he could not know if the other six in Merovingen itself
remained in that custody or if they had fallen into
other hands.

One could do worse, short-term, than attract the
attention of the sharrh.

No questions, Richard hammered on the spark-key.
We're safe. That's all. And concluded with an
emphatic request for quiet, which Bosnou, for the
moment, respected. Richard leaned on his elbows and
pinched the bridge of his nose. A fainter message
came to his ears:

*First watch. Farm quiet. Nothing moving on the
Greve. Murfy he's got a heavy—*

ONCE WAS ENOUGH (REPRISED)

Richard put his own fist on the spark-key to quiet Paul, then listened as one of the Wex estates identified itself and pleaded for information. Richard's hand hovered above the spark-key before he changed his mind and closed the toggle switch to reconnect the recording device. He was fixing the paper jam Bosnou's heavy fist had caused when he realized he wasn't alone in the room: Denny Tai, born Deneb Takahashi and destined to be head of that house if he lived long enough, stood in the doorway with his arms wrapped around a wooden crate both longer and broader than he was himself.

Denny's mouth was open. When the brass arm began to rise and fall for no reason or cause the boy could possibly fathom, he jumped and lost control of the crate. It crashed to the floor, shaking the whole spire and jamming the paper strip. Eleanora came up behind Denny at a run.

"What's wrong?" she asked, though the answer was obvious.

Richard sank heavily onto the stool, the wood-on-wood crash still echoing inside his head. Murfy— Murfy understood and, maybe, Murfy *caused* moments like this when one's self seemed a small frantic creature, utterly powerless against the circumstances of one's life. Circumstances which ranged from the green nausea billowing in his gut to the jammed recording device, to Eleanora's worried, disapproving face, to Denny himself, who was now a party to the wireless conspiracy, and that box lying at his feet, half-open and spilling sawdust, steel, and crimson velvet onto the carpet. One forgot, for the moment, the primary cause: Merovingen, Nev Hettek, the Sword of God, the Kalugins, anarchy, fire, earthquake, and the

265

spate of gunshots once again reverberating through the canals.

"Nothing," Richard murmured, pinching his nose again as he drew a deep breath which was supposed to help and didn't. The nausea shifted color to red and became a sharp pain that made him want to do nothing more than crawl into a corner to die.

"You're ill," Eleanora said, seeking a way past the boy and the box. "Come, your food's waiting."

"No. It's nothing! Go back downstairs. I'll be down to eat when I'm ready to eat." His voice was cruelly sharp, and he didn't care. The pain ebbed to bearable—and familiar. He had plaster-y pills in his lavatory below, that helped sometimes, and an amber elixir that was mostly brandy. The last thing he wanted right then was food.

Eleanora retreated as if she'd been physically assaulted. The door to their shared bedroom slammed shut. At least she hadn't gone running all the way down to the servants' quarters as she sometimes did when his frustration made her the tempting target.

In the meantime, the paper had backed up until it triggered a nerve-rattling, thought-scattering buzzer. Richard flailed behind him until he found the main switch and shut everything off.

Denny danced from side to side in the doorway. He was canny and clever. He had a fair idea of what he'd stumbled into and the instinct to run far and fast. But he was fascinated, too, and that, in a boy his age, was stronger than instinct.

"What is that?" His eyes were riveted to the device-filled table behind Richard. *"Wow—"* He came across the carpet like a hooked fish.

"It's a wireless transceiver," Richard said flatly, and told, by rote, its history.

How after Willa Cardinal Exeter closed the College library to curb the overflow of progress and technology, students had begun smuggling the books themselves. And yes—Denny's older brother Raj probably smuggled a few himself. And no—Raj had nothing whatsoever to do with the books, or the conspiracy to build the transceivers, which brought an oddly mature sigh from the boy's bony chest.

"Raj gets hisself *involved*," Denny said.

Richard didn't respond, but concluded the much-abbreviated, nameless tale: "Once was enough, Deneb—" The boy was, after all, the heir of a trade house and in desperate need of education. "When we couldn't rely on civil authorities to look after our interests, we had to arrange to look after them ourselves. The Det Valley is too vital to all Mcrovin to become a political pawn. Karl Fon, the Kalugins—the whole lot of them—stand in the way of trade. And we will not—" Richard's eyes focused beyond the boy. "We will *not* lose what little we've gained in the past six hundred years."

Denny nodded. "But no *wires*? How's it work?"

"It sends messages," Richard said with a shrug. "Electrically . . . On waves through the sky." The principles of operation had never been clear to him. Truth to tell: Richard had not tried very hard to understand them when Juarez Wex—disillusioned Juarez Wex who tried to teach physics at the college—had explained them. Richard didn't need to know how the wireless worked, any more than he needed to know how the phosphorescent plankton in the new moon tide fixed Kamat's indigo dyes into their trademark First-Bath blue. It was sufficient to know that they were reliable.

A boy, however, had different priorities: "Like when you see your voice in the air on raw, damp morning?" Denny examined the apparatus at close range with his hands clasped tightly behind his back.

"Like that, I guess," Richard replied absently, as interested in Denny's abandoned box as Denny was in the transceiver.

"So—where do you talk into? What's the paper for? I mean, I seen tappers, but not like this. How come—?"

Richard grabbed a thick sheaf of paper and waggled it in front of the boy's face. "Read this, if you're so damned curious—and don't *touch* anything. And stay right here until I get back."

" 'The Starscout Explorer's Manual. Part Four. Radio—' Did you copy this? Is this your writing?—I can hardly read it—"

Richard flinched midway between his stool and the door. His script had always been labored; he never wrote unless he had to, and since becoming Househead he could pass almost everything to a secretary. But copying Juarez's manual had been one of the conditions for receiving the transceivers; he wanted the apparatus, so he'd dutifully copied each page and diagram—paying scant attention to its legibility.

"Read it or not," he said irritably, thinking mostly of the white pills on the shelf in the lavatory and the hot-water plumbing that reached across the roof to his Househead's quarters but not as far as this office. "But don't touch anything!" He turned and tripped over the box, lunged to catch his balance on the doorframe, then stayed bent-over with his hand clutched over his gut until the knifing pain passed.

"Dammit, Deneb!—what is *this* you've hauled up here?"

The boy was off the stool in a flash, leaving the manual to flutter page by page to the carpet. "The sword, m'ser Richard." Meaning the sword of his own house, the Takahashi of Nev Hettek, forged on Old Earth and sent to Kamat of Merovingen for safekeeping. "I waited for Raj to come—t' show me how to pack it up. He remembers, y' know, but I don't; I was too young. But Raj ain't here and he isn't at the College—"

Richard blanched at the thought of Denny spying out the College earlier this afternoon, and blanched with the pain that followed the thought.

"I should've gone with Great Uncle Bosnou. I should've taken the sword with me."

Denny's shame and despair were real enough. Bosnou had a gift for taming wild creatures, including teenage boys He'd offered to take the boy back to the *stancia*. Denny wanted to go as he hadn't wanted anything just for himself in a long time, but Raj was mooning over a girl again and Denny felt obligated to stay behind. Raj, as he said, got involved, and more than once Raj had needed his younger brother's canniness to get un-involved.

"But I couldn't find Raj, and I didn't get the sword wrapped and into the box until *after* m'ser Greg left so I couldn't give it to him to take with him to the Chat ship in the harbor—"

God help us, Richard thought, imagining the consequences if Denny's plans had not gone awry. Takahashi's sword with Greg bound for the Chattalen: the mind boggled, and he'd been a fool not to spare one thought for the brothers since this whole fiasco began.

"—So I was bringing it to you—to put with the Kamat jewels while I went lookin' for Raj—just in case something happens—"

"Nothing's going to happen. You're not going anywhere." The knife spun in Richard's gut. "Just stay here—right here—until I get back." He stumbled down the twelve steps to his quarters.

The regulator clock on the mantel in Richard's office marked off an hour before the downstairs door reopened. Eleanora, it seemed, was in league with Dr. Jonathan, and not about to let her beloved escape without proper care. She let him take the chalk pills and insisted he eat the bland, acid-absorbing meal the cook had prepared for him earlier. She wanted him to lie down and rest, if not sleep.

"Merovingen can get by without you for the night. You know what'll happen if that ulcer perforates."

Richard did: blood poisoning, peritonitis, and a hideously lingering death. Courtesy of history, Dr. Jonathan could diagnose most of humanity's infirmities; courtesy of the Scouring he lacked the skills to heal them. Ulcers were not something to be taken lightly or ignored.

"Denny's still up there—with the transceiver and with his family sword."

Eleanora accepted defeat graciously. "Try not to be long, and try not to get upset with him."

The boy didn't hear Richard coming up the stairs. He was hunched over the spark-key, with the headset clamped over his ears, scribbling in the margins of the Starscouts' manual. Richard's inclination was to get upset, but he took pity on his gut.

"You've just been *listening*, haven't you?"

Denny was properly startled and chastised. "You was gone so long—"

"But you didn't send anything?"

"No, m'ser. I thought—I put it together that if you had one o' these, maybe all the other Houses did. And I was going to see if maybe somebody knew where Raj was." Richard glowered and Denny hurried to reassure him. "But I didn't, m'ser—honest. I just been listenin'. Ever'body else's been sending stuff. . . ."

Richard believed the boy. "It can get pretty thick sometimes," he agreed. He began to scoop the sawdust from the carpet back into the sword box.

"I'll say. And sneaky, too."

"Eh?" He froze with his hands full.

"Yeah, somebody'll start something, and then somebody else'll sort of slide in on top to try to finish it. I'll tell you one thing, m'ser Dick, I wouldn't make secrets on this thing. Not the way it is now."

"I figured that the moment I saw the recorder. It's like whispering in a crowded room, Deneb: you only say things you want everyone to hear. The wireless is useful, but it surely isn't confidential."

"Not the way it is now," the boy agreed, "with ever'-body using the same fre-quency."

He'd read the manual carefully, but not—Richard decided—carefully enough.

"We've got to use the same frequency to receive and transmit," he said, joining Denny at the table. "There's no other way."

Denny hesitated, he was bold and brash, but not stupid, and not knowing how Richard Kamat took correction he wasn't sure he should say anything at all.

Except for Raj—who wasn't where he was supposed to be or anywhere else—and Tom and Jones.

"There's two things you could do. First you could make another code, instead of this 'un, that'd fool whoever was listenin'. But you could also change the freq'ency—" Deneb got excited and his hard-won grammar went to hell.

"Who'd be able to listen?"

"Anyone who knew what we'd changed it to; anyone you told. See—look here:" Denny pointed to one of Richard's sloppily transcribed schematics. "That's supposed to be a modulator, and you can set it wherever you want. You could have as many different waves as you wanted, and no one'd be able to spy on ye 'less you told 'im what your wavelength was. I can't find the real 'un by looking at this thing—but it's got t' be here, 'cause everything *else* is. Unless whoever made these left it off—" Denny swallowed the rest of his words when Richard moved away from the table to stare out the windows at the early evening light.

"A modulator?"

"Yeah," Denny said, then added, softly: "Didn't ye read what ye wrote, m'ser?"

Richard shook his head. "No, I didn't." He was certain Juarez Wex hadn't said a single word about modulators or wavelengths when he demonstrated the transceivers. And he was just as certain Juarez knew about them and all the boy implied with them, and so, therefore, did all of Wex which wouldn't be above taking advantage where advantage was to be taken. "Dammit."

"M'ser? M'ser, I'm sorry—but you said to read it, and I did. Maybe I don't read so well, and you don't write so well, neither. And this Starscouts' manual—

it's *old*, m'ser. It's got a lot of words I never saw before—so maybe I'm wrong about it all."

"You're not wrong, Deneb. You're smart. Your grandfather knows what he's doing. He's got one of these machines, too—you should know that, along with the rest. . . ."

There was an explosion to the west. Thick black smoke shot into the sky. Night was coming and it was starting again.

"What's goin' t' happen to us, m'ser?" Denny left the wireless untended and stood in front of Richard, watching the smoke billow.

"I don't know." Richard draped his arms over Denny's shoulders. "I've got to get you out, though, you and the sword. I owe that to your grandfather. I'll send both of you to Uncle Bosnou. You'll—"

Denny twisted free. "You can't. I won't go—not without Raj."

They bargained then, and swiftly. Denny wanted to find Raj only so they could leave Merovingen together. Richard promised he'd search Merovingen island by island until they knew where Raj was, or where he had gone. Besides, the Kamat packet boat wasn't due for four days. Denny figured—silently, of course, that he could find *anything* in four whole days. The agreement was sealed with a man-to-man handshake.

Together they closed the sword crate and stood it carefully by the mantel.

"What about the wireless?" Denny asked. "Shouldn't somebody stay up here listenin'?"

Richard nodded. He hadn't settled in his mind who that would be. It wouldn't be Denny—though desire burned in the boy's eyes and he seemed to have an aptitude for it. He put a hand on the boy's neck and herded him to the door. Uncle Bosnou could deal with that enthusiasm, Richard thought; and formed an image of the two of them in a shepherd's hut hunched over the Voice of Doom. It would probably come to pass, given the personalities involved, and Merovin would never be the same.

Karma. Endless, cyclic karma harnessed to the dynamic of change and progress.

Once was enough for anything.

ENDGAME (CONCLUDED)

by C. J. Cherryh

The weapons-fire was light through the day, desultory shots from one position toward movement in another. And there was movement going on. Mondragon listened to it with half an ear, from his own position on Spellbridge—a resting position, lying on a slanted timber brace of Spellbridge East High, catching a kind of drowsing sleep in the shadow—never deep sleep, just the kind that an exhausted body imposed on a distraught and busy mind.

He'd lost Min's skip. It had gotten him through the fire, across the Grand and onto Archangel, before the shelling and the rifle fire had gotten too thick: it was Anastasi's yacht he wanted, that black boat that was blasting away with its cannon at the Justiciary, while Tatiana's forces, trying to maneuver from the Justiciary, where they held all levels, invaded the College and battled Anastasi's same-uniformed militia for control of the roof. Won that fight, by what he could tell.

Rooftops and high bridges were the matter under contention just before the dawn made movement difficult, and from what Mondragon could tell, the militia had the roof of Spellbridge, maybe Kass, and the College bottom floor; Tatiana's forces had the Justiciary, were fortifying themselves on the College roof, while, the way Mondragon saw it, the governor's personal guard still probably had the Signeury, and what was probably going on out there in the daylight was setting up better cover and emplacements on the roofs; not mentioning delegations from one faction and the other scurrying about to Signeury making offers to papa Iosef—if Iosef would listen to either of his surviving offspring. Either was offering papa the other's head. Doubtless.

And Mondragon lay up here on a timber broad enough to support most of his shoulders and his feet, wrapped in Min's old gray patchwork cloak, that was the best camouflage he could come up with, and a defense against the chill that blew up from the canals. Mondragon felt a little flutter of his heart when a mild quake shook the timbers: it made a man think of that fall at the edge of sleep. But it wasn't illusion, it was Merovingen settling that much deeper in fear and chaos.

He had resources he could draw on—Kamat, perhaps, but Kamat had betrayed him, Kamat hadn't seen Jones to safety, and maybe that wasn't Kamat's fault: Jones was hard to catch—or maybe Kamat had come through at the last and gotten Jones away. He could construct a scenario in which Jones, straight from a near miss with Chance's men, might have gone to Kamat and gotten snatched upriver—exactly what he'd paid Richard Kamat to do, if Kamat could lay hands on her.

But Jones had never quite trusted Kamat, perhaps because Richard didn't deal with her, only with him, which might suggest to Jones where Richard might get his instructions in her case: which might suggest to

Jones that she'd be a fool to walk in on Kamat and trust to get out again.

And he wished he could think that Jones would think the same thing about Anastasi Kalugin. But Jones had never understood Anastasi as well as he had. She had never had the occasion. Thank God.

He turned his head. From where he was, on Spellbridge High, he could see the black yacht lying across Spellbridge West entry off Archangel—he'd learned the cant and the nomenclature of the canals. He'd learned to think canaler and breathe canaler and to understand why canalers hated that black ship, that had as soon run them under as give way.

But Jones only knew that he had ties to Anastasi and never understood how Anastasi threatened her— he very much feared that she didn't; because, dammit, he hadn't explained to her *why* he couldn't trust Anastasi without getting into things he didn't want her to know—he'd asked her just to believe him; and that, with Jones, wasn't enough. She was like him. She knew how pressure made people do things they wouldn't do, and lie to people they loved, and every damned, damnable thing that might make a person do or say something that hadn't a thing to do with love, and everything to do with self-esteem, or necessity, or whatever else was tangled up in his dealings with Anastasi—

And Fon. One triggered what the other had set up somewhere deep inside and he wasn't rational, Karl hadn't left him rational, rational had died somewhere in prison, in hopes held out and snatched back, in attachments offered and taken away—

He couldn't make her understand that. He couldn't tell her and not telling her—he might have killed her.

That was the thought that went around and around in his mind, that was the thought that had him here instead of down at Moghi's looking. The fact was that Anastasi could have her, and if he didn't she could still turn up here, on that harborside, slipping past him in the multitudinous routes a skip could travel, and if there was a game yet to play, with the power he had left—it was down there, on that black yacht . . .

. . . because Anastasi wouldn't kill him till Anastasi knew what he did know, knew what he might have told Chance, or through Chance, Tatiana. For a man whose intention was war with Nev Hettek the moment he was in power—what Thomas Mondragon might have held back from 'Stasi Kalugin could be critical; and what Thomas Mondragon might have heard inside the Nev Hettek embassy or why Thomas Mondragon was loose now was all information Anastasi would want to have before he signed off.

Which meant the people closest to 'Stasi wouldn't shoot him on sight. Tatiana's folk wouldn't either. An ignorant militiaman might. Which was what he was doing up here in the timbers of Spellbridge High East, looking down on canalside, where he had a view of the gangway that let people come and go from the yacht, and the deck around it; and a hope of seeing someone who could get him to Anastasi.

Couldn't plan on picking 'Stasi off from here, though he had a rifle on that slanted beam above him—a militiaman had provided that last night. He'd tested it during the firing, thought he hadn't that much ammunition, and it was no marksman's rifle. It was a contingency—in the remote scenario that he had 'Stasi in clear sight and standing still, or that he had to discourage someone climbing up here. The rifle was a remoter chance than he liked; and more noise than he liked; and more immediately provocative than he liked—'Stasi liked his victims more compliant, and more afraid—'Stasi *liked* scaring hell out of you, and the more dangerous you were and the more he scared you, the better it was for 'Stasi—just like Karl.

That was one thing about Karl he'd explained to Chance. Told him things Karl didn't put out in public, and if Chance had known all of it, he'd no way to tell. He didn't think so. Chance was a professional and Chance didn't have damn much patience with fools— as Karl was, on a personal level. That was the great secret: Karl was ultimately a fool. Ultimately someone would find his self-indulgence and kill him with it. But not before Karl had run his course, and alienated enough of his own elite, or chosen an elite who'd alienate the people, and kill the revolution they'd used to believe in. Then there'd be another revolution. Or somebody would just pick off Karl, somebody who had access, and no scruples, and no hesitation.

Somebody Karl wouldn't expect, somebody Karl was still being public Karl with.

Somebody, if he hoped to survive that act, who'd formed a cadre to back him before Karl got wind of it—that was how you could survive: be prepared to take power yourself and ride the storm.

Which Chance Magruder might be, now, coming back from business in Merovingen—if Chance didn't think it over and head elsewhere. If Chance wasn't fool enough to go back to Nev Hettek and pretend he'd never debriefed Thomas Mondragon or heard things Karl wouldn't want him to hear. And he didn't think Chance was that kind of fool at all. Chance Magruder was the best chance the revolution had now.

Thomas Mondragon didn't have a cadre at all, unless you counted the canalers, who'd die in too great numbers, or Jones, who might already be aboard that ship; or old Min, who (God forgive him) was running around somewhere (he hoped) with that fancyboat—the sight of old Min at the helm might get her boarded, might get her searched, might tell whoever was interested that Tom Mondragon was loose somewhere less noisy—and worry Chance and worry Tatiana, and worry Anastasi if Anastasi had anybody deep in Chance's organization. . . .

Couldn't count on that. And he was most thoroughly ashamed of what he'd done. Jones would never forgive him, making Mintaka Fahd a decoy. There was part of him Jones had never understood, Jones being honest and Jones being willing to die for abstracts like friendship and right and fairness and all: and the fact was there was only one human being in the world Tom Mondragon was willing to stay alive for—when he'd had the impulse to kill 'Stasi Kalugin; and there was only one human being in the world he'd protect at all costs, and that meant any human cost. That was the equation Jones wouldn't figure, because Jones liked honest people, and Jones loved him, and Jones wouldn't understand the man who'd come out of Karl Fon's prison and into 'Stasi Kalugin's hands— she only understood the one she'd pulled out of the Det, and made love to in Dead Harbor, and saved from hopelessness. That was the Mondragon that had been, that was the one Jones was in love with, and he never wanted her to meet the one that'd use Min Fahd the way he had, or get in deep with 'Stasi Kalugin— she couldn't imagine 'Stasi because she wasn't, in 'Stasi's mind, powerful. 'Stasi couldn't be afraid of her.

And it was fear and control of fear that was 'Stasi's game. So Jones would only be the means. Tom Mondragon was the object, what he knew and what Chance knew was what 'Stasi would want from him, and whether or not Jones was in that boat, Jones was in dreadful danger—a threat against him or a lure or, if he'd dared to get the better of Anastasi Kalugin, the shot to the heart that would leave him dead on his feet: 'Stasi knew that. 'Stasi'd figured that out the first time he'd seen them together. And 'Stasi'd made him believe he'd do; left him the impression Stasi'd reach out from a Merovingian's watery grave to do it, if Mondragon failed him in the least.

But 'Stasi had made one mistake—he'd taken up a man Karl had made expert at evasion. And made Jones' survival contingent—not on his fear of 'Stasi; but on his patience with it. *That* was 'Stasi's error.

And fire and quake and the coming firefight made the situation different for the first time: if 'Stasi won the firefight that was coming tonight—there'd be war with Nev Hettek, no matter who was at Nev Hettek's helm; and Tom Mondragon might be too useful to kill—in which there was still a failsafe for his walking in there.

He figured he'd live at least until things sorted themselves out, until 'Stasi won or lost; and if Jones was in there, he'd save her the same way he had; and if she wasn't, 'Stasi wouldn't waste him till 'Stasi knew Jones was dead and he had no hold over him—'Stasi was at least that self-controlled: so he had a free shot at 'Stasi, no penalties, no danger to Jones worse than was, no matter where she was.

Only if Chance had told half the truth—if Chance's men had killed her and she wasn't available to be

'Stasi's pawn, then he'd have to sort that out from 'Stasi's behavior—which wasn't altogether easy to read; and take his shot at 'Stasi from the first instant he knew the truth.

Same business as Chance getting a shot at Karl. You had to get close and you had to get inside. And you either had support or you didn't, and in one case you died. He just wanted to make sure Jones wasn't in there. And to get her free if she was. And maybe put things back to zero, and stand at 'Stasi Kalugin's side while he fought Chance Magruder at the helm of Nev Hettek, if he could convince 'Stasi Kalugin he was still useful.

Or if Chance still had Jones—convince 'Stasi Kalugin he'd kill Chance to get her back.

Fool if you believe that, 'Stasi. And fool on Chance's part not just to tell me so and own me outright. So Chance didn't have her and couldn't get her.

Which means she's free, dead, or where Chance said, on that boat or in the Signeury.

And if she's free, good luck, then, Jones. There won't be a 'Stasi Kalugin. You won't matter in hightown. They won't even remember your name. Even if Kamat double-crosses me and never gives you that money—you'll be no worse than before I came.

Sky's going to fall tonight. But so's 'Stasi Kalugin— if his power's gone, *Tatiana* will take out the ones that carry out his orders in this chaos; and if I see the morning I'll go to Tatiana, see if she's any different kind of fool. Go to Iosef, maybe. The old man wants to live. But he won't live long, and his power's fragmented, last night. His militia's deserting. He *might* sweep up 'Stasi's, if 'Stasi were out of the equation, and take on his daughter. Or declare her his heir and hope for a cease-fire.

Hell, it's too damned dangerous. And taking out 'Stasi isn't survivable. Not my damned concern, what happens to those two. Just Jones. Just Jones.

Damn the luck that made Min Fahd the only source of information he had. The woman's loose tongue had spread the news of his being loose from Rock to Rimmon, and that Jones hadn't done something stupid yet was only reason to think she *was* down there; but you couldn't depend on Min knowing what century it was, or where she was in it: she could have been talking about Jones' mama, or Jones, or now, or a year ago. She was only a telegraph. Tell Min and it was public. Depend on it.

One constant in the world. Granted Min hadn't gotten sunk last night.

And if Min had said Jones was waiting for him?

He'd have been a fool. He'd have gone for her. And involved her again.

The only thing he was wrestling with now was that— whether he had the nerve finally to let go of life, take out 'Stasi and leave Jones to survive on her own.

Trust she could do it. Trust he had the courage finally to believe in someone else's competence and quit living her life for her.

Hell, she was seventeen. Eighteen, maybe. She didn't need a Sword of God agent throwing her out of bed in his nightmares or making her a target when Chance won Nev Hettek and decided to collect a stray who could be useful to him.

He didn't want to be used again, dammit. One last job, Chance had said. One last time, Tommy-lad.

There was a lump in his throat when he thought

about that. He didn't know whether it was anger or gratitude or whether he wanted to think about it at all. Just do it, that was all. And don't do it if they've got Jones in hand. So they probably didn't. And Chance had lied. Which left dead—or out there somewhere trying to find him and involve herself again.

Find her and lie low till things in Nev Hettek could sort themselves out again? Chance could have offered that—if Chance had let him in on his plans. Which Chance wouldn't. But Chance didn't offer charity.

And take Jones off the water?

He'd tried that once. Jones would die, shut away from sun and wind and the deck under her feet. He'd watched her. He'd felt it in his gut. And *that* was all he could offer her in Nev Hettek even if he could go home.

So solve the problem, Tommy-lad. It only adds up one way. Give her Merovingen to live in. Give it to her without politics or the Sword in her life. Let her go, stop fouling up her life: she never asked for you.

The ships were gone. That was plain enough. Fire and quake and they'd slept through it, waked to the smell of ash on the wind, an unnatural quiet in the town, and Rat had gone out on canalside and had a look at the Grand without hardly a boat on it, and smoke lying low over town.

Which was when the Falken lad, what was his name? Pavlos? Pavel? had grabbed up his pants and declared he'd better look to harbor.

Good idea, had been Rat's thought. If there was fire in town, if there was quake, then you got to somewhere—if there was fire you got to the harbor; if there was a quake you got up to the Flat, if there was the *big* quake, the quake to raise the Ghost Fleet and bring the Retribution, then you prayed to whatever gods you thought were listening, because the wave from the big one the Astronomer foretold would come, would sweep Merovingen to kindling and its souls to rebirth or to New Worlder hell.

The quake she *hadn't* heard about—till she and Pavel got to the harbor, running from the smell of smoke, and found crowds thick on high Eastdike and up and down the wharves, and small boats thick in the harbor.

No sign of the Falkenaer ships, not one. The tall masts were gone from the end of the pier, and the pretty fair-haired lad beside her on harborside stood staring and said, "Gawd, they've off an' lef' me. . . ." as if his heart was broken. "Gawd, oh, Gawd, th' cap'n'll 'ave me skinn't f' this 'un—wot day is it? Wot day c'n it be?"

"Retribution day," Rat said, because that was what it looked like, with the smoke pall over the town. "What's happened?" she yelled at a skip-freighter, and the freighter yelled back,

"Where?"

She waved her hand at the harbor, at the boats, at all of the city. "I overslept! We just waked up—what happened?"

The skip-freighter stared at her with his jaw dropped, and said to his mate, "Vishnu save, slept *through*, d' ye believe, Rish? —Mikhail's dead, Tatty an' 'Stasi been slammin' away at each other wi' cannon, Zorya burned t' th' waterline, the College doors is down an' they're sayin' Bloody Exeter is dead!"

"God," Rat said, and Pavel. Or Pavlos:

"W'ere's me *ship*, f' Lor'sake? W'ere's me ship gone?"

The skip-freighter pointed to the open harbor, to the horizon, where clouds gathered and thundered. "T' wherever th' rich folk bought. They was usin' sticks and guns t' keep th' gangway from bein' over-run. Gone an' left ye, lad?"

Wasn't a lot of sympathy Falkenaers got from townsfolk. But there was sympathy on the canaler's face that hadn't been there before the boy said that. The boy said, pleading, as if please would help,

"But th' cap'n *needs* me."

Moment of silence then, the canalers bobbing there, the boy standing there, and Rat trying to make a hangover headache think.

She said, desperate herself, "There's others need us. —Can y' tell me, seri, I'm lookin' for a skip-boat—"

The canaler waved harborward. "We got plenty in this pot."

"Jones?"

"That 'un. Yey." Real sober now. "You a friend or a hire?"

"Friend. And a hire if I can find her."

Shake of the head. "Jones ain't takin' any. You ain't seen Tom Mondragon, have ye?"

"You expecting him?"

"The Trade's lookin'. The Nev Hettek embassy burned last night. It don't look good." The canaler frowned, lifted an elbow against the sun-glare. "What's yer name?"

"Rat. Name o' Rat. Singer at Hoh's. Partner's name is Rif."

"Yey. Now I know ye. Yey, Rif, I seen. Her an' that blackleg cap'n. You want them—" He pointed, out across the harbor, and a bobbing soup of boats, where—Rat shading aching eyes—she could *see* the boat, nosing along the harborside.

"God," she said, putting pieces together, the quake, the fire. She grabbed Pavel's hand, said, " 'Scuse," and thought of running. But the canaler said, right off, "Ye want a lift?" and she looked in her pocket for what she hadn't spent. Found a silverbit. "This enough?"

"Yey," the canaler said. "Can ye ease down?"

" 'Oo's this we're meetin'?" the Falken lad objected. "Where're we goin'?"

She said, "Only place I know t' go," thinking— damn, Rif's going to skin me. Slept through it. God!

She'd spread her rumors, she'd gone the rounds, she'd done that part. But be where she was needed last night—that, she hadn't been. Dammit, something had jumped the schedule. Or it *was* the Retribution.

She slid down from the wharf into the skip's well and caught her balance, caught it again as her Falken lad came aboard with a grace that wasn't born ashore—Lord, he was beautiful. She had to think that even while she was squatting down and grabbing the side of the skip, how Pavel and the canalers didn't have to do that, while the canalers fired up their engine and chugged into reverse, swung about in the crowded, choppy harbor and put their bow about for that fancyboat the Trade thought was Cal's.

But Cal was Rif's. So that was about the same.

She thought, but she didn't say it, Better not stand, Pavel, lad, my partner's like to shoot at me on sight.

God, what've they done, what's this about Zorya burning? And Mikhail and Exeter dead?

That wasn't in the plan.

A fuse running from those barrels, all up through the well. And a slow match that made Raj nervous even to think about it, even if it wasn't lit. Jones had showed him that. And Jones was just waiting now, waiting for dark. They'd gotten their fuel aboard, tanks were filled—taken a little bit from this skip and that and some wouldn't charge but a copperbit to avoid the karma—family folk, thinking of their kids, Raj thought, who might risk it for themselves, but who had innocents to think of: Jones was a kind of karma you might not want in your next life, unless you wanted a wild one—good karma, Father Rhajmurti would say, but tied to Merovingen as close as the bandit-birds and skimmers that looked for pickings off the boats. Or maybe she was *paying* karma from past lives, who could know? Something like Jones came through your life, you got tangled; and got to thinking about involvements, and karmic debt, even if you took the Revenantist catchism at skin-deep—

Even if that part of your life had gone toward the dawn. That big Falkenaer ship had stood off from shore a bit, folk said—for fear of riot, and sat there along time in a harbor full of little boats. Time enough for more than one fancy boat to come alongside it, and skip-boaters to help steady the folk climbing that scary heaving distance up—not that they loved rich hightowners that much, but because, poor rich folk, they had to run, they didn't know how to live in troubled waters—going to their estates in the country, they were. Or further. And some dropped coin, to be kept from the crowds ashore, and some paid to be ferried out and some had taken themselves.

Malenkov fancyboat was one, the rumor was. Canalers noticed such things, accounting debts; and passed him the message—it came through the Suleiman's Tommy—Justice says he's all right. He and Rhajmurti and Sonja are all right. No, the Malenkovs were staying. There were still Malenkovs on Rimmon Isle. And canalers gossiped that, too, who was holding fast and who was running, and they began to talk about *their* hightowners, and who were *real* Merovingians, and who were cutting line and running.

Couldn't count the Nev Hettekkers, of course. Toward dawn, the canalers said, the shore wind had come, and the Nev Hettek riverrunners that had had their gangplanks withdrawn long since had stoked up their engines and their paddles began to turn. And the Falken ships had spread their sails and gone out of harbor, and the Nev Hettek riverboats had churned out behind them, with their smokestacks spitting sparks like demon's eyes in the dark, they'd gotten there only in time to see that, to Jones' complete despair, gotten there only in time to see those smokestacks, and their running lights, and their paddlewheels churning up a white froth and a chop in the harbor.

Weren't so many folk sought passage on those. Talk was half and half, how the Nev Hettekkers might be behind what was happening; or whether it was Exeter's slinks had set the embassy afire. Or whether it was some follower of Cassie Boregy who'd done it, distraught about Mikhail and wanting war—

He didn't know, himself, and you didn't talk to Jones right now, not about that. Jones damned the Nev Hettekkers on those ships. Jones hadn't talked much for a long time after that, and all day Jones'd talk about the weather, Jones'd say how the Singh's had gotten out all right, she'd spotted them over there. Jones'd see some skip edge close bringing her a message and Jones' face would be all guarded and grim—

But every time she was hoping, Raj knew it, and every time there was no news of Mondragon, and Jones would look a little grimmer and more desperate till she could remark about the birds, or the sky, or how the smoke was clearing, maybe, and how if she saw tomorrow and she'd got through this, she might sell the boat and go shoot Karl Fon.

Didn't sound reasonable to him. But Jones' opinion about tomorrow shifted like the wind, and he got the feeling in Jones' mind there wasn't going to be one, and if she got one by total surprise she was trying to settle in her mind what she was going to do with it.

He didn't know how to argue with that. He'd said, "You could go to Kamat," which was the best advice he knew. "Jones, Tom's left money for you there. . . ."

And that had gotten him a look like a dagger and a quiet, "Ain't walkin' in there. If I need it—you get it. You get it f' me, hear?"

"Yey," he'd said, last time she'd brought the matter of tomorrow up. And shut up, because thinking of Kamat he thought of Denny, and thought of the riot and the burning, and his—Tom's daughter. He thought of saying, "Jones, Tom's left a baby," but he shut up on that: it was Marina Kamat's baby, and Jones and Marina didn't get along. *Take* that baby, she might. And, God, he might help her. He'd thought he'd loved Marina; but he'd loved love, not flesh and blood, and if Marina's baby would keep Jones alive, he'd betray Marina, and Richard, and keep a promise to Tom.

Wasn't anybody moving back into the canals yet. You could hear the gunfire even this far away, just little pops that made you know it was still going on, and it was only stage-setting for this evening. "If he's anywhere," Jones was saying now, "he's up there. Possible 'Stasi's snatched 'im.'"

"So what'll we do?" he asked, because the silences were awful, and all day Jones had talked alternately as if Mondragon was still alive and then as if he wasn't, and never had said where she was making delivery of this powder.

"You don't do a thing," she said. "I do."

"Jones. . . ."

"Kat'd skin me," Jones said, and gave this funny, awful laugh. "If she could sort us out. Ney, ye're gettin' off this skip. Ye want t' help, you get t' Kamat an' get me that money out."

"Jones, —Tom wouldn't want you to kill yourself."

"Yey, well, a lot o' things've happened 'e wouldn't o' wanted, ain't they?" She was whittling on something. Shavings piled up in the well between her bare feet.

He felt like a coward, but, dammit, Kat might come after him if he went off being a fool. They could drag all Merovingen to hell after them, karmic debt by karmic tie. He said, "I'll get it, Jones."

"What?" she said without looking at him.

"The money," he said. And she made a funny move of her mouth as if it had been the farthest thing from her mind. That was how much she thought about it.

He said, desperate, his best throw: "You going to leave Tom's baby in Kamat?"

She said, cold-eyed, "You'll take care of 'er. I'm *my* mama's daughter. Retribution's. And she's hers."

Dark came by bits and pieces to Merovingen—first to places like Spellbridge Cut, and Spellbridge canalside; and then to middle tier, and finally to high, about the time it came to canalside out on bright Archangel, where that yacht was tied, and about that time Mondragon began thinking about moving, flexing this small muscle and that, making sure when he moved he wasn't going to raise the alarm—because there was militia on Spellbridge roof, traffic going right over his head, a thumping on the wooden bridge, the giving of orders. If he'd been Tatiana's, lying where he was, he could have taken out the emplacements on two rooftops before they got him, and maybe gotten away clean. As it was, he had no quarrel with the militia and no interest in the maybe: when dark came, he just climbed back the way he'd gotten up there, back along the underpinnings of Spellbridge High walkway, not into Spellbridge North Cut: they spanned that and left the three tiers of the waterstairs to the Family. But to a small, dirty shutter, which had been obscured when the walkway'd been extended on this upper tier, and which had gotten jimmied last night. From the inside, when he'd been looking for a way out to a vantage-point. Nobody had found the window open. Nobody had occupied the storeroom, but he didn't give odds about the stairway. He just got a dusty coil of rope from the floor where he remembered it, tied knots in it at convenient intervals—it'd been too long since he'd done this one, and his hands were callused from Jones' boat, but not enough: he needed the knots and hoped it reached, measuring it with each knot and counting, while the evening's shells and bullets began to fly.

Close enough. Out the window again, a fit that would have been better on Denny Takahashi; and a quick snub of the rope around the timbers.

Straight, easy climb, then, thank God the rope held—a fast descent past second tier to canalside and a cat-footed, careful passage as shots echoed and rattled off Kass and Spellbridge.

He made himself part of the building for a while, in Min's cloak. He moved. He waited. He looked up and out at the shell-lit smoke that canopied Archangel, and saw what he'd thought, militia on the bridges, including the one he needed; and that was a problem. But not an insurmountable one.

He slipped the cloak and left it on the canalside walk; he slipped the scarf and pulled off Min's dark sweater.

Bright as a candle he was, then, blond hair and lace collar and cuffs, velvet and leather, and the wink of a sword-hilt. And he still got close enough to the soldiers on Spellbridge corner, in the cover and shadow of that black yacht, that he could say, "Courier for 'Stasi," and still scare hell out of the kids in the black-leg uniforms.

Weapons pointed straight at him, click of hammers. Cheap numbers, those. 'Stasi's gunsmiths had the College censors to deal with. Poor 'Stasi. He had time to think about that while the boys were deciding not to fire on a man with both lace-cuffed hands in sight; and if he'd had help, they'd have been on their faces dead or out cold.

As it was, they said, "Let's see a pass," and he showed a ring, that was 'Stasi's, with the Kalugin crest. Chance had let him keep that. Exeter's interrogators had let him keep it—incrimination stored with the evidence; they'd wanted it *on* his finger, if they brought him visitors. And the visitor they'd brought had been Chance, with a release to Nev Hettek custody.

And maybe he could have talked his way past without it, he had his story ready if they didn't so much as recognize it; but they made up their minds then to do the soldierly thing and ask the sergeant.

Meanwhile he was to face the wall and put his hands on it in plain sight.

M'ser.

"Ye get out here," Jones said. Spooky, it was, the Grand with no traffic. And Kamat bristling with guns.

But there was traffic behind her. Kat Bolado was coming up, slow as she was moving, using just the pole, like the first wave of canalers that might be venturing back into the city, just a little early—just a little suspiciously early, Kamat evidently thought: shots banged, hit the water just shy of her gunpowder-laden bow; and Raj yelled up:

"It's Raj Takahashi, ye fool! Hold your fire! Where's Richard?"

"Sorry," someone said sheepishly. "Sorry, m'ser Raj."

Jones let go a breath she'd been holding, said, shakily, "Luck t' ye, Raj," and shoved off while Raj was still trying to say something. Just poled right along the Grand, with Moghi's astern. Wasn't any likelihood Moghi'd agree to this 'un, she thought. No use askin'.

Only fools big enough was behind her in that fancy-boat. Rat'd showed. With a pretty Falkenaer lad in tow, who *didn't* know what he was getting into—hard enough to get past the accent. Maybe he hadn't understood Rat was going to hell. Maybe he hadn't understood words like *blown up* and *shooting* and *Kalugin*, but maybe again he and Rat had, they said, slept right through the quake and the shooting. And maybe they'd had reason. And maybe a lost, left Falken lad who'd experienced that, was just keeping himself in staring distance of Rat—

She could figure it. She'd stared a lot at Mondragon when she'd first seen him by daylight. Just looked and looked till she knew she'd never see anyone else the same.

The hook's in, boy. Ye got no chance in hell, you start lookin' at anybody that way.

Yey, mama, ye didn't tell me that. Can't look away, can't turn away, if he's up there I'll find 'im. If he ain't, 'Stasi Kalugin won't see th' dawn.

Lot of shootin' up there, mama.

Damn, that Kamat fool. Give me th' shakes, them bullets. . . .

I got t' get there first. Got t' get this load *through* that gunfire.

Ye got any suggestions, mama?

Mondragon knew the drill. Strip-search reminded him of prison and 'Stasi had to know it; they got the knife, they got the sword, most obviously, they let him dress again, which he did at his own pace, while the cannon shook the yacht's frame. Tatiana's forces didn't have a heavy gun on the rooftops; didn't yet, but he'd lay whatever he had on it, that heavy piece he'd heard last evening had either blown up (not an unheard of thing with Merovingian cannon, last century, and it might well be an antique) or they were moving it, remounting it in the best position they had—couldn't get it to the College roof. Stasi's forces still had canalside. So she had to get papa's permission, one could guess, to fire it from Signeury, or she'd lost the College roof today—one or the other. He guessed it was in transit somewhere. Maybe even to something south of Kass. They could boat-freight it to the Grand and around.

But if it ever opened up from a rooftop, with a clear trajectory to Archangel, Anastasi could be in deep trouble. They had to get that gun. And if Anastasi did—then kiss Tatiana good-bye, or quick passage to Nev Hettek.

Leisured adjustment of the lace. He was thinking again. He'd shaken like a leaf a moment ago, embarrassing that it was, but he was that much on edge. Min's skip hadn't had much food aboard, hadn't much of anything. And he felt cold. Constantly cold, as if he'd never be warm again.

"M'ser," the sergeant said, and showed him to the guard who showed him down the tight companionway to Anastasi's cabin—two before, two behind; and he might have taken them, on a better day, taken them, and maybe Anastasi, in his cabin, and maybe found Jones if she was aboard, but his timing was off, he felt it right now—they were hair-triggered, the whole atmosphere was tense enough a stray shot might get Anastasi or him, and he was still feeling that chill the search had made, still *thinking*, dammit, when it might have been time to move, take the chance, take the shot and die for it. They'd taken his sword, but there were guns he could have all around him, and he was walking down this passageway, he was letting them open doors for him and show him in.

Anastasi, in blood-red silken shirt, in jeweled collar and cuffs, was pouring brandy. Anastasi offered him a glass.

And a chair. He said, "I'll stand. I'll skip the drink, if you don't mind. I've a message for you from Chance."

"None from Tatiana?" Mikhail had been the awkward one. Tatiana was some fair-haired mother's daughter. 'Stasi was dark, with eyes like a skit's, always looking for prey—handsome skit, 'Stasi was that. But still a skit.

"I don't come from Tatiana. Chance sends his regards. There's some likelihood they'll be important. That Chance Magruder will be running Nev Hettek."

He'd hoped to shake Anastasi. He hoped. And Anastasi let it hang there a long, long reactionless time. The cannon thumped. He kept thinking away the connections between his face and his brain. No nerves. Nothing.

Anastasi said, to the guards, "Stay here." Those guards had just gotten promoted. Or might meet with accident tonight. And to him: "Have the brandy, Tom."

'Stasi offered it. 'Stasi's hand didn't shake. His did. He let it. He let his breathing give him the air he needed, light-headed as he was. 'Stasi liked fear. 'Stasi liked people wondering what he'd do.

He took a sip of the brandy, wondering was it poisoned, or drugged. It left no suspicious aftertaste. But one could be surprised.

'Stasi said, still standing, "So Magruder's confident of this?"

"Say I held back on you. Say there were things I know that he knows now. They weren't significant before. They *are* to Magruder. Now that Magruder knows what I know—Karl's in danger. And Magruder knows Karl *will* know."

"Held back on me."

A shrug. A nervous one. "Details that didn't mean anything—to someone who wasn't in Fon's close circle. You couldn't have used them. Might not have appreciated them. Your agents could have botched something and let it out and Karl'd have had a cover by sundown, one Magruder couldn't breach. I'm still acting in your interests."

"Maybe I prefer Fon to my sister's *lover* at the helm!"

Anastasi's anger slipped. The mask did.

Mondragon said quietly, "Not her lover now. There's Dani Lambert."

"Who?"

"Dr. Dani Lambert. The Nev Hettek doctor, in Boregy. I'd move, if I were you. Get Lambert, if she hasn't flown."

"See about that," 'Stasi said sharply, and one guard left. Mondragon ticked that down.

"On the other hand," Mondragon said, "your sister isn't one to lose gracefully. I know."

"What do you mean you know? Been sleeping with my sister?"

"No. But I've heard Chance talk."

"Chance, is it?"

"Say we've gotten closer acquainted. Say Chance doesn't think your sister's going to be that pleased—

Chance upriver, with Lambert, Tatiana down here, in charge of policy . . . old lovers can be the devil. *Not* clear thinking. Chance is making an offer, through me. And I'm making one."

A long, long stare. "What do you have to offer?"

"Same thing I always did. I want to talk to Jones."

'Stasi's pupils dilated and contracted. That was all the sign he gave. But maybe 'Stasi realized that eye to eye with him he couldn't lie. 'Stasi said,

"Hard item to deliver." Which didn't tell him enough, dammit. *Dead*, could be hard to deliver.

"I've never changed my price. Where is she?"

'Stasi said, "Ask me in the morning."

"You haven't got her."

'Stasi said, "I know who has."

Lying, he thought desperately. Tatiana couldn't. Tatiana wouldn't know.

Would she?

Anastasi said, "Put him in safe-keeping. See he's secure."

Guard behind him had a gun and a sword. He turned slowly, caught sight of his target and struck fast, blocked the gun up and grabbed the sword hilt. Smashed it into the guard's chin on the way up and whipped the guard around.

'Stasi's shot got the guard. And he *had* the pistol—his got Anastasi, blew him backward as he heard militia thunder down the companionway—

He shot through the door—and there was chaos outside, men yelling. He gave it another round, and somebody got the door open. A dead man, that sprawled inside, and a deserted companionway.

You didn't walk off from a job half-finished. He turned toward Anastasi, where he was lying—but

'Stasi wasn't, 'Stasi shot back and the bullet burned past him, or hit, he couldn't tell—he fired, but 'Stasi was behind a solid buffet, and chairs, and he wasn't: he whipped back for the little cover the doorframe offered, in the companionway, and fired again.

Get clear, his brain was telling him, get hidden, there's going to be militia behind any second.

There were. He stayed tight against the wall, slim profile as a fencer, and fired straight on, heavy gun kicking at his wrist, while shots missed him on either side from both directions, best he could hear. And 'Stasi's that went past his ear might have got a militiaman or two.

He had a breath to think, decided 'Stasi might chase a running man, if he could. Or get curious. He grabbed up another spring-clip pistol, made a quick move over bodies to halfway along the wall, plastered himself there and felt the sting in his arm when he did that. Close one, there. He waited, catching breaths, waited for another rush of militia down that companionway at his right or for Anastasi to come out of cover on his left to find out where he was. One shot left in the clip on this one. That meant one in the chamber.

Shot went down the corridor past him. The woodwork was a mess. Men on the floor were in worse shape. He blinked sweat, shoved the clip back in. Heard running on the deck, people yelling.

The whole ship rocked, violently, to water-motion. He caught his balance, had a shot go past him as the motion flung him from the wall, and fired back.

Saw 'Stasi duck. And waited, with the pistol in both hands and his back naked to the corridor behind.

'Stasi couldn't stand a challenge. Couldn't let well enough alone. Curiosity killed the cat, 'Stasi.

Bang!

Cannonball churned the water up and Jones fought the tiller, throttled up and powered through—couldn't believe what she was doing, couldn't believe what she was seeing, but there was calm water ahead, as she'd come in on Spellbridge West and come around the corner—the flash of fire off the roofs, all hell breaking about 'Stasi's black yacht, and she just went on as she could, put that boat right up against 'Stasi's stern—she'd 've preferred to go midships to be sure, but Cal swore Spellbridge Low was too tight, and once she'd got to thinking on that—

Splash! Rocked the whole canal, that one did. Put her heart in her throat. Get right up there, little boat, ever'body taking cover—

Yey, mama, won't see us, maybe, with all the lights bein' out—

Right up again' 'Stasi Kalugin's hull an' then tell 'im I got to talk to 'im. Fast-fuse and the slow match was one thing, but there was this transmitter Rif had rigged, to a detonator in those barrels, and scary as it was, needing only the flip of a little switch and the press of a button, that was what she had in her pocket and that was what she was counting on if she could get ashore at all.

Rif and Rat and Cal in that boat of theirs, *they* were coming up Spellbridge. Cal with that hand-cannon of his. Rif with her pistol. Rat had said she'd steer, but her Falkenaer lad had said, Ne, he'd do 'er—probably in fear of his life. . . .

Give Mondragon half a chance if he was there,

make a little noise, if their little noise was hear-able over the banging and the thumping of two militias.

Water splashed on her. Wave rocked her against Spellbridge North buffers as she eased up in the dark and scrambled out to make the bow tie, tucked low—

Shot hit the boards by her. Another hit the bow. She yelled, "Ye damn fools!" and went overside, slipped along the edge in Det's dark water until she was at that dangerous point where the yacht rocked and bumped against the buffers and the pilings. But a skinny somebody could just fit into the nooks between the pilings, if she kept moving, if she timed her advances along that line just so that the hull was swinging outward when she was moving and she was tucked in tight between the pilings when it hit.

Tight fit, there, mama, yey—

Rattle of guns. People looking up and down in the shadows, not sure whether she'd been hit back there. Touch that toggle now and five or six were going to the rebirth.

Thump of tons of boat against her back. Enough to make breath tight a moment. But she was crossing Spellbridge now, duck down and swim, gun was wrapped in wax-seal; so was the detonator battery. Rest was all right. She came up on Kass-corner pilings, wondering where in hell was Rif, was peeling the wax covers off from where she was in the water, when of a sudden you could see the flashes of guns off Spellbridge Low, and guns flashing on the water, and hear that fancyboat roar. *Big* burst of rifle fire then, Lord hope it didn't hit the tanks. . . .

Lord, it was still coming!

She made the shadow of the gangway, as Kass bridge went up in a blinding flare—the tanks, she thought, with a thump of her heart, God, they were gone—she didn't *have* any help—

So she scrambled up ashore while the gangway guards were taking cover from raining debris—ran up the gangplank and onto the deck, tucked low, about the time fire broke out down on canalside and she was sure an army was coming up the gangplank after her.

There was, but one was Rif and one was Cal, and Rat and the blond Falken lad. She cried, "Get low, ye fools!" because shots started coming every way, some slamming into the railing over her head. "Haul th' gangway up!" the Falken lad cried, and that was smart: she dropped the pistol and the detonator and hauled on this side, on her knees, while the Falken lad hauled on his, and Cal and Rif and Rat blazed away covering them.

But of a sudden shots were coming from out of the doorway to the cabins and it wasn't militia, the shots were hitting militiamen, and militia was running for the water-side. Some made it and jumped, some didn't, and she heard a hoarse voice call out:

"Jones? Jones, is that you?"

"Mondragon?" God, she was going to sit down where she was and faint. It was him in the doorway. Was him coming across the deck—blond hair loose in the wind.

Movement in the doorway. She didn't even think. She had the pistol up and between her knees sitting as she was and she let fire.

Mondragon hit the deck and looked back, as a whole handful of shots from their side went that way. But whatever it was back there she hoped to hell it wasn't friendly, because it was gone.

Cannonball hit. Close. Rocked the boat.

"Jones!" Mondragon yelled from where he was, flat on the deck, next to the unstepped mast. "Jones, cut the ties! We're under fire from the roof, let the current carry us out of here!"

"Yey!" she said, but Rat and the Falken lad were already moving for the cables: she had better than drift in mind, and crawled toward the bridge.

As shots knocked splinters off the deck and she thought about that boat out there.

"You all right?" Mondragon yelled at her.

"Fine," she yelled back, and got to the door. Opened it from ground level, and that was a good idea—shots came out, and Mondragon's bullets came past her, right inside.

So did Mondragon, damn man was in there, down those steps in the dark and punching buttons on the panel before she could get her wobbly knees to carry her down to him. He said, "Damn thing!" and she figured it was like a barge, different kind of start, and held one button down and pushed another and heard the engine turn over.

Cal's voice then: "They're coming up from the west!"

And a whole volley of shots. She just kept pushing. Engines both caught. 'Ye got those cables, yet?"

"Go!" Mondragon said.

Two throttles, two engines, she remembered that about this boat. She throttled up easy, feeling it out, had, beyond the glass, a shadowy view of Borg North picked out against the night-glow and the smoke. Signeury Bend was right at Borg, and you made it smooth or you'd stove her in on the triple pilings of Signeury Bridge.

Mondragon was trying to keep her down low. She

needed to see. She upped the engines, the yacht straining and getting nowhere.

"They're coming!" Cal said. "Hurry, dammit, Rif!"

Stern was swinging out, bow was still tied and they were like to ram the shore. She reversed the screws. *Then* the bow cable went, all of a sudden, and Jones throttled to neutral, spun the wheel over hard to correct, and throttled up, as a shot splintered the wall.

She said, on a breath, "Here!" and hauled the detonator out, laid it on the counter. It slid off and he caught it, didn't have to ask what to do with it.

Whump!

Too close, she thought. Whole ship lurched, God hope it didn't get the screws. And she was steering hard, the way you had to when you didn't dare carry enough way. But she was bow on to the Grand, didn't need to back, just get round that damn Signeury Corner and take her on.

"I can't make the bridges," she said, thinking of those pilings that you had to skin this huge ship by, and she heard the panic in her voice. "I can't handle her, Mondragon, I'm going to crack her up, you better get ready to jump, better warn 'em—"

"Give you a damn boat and you want to complain, *steer* it, Jones, you know the currents, give her some way and *steer!*"

Man was shaky-voiced himself. She punched buttons. She got deck-lights. She didn't want that. She got the warning horn, and, God, she wanted that one. No knowing what boats might be in her way if she got to the harbor. Running lights. Yey, mama, bow-light's all right, but I run all my life in th' dark. Cut 'er out and use the eyes.

Signeury Bridge. A scrape there. Terrible scrape.

Need more way for Bucher-Borg. Engines throbbed like her heart. Thump-thump, thump-thump. Blast of the horn, let whoever know she was coming.

You carried way or the currents got you. Carried way enough to crack your bow and sink you. Mondragon's hand was on her shoulder, fingers pressed.

"You got it, Jones," as bridge shadow passed with so little to clear overhead it stopped your heart.

"Scrape this damn deck-house right off and stove us with it—let me stop this thing—"

"Keep going. You're all right."

"The damn overheads are *tight*, they ain't even, Mondragon, if I miss a center I'm going to rake this bridge an' us right off, won't know what hit us—"

"Keep *going*, Jones. We're all right, we're—"

God!

She shut her eyes. She felt the current, she opened them and she was on. Right under Foundry. Fishmarket ahead, treacherous deep wash in the middle pilings, but that was where this big wide boat had to go, with its deep draft. Right through the current. Little whip at the end.

Big ship powered right through it, hardly felt it. Slow up, now, Mantovan corner coming, couldn't chance this big boat there—big push where the Gut let out. . . .

"You got it, Jones. You got it."

She blew the horn. She eased right out into harbor and slowed down, scared of hitting some poor skip freighter. There she was, Altair Jones, in 'Stasi Kalugin's big black yacht, reversing the screws to stop and letting the boat toss in the stirred pot that was the harbor—

Had Mondragon's arms around her and she didn't

mind she was soaking wet and sweating weak, and being kissed out of the breath she had. She held onto him and gave it back, good as she got, the two of them like fools in the dark and the toss of an unhandled ship.

He said, out of breath, "You made it, Jones."

She said, "Figured where t' find ye." Then she thought about her skip, mama's skip, blown to hell out there, and felt sick. "I lost my boat—"

"I got you another, Jones, what're you complaining for?"

"Let us off," Rif said; and Cal. "We got work to do."

And what they were going to do or when or how, the Lord knew, but they said this morning that Tatty was governor up in the Signeury, Lord only knew about papa Iosef. And Jones didn't say a thing about what was under Dead Marsh, wouldn't say it even to Mondragon, that was the way she felt about it: they'd bought her silence with what she couldn't get, else, and she had him back and for her mind, they were just going to pull out a while and let the winds blow clean.

"Go fishing," she said to Mondragon.

Odd things turned up in the dawn. There was Min Fahd in a fancyboat, with an old hightowner man, the both of them like kids, Min waving and calling out to all her friends.

Waved up to the big yacht, too, and laughed and laughed, her and Mondragon leaning over the side. It was m'ser Elgin with her, the Lord only knew how— seein' what was to be seen, Min said.

But came the rush of folk to Eastdike and the cry of blacklegs coming to the harbor, it seemed time to start the engines up and put a little distance between them and Tatiana Kalugin.

"Ain't gettin' *my* man," Jones said, and said to Rat and her Pavel fellow, the Falkenaer, "Better get off if you're goin'. We're goin' out a ways."

"Wot's y' course?" the Falken lad asked, blue-eyed and interested.

"Dunno," she said honestly. "Just keep in sight of land and out of trouble, all I know t' do."

Mouth pursed, head shook. "Na, na, ye want t' keep her t' good len'th out, ye got a shoal t' sout'. . . ."

"Ye *know* the coast?" she said.

Lad tapped his head. "All th' charts. Fuelin' stations. 'Ell, I do. Secont navigator, I was on th' *Coldsmith*."

"Ye're stayin'," she said, with a jab of her finger. And to Rat's objections, "Ye're th' bribe, Ratliff. Ye're comin' with. Just a little fishin' trip. We'll bring ye back, eventu'ly."

"Jones!" she heard Mondragon yell. "Jones, better get us out of here! Launch is coming, they don't know us from 'Stasi!"

He came running. Heavy gun boomed out. But she was throttling up by the time he got inside.

"Ain't no problem. How's th' Chat sound for winter?"

"Fine. The Rim's fine, right now. Somewhere that launch can't reach. Thing's got a deck gun of some kind—"

"Chat." She looked aside at him as the ship gathered way. "Think I can find 'er. There or somewheres. What d' ye say?"

"Just kick her up a bit."

She did that. Right out harbor-mouth, and straight on as she bore.

INDEX TO CITY MAPS

INDEX OF ISLES AND BUILDINGS BY REGIONS

THE ROCK:
(ELITE RESIDENTIAL)
LAGOONSIDE

1. The Rock
2. Exeter
3. Rodrigues
4. Navale
5. Columbo
6. McAllister
7. Basargin
8. Kalugin (governor's relatives)
9. Tremaine
10. Dundee
11. Kuzmin
12. Rajwade
13. Kuminski
14. Ito
15. Krobo
16. Lindsey
17. Cromwell
18. Vance
19. Smith
20. Cham
21. Spraker
22. Yucel
23. Deems
24. Ortega
25. Bois
26. Mansur

GOVERNMENT CENTER
THE TEN ISLES
(ELITE RESIDENCE)

27. Spur(militia)
28. Justiciary
29. College (Revenant)
30. Signeury
31. Carswell
32. Kistna

TIDEWATER (SLUM) FOUNDRY DISTRICT

INDEX TO CITY MAPS

MAPS

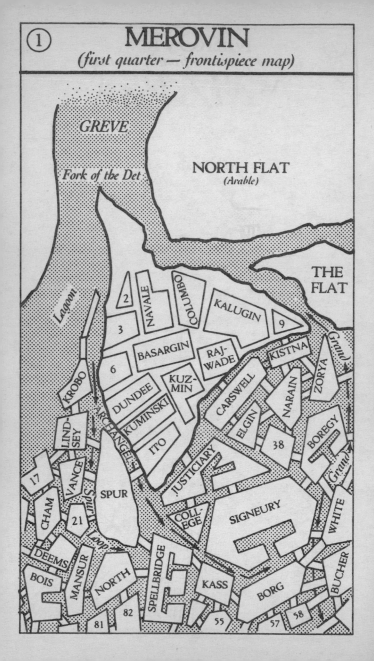

MEROVIN
(first quarter — frontispiece map)

①

GREVE

Fork of the Det

NORTH FLAT
(Arable)

THE FLAT

Lagoon

2

NAVALE

COLUMBO

KALUGIN

9

3

Grand

BASARGIN

RAJ-WADE

KISTNA

ZORYA

KROBO

6

KUZ-MIN

CARSWELL

ELGIN

NARAIN

LIND-SEY

DUNDEE

ARCHANGEL

KUMINSKI

38

BOREGY

17

VANCE

ITO

JUSTICIARY

Grand

CHAM

21

SPUR

Spur

COLL-EGE

SIGNEURY

WHITE

DEEMS

Ton

BOIS

MANSUR

NORTH

SPELLBRIDGE

KASS

BORG

BUCHER

82

81

55

57

58

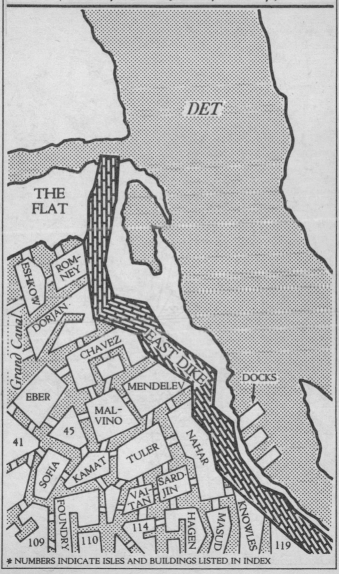

② MEROVIN
(second quarter—frontispiece map)

DET

THE FLAT

ESHKOW

ROM-NEY

DORJAN

Grand Canal

CHAVEZ

EBER

MENDELEV

MAL-VINO

EAST DIKE

DOCKS

41

45

SOFIA

KAMAT

TULER

VAI-TAN

SARD-JIN

NAHAR

FOUNDRY

109

110

114

HAGEN

MASUD

KNOWLES

119

* NUMBERS INDICATE ISLES AND BUILDINGS LISTED IN INDEX

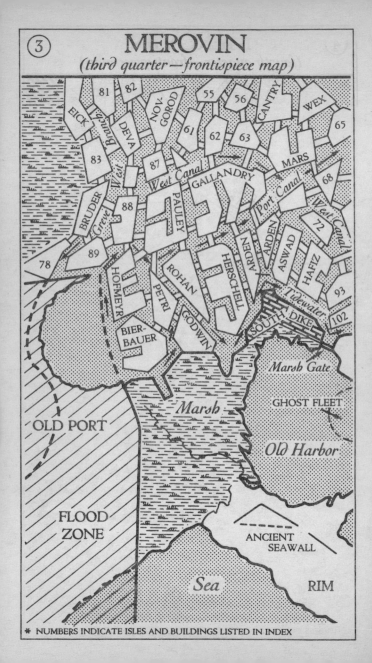

MEROVIN
(third quarter—frontispiece map)

③

EICK
81
82
Branch
DEVA
NOV. GOROD
55
56
CANTRY
WEX
61
62
63
65
West
BRUDER
83
87
MARS
68
Greve
West Canal
GALLANDRY
Port Canal
West Canal
88
PAULEY
72
89
ARDEN
ASWAD
HAFIZ
78
HOFMEYR
ROHAN
HERSCHELL
ARDEN
93
PETRI
Tidewater
102
BIER-BAUER
GODWIN
SOUTH DIKE
Marsh Gate
Marsh
GHOST FLEET
OLD PORT
Old Harbor
FLOOD ZONE
ANCIENT SEAWALL
Sea
RIM

✴ NUMBERS INDICATE ISLES AND BUILDINGS LISTED IN INDEX

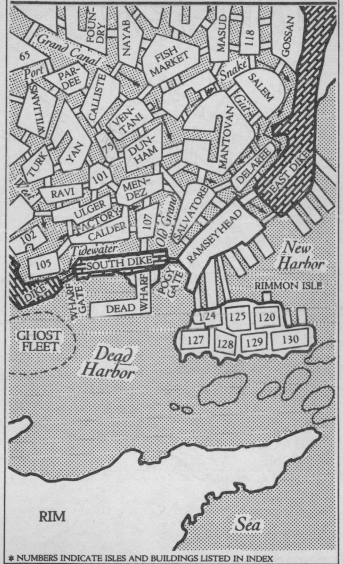

MEROVIN
(fourth quarter—frontispiece map)

④

FOUN-DRY

Grand Canal

Port

65

NAYAB

MASUD

118

GOSSAN

FISH MARKET

PAR-DEE

WILLIAMS

CALLISTE

VEN-TANI

Snake

SALEM

Gulf

MANTOVAN

TURK

YAN

75

DUN-HAM

RAVI

101

MEN-DEZ

DELAREE

EAST DIKE

ULGER

FACTORY

CALDER

107

SALVATORE

102

Old Grand

RAMSEYHEAD

New Harbor

105

Tidewater

SOUTH DIKE

RIMMON ISLE

DIKE

WHARF GATE

DEAD WHARF

POST GATE

124

125

120

GHOST FLEET

Dead Harbor

127

128

129

130

RIM

Sea

* NUMBERS INDICATE ISLES AND BUILDINGS LISTED IN INDEX

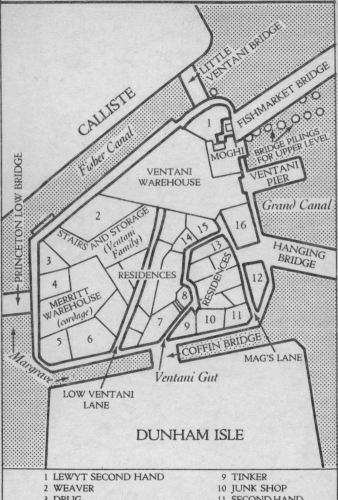

VENTANI ISLE
(Canalside Level showing Moghi's Tavern)

LITTLE
VENTANI BRIDGE

CALLISTE

FISHMARKET BRIDGE

Fisher Canal

PRINCETON LOW BRIDGE

1

MOGHI

BRIDGE PILINGS
FOR UPPER LEVEL

VENTANI
WAREHOUSE

VENTANI
PIER

Grand Canal

2

STAIRS AND STORAGE
(Ventani Family)

15

16

14

13

HANGING
BRIDGE

3

RESIDENCES

RESIDENCES

12

4

8

MERRITT
WAREHOUSE
(cordage)

7

9

10

11

5

6

COFFIN BRIDGE

MAG'S LANE

Margrave

Ventani Gut

LOW VENTANI
LANE

DUNHAM ISLE

1 LEWYT SECOND HAND	9 TINKER
2 WEAVER	10 JUNK SHOP
3 DRUG	11 SECOND HAND
4 DOCTOR	12 SPICERY
5 CHANDLER	13 LIBERTY PAWN
6 FURNITURE MAKER	14 TACKLE
7 KILIM'S USED CLOTHES	15 MAG'S DRUG
8 JONES	16 ASSAN BAKERY

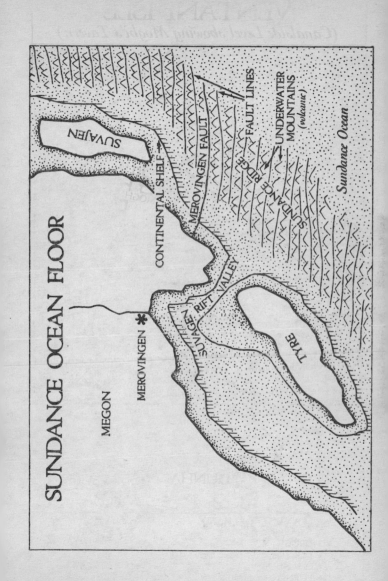

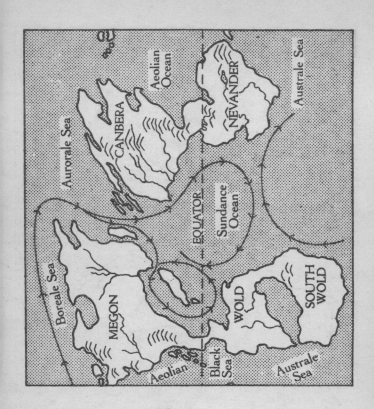

MAJOR EASTERN OCEANIC CURRENTS *(affecting climate)*

N

Aurorale Sea

Aeolian Ocean

CANBERA

NEVANDER

Australe Sea

Boreale Sea

EQUATOR

Sundance Ocean

MEGON

WOLD

SOUTH WOLD

Aeolian

Black Sea

Australe Sea

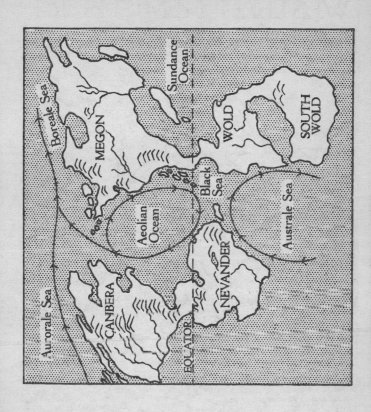

WESTERN

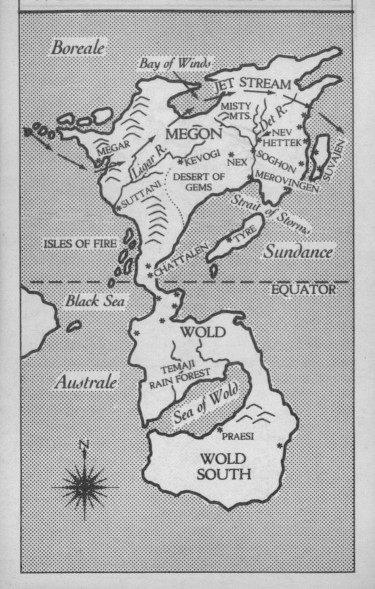

WESTERN HEMISPHERE

Boreale

Bay of Winds

JET STREAM

MISTY MTS.

MEGON

Det R.

NEV HETTEK

MEGAR

Ligar R.

KEVOGI

NEX

SOGHON

SUVAIEN

MEROVINGEN

SUTTANI

DESERT OF GEMS

Strait of Storms

ISLES OF FIRE

CHATTALEN

TYRE

Sundance

Black Sea

EQUATOR

WOLD

Australe

TEMAJI RAIN FOREST

Sea of Wold

PRAESI

N

WOLD SOUTH

C.J. CHERRYH
THE ALLIANCE-UNION UNIVERSE

The Company Wars
- [ ] DOWNBELOW STATION   (UE2431—$4.50)

The Era of Rapprochement
- [ ] SERPENT'S REACH   (UE2088—$3.50)
- [ ] FORTY THOUSAND IN GEHENNA   (UE2429—$4.50)
- [ ] MERCHANTER'S LUCK   (UE2139—$3.50)

The Chanur Novels
- [ ] THE PRIDE OF CHANUR   (UE2292—$3.95)
- [ ] CHANUR'S VENTURE   (UE2293—$3.95)
- [ ] THE KIF STRIKE BACK   (UE2184—$3.99)
- [ ] CHANUR'S HOMECOMING   (UE2177—$4.50)

The Mri Wars
- [ ] THE FADED SUN: KESRITH   (UE2449—$4.50)
- [ ] THE FADED SUN: SHON'JIR   (UE2448—$4.50)
- [ ] THE FADED SUN: KUTATH   (UE2133—$4.50)

Merovingen Nights (Mri Wars Period)
- [ ] ANGEL WITH THE SWORD   (UE2143—$3.50)

Merovingen Nights—Anthologies
- [ ] FESTIVAL MOON (#1)   (UE2192—$3.50)
- [ ] FEVER SEASON (#2)   (UE2224—$3.50)
- [ ] TROUBLED WATERS (#3)   (UE2271—$3.50)
- [ ] SMUGGLER'S GOLD (#4)   (UE2299—$3.50)
- [ ] DIVINE RIGHT (#5)   (UE2380—$3.95)
- [ ] FLOOD TIDE (#6)   (UE2452—$4.50)

The Age of Exploration
- [ ] CUCKOO'S EGG   (UE2371—$4.50)
- [ ] VOYAGER IN NIGHT   (UE2107—$2.95)
- [ ] PORT ETERNITY   (UE2206—$2.95)

The Hanan Rebellion
- [ ] BROTHERS OF EARTH   (UE2290—$3.95)
- [ ] HUNTER OF WORLDS   (UE2217—$2.95)

DAW

More Top-Flight Science Fiction and Fantasy from
C.J. CHERRYH

SCIENCE FICTION
☐ HESTIA   (UE2208—$2.95)
☐ WAVE WITHOUT A SHORE   (UE2101—$2.95)

The Morgaine Cycle
☐ GATE OF IVREL (BOOK 1)   (UE2321—$3.95)
☐ WELLS OF SHIUAN (BOOK 2)   (UE2322—$3.95)
☐ FIRES OF AZEROTH (BOOK 3)   (UE2323—$3.95)
☐ EXILE'S GATE (BOOK 4)   (UE2254—$3.95)

ANTHOLOGIES
☐ SUNFALL   (UE1881—$2.50)
☐ VISIBLE LIGHT   (UE2129—$3.50)

FANTASY
The Ealdwood Novels
☐ THE DREAMSTONE   (UE2013—$2.95)
☐ THE TREE OF SWORDS AND JEWELS
                                  (UE1850—$2.95)